M000202398

Catch Me When I Fall

A.L. Jackson

NEW YORK TIMES BESTSELLING AUTHOR

Copyright © 2020 A.L. Jackson Books Inc.   —
First Edition

All rights reserved. Except as permitted under the U.S. Copyright Act
of 1976, no part of this publication may be reproduced, distributed,
transmitted in any form or by any means, or stored in a database or
retrieval system, without prior permission of the publisher. Please
protect this art form by not pirating.

A.L. Jackson
www.aljacksonauthor.com
Cover Design by Silver at Bitter Sage Designs
Editing by Susan Staudinger
Proofreading by Julia, The Romance Bibliophile
Formatting by Mesquite Business Services

The characters and events in this book are fictitious. Names, characters,
places, and plots are a product of the author's imagination. Any
similarity to real persons, living or dead, is coincidental and not
intended by the author.

Print ISBN: 978-1-946420-76-3
eBook ISBN: 978-1-946420-45-9

Catch Me When I Fall

More from A.L. Jackson

Redemption Hills
Give Me a Reason
Say It's Forever
Never Look Back
Promise Me Always

The Falling Stars Series
Kiss the Stars
Catch Me When I Fall
Falling into You
Beneath the Stars

Confessions of the Heart
More of You
All of Me
Pieces of Us

Fight for Me
Show Me the Way
Follow Me Back
Lead Me Home
Hold on to Hope

Bleeding Stars
A Stone in the Sea
Drowning to Breathe
Where Lightning Strikes
Wait
Stay
Stand

The Regret Series
Lost to You
Take This Regret
If Forever Comes

The Closer to You Series
Come to Me Quietly
Come to Me Softly
Come to Me Recklessly

Stand-Alone Novels
Pulled
When We Collide

Hollywood Chronicles, a collaboration with USA Today
Bestselling Author, Rebecca Shea
One Wild Night
One Wild Ride

prologue

Royce

*R*ed and blue lights whirled through the deepest night, reflecting against the heavy clouds that hugged the city in a hazy glow.

I raced down the dank alley, my footsteps pounding through the black puddles and dirt and debris. Maybe if I ran hard enough, I might be able to escape.

Jagged panting rose into the dense air, aggression and fear and hatred a pulsing ache in my arteries.

Thunder rumbled, a dark, ominous warning that twisted through the heavens, and I lifted my face to the tiny droplets of rain that began to pelt from the sky, burning cold against my heated skin.

What had I done?

I pushed harder, desperation seeping all the way to my bones as the sound of sirens grew louder.

Agony clutched my spirit, time slipping as I darted through a tunnel of hopelessness that I knew led to a dead end.

I skidded out of the alleyway and hit the sidewalk.

My ribs were gripped in a searing blaze of pain from the blows I'd sustained.

I sucked for breath. For relief.

It didn't matter. It had been worth it. There'd been nothing that could have stopped me from seeking this revenge.

The taste of vengeance still danced on my tongue.

Violence lighting a path through my veins.

Whirling lights closed in from behind, and another cruiser came at me from ahead. Blocking me in. Nothing left to give, I dropped to my knees in the middle of the street.

I tipped my head up to the rain that began to pound harder, and I roared.

Roared in surrender and anguish.

But with it was a shout of victory.

Blood dripped from my mangled, torn knuckles like evidence signed on the pavement.

I had no place to go.

No place to escape.

I'd already been convicted.

The reason didn't count.

None of it mattered, anyway, because I'd do it all over again.

A thousand times.

Give up everything like an offering.

Condemning myself was the one sacrifice I could make.

Royce
Present Day

I crossed an ankle over my knee where I sat in the high-backed leather chair situated on the far wall of the office, focusing on readjusting the cuffs of my button-up rather than the rage that blistered across my skin.

Tension radiated through the massive room that was as pretentious as an eighty-dollar bottle of water, all carved wood and original first editions and the pungent stench of arrogance and BS.

I angled my head at the man who sat on his pompous throne on the opposite side of the desk.

He wore a suit and a tie, as per usual, hair perfectly styled and parted to the side, though his stomach was beginning to paunch, like it was trying to keep up with the pride that overtook his conscience.

Karl Fitzgerald.

Owner of Mylton Records.

Prick extraordinaire.

My piece-of-shit stepfather.

Yeah, my mother hadn't had hearts in her eyes. She'd had dollar signs.

"Royce," he said, like he was giving me permission to speak.

I cracked a grin. "Father. So nice to see you."

The words dripped with sarcasm and disdain.

I couldn't stand the sight of the bastard, which was an unfortunate circumstance considering he was my boss.

But it was all part of the plan.

You know what they say—Keep your friends close and your enemies closer. Believe me, I was right on his tail until the moment I overtook him and trampled him underfoot.

He'd stolen everything from me, crushed it in his fat, greedy fist.

I couldn't wait to return the favor.

"I just wanted to be sure we were clear on the situation. I wouldn't want there to be any further . . . mistakes," he jeered.

"I think you made it plenty clear."

"Did I?" he shot back, angling his head. "You failed the task the first time. I won't accept a repeat."

Incredulous laughter rumbled in my throat, and I turned my attention out the window to the sprawling grounds of his estate, the lawn meticulously manicured and a negative-edge pool stretched over a cliff like it touched the tops of the skyscrapers in the city below.

I tapped my tattooed fingers on my knee that was bouncing at the speed of light, agitation curling through my senses and setting fire to my veins.

Slowly, I swiveled my focus back to the man who overshadowed this family like a wraith. A monster at the helm.

"There was a . . . difficulty." I refused to gift him with more information than that.

He scoffed. "A difficulty? Your job is to eradicate difficulties. Your job is to seal the deal. Get it penned in ink, in blood, or

4

whatever the fuck it takes. Taking no for an answer is not acceptable."

Bitterness tightened my chest in a fist. Of course, he would think *no* wasn't a sufficient answer. Money the solution to every obstacle. To every reservation and fear and question.

To every crime.

Cover it up with a little dough.

I just wondered how deep it went. The depravity. The sickness he poured into the world.

Slowly, I pushed to my feet, unable to stop the aggression that lined my bones. I prowled across the floor until I was standing at his desk and planting my hands on the gleaming wood. "I am very aware of my job description. But I do it *my* way, and I'm fucking good at it. You have a problem with it? Feel free to cut me loose."

He wouldn't.

He needed me. I'd seen to it that it was a fact. That I was the best.

Indispensable.

Didn't mean he liked me for it.

Redness colored his ears and hatred darkened his eyes. "You're standing here today because of me. Don't forget that."

I leaned in closer, spitting the words, "I'm standing here because you need me. I never asked for any favors. Don't pretend like I did."

My position was the one thing my pathetic mother had offered. She'd done it out of guilt. I'd jumped on it, salivating at the mouth as I'd plotted for revenge.

Venom fueled his smile. "So angry, aren't we? A hothead getting ready to snap." He tsked like the smug old bastard that he was. "Maybe they should have left you locked up after all."

I grinned. All teeth. "You never know. Maybe they should have."

Air huffed from his nose, and he rocked back in his chair.

I cocked my head. "Are we done here? Because I have work to do."

He gave me a tight nod, and I turned on my heel, my dress shoes echoing on the marble floor as I left him sitting there.

"Don't come back here until it is finished."

I froze when his voice hit me from behind. I tossed a glance at him over my shoulder, anger seething in my blood, disgusted that we both wanted the same fucking thing though it was for entirely different reasons.

"Trust me. This deal is as good as done."

"That's my boy." He said it with a derisive gleam in his eye, like he'd ever given two fucks about me.

Without giving the prick the credit of a response, I turned and strode out into the foyer.

I stumbled a step when I saw my baby sister, Maggie, pacing at the bottom of the stairs. Mahogany hair, two shades lighter than mine, swished from the ponytail she wore it in, the girl petite and oozing a fear that I would give anything to hold for her.

She took two steps in my direction.

Rage that would never abate thrashed in my spirit when I saw the scar that slashed across her chest. Permanently as red and angry as I was.

Hugging herself, she angled her head, an innocent petition written into her expression. "I don't know why you fight with him. You know it's not going to change anything."

I went right for her and pulled her into my arms, pressed a kiss to her forehead. "There are some things I can't seem to control."

Hating Karl Fitzgerald was one of them.

"You're so angry. So sad," she whispered into my heart, the girl so short she barely came to the middle of my chest.

"I'm not."

"You're a liar," she returned. "I can hear it. *Feel* it." Affection tightened my chest, the love I had for my sister the only love I had left. The rest used up. Burned to ash. Scorn in its place.

I hugged her tighter. "I'm the last person you should be worried about."

"I want you to be happy."

"You make me happy," I murmured against the crown of her head.

Fists in my suit jacket, she edged back and blinked up at me. "You know that's not enough. Not when I was responsible for you losing everything."

I gripped her by the outside of her arms. "Bullshit."

Tears gathered in her eyes. "You know it's true."

Violence flashed across my skin, and I struggled to hold it together. To stop myself from marching back into my stepfather's office and making him confess whose fault it was.

To end this now.

I had to remember my purpose. That attack I'd been setting into motion for the last four years.

"No, Maggie, it's not. None of the blame is yours."

The greedy bastard who was her father made sure the one responsible didn't have to pay.

I touched my baby sister's cheek, wiped the tear that had fallen. "I won't fail you again, Mag-Pie. I won't. I promise you that."

"I just want to be safe. For this all to end."

I pressed my lips to her temple, whispered, "The end is near."

Then I turned and strode out the door to my car waiting for me in the circular drive. I slipped into the backseat.

"Mr. Reilly." My driver glanced in the rearview mirror, waiting for instruction.

I sat back in the seat. "Airport, please."

Releasing the button of my suit jacket, I blew out a sigh and roughed my hands through my hair, trying to calm the riot that was pounding my heart into mayhem.

My driver weaved down the long drive of Karl Fitzgerald's estate before maneuvering the winding road that led to the bottom of the hill. He headed directly to the airport, taking me to the private hangar where the jet was waiting.

I slipped out of the car, and the concierge gathered my bags from the trunk.

I climbed the stairs, nodding my head to the pilots and flight attendant who were waiting to welcome me aboard. I took a seat, accepted the tumbler of whiskey I was offered, pulled my phone from my pocket when it buzzed with a message.

We need you to make this happen.

I tapped out a response.

I'm on my way..

Emily

"Emily!" My brother shouted from behind me, trying to push his way through the group of people that had descended on him the second we'd come off stage.

Backstage, the energy was alive, the way it always was, only dim lights illuminating the wings. Roadies hustled to tear down our gear and set up for the next band, local reporters vied to get the scoop, and fans tried to get a closer look. To brush up against the only world that I knew.

I ignored all of it.

Feet pounding the floor, I fumbled over cords and pushed through curtains and dodged equipment.

"Emily," Richard shouted again, "would you fuckin' wait?"

I didn't want to face him. Didn't want to turn around and see the questions in his eyes.

Without looking back, I pushed myself faster. Fought to get away.

Hide.

As if there were any hope to change any of this.

Fear pulsed like wildfire through my veins, lungs burning with panic and exertion.

Where I was going, I didn't know.

Searching for a solution.

A safe place, I guessed.

A way to scrape the ugliness that had seeped into my consciousness, this gross feelin' I couldn't escape.

Trapped.

And God, I hated it. Hated it so much that I was doing my best to outrun it.

Keeping my face down, I slinked around a group of fans with backstage passes, their excitement a palpable brand of anticipation and suspense.

I said a silent prayer that they wouldn't recognize me, though I figured they were probably there to see Civil Stone, the headliner on the tour, anyway.

There wasn't even a rustle of awareness. Thank God.

Increasing my pace, I rounded into a narrow hall that ran along the back of the old club. With every step that I took, my heart rate spiked, amplifying the suffocating sensation that pummeled me in nauseating waves.

I almost shouted in relief when I found a side door, my hands planting on the heavy metal latch as I shoved it open to the waiting night.

It banged against the wall, and I stumbled down the three steps into the dark alleyway, gasping for breath and wondering how I thought isolating myself in the shadows was any better.

Humidity slapped me in the face, clogging my lungs, and the panic only intensified.

Footsteps clamored after me, my brother slowing when he found my hiding place. A shiver of unease rolled across my flesh as he eased down the steps, stopping two feet away.

"What the hell is going on with you, Em?"

My throat grew tight, locking up the confession. One I wasn't sure I wanted to make anyway. I shook my head. "Nothing."

"Nothing?" Richard grabbed me by the wrist and spun me around. "That wasn't fucking *nothing*," he spat.

Frustration and confusion and anger marred his attractive face. My brother was about as handsome as they came. One-hundred-percent masculine with a striking, unforgettable face, the guy was nothing but charisma and drive and a talent unlike any other.

Night after night, he won over crowds, and they worshipped at his feet.

They liked to say I was the face of Carolina George.

I knew better.

It was him. My older brother who I respected more than anything. I still couldn't believe he'd get mixed up in what he had. That he could be partner to it. I wondered what he'd say if he found out that I knew.

If it would change anything.

"I just . . . I think I'm tired."

Tired of pretending.

Tired of covering up this hurt.

Tired of being afraid.

Doubt pinched his face, and he roughed a hand through his dark blond hair. "Are you joking right now, Em? You're tired? You fucking blew the call with the record company this morning, and then you ran off the stage in the middle of our last song . . . because you were fucking tired? Is that what you're tellin' me?"

He kept angling closer with each word he shouted, the anger in his voice echoing against the brick walls and pelting against the dingy, dirty ground.

Tears burned in my eyes, and I struggled to hold them back.

Didn't he get what I had done for him? What I'd gone through for him? But I knew he didn't have the first clue, and I had no idea how to tell him. Terrified for him to know what I'd endured. Almost more terrified of what he was hiding.

Wrapping my arms over my chest, I took a step back, as if it could shield me from his anger. Protect me from the pain ripping me apart.

"I'm not sure I can do this anymore."

Richard grabbed me by the upper arms and shook me. "What the fuck does that mean?"

I knew he wasn't trying to hurt me, that he somehow thought he could shake some sense into me, but it didn't matter. I felt it like a blow, terror ridging my spine, my nerves racing as my breaths turned shallow.

Struggling for air.

"We've spent our whole damn lives working toward this, Em. Our whole lives. And now, everything we've wanted is right there, waiting on us to take it. And what? You're just going to walk away? Give it up? After everything?" His words were a rush of resentment and confusion, as if he'd gotten swept up in my turmoil and didn't know how to get free of it.

But that was the problem.

We were tied, our success wound up in my decision.

Agony raked my throat, and my voice scraped with uncertainty. "I don't know, Rich. I don't know what I want or if I can keep going on like this. I'm so sorry."

Disbelief pulled through his expression, disgust coming in right behind it. "So, you're just gonna make that choice for us all?" His green eyes blinked a thousand times, as if he were trying to see me.

As if maybe he no longer recognized me.

It seemed about right because I no longer recognized myself.

"What about Leif and Rhys?" he demanded.

The faces of our drummer and bassist spun through my mind.

My best friends. The two guys who were as close as family and just as important. I was struck with the truth that I was letting every single one of them down.

"They have given their whole fuckin' lives for this band." Richard's voice was low and severe, conveying a message my spirit didn't want to receive. "What about every fucking mile we spent on the road? Every venue we ever begged to let us play? The nights we went hungry, so goddamn broke we had to choose between food and the gas to get us to the next city so we could play? What about the pact we made that the most important thing to all of us was chasing down a dream? What about that?"

"I don't know if I can do it," I whispered, trying to hold myself together and not come apart right there. Trying not to throw the blame at him. To demand that he take some responsibility. But I didn't know how to form the words. Didn't know if I could admit what had happened because of it. I was terrified that would be the last fallen brick that sent me crashing.

Richard turned away for a beat, scrubbing his face with his palms and tipping his head to the night sky.

His muscled body vibrated with indignation and ire. Barely constrained. Getting ready to burst.

As if he couldn't contain it a second longer, he flew back around, fury flooding from his mouth. "You don't get to do this, Emily. You don't. This is bullshit. You were all in, just like the rest of us, and you don't get to walk now."

"I just . . . I need a little time," I begged.

Time to figure this out. To fix this. Repair all those broken bits floating free.

"We don't have any time left. This is our big break. The culmination of years of blood, sweat, and tears. You have cold feet, Em. That's it. It's going to be fine." This time, it was his turn to plead.

Cold feet.

I only wished.

I backed away another step. "I'm not ready. I'm sorry, but I'm not."

My brother roared, shouting his disgust and disbelief in the empty, stagnant air. He snatched a discarded beer bottle from the ground and threw it against the brick wall. It crashed, shattering into a million pieces, raining to the ground like the dreams I could feel coming apart around us.

"Fuck this bullshit!" He whirled on me and jabbed his index finger in my direction. "And fuck you."

"Richard," I said through the lump in my throat.

He backed away, putting up his palms, his mouth twisting in outrage. "No, Em. Don't try to cover up what you're doing with a lame apology. It's not enough."

Didn't he get it?

I'd already given more than I could take. For him. To protect him.

He left me standing there, gasping and bent over. He flew up the steps and disappeared inside. The heavy door slammed shut behind him, a wall that went up between us and left me bitterly alone.

Alone and afraid.

My hands found my hair, and I yanked hard, and I screamed as if it might expel the loathing invading every cell. It just echoed back like a vacant, endless silence.

Unable to remain in it, I ran, racing out of the alley as if I might stand the chance of leaving it all behind. Just more crap tossed into the dumpsters.

I doubted I could run that fast, but oh, was I going to try.

I hit the sidewalk, my wedge heels slapping the concrete, the hazy glow of lights coming down through the dense Savannah summer night and infiltrating the air with an eerie glow.

It was just after ten, and the Historic District was alive, roiling with bodies and voices, a bated disorder that clung to the atmosphere.

I felt hostage to it.

Wanted to get lost in it.

Outrun it all.

Forget.

Or maybe what I really wanted was to remember who I was.

Making a mad dash to find myself.

A familiar neon sign shone from up ahead.

Charlie's.

It was an old dive bar that we'd played in what seemed a thousand times, back before we'd gotten hooked up with that big-name band that was gonna take us places, and then I'd been taken places that I didn't want to go.

Swinging open the door, I rushed through it, breaths still heaving from my throat. Inside, it was packed, a crush of bodies dancing at the foot of the stage where a band played, live music the life beat of this place. The round-top tables were surrounded by smaller groups, the plush, darkened booths lining the far-left wall overflowing with obscured faces.

Eyes making a quick sweep, I made a beeline for the bar and slipped onto the one free stool. The young bartender slinging drinks as fast as they were ordered.

The bartender tossed a paper coaster with the Charlie's logo on it in front of me. "What can I get for you?"

"Two shots of tequila."

He arched a brow.

I swallowed around the lump in my throat, the nerves and fear and terror that wouldn't let me be. I wanted to silence them more than I wanted my next breath.

"Make it three."

I guessed he saw the way I was trembling because he dipped his head really quick and lined up three shot glasses that he rimmed in salt. He poured the bottle over them and garnished each with a lime.

I didn't take the time to prime my taste buds. I just slammed one back, then the second, then the third.

Fire burned down my throat and pooled in my belly, and my trembling spirit began to calm.

I didn't care that I looked like some kind of lush.

The only thing I cared about right then was forgetting. The desperate need to feel something different than hopeless, the way I'd been feeling the last three months.

I wanted to reclaim.

Salvage the pieces that had been scattered.

Maybe I was going about it the wrong way, but I had to take a step before I went and lost everything.

I lifted my finger in the air, indicating one more. There was no missing the look of worry that passed through the bartender's expression. "Can I call someone for you? Looks like you're having a bad night."

Humorless laughter rolled out. "I'm just fine."

Lies.

All lies.

But who was I gonna call? I could call Mel, but then she'd be pissed at Richard, and the last thing I needed to do was get our assistant who was also my best friend mixed up in this. After all, her future was riding on me getting my shit together, too.

All of them were. Reliant upon me.

Oh God.

Another round of regret and hurt and bitterness went stampeding through my senses, and I slumped over, pressing the back of my hand to my mouth in an attempt to keep the sob bottled in my throat from gettin' free.

The bartender eyed me, questioning his judgement before he grabbed another shot glass. "One more for you, gorgeous, then you're done."

Redness clawed. God, ten minutes in, and he thought he needed to cut me off.

Apparently, I needed an intervention, but not the type the guy was thinking.

"Thank you," I told him with a shaking voice, trying to play it cool, as if I couldn't feel the warmth of the alcohol gliding through my veins, warming me from the inside out, at odds with the cold, stark loneliness that covered me from the outside.

He slid the glass my direction. "No problem."

He turned away to focus on other customers.

"You don't have anyone to call, I'd be glad to take your number." The slimy pickup line came from the stool to my left, and I lifted my eyes to the guy who was leering at me. Ratty, unkempt beard and stained tee shirt.

Awesome.

"Thank you, but I really want to be alone right now." I tried to turn away, but he leaned forward, forcing himself into my line of sight.

His brow lifted in suggestion. "Huh, you sure look like you could use some company. Why don't you come over here and sit on my lap, and I'll make it all better?"

He grinned a vile, disgusting grin.

Nausea churned in my belly, revulsion and fear flickerin' through my senses that were barely dulled by the liquor.

Maybe I should have thought better about this.

I was still wearing the dress I'd worn onstage, red and short and cut deep between my breasts. Much more provocative than anything I'd ever pick for myself—my wardrobe was completely in the hands of Mel, considering I'd probably be wearing sweats up there if the decision were left to me.

And God, I didn't have my phone.

This was stupid.

"I'll pass," I said, dread crawling through my being.

He set a hand on my knee. "You sure about that?"

I sucked in a staggered breath at the unwelcome contact, trying not to gag.

Then my heart fully seized in my chest when I felt the dark cloud descend from behind us.

A voice that could only be described as menacing rumbled into the space, "Only thing sure around here is you're about two seconds from losing your throat if you don't take your hand off her. Got me?"

Dark and cold, the words penetrated the din of the bar, and the guy who'd had his hand on my knee glared behind me, clearly getting ready to spout out something aggressive, and then froze, words dying on his tongue. I was pretty sure it was fear that took hold of him as he slowly removed his hand and slipped off the opposite side of the stool.

Unsettled, I kept my attention trained on the tiny glass still clutched in my hand.

The man who'd sent the asshole running slipped into his place.

Was it the ground shaking or the slosh of alcohol beating through my brain that made me feel as if I were tipping sideways?

I was almost afraid to look that way, not sure of what to make of the feeling that crawled over my flesh.

I stole a peek at the man.

My belly tipped.

Capsized.

Tossing me into an ocean of instant fascination.

The eyes of what had to be the most intriguingly beautiful man I'd ever seen were trained on me. Eyes so dark they were the color of onyx, though somehow, they glinted like cracked, black ice that held a seething ball of white fire within.

Anger and fury raving in the depths.

His sharp jaw was clenched, and his full, full lips were set in a grim, threatening line.

"Are you okay?" he demanded. His voice rang like the lash of a raging song. Heavy and grating and seductive.

"I . . . I—" It was all a stammer as I contended with the lump that had grown thick in my throat, all of my attention trapped, snared by the face that glared back.

I couldn't even blame it on the alcohol because the man was prettier than any soul had the right to be. His eyes so deep, burning with a thousand wicked secrets, lips nothing but seduction, body so intimidating that it made my heart thunder out of control.

He faced me where he sat on the stool, one hand clinging to the back of the seat and the other planted on the bar.

His hair was just as black as his eyes, wild and disordered, and I got the distinct sense that he'd been roughing agitated fingers through it the entire day.

"I . . . I . . . thank you," I managed, my voice raw and unsure and riddled with attraction. A spark fired in my chest. I was sure, sitting there, it was the first time I'd felt alive in months.

Dressed like some kind of powerful CEO, he wore a perfectly fitted white button-up and gray suit pants that hugged all the lean, sinewy strength that oozed from his body, though somewhere along the way, his jacket had been discarded.

But it was the way every exposed inch of his flesh was covered in designs and colors, shapes and shadows, that held me rapt.

All of him.

Arms and hands.

Chest and throat.

I felt as if I were looking at a mysterious painting and had been charged with deciphering the meaning.

The man written in opposition.

Rebel and ruler.

Contradiction and conflict.

A bottle of discord and mayhem and destruction.

A very expensive brand of sin.

Something you didn't dip your fingers into without signing a waiver, accepting the outright risk.

And somehow, I was stuck there, throat dry and eyes devouring him as if he might be the one to remind me exactly of who I was.

He edged forward, intensity fierce. His attention skated over the three empty glasses sitting in front of me, lingering on the one I still had clutched in my hand.

"Drowning your sorrows doesn't work. Believe me, I've tried."

Those eyes swept back up to me when he murmured it, and there was no amusement there.

My heart thudded in my chest, emotion fisting tight, and my gaze roved his face, trying to get a read on this man who'd stepped in to save me and looked like he could destroy me in the same breath.

"It doesn't hurt to try, does it?" A tremor filled my words.

"Doesn't it? It looked like you were a couple seconds away from regretting it to me."

Unease twisted through my body, a flush rising up my neck and hitting my cheeks.

He was right.

But I was feeling desperate. Trying to fill the hole that couldn't be filled.

I dropped my head, staring at the amber in the glass before I mustered the courage to look back at him, where a wayward lock of raven hair cast one side of his gorgeous face in shadow. "I wasn't askin' for that . . . for that . . . jerk. Just because I'm sitting here by myself doesn't mean that man had the right to touch me that way."

Dark eyes flashed fury. "You're right. It doesn't. I should follow him out of here . . . show him the cost of touching what isn't his. Say it, and it's done."

Anger radiated from him. Fierce and ferocious. As if he were my protector and standing guard over me was his job. A wraith that would lay waste to any threat. I wasn't sure what to make of that, why I suddenly felt safer than I had in forever. At the same time, I was one-hundred-percent certain I was standing at the shore of a stormy, churning sea.

Wrought with danger.

The man written in peril.

And there I was, wanting to wade deeper, reach out and dip in my fingers, pull a little of it into my mouth to wet the thirst growing by the second.

God, what was goin' on with me?

I didn't do this.

Fumble all over a stranger. Wonder what it might be like to have his massive hands takin' possession of my body. Those were the last kind of thoughts I should have been entertaining.

"I appreciate you steppin' in, but I would have been okay." I didn't even know why I was trying to front that assertion. Because I was shaking. Shivering all over the place. Runaway nerves that didn't know where to go.

The fact that I wasn't okay abundantly clear.

But I was pretty sure if I sent this man on that kind of mission, he would end up in jail.

"Would you really?" he challenged, still so close that I was breathing all his breaths. He smelled like whiskey and cedar and the faintest vestiges of cigarettes.

I should have been repulsed.

I wasn't even close.

Intrigue and attraction had me parting my lips, wanting to inhale him, suck him down.

Experience something profound.

To get zapped by the current I could feel running a circuit between us.

"You think I didn't see you come running in here, looking for a place to hide?" His mouth brushed my jaw, his words just loud enough to be heard over the roaring din of the bar. "Right out in the open. Is that what you wanted, to be found?"

A wicked sort of seduction was falling from his tongue.

Entrancing.

Mesmerizing.

My gaze flickered up to meet his, wavering and returning, wanting him to see me and terrified that he might discover who I was at the same time. "I think that might depend on who it was that found me."

Onyx eyes flitted over my face, as if he were tracing the lines, as if he were peeling me open and getting a good look at what was hidden inside.

"Is that so?"

I chewed at the inside of my cheek, feeling so out of sorts that I no longer understood up from down.

"And who was it you were hoping would find you?" he pressed, his tattooed throat bobbing as he swallowed, his lips moving slow.

Hypnotizing.

I gathered up all the courage I had, and the words came rolling out like a plea. "Maybe I came here hoping for you."

A rough chuckle rumbled up that thick throat, and my eyes got stuck on the action, my mouth going dry.

"I'm pretty sure I am exactly the opposite of what you're looking for, beautiful."

He said it to repel, a clear-cut warning, but the only thing I could really process was the fact that he'd called me beautiful.

"I think maybe you are exactly what I need right now." I didn't even know how I'd managed to get it out, but it was true.

I needed him.

For a moment.

For a night.

Even if he used me up, I knew it would feel right.

"You don't have the first clue what you're asking."

There it was again.

Another threat. A risk I wanted to accept. This was one time where I was happy to sign on the dotted line.

"Maybe I want whatever it is you can give me." God, I sounded like I was beggin'.

A smirk ticked up at the corner of his delicious mouth, and he angled in closer and lifted a tattooed knuckle to trace along my bottom lip.

Shivers raced.

"Do you want to know what I think?"

Did I?

"Yes," I whispered, my gaze jumping around, not sure where to rest my eyes, wanting to take in every inch of this compelling man.

He let a fingertip traipse down the side of my jaw. "I think you're feeling reckless. I think you're looking for someone to take away the pain you're drowning in. I think you're itching to experience something different . . . to dip your pure, cute little toes into something dirty. Is that what you want . . . to get dirty?"

A shockwave of need slammed over me, and my belly twisted into a thousand knots.

I swallowed around the lump he had wedged in the base of my throat, going for brave when my knees were knocking so hard I wasn't sure how I remained sitting on the stool. "You say that like it'd be a bad thing."

He dipped down faster than I could process it, his lips brushing mine. Chills zapped and energy flashed and a rush of dizziness swept through my head.

"It would be a very, very bad thing."

He edged back, and I could feel the space between us simmering with something mysterious.

"I'm not scared of you," I murmured, wondering just who it was that I was tryin' to convince.

"You should be."

A frown pulled at my brow. "You just saved me. Stepped in and stood up for me."

"I touch you, and you won't ever forget it. I'll wreck you, beautiful. Looks to me like your heart is banged up enough."

"I'm not broken," I whispered in a rush.

"Are you looking to be?"

"I . . . I . . ." All I could do was blink at him, trying to make sense of *this*. Of this attraction.

Because he felt like instinct.

I believed in love at first sight. With all of me.

But this wasn't close to being it.

This was fascination. This was climbing a mountainside with the sole purpose of diving off a cliff. Risking everything to experience a free fall.

"I don't think my coming here was a mistake."

His voice lowered. "Watch yourself because those are the only kind of choices that I seem to make."

I peered at him in an attempt to see through the veil of words he kept tossing at me. "I don't understand."

He angled his head, that black hair falling to one side, his gaze so severe my heart rate spiked. "That's because you're too good to see what's staring back at you."

"Or maybe it's you who sees himself all wrong."

A roll of coarse, dry laughter escaped him. "Precious girl."

He said it like an insult dipped in affection.

God, this man was too much. Too forward and too compelling, and I was contemplating all kinds of things that I didn't do. Maybe he was right. This was a very bad idea.

"I should go," I told him.

"Yeah, you should."

I started to fumble for my credit card in the zipper pocket of my dress, thanking all the stars I sang to that I actually had one along with my hotel key. The last thing I wanted was to have to go crawling back to my brother.

The stranger set a tattooed hand on my wrist.

My attention dragged down to where we were connected. The muscles of his forearm were twitching, the skin covered in shadowy ink that looked like some kind of ripped-up, intricate treasure map interwoven with landscape and faces. It shifted into the portrait of a king on the back of his hand, the image surrounded by roses, fading into the pawns stamped on his knuckles.

The entire scene screamed power and still somehow felt incredibly sad.

I suddenly had the devastating need to climb inside of this man. To touch him and feel him and know him.

He was right. I was a reckless, careless girl.

"I've got this," he grated.

"You don't owe me anything."

He looked at me with something in his expression that I couldn't quite make out. "It's the least I can do."

He handed the bartender his card, and I was whispering a wispy, "Thank you. I'm Emily, by the way."

A twitch of something that looked like disgust pulled at one side of his mouth. "Royce."

He said it like his name was an issue of condemnation, the man staring me down for a beat, as if he were waiting for something, for a fallout maybe, before he turned to the slip the bartender handed him and signed it.

He returned the card to his wallet and tucked it into the back pocket of his pants.

Unable to remain under the potency of him for a second longer, I fumbled to stand, swaying a bit when I got to my feet.

His hand shot out to steady me. "Watch yourself, Precious."

A shiver raced over my arms. "I'm fine . . . I'm just . . . going to use the restroom. It was nice to meet you," I managed, taking two steps as if I possessed an ounce of calm, and then for the second time tonight, I rushed through a crowd to get away.

Though this time it was because I wanted to stay.

Because I wanted to experience those dark waters washing over me.

I shouldered through the crush, fighting the sting of tears.

God, I really was pathetic. But I couldn't help it. The only thing I wanted was for someone to see me for me. All I needed was one second of truth. A taste of freedom. To be loosed of these chains.

Maybe then I would be willing to give it all away. Stand up and be brave.

Forget and remember.

Accept all the possibilities and reject what had been haunting me.

A surge of power rustled over me from behind, and I sucked in a staggered breath when I realized he was there, right behind me, following me through the crowd. My pulse raced in anticipation, though I increased my pace.

The man did the same.

Royce.

I wondered what the sound of it might be like coming from my tongue.

I stumbled when I broke out of the crowd and into the narrow, dimly lit hall, the decibel of the bar diminishing to a dull thrum. The only sound I could make out was the thunder of my heart pounding in my ears and the man's footsteps edging up from behind.

"You don't have to watch over me," I whispered into the hollow vacancy.

A tattooed hand snaked around to palm the front of my throat. I felt it like a rough caress to my soul.

"I don't know how to let you walk away."

Oh, God.

My knees went weak, and the plea was spilling out, "Then don't."

He exhaled a shaky breath, and he was slowly turning me around and edging me deeper into the hall, the shadows swallowing us as we moved farther into the recesses. He backed me into the wall, and a tremble ripped down my spine when he planted both palms over my head.

Heat surged as he covered me in the shroud of his gorgeous body. A whimper of need bled from my tongue.

"Royce." I murmured his name like it was a dream.

He ran his nose along my jaw, and my chest was heaving, my wayward heart reaching out for him.

"You're going to regret this," he grated.

I probably would.

This was so not me.

But tonight—tonight I didn't care. The only thing that mattered was this.

Feeling.

And I wanted to *feel* with him.

"Please . . . just . . . kiss me," I begged.

Royce wavered.

Rocking forward then edging back, needy pants ripping up his tremoring throat.

"Please," I said again.

"Shit," he muttered, then his mouth crushed against mine.

Three

Royce

*S*hit.

Motherfucking shit.

What was I doing? What was I doing?

Making another one of those huge, massive mistakes, that was what.

Didn't understand why I couldn't stop. Why I didn't fucking want to.

Nothing made sense. Nothing but driving my fingers deep into long, thick curls of blonde hair as I kissed her like a madman.

A lightning bolt ridged down my spine, my cock steel, a boatload of lust dumped into my bloodstream, so thick, it obliterated all reason.

Chased out all rationale.

I was going to regret this. But sometimes one moment was

more important than a thousand others.

Unforgettable.

Impossible.

Because there was no chance I was actually *feeling* this.

Emily exhaled in surprise, and I swallowed the needy sound, my lips slanting over hers in frantic possession.

Those little hands fisted in my shirt, the girl trying to keep up with the assault, gasping for air as she fought to kiss me back.

Could feel the heat, the need, the way she struggled to get closer. No chance that either of us could get close enough.

For a desperate beat, I edged back to look down at her, the girl so gorgeous it knocked the breath from my lungs, my mind canting to the left, disconnected from all logic.

She was cut in sharp, defined angles, cheeks high, her mouth the only contradiction, a soft, silken bow that I wanted to lose myself in forever.

But it was those sage-colored green eyes that gutted me, the trust that swam in their lapping depths, the storm of gray that rimmed the outside.

"Royce," she begged.

All it took was my name raking up her throat for me to completely lose it. No control left.

Fuck it.

Only thing that mattered was getting closer.

I lifted her from the ground, one arm around the small of her back and the other wrapped up in her hair. I pulled her to my hungry mouth, kissing her wild, lips and tongues and teeth.

Cherry coated her sweet tongue, and need thrummed her heart into a fury.

"You were right, what you said. You were right," she whispered frantically. "I want you to take away the pain. Take it . . . just for a little while. Just for tonight."

Fuck.

I was a bastard.

A monster.

But I couldn't stop.

On a groan, I spun around and rushed us five steps deeper into the hall, like that was going to do anything to keep us concealed.

Her upper back hit the opposite wall with a thud, and she wrapped her legs around my waist.

Flames licked, friction rising from the barest connection.

I dove in deeper, possessing her mouth, and my palm greedily slipped up the silky bare flesh of her long, toned leg. The material of that red country dress that had driven me out of my mind all night bunched up over her thigh.

A warning screamed from the depths of my mind that this was spinning out of control.

Realization that I was devouring her right out in the open. The shadows had nothing against a powerful camera lens.

God, this was stupid.

Reckless and foolish and brash.

I knew this girl was out looking for a reprieve. Sanctuary. To find something that was so clearly lacking, but I didn't think she had the first clue what she was signing up for.

Me.

The fucker who would take it all. Ruin it. Destroy her.

Her tongue stroked mine, desire wrapping us in a hazy cloud of delirium.

"Goddamn delicious." I rumbled it into her mouth, just like I'd known she'd be. "Precious."

She was fucking precious.

I kept kissing her, my hands grappling to get closer, to touch every inch of her sexy body. Running over her small, firm tits, cleavage just peeking out along the plunge of the dress.

Palmed her slim waist and gripped her lush ass.

I pressed my aching dick against the sweet heat of her pussy, my mind going fuzzy at the pleasure that threatened to erupt.

Fuck.

This girl was too much. Too perfect and too right and everything I shouldn't want.

She whimpered and sank her nails into my shoulders. "I don't do this," she rasped.

My hand fisted in her hair, and I angled back to look at her, our chests heaving in sync, her back hiking up the wall as she clawed to get closer.

I nipped her bottom lip. "What's that? Kiss strangers in dark hallways?"

"Yes." The word blustered from her mouth, and I devoured that, too. "But . . . but you feel so familiar. So right. I feel like you can see me. See me for who I am. I want this."

Guilt gripped me in an iron fist.

Lungs squeezing tight.

There was that innocence, what had hauled my ass off that stool when I'd spotted the wolf that had scented her, bastard salivating all over the girl, going in for the kill.

Couldn't stomach it, the thought of someone touching her.

Couldn't sit aside and watch it go down.

Fucker had been lucky I couldn't seem to leave her side, because I'd been about five seconds from hunting him down.

Then I was the twisted fuck who'd turned around and gone for her instead.

Now here I was, pressing her against the wall like she belonged to me. My dick begging for reprieve.

"I don't think you know what you're saying."

"I do . . . I do," she whimpered, rubbing her tight body all over mine, inciting a fire that flamed and burned any good judgement into the ground.

Turned it to ash.

I let my lips travel over her jaw and tumble down her throat, both my hands holding her by the face. The girl's head rocked back on the wall, gasping and panting for air as I devoured her sweet flesh.

The girl completely surrendered.

Shit.

This was bad. So bad.

I ripped myself back, which was a goddamn travesty in itself. "We have to get out of here. Right fucking now."

"Okay," she said without reservation, and shit, that ruined me, too.

Trust bubbling from her like a spring.

I set her on unsteady feet, and my hand shot out to keep her from falling when she swayed. "Are you good?"

"I need you," was all that she said, and I gripped her by the hand and hauled her back down the hall and into the throng that had grown rowdy, the bar alive and thrumming.

Thrumming as violently as my heart.

I managed to pull her outside onto the street. Humidity clung to the night, the Savannah summer thick as it moved through the air, streetlamps hazy where they glowed through the mugginess that draped the city.

It made it hard to move.

Hard to breathe.

At least, that was what I was blaming it on and not the girl who had her hand wrapped in mine.

I lifted my free hand for the cab sitting on the opposite side of the street. It pulled from the curb, whipping around to our side. I pulled open the door, trying to keep my eyes off the curved lines of those legs as she slipped in. She angled to the side, one knee coming up, the material slipping up her thigh like a tease.

She leaned back, both palms pressed to the seat, begging me to go for her, all the while shaking and shivering with nerves, a slick of heat radiating from her skin.

Energy flashed, attraction and greed, and I clenched my teeth against the force of it.

Fuck.

She was hotter than a thousand suns.

Sweeter than an orchard of dark black cherries.

Trying to keep my cool, I slipped into the seat beside her, fighting the aggression that bottled in my chest when I saw the way the driver was looking at her through the rearview mirror.

I cleared my throat.

His attention snapped to me.

That's right, asshole. Don't look at the girl unless you want to lose your teeth.

With a glare that could kill, I gave him the order of where to drive. "Bohemian."

He gave a tight nod and flipped a U, taking the half-mile drive to the upscale hotel. The whole time, jade eyes with flecks of gold watched me from where she was angled on the seat, her breaths filling the air with cherries and sweet and desire.

Could smell it coming off her, could feel it as she rubbed her thighs together. A fresh round of lust went pounding through my body, hammering my heart into mayhem, and I was desperately searching around inside myself for one moral bone.

For one sliver of decency.

I might be a dick, but I refused to be a creep.

Problem was, she was looking at me like I was the one who'd saved her. Found her when she'd been wandering lost for years.

Two minutes later, the cab pulled into the drive at the hotel, and I tossed a bill at him.

Asshole was lucky that was my only parting gift.

Climbing out, I turned, dipped down, and extended my hand.

Emily took it, those legs so long as she slid to the side and stepped out into the night, and I wondered if she'd even noticed that I hadn't asked her where she was staying. She just let me lead her into the posh lobby of the boutique hotel in Historic Savannah.

Old brick walls and dark hardwood floors made it feel like we were stepping into another time, like one of those old romance movies that screamed scandal and temptation.

Guessed it was no accident she was staying here.

I dipped down to murmur in her ear, "What room?"

"Four-Seventeen."

I punched at the button of the elevator. A river of anxiety pulsed through my blood as I waited, that feeling only intensifying tenfold when we stepped onto the lift and the doors swept closed.

Boxing us in.

Sealing us off.

Just the two of us with our pulses pounding and our breaths filling the confined space.

Mirrors surrounded us on all sides.

I pried myself away, needing to put about two states between us.

Emily turned to face me, those blonde waves a sexy disorder where they'd been mussed by my fingers, her lips bruised and swollen from my kiss. Girl taunting me in that short red dress that screamed country and a pair of wedge heels, legs bare and leading to the promised land underneath.

And there she was, staring at me with all that innocent seduction she wore like a brand.

She looked like heaven.

Tasted like it, too.

I leaned against the railing, holding on to it like I was shackled by chains.

Forever condemned to hell.

Sounded about right.

"You are gorgeous. I hope you know that. I hope you look in the mirror and you see exactly what I see. I hope you know exactly how much you're worth. Don't you ever sell yourself short."

My words were hard, coming across like a threat.

It was exactly what I meant them to be.

A frown pulled across her face just as the elevator jolted to a stop on the fourth floor. The doors slid open. I took her hand, and my body was assaulted with the shiver of anticipation that rolled through her.

Luckily, her door was a straight shot off the elevator, and I waited behind her as she fumbled into her pocket and retrieved the key. She slipped it into the slot and clicked open the door, not looking back at me as she pushed it open.

But with the way she was trembling, I knew she was expecting me to follow.

Anxious and nervous and needy.

I pressed my hand up high on the door to hold it open for her so she could go all the way in, and when she didn't feel me enter, she turned around. Confusion filled her expression.

"Good night, Emily."

She looked like I kicked her, but this girl didn't have the first clue that I was doing her a favor.

"What?" It quivered from her mouth, a plea that hit me like a bullet to the chest.

"I think it'd be best if we call it a night."

Her head started to shake, as much as her hands, and fuck me, a tear slipped from the corner of her eye.

Didn't know how it was possible that a girl who was so voraciously sought after, wanted, could feel the amount of rejection that had visibly struck through her spirit.

The palpable pain that filled the air and clenched my chest in regret.

I wanted to ruin every fucker who'd ever damaged her. Vindicate every scar.

"Please . . . don't leave me here like this."

"Emily." It was a groan. A petition for her not to do this.

Her eyes dropped closed, and her little hands clenched at her side.

"Please. Don't do this to me. I can't handle it tonight. I need . . . I need . . ." she trailed off as more moisture went gliding down her face, glinting in the bare light of her room, while the girl stood there pressing her thighs together, desperate for relief.

For something to fill up the void.

For an escape.

Motherfucker.

There was nothing I could do.

I broke.

Restraints coming apart.

I pushed through the door, and it slammed shut behind me.

I swept her off her feet, and surprise was rocking from her mouth just as I was diving in to swallow it. Her hurt and insecurities and fears.

I kissed her mad. As mad as she was driving me, my hand in her hair and the other at her back as I lifted her to prop her on the high foyer table of her suite.

A rasp of need moaned from her mouth as the cool glass hit the back of her thighs, and I continued to devour her, muttering the words in between, "You think you aren't wanted? You think I don't want you?"

I shouldn't.

It was so fucking wrong. So twisted and at odds with everything I'd been fighting for. Right then, it didn't matter.

Frantic, I held her by one side of the face, our lips grasping for the other, my other hand pressing her legs apart by one knee. I slid my fingers over the soaked fabric of her underwear. "You think I don't want this?"

I shoved the fabric aside and pressed two fingers into the wet well of her body. I fucked her tight little pussy with them, driving her right into delirium as I consumed her mouth like the greedy bastard that I was.

Yeah. I was going to regret this.

But I might have regretted walking away more.

She rode my hand, gasps ripping up her throat as I rolled my thumb over her swollen clit. As I worked her into a frenzy. Shot her straight into oblivion.

"Fuck, you are the hottest thing I've ever seen. You are every fantasy I've ever had. Did you know that, Emily? Do you have any clue how damn sexy you are? I would sell my soul to get into this body."

Thing was, I'd already sold my soul a long time ago, and it no longer belonged to me.

Her hands were everywhere, whimpers coming from her mouth, fingers going for the buttons of my shirt. "Take this off. I want to see you. I want to feel this. Know you."

Grabbing her by the wrists, I pinned both of them over her head to the mirror on the wall behind her.

"No," I grunted, thrusting my fingers deeper and harder and faster, the whole time wishing it was my aching dick that was getting to experience all that slick, tight heat.

"Please," she whimpered, but then she was forgetting all of that when I pressed down on her engorged clit, swirling my thumb over that sweet spot. I curled my fingers deep inside her and shot her to the stars.

Her back bowed, her covered tits arching out, my tongue thirsting to get a taste, my eyes raking over the most beautiful sight I'd witnessed in all my life.

The girl was a fucking oasis.

A song written in seduction.

She cried out, my name a plea and praise on her tongue, her entire body stretched taut, wracked in bliss.

She gasped and writhed, pants heaving from her chest as she came back down.

Slowly, she peeled her eyes open. Lost in them, I pulled my fingers free and readjusted her skirt, my heart a jackhammer in my chest as I helped her down onto unsteady feet.

Like a fool, I leaned in and brushed my lips against hers, relishing her for one second more.

"It's so fucking wrong how bad I want to keep you," I murmured to her forehead, squeezing my eyes, memorizing this.

Then I peeled myself away, turned, and headed for the door.

"Royce." Pain bled through her voice. Like a sucker, I turned around to look at her because apparently there wasn't a damn thing I could do to resist this girl. "I . . . I don't understand."

Taking the three steps back her direction, I swept back the lock of hair that had fallen into her face, stared her down, my words grit. "Just remember in the morning that I warned you the only thing I do is make mistakes."

And I was pretty sure this was the worst one I'd ever made.

Before I could make this worse, which was pretty much a fucking impossibility, I tore myself away and forced myself into the hall, pulling the door shut behind me.

The click of the lock engaging rang with finality, and I headed down the hall, heart raging like a beast, cock so hard it was painful to walk.

Derision huffed from my nose when I stopped three doors down in front of my suite, and I dug into my back pocket and pulled out my key.

Wondering how it was possible I'd fucked up so badly on day one.

Standing there, I promised myself I would never touch her again.

Didn't matter how fucking bad I wanted her.

I had a job to do.

And I was damn sure going to see it through.

four

Emily

The phone ringing from the nightstand pulled me from sleep.

From what had been a really incredible dream, or a really bad one, I couldn't decide.

All I knew was I felt completely wrung out as I lifted my head from the pillow where I'd been passed out facedown, my hair a ratted mess that obstructed my view as I fumbled around to find my cell.

Finally getting hold of it, I flopped onto my back and shoved the mess of hair from my face so I could see who was screaming for my attention.

Sunlight poured in through the massive windows overlooking the river, and I squinted through bleary eyes. Sickness bloomed in my stomach when I saw the name on the screen.

Of course.

At seven in the mornin'.

Who else would it be?

As if I didn't have enough to deal with.

Flinging my arm over my eyes like a shield, I accepted the call and pushed the phone to my ear.

"Nile." I gave it my all to keep my voice from shaking.

"Emily." He breathed out in what sounded like disappointment and relief. "I haven't heard from you in weeks. Why haven't you returned my calls?"

I swallowed around the knot of irritation that burned hot in my chest. Was he serious? After everything?

"I never said that I would."

Silence traveled through the distance. His anger was almost palpable, though I knew he was trying to rein it in considering he sure didn't have a right in the world for it to be there. Still, there was an accusation in his tone. "You used to call every day."

"Yes, Nile, that was when we were engaged. When I was committed to you and you were committed to me. We aren't anymore. Do you see how that works?"

Couldn't keep the snippiness out of my voice.

I mean, really, who did he think he was?

"I care about you. I was worried."

Resentful laughter rippled out. "You cheated on me."

Wasn't there when I needed him most. When I'd gone to him at the worst time of my life, and I'd found him with her.

An indignant huff came through the line. "Because you were gone for three fuckin' months. Had guys drooling all over you every time you got up on that damn stage while you left me here alone. What else was I supposed to do?"

Right. All of that made it just fine?

"Oh, I don't know . . . respect me? Cherish me? Realize I was worth the wait?" I spat at him, hurt and hatred bleeding out.

He sighed. "You are worth the wait."

I laughed again, no amusement in the sound. "You should have thought about that then."

"Maybe you should come home. Where you belong. We'll work it out. You know how good we are when we're together."

"There's no working this out, Nile."

Sadness pulsed through my spirit, cracks that throbbed where everything good had leaked out and left me hollow.

Dreams that had been lost.

Love that had been crushed.

"Emily," he murmured, his voice turning low and pleading, and I fought the threat of tears I could feel pricking at the backs of my eyes. I couldn't do this with him. Not again. Not anymore.

"Please . . . just don't, Nile. What's done is done. It's over."

"We aren't finished. You know we're not. Tell me you don't still feel this."

Grief bound my chest.

"You want to hear that I still *feel* it, Nile? Fine. You're right. I do. I still feel it. I still feel the remnants of the devastation I felt when I came home and found you with her. I can still feel the split right down the middle of my heart. I still feel the betrayal carved into my soul. And I promise you, I don't ever want to feel that again."

Without allowing him to say anything else, I ended the call, needing to cut off that train before he pushed me any further. Before he backed me up against a wall, and I completely lost it.

God, I wished there was a way to eradicate everything.

Start over.

Before I let myself drown in an ocean of turmoil, I forced myself up to sitting, knowing I had so many more things to face this mornin' than just my ex-fiancé.

Instantly, I was hit with a rush of dizziness. The residual of last night's alcohol slugged nausea through my veins, and a vague memory was pressing into my mind.

My hand slid down my trembling body, checking to see that I was still whole. That his touch hadn't shattered all the pieces I was trying to hold together.

Royce.

I'd fallen into bed still wearing the red dress that was now wrinkled and crumpled to shame, so confused and unsettled by the stranger who'd made me feel different—reminded me that *I* was still inside, maybe beaten and shackled and a little bit broken, my spirit dimmed, but I was there.

Alive.

A tinge of hope still burning in the depths.

I'd be a fool to deny it wasn't more than that, though. That was shocking in itself. He'd touched me in a way I was sure I'd never been touched before, passion boiling over and inciting a raging storm that had come from out of nowhere.

As beautiful as it was devastating.

Then he'd just . . . left.

Left me standing there aching and needy and more bewildered than I'd ever been. Offering myself to a man who I'd sworn had wanted me every bit as badly as I'd wanted him. I'd been desperate to stand in his flames, to experience the rush and thrill.

To experience the darkness that surrounded him.

Okay, maybe that was a problem, too. A flicker of worry traipsed through my spirit. Just because I was struggling didn't mean I should turn around and go after things that I shouldn't.

Choosing danger rather than allowing it to come after me.

I blinked through the images from last night, trying to process. I pressed the heel of my hand to my eye as if it might offer some clarity. My brain was a muddled, hazy mess.

No big surprise there.

But that didn't mean it wasn't ingrained with the perfect imprint of that unforgettable face.

Ugh. I needed to shake off the encounter. Accept that fixating on it wasn't going to make a difference.

Like I'd told Nile, what was done was done. That went for the stranger, too. I'd be gone this morning, and I wouldn't be seeing him again.

A chance missed.

Or maybe it was one of those blessings after all. I was pretty sure the sunlight pouring in through the window was casting a spotlight on my bad judgement.

I knew myself well enough to know I would have regretted it.

No one-night stand was going to fill up this hollowed-out vacancy that throbbed inside of me, and it sure wasn't gonna heal the cracked, brittle pieces that I was barely holdin' together.

Pounding thundered from my hotel door.

My heart jumped into a riot.

I wasn't sure I was ready to face my brother and the rest of the band after what I'd done last night. And I was more than certain I wasn't ready to answer their questions or succumb to the pressures.

God, maybe I really should pack up my things and make a run for it.

All the way back to South Carolina. Curl up in the warmth of my mama's house and the safety of her arms. She'd know what to do. That was if I ever garnered the courage to confess it, which hurt all the more considering it wasn't even my own sin.

But I'd kept it as my own.

Bottled it.

Let it fester.

Last night onstage, it'd almost burst.

Another round of pounding echoed from the door.

Groaning, I shut down the disturbance of thoughts and forced myself out of bed. I padded barefoot across the posh room and out into the living space.

My attention caught on the glass table where he'd had me pinned.

Redness streaked across my flesh, as red as the dress. Maybe I wasn't gonna get over the memory so easily.

Another bout of impatient knocking.

"Comin'," I grated, voice scratchy from sleep, wary of who was going to be on the other side.

I popped up onto my toes and glanced through the peephole.

Relief blew through my body, and I quickly worked the lock and opened the door.

"Mel."

With a smile that was partway a frown, she shoved a paper cup of coffee in my direction. "I figured you were gonna need that this mornin'. My keycard didn't work since you had the deadbolt engaged. What's that all about, anyway? You know I should have access to you twenty-four-seven." She issued the last like a tease, edging right in without an invitation. It wasn't like she needed one.

She was my best friend, my closest confidant, but I'd done a bang-up job of keeping her at bay, too.

Why was it we hid our hurt when those who cared about us would gladly hold some of our pain?

She eyed me with her dark brown gaze as she passed, her voice held low, as if she were letting me know this was just between us. "Where in the hell did you run off to last night? I was worried about you. I called at least fifteen times and texted what had to have been a million. And what did you give me? Zip. Zero. Zilch. I thought you were dead in a dumpster somewhere. Not cool, Em, not cool. You're lucky I didn't have the cops out lookin' for you."

Cringing, I blew at the steam escaping the sip hole, focusing on that rather than the warranted anger I could feel radiating from her. "I just . . . needed to get some air."

Her brows disappeared behind her bangs, and a slew of incredulous words started tumbling from her mouth. "You needed air? You ran off the stage in the middle of a song . . . which is like . . . the biggest WTF you've ever hit me with, and I had to spend the entire night dodging questions about what went down. I'm pretty sure the gossip columns are having a field day, half of them claiming you are sufferin' from morning sickness and the other speculating you've got a thing for little white pills and we have to make the hard decision of checking you into rehab."

Frustration twisted up her expression. "And then you took off without a word, and that's all you've got? You needed air? What is goin' on with you, Em? And don't you dare tell me you actually have gotten yourself messed up in that shady business because I will personally kick your ass from here to the Betty Ford Center."

"Of course not."

"Then what?" she pleaded, taking a step toward me.

"I'm just having a bit of a rough time."

A frown pinched her pretty face, her tawny red hair swept up in a ponytail and her makeup done to perfection. The girl was all of five-foot nothin', but her personality more than made up for her size.

She was a spitfire.

A powerhouse.

Managed to keep four creative spirits focused and on task.

She also loved like crazy.

She never hesitated to tell it exactly as she saw it, either.

Zero filter.

She brushed back a tangle of hair hanging in my face. "Is it that bastard, Nile? God, I was hopin' you would've ended up being thankful that pencil dick finally showed his true colors. I always knew he was a slimy motherfucker. You deserve so much better than him," she drawled.

I wished that was it. It was the rest of the rubble I was trapped under that was crushing me.

I forced a small smile to my mouth. "Oh, I saw his colors, all right. You don't need to worry about that."

I got an eyeful of plenty of other things I'd have preferred not to be subjected to, too.

"He stole enough of your time, Emily. Don't let him go and steal your dreams."

Her brown eyes filled with sincerity.

"I'm tryin' not to. I promise, I'm tryin'."

Only thing was, it wasn't Nile who I was trying to outrun.

Her expression shifted into playful sympathy. "Well, just because you wanted more to deal with, a word to the wise—your brother is in rare form this morning. Prepare yourself. He's pacing around like a caged beast."

Nerves rattled through my senses. I knew the reason for that. The fight we'd had last night. He hated when we were angry with each other every bit as much as I did.

We were going to have to hash this out. I just didn't know what I could give him. Promise him. What I could confide in him and he could confide in me. It felt like we were going round and round on opposite sides of a circle, and we were never going to meet.

"I got a text that he wants the whole band in his room at nine. Something about an important meeting that came up. You better get into the shower. You look like you went a round or two last night."

She let her attention travel down my body. "Holy shit. What did you get up to last night? Or I guess the better question would be, what got into you?"

She was clearly only teasing considering she knew me a whole lot better than that. Which was precisely why embarrassment quivered in my belly.

"Nothin'," I said far too quick, spreading my hand over the skirt of my dress in a futile attempt at ironing out the evidence.

"Nothin'?" she returned.

I shifted on my feet and took a fumbling sip of the steaming coffee to bury the guilt I knew was written all over my face. "I said, nothin'."

"If that's nothin', then I sure would like to see somethin'." She gestured at me like my state was the proof in the pudding, a taunt riding through her demeanor.

A blush went racing again.

Mel caught it, and she angled her head and lowered her voice when she realized something had really gone on. "Oh my God, Emily Iris Ramsey, did you actually have a one-night stand?" she demanded through the quietest whisper, her gaze darting around as if I still had the guy hiding in my bed.

God, was it wrong that I wished I'd woken up with that body wrapped around mine?

"I did not," I whisper-shouted back, my gaze jumping around behind hers, as if I was going to get caught.

Her eyes narrowed. "Don't you dare keep the good stuff from me. Here I was, up all night, worried you were in some dark corner crying your eyes out or maybe facedown in some ditch, and you were with a man, weren't you?"

"Fine . . . I brought a man here, but we didn't sleep together."

Her eyes went round with glee. "Oh my God. I can't believe it. This is the best news I've gotten all year. Forget the whole record deal possibility. Was he hot?"

His face flashed through my mind, that body and those hands and those eyes. A fever blistered across my flesh, scorching my legs as if I were still standing in the vestiges of his flames.

"He was unlike anyone I've ever met," I admitted with a tremble in my voice.

Confusion pulled through her expression. "And you didn't

sleep with him? What in the world is wrong with you?"

It was all a joke, but it had me fidgeting with the lid on the cup, wondering that very thing. Why he'd touched me with all that passion, looked at me that way, and then walked out the door, disappearing in the night. "I guess he wasn't that into me."

She scowled as if I were speaking nonsense. "You are the prettiest thing between here and the Pacific. Men would die for a chance to be with you, and you turn your nose up at everyone."

I shrugged a little. "Sometimes people connect. Sometimes they don't."

Except, in that short time, I'd felt more connected to him than I'd ever been with anyone before. I'd run into thousands of men in the years of touring. I'd been flirted with. Coaxed and fed a million lines, a nonstop parade of attractive men at my feet.

My whole heart and devotion had belonged to Nile the entire time. Never once had I been tempted. Never once felt a spark.

After everything that happened, the loss and the torment, I was sure the life had been stamped out of me, trampled into nothing.

Then there was Royce.

Mel rolled her eyes. "Yet he was here."

"And he left."

She huffed out a sound. "Maybe he connected with you enough to know you probably would have been freaking out this morning if things moved too fast. I mean, seriously. We are talkin' about Emily Ramsey here. You bring someone up here? You're goin' to be all in. Hell, the poor asshole would probably have a whole album written about him."

I scowled at her for pointing out the truth of who I was. That was the thing about your assistant being your best friend. She knew you better than you knew yourself.

"Or maybe he was just toying with me," I said, wondering if he just wanted to see what it would take to make the good girl crack.

"Yeah, that's probably it, Em. Most guys bring a gorgeous girl to their room, tease them a bit, and then walk away. Cock-block themselves. Sounds like some good, old-fashioned fun to me."

"Well, it doesn't matter now, does it? We'll be back on the road today."

Moving on.

Connections lost.

Just a blur of cities and faces and venues.

My stomach sank.

I knew that was a part of the problem.

Mel released a heavy sigh, catching on to my mood. "Sorry, love bug. You're gonna find someone. Someday. Someone who means everything."

I forced a smile. "I'm fine. I don't need anyone."

"Are you fine?" There she went. Calling me on my bullshit.

"I will be. I promise."

"I'm pretty sure it's you who needs to believe that."

Emily

*F*orty minutes later, I was being herded out of my room and down the hall toward Richard's. Mel had dressed me in a wispy, floral tank, all straps and bare shoulders, and super-short white shorts. She'd paired it with the same wedges I'd been wearing last night.

I'd rolled my eyes at her when she'd told me they were good luck.

Carrying a tray of coffees, Mel knocked on Richard's door before producing her own key and shoving it into the lock. She threw the door open to the suite. It was decorated the same as mine, all dark woods and marble surfaces and luxurious, rich textures, though Richard's had a big dining table and a kitchen at the back that we used for meetings, song writing, and business.

It was our favorite place to stay when we came into town.

I think it reminded Richard of how far we'd come.

Rhys and Leif were already at the table.

Rhys was in an old holey tee, the guy as country as they came, a trucker cap on his head and a big ol' smile on his face. Although today, that smile was filled with worry as he watched me come in.

Leif had his back to us, and he slowly swiveled. Nervously, he tapped the drumsticks that he carried with him on the table. Brown eyes keen, sincere, and concerned.

"Hey, guys," I offered warily with a tiny wave of my hand as if it were a gesture of surrender, guilt grabbing hold.

"Em-Girl. How's it, sweetness?" Rhys asked in his southern way, rocking back and tucking his muscled, tattooed arms behind his head. "You caught us a bit off guard last night. You good, baby girl?"

His voice was pure care, his expression telling me he was gonna have my back, no matter what. Rhys was Richard's oldest friend, treated me like his baby sister, as protective as he was playful.

Careless and fierce.

Not a whole lot mattered to him except for the very few things that mattered most.

Family and music.

He treated the rest of life as if it was nothing but a big joke.

I blinked and tried to swallow around gratitude and unease. "Yeah. I'm . . . I just got a splittin' headache, and I needed to get some air. I knew you all could cover for me just fine."

Awesome.

There I went. Spoutin' a few more lies.

Rhys cracked a grin. "We all have bad days, love. Look at our poor Leif here. Guy has one every show," he razzed, smirking at Leif.

Leif rolled his eyes, which always seemed to smolder. The guy was wearing a tank and shredded jeans, his lean body muscled out from banging on drums all day and all night. Richard had stumbled upon Leif playing drums for a failing heavy metal band and had snatched him up after that band fell apart.

Leif had just gotten married this last winter. He'd had a rough past, but he'd finally found peace in Mia, the woman who had been meant for him.

He lifted his arms out to his sides. "Sure, blame it on me, man. Everyone knows when we're off, it's because of you. Who even told you that you could play bass, anyway? Problem is, you can't keep up."

The two of them went round and round. Enemies and the best of friends. Always challenging the other. It made for interesting days, that was for sure, and the music never, ever got stagnant.

Rhys hooted and tossed his booted feet onto the table, crossing one ankle over the other. "Keep dreaming, Banger. You just don't get the rhythm of a good country song."

"Head Banger to you," Leif told him, sipping from the coffee Mel handed him. "And that's what I'm here for . . . to get a little of the country out of you."

It was true. Rich wanted him to add a different element to our sound. He didn't want us to just be another country band. He wanted us to stand out from the crowds. Write music that all different sorts of people and tastes would gravitate toward.

"God, can you get your feet off the table, Rhys? I swear, you were born in a barn," Mel chastised, swatting at his boots as she tried to find a spot to set his coffee.

Rhys laughed harder. "That's because I was, in fact, born in a barn."

I rolled my eyes. "Sorry, Rhys, but the barn that was torn down on the old farm where the city hospital was built does not count."

"'Course it does. I feel that country dirt all the way to my bones."

"The only dirt around here is your dirty dick. I saw those two chicks you snuck into your room last night." Mel glared at him as if she were his keeper.

Rhys cracked up. "No sneaking to it, Mells Bells. Could hear those two all the way to Atlanta."

"Gross," I muttered, laughing under my breath.

My nerves came rushing forward when the bedroom door opened to my freshly showered brother. The room instantly grew quiet, the two of us staring at each other.

Discomfort bounded.

Filling the space.

Richard swallowed hard and roughed a hand through his damp hair. "Hey, Em. Can I talk to you for a minute?"

My throat felt swollen and achy, and I peeked at the rest of the band and Mel. All of them watched us with worry, apprehension thickening the air.

I gave a tight nod and walked toward his room, the space only lit by a slice of sunlight slanting through a thin strip in the drapes. He stepped to the side to let me pass and shut the door behind us.

Closing us off.

Turning back to face me, he blew out a strained sigh and rubbed his palm over his mouth. The uneasiness was so dense I was choking on it.

"Listen," he said, his voice low, "about last night."

My heart gave a tremble. "I'm—"

He held up a hand. "Let me get this out, Em. I . . . fuck . . . I'm fucking sorry for what I said. I was pissed that you ran off stage after what you said on the call with Fitzgerald yesterday morning, but I'm more pissed at myself for the way I handled it."

Warily, I nodded acceptance. "I'm sorry, too."

He looked to the floor, wavering, hesitating, and my nerves were getting bound up again.

I could just feel somethin' coming that I knew I didn't want to hear.

"But you can't keep dragging your feet. It's not fair. Not to Rhys and Leif. Not to Mel. Not to me. And it's damn sure not fair to you."

He pinned me with eyes that were the same color as mine. "We've worked too hard for this, Em. Too fuckin' hard."

I blinked at him, conjuring enough courage to at least get a small confession out. "The songs have dried up, Rich. I . . . I can't write . . . can barely sing . . . and I don't know how to fix it. I would if I could. I just need time."

"We don't have the time, Em." He glanced away, looking at the wall as if he had to prepare himself to deliver bad news. "Fitzgerald is pissed that this deal isn't done. Angela said she's left you a bunch of messages that you haven't returned, and she's getting pissed, too. This isn't the way business is run."

Regret pulsed in my chest. I tried to inhale around it. Angela was our manager. She'd worked every bit as hard as the rest of us to ensure our success, believing in Carolina George when no one else did.

"I'll call her," I promised. Somehow, I'd smooth it over. Make it right.

Rich shook his head. "It's too late for that. Fitzgerald sent the head of Mylton A & R. He's going to be here this morning."

"What?" It came out sounding like a defense.

We already had the offer.

I already knew what it meant.

I didn't need someone here trying to convince me to sign something when I wasn't ready.

Not when I didn't know if I could work in the same world as Cory Douglas. Just the thought nearly sent me into a panic attack.

The doorbell to Richard's suite rang. That feeling amplified by ten, anxiety chasing all the air out of my lungs.

"Richard," I begged.

He took a step back. "Just, hear him out. Please. For the sake of this band."

What was this guy going to say that hadn't already been said? What would it change? They represented everything I was running from.

Literally.

Richard swung open the door and stepped out into the bright, shimmering light, turning his attention to the door that Mel was opening.

Tentatively, I stepped out behind him, then I nearly dropped to my knees as all the blood drained from my head.

"Just remember in the morning that I warned you the only thing I do is make mistakes."

Only I was the one who had made the biggest mistake.

Was the biggest fool of them all.

Because my beautiful stranger was standing in the room.

As dark and deadly and dangerous as last night.

Royce.

six

Royce

*T*hey say there are seven deadly sins.

Bullshit.

Emily Ramsey was number eight.

Although this sin?

This sin came with immediate condemnation. I could feel the consequence of it quivering through the air, quakes of a warning trembling underfoot.

I knew I'd regret it. Knew it with all of me. But sometimes you wanted something so damned bad that any other reason ceased to matter.

Now she stood across the room in all that perfect, delicate flesh. Her expression one of horror, etched in bold, glaring lines; her face so ashen I was pretty sure she was trying not to spew her guts out onto the floor.

Repulsed.

Disgusted.

I was a bastard. I knew it. But there wasn't a goddamn thing I could do about that now.

Like they say, it was time to face the music.

Refusing to back down, I kept my attention pinned on her, watching the way her face twisted and contorted and pulled through a thousand different emotions.

Shock.

Hatred.

Attraction, every bit as strong as it had been last night.

Only growing when I took another step farther into the room.

No one said anything.

I wondered if they could feel it, too.

I reached up and adjusted the tie cinched too tight around my neck.

Finally, Richard Ramsey cleared his throat and approached me, appreciation and hidden understanding in his eye. "Royce Reilly, in the flesh. It's good to finally meet you face-to-face."

He offered his hand, and I shook it, words rough when they scraped up my throat. "Glad to be here. Thank you for meeting with me on such short notice."

Only, he'd been well aware that I was coming. He'd jumped at the idea when I'd suggested it, though I'd prefaced it like a requirement. A little gift to let him off the hook. To take the pressure off his shoulders.

Thing was, I got his frustration. It was plenty warranted, and the care he had for his band was clear.

He was a cool guy. A good guy. On top of that? He was fucking off-the-charts talented. And it was my job to sort the talent from the hacks. The exceptional from the expected.

The only thing you could expect from him was greatness.

No mediocre songs or riffs or lyrics or shows.

"Hey man, not a problem at all. We had nothing going on this morning, and we don't have to be on the road for a couple more hours." Rich's words rushed from him, the guy clearly anxious, not sure which way this meeting was going to go. Swiveling on his bare feet, he gestured for me to move deeper into his suite where the rest of Carolina George waited. "Come on in and have a seat."

I wondered if he'd be so earnest if he knew what the full extent of my intentions were.

"Everyone . . . this is Royce Reilly, head of A & R at Mylton Records. I asked you all to come here because he wanted to meet with us this morning."

A ripple of raw energy blasted from the tight-knit group.

Rhys and Leif, who were easy to recognize, shared a glance of speculation, unsure what to make of my appearance.

Trying to deduce if I was a benefit or a threat.

Let's just say I didn't exactly come across as a friendly guy.

"Good morning," I said curtly, moving deeper into the room, doing my best to ignore the way the air crackled the closer I got to Emily. My footsteps coming heavy, in sync with the breaths punching from my lungs.

Fuck.

This was going to be a problem.

"Well, well, well . . . If it isn't a new face from Mylton Records. Can't say I'm surprised. Looks like they're pulling out the big guns," Rhys said with one of his signature grins, eyeing me with a gleam, clearly hoping I was coming with a more enticing offer than the one my stepfather had presented them with three months ago.

No, more money wasn't on the table today, even though they'd be worth every cent.

Richard Ramsey wasn't the only talented one.

The entire room was loaded with it.

Each member possessed their own unique style.

Their own distinct sound.

Contributed a piece that couldn't be replaced.

It made Carolina George a name that couldn't be replicated.

Which was why *Daddy Dearest* was salivating to get his grubby paws on them.

Not a fucking chance was I going to let that happen.

I returned a rigid smile to Rhys Manning. The guy played bass like he was roping a bull in a rodeo. Wild and reckless and so skilled you didn't know what hit you. Country all the way to the dusty boots he wore on his feet and a face that made innocent girls lose their minds.

I let my attention drift across the table to where Leif Godwin sat.

He was precisely that.

A god in his own right.

Drummers tended to fade into the background. Secondary. Songwriting far from their repertoire.

Not Leif.

He was just as enigmatic and indispensable as the rest.

And then there was Emily.

Emily Ramsey.

The girl was crucial.

Essential.

A necessity.

She possessed what had to be the sultriest, sexiest voice on the planet.

A face and a body to match, all wrapped up in a sweet southern shyness that made good men want to do wicked things.

Thing was, wicked ones wanted to do worse.

And every fucking component of this was riding on her.

Then she had to go and shock me with the way she'd affected me, the first girl since *her* who made me feel like I couldn't breathe.

That should have been enough of a warning.

This girl was the one who was the threat. The first with the power to cloud my judgement.

I wouldn't let it happen. Wasn't going to mess this up any more than I already had.

Touching her again wasn't an option.

Didn't mean I wasn't going to be fantasizing about it.

"Let's get started." I kept my voice low and indifferent, like I hadn't had her propped on a table last night. Like I couldn't still taste her on my tongue or feel the scratch marks she'd left on my shoulders.

She gasped out a small, shocked breath, clenching and unclenching her fists, chest jutting with pants where she stood trying to rein in the disbelief and disgust shimmering in her eyes.

I deserved it all.

The woman who'd opened the door all of a sudden rushed to catch up with me, like she'd, too, been locked in a trance and had just broken free. "Mr. Reilly. Welcome. I'm Melanie, assistant to the band. Please, have a seat. Can I get you a cup of coffee?" She cocked her pretty head, taking me in, something wry pulling into her expression. "Or maybe a whiskey or a scotch?"

I got the feeling she was stamping me with the label of *bad*.

Smart girl.

"No, thank you, I'm fine." I unbuttoned my suit jacket and slipped into the chair at the head of the table. Just to let them know where I stood.

I let my attention bounce around all of them again. "I apologize for interrupting your busy schedule, but I was in Savannah on business, and I thought it would be a good idea to meet with you while I was here."

I'd left Sebastian Stone's house a half an hour before. A legend who I'd idolized as a teenager before he'd become a friend.

He'd warned me that this was messy.

I'd told him I didn't care.

It was worth it.

"Nah, no apologies, man," Rhys said, rocking forward with an easy smile. "There are things we obviously need to talk about."

He glanced at Emily, gauging her reaction, like he was hoping she would take one look at me and jump on board.

Highly unlikely.

Not with the stupid fucking stunt I'd pulled last night. Knew I'd regret it. Didn't know it so much until right then.

"Yeah, no worries." Leif waved a hand, watching me like he didn't know whether he should trust me or not.

"Thank you," I told him. Honestly, it wasn't either Rhys or Leif that I was concerned about.

Richard followed me in, though he remained standing. He hung onto the back of a chair, letting his wary gaze jump around the members of his band. "So, guys . . . you all know we're coming up on having to make a decision soon."

Every eye turned to Emily.

Discomfort had her shifting on those toned, bare legs.

What the fuck was she wearing, anyway? Flimsy material caressing her shoulders and those tits, shorts so short she looked like she was ten feet tall, all legs and seduction. It was almost worse than the tease of that dress from last night.

I cleared my throat, drawing the attention from her. Clearly, she didn't want it.

She probably wasn't going to like what I was getting ready to say any more than having all eyes in the room on her, though.

I went all business. "You have a contract you're sitting on. I get it . . . it's a big decision. You're smart not to take it lightly."

"Our songs are being downloaded at warp speed, man. Not sure if there's a whole lot more you can offer us," Leif said, though I got the feeling he was just making room for the conversation. That he wanted one more person at Mylton Records to make him big promises. Assure him they were taking the right step.

I eased back in the chair, crossing an ankle over my knee. I met his eye. "Yes, they are. We have the reports. Which is why we're offering the amount that we are. You've amassed a huge, devoted following. It speaks volumes about your talent and drive. But I think everyone here is aware you've only touched the tip of the iceberg. There are millions of people who've never heard the name Carolina George. My job is to change that."

It wasn't a lie.

Leif nodded. "And you think that you can?"

"I know that I can."

My attention moved on from him, hitting Rhys then Richard, before dragging all the way up the lush lines of Emily's body to meet the turmoil in her eyes, her lips moving in silent disbelief.

My chest tightened like a fist.

I was pretty sure she wanted to call me out.

Shout that I was a fraud.

"I realize you're not ready," I said, voice raw as I stared directly at her. "That you may not trust what we are offering. So, I've decided to hit the next couple tour stops with you so you can get to know me."

Those green eyes flared with another bout of shock. A rustle of movement filtered through the bodies around me.

Unorthodox.

Yeah.

But this was worth it.

Rhys smacked his hand on the table like it was settled. "Sounds like a damn good plan to me. We need to get this thing settled."

"It's reasonable," Leif agreed.

Cool.

I was glad they were on board.

But it was the storm of energy pounding me that I was really interested in.

Wave after wave. Surge after surge.

I stood in the middle of it, pinning her with my stare, wishing I could erase the doubt I could see spinning through her mind. Thing was, I wasn't sure her reaction would be any different if last night hadn't happened.

She probably would have been looking at me with the same distrust. With the same fear in her eyes. I wasn't the one who'd put it there in the first place.

Emily gave a fierce shake of her head and hugged herself over her middle. "No."

More rustling. This time disgruntled.

"Emily . . . come on, baby girl. This is super cool. I mean, what can it hurt?" Rhys was sending her one of his smiles that had clearly won him his way on more than one occasion.

All the guys in this band possessed that power.

You couldn't only play.

Charisma was a key factor of success in this business.

It wasn't just music.

It was entertainment.

I knew that firsthand.

Except the one he was trying to charm wasn't buying it.

She knew exactly how badly it could hurt.

"I'm not comfortable with this," she whispered, rubbing her hands up her arms, looking to her brother to back her up.

Guilt tugged at my spirit.

Fuck.

I swallowed it down, remembered my purpose. "You won't even know I'm around. Unless of course you want to ask me questions. That's all I'm here for. To answer your questions and assure you I have this band's best interest at heart."

Her brow twisted, like she couldn't believe that I would sit there and spew this bullshit.

I really couldn't believe it, either.

Richard huffed out a breath. "Emily . . . you have to give something. He's here because of you."

Chewing at her lip, she stared at her brother, trying to keep it together as she rushed to whisper the words, "What he's here for is to talk me into what I've already said I'm not ready for."

"I'm here to offer you that time," I interjected, capturing that sage-gaze that was making me itch. Fingers twitchy and dick antsy.

What the fuck was she doing to me?

She scoffed out an enraged sound. It rang of discord and disbelief. "Is that what you're here for?"

"Yes." It came out resolute.

"Emily . . . please . . . just give him a chance. Give us a chance." Her brother edged toward her, pleading, trying to get through to this girl who was so confused and uncertain and broken down that I was pretty sure all it was going to take was one more blow for her to crumble.

My soul shook.

Fuck.

This was bad. Everything was getting distorted. Pen strokes breaching clear-cut lines. I had to keep it together.

Her attention bounced around the room. "Is that what all of you want? For him to come along? Get into our business?"

"It's not a big deal, Em. He's just doing his job," Rhys said, lifting his hands out from where he held his coffee cup, looking at her like he couldn't make sense of her.

Not getting that there was something bad going on in that pretty head.

So clear it was giving me a heartache.

"Leif?" she asked, voice soft and unsure and pleading.

In discomfort, Leif fiddled with the strings from a massive hole in the thigh of his jeans, glancing down before he looked back at her with a sigh. "I think we've got to give this thing a chance, Em. Know you're dealing with something right now, but I don't think we can just turn our backs on this opportunity, either. I'm sorry."

She looked at Mel, who shrugged her shoulders hopefully.

Emily didn't need to look at Richard to know what his vote would be. He'd already made that plenty clear.

Warily, she gave a tight nod, giving in.

Got the feeling that was what she always did. Looked out for everyone else rather than herself.

"If it's really what you want, then okay."

Richard blew out a relieved breath. "Thank you, Em. You're not going to regret this. You'll see." He looked around at the band. "Bus leaves at 11. Get your shit together. We have to be in Birmingham tonight."

"You made the right decision." I issued it to all of them, though I was directly speaking to Emily.

Wishing there was a way to convince her she could trust me. Knowing she shouldn't.

"Thanks for doing this," Rhys said, clapping me on the shoulder as we stood.

"I fight for the things that are important."

Emily sucked in a haggard breath. That overwhelming connection I'd felt to her last night was a throb in the air, though it was mangled and meshed with hostility and doubt.

Leif lifted his chin to me. "See you on the bus."

The guy strutted out behind Rhys, two of them followed by Melanie who was barking a bunch of orders. She only glanced back once as I headed out behind them, eyes narrowing for a flash like she was issuing her own warning, before she let the door close behind her.

No doubt, she was a force to be reckoned with.

I glanced at Richard.

He barely nodded.

Knowing.

Grateful.

I just prayed this bullshit wasn't going to backfire on us all.

Opening the door before I said anything more, I strode out to head for my room. I froze when I felt the presence come over me from behind, potent and raw and sweet.

It was a dangerous, dangerous combination.

"I can't believe you." Her voice shook like a crumble of stones, and I slowly turned around.

My chest clutched, the sight of her a constant kick to the gut.

I shouldn't be attracted to her.

It shouldn't be possible.

Couldn't be.

But my heart fucking pounded a wayward, mindless beat.

"I'm just doing my job, Ms. Ramsey."

"Is that so?"

I took a single step her direction, cocking my head and lowering my voice. "I told you that you would regret meeting me last night."

Her lips trembled. "You're right. I do. But I didn't have all the information then, did I?"

It was straight accusation.

Drawn, I edged forward, one step and then another. Tension ricocheted, alive in the narrow hall.

Those eyes widened in surprise.

Seemed it was impossible to stay away from her.

Nervous, she fumbled, backing into the wall, pants jetting from her throat.

My gaze swept across her gorgeous face, getting distracted by those full lips covered in more of that cherry gloss I had the sudden, overwhelming urge to lick off, our noses so close they almost touched. "Don't pin this on me, Precious."

She stared up at me, and I worried it just might be hope that shone in her eyes. "Tell me one thing . . . when you came up to me last night, did you know who I was?"

Lips pursing in a thin line, my head angled back, eyes narrowed, tongue held.

A silent confession.

She didn't need to know there was no chance I couldn't have stood up for her.

A roll of low, horrified laughter ripped up her throat, and she slowly shook her head. "Wow. I guess I really was an easy target, wasn't I? Is that what you wanted? To sleep with me to form some kind of connection? Make me think I knew you a little better? Get me right where you wanted me so you could manipulate me into doing what I don't want to do?"

"Last night was a mistake. But this isn't. I'm here because I'm going to sign your band."

An incredulous sound left her. "Maybe I won't sign."

"And maybe you can be replaced."

She blanched, hurt streaking across her face like she'd been punched, anger riding in right after.

That's exactly what I needed.

Her passion.

Her ferocity.

For this girl to stand up and fight for her band.

To let devotion consume her rather than her fear.

Pushing out from under me, Emily whirled around on those strappy heels, taking two steps back to put space between us. "You really are an arrogant bastard, aren't you? You think they'll just drop me? That I'm just . . . replaceable?"

She clutched her chest. "They would never do that to me. They are my family." She pointed down the hall. "Those boys are loyalty and integrity, but you don't have the first clue what that means, do you, Hollywood?"

"Integrity was me leaving your room last night."

Disbelief rolled off her tongue, and she shoved her keycard into her lock and flung open her door. Halfway through, she stopped to look back at me from over her shoulder. "No, Royce. Integrity would have been you never stepping through it in the first place. Integrity would have been you telling me who you were. Luckily, I know who that is now."

"Yeah, and who is that?"

"You're a sick bastard who is willing to do whatever it takes to get what you want. You are just like every other asshole who thinks they can reach out and take what they want of me. Steal parts I'm not willing to give. I'm not about to let that happen. The rest of the band might be blinded, but I can see right through you."

Then she flung open her door the rest of the way and stormed inside. It slammed shut behind her. My eyes squeezed closed.

Anger and regret tied me in knots.

She was right on most accounts.

I was manipulative.

After one thing.

And I was positive she could see right through me. Right into me. God knew, she'd gotten under my skin.

But she was wrong on another.

This was going to happen.

Whatever the cost.

Seven

Emily

$\mathcal{I}$ frantically tossed the few things I'd hung in the closet into my suitcase. Fighting tears of anger and shame and disgust.

I couldn't believe I'd let that asshole touch me.

God. What was wrong with me?

I wanted to scream.

Worst part? The second I'd seen him stroll through that door, arrogance rolling from him like a drug, wearing that stupid perfect suit that showed off that stupid gorgeous body and that stupid perfect face, I'd gone *stupid*.

Like an ignorant fool, wondering what it might be like for him to touch me again.

That was all of two seconds before reality had come stampeding in, and I caught up to what he'd done. The game he'd been playing. Sure of it. Praying at the same time it'd only been a coincidence, that he hadn't realized who I was last night.

I shouldn't have been such a fool to even have hoped.

He didn't even deny it.

God, why did that piss me off, too?

Dizziness swirled, and my heart raced faster. A crazed frenzy was taking me over. I was losing it, I was sure, lost to waves of dark, perilous waters that rose higher and higher.

I'd been treading them for so long.

I knew it was only a matter of time before they finally took me under and I drowned.

Up front, the door banged open, and the telltale sounds of Mel letting herself in echoed through the room.

"Knock much?" I mumbled, unable to keep the irritation out of my voice.

She didn't even notice. "Oh my god," she squealed as she flew into my room and flung herself on top of my unmade bed.

Clearly, she was in best friend mode.

"It was him, wasn't it?"

In shock, my eyes darted to her, a flush flashing across my skin, hating that I'd been so transparent. Jerking my attention back to my suitcase, my movements became more frenzied as I stuffed all my things into my bag. "I don't know what you're talkin' about."

She hopped onto her knees, bouncing on them like a five-year-old and waving her hands in the air. "Oh, come on, Em. You think I wasn't standing right there, watching it go down? You looked like you were gonna puke the second you saw him, and that man looked like he was about two seconds from taking you right there on the table, out in front of everyone. Two of you nearly set fire to the room."

I tried not to get all hot and bothered at the thought.

That feeling there, so thick in the air that I'd been sure I was suffocating. I was content to fully blame it on my anger.

Mel's eyes were wide with the scandal. "I can't even believe it. I mean, he's so not your type. The last kind of guy I thought you'd go after."

"Nope, he's not. Not at all," I was all too quick to agree.

"I mean, you said he was hot, but that man is ungodly. Did you see those hands?" She threw back her head with a dreamy groan. "Can you imagine the size of his dick?"

I was halfway to stuffing a pair of shoes into my bag when she said it. With a gasp, I threw one at her. "What is wrong with you?"

Deflecting it like a pro, she rolled her eyes. "Like you weren't thinking about it. Or do you already know? Oh, I bet you do. Give me all the dirty deets." She edged forward on her knees like an eager puppy dog.

"There's nothin' to tell. I already told you it didn't come close to getting that far."

She squealed. "So, it was him! I knew it. God, I'm good. I can sniff out a good romance like nobody's business."

"It isn't your business."

"Um, hello. Best friend." She gestured to herself. "It is the very definition of my business."

This was going nowhere and fast. I needed to shut her down.

"Fine. It was him. I was attracted to him, but that ended the second I figured out he's only here to play me. Any romance between the two of us would be the very bad kind."

"Oh, yeah, he does look bad. So wrong he's right." She actually waggled her brows.

God, she was infuriating. Was it wrong I wanted to toss her blabbering, smiling face out the window right then?

"Goodness, did you feel the way he seemed to fill up the whole room? I thought I was gonna go off just lookin' at him."

"Have at it," I told her, storming into the bathroom and tossing my toiletries and makeup into my travel bag.

I probably broke a mirror or two.

At this rate, I was gonna have a hundred years of bad luck.

I zipped it up with a flourish.

"Um, no thank you. Not about to fight with my best friend over a boy. Sisters before misters. I'm in for the long haul."

I was sure I was wearing a scowl the size of Texas when I rounded back out into the room. "I don't want him, so you can do whatever you want with him."

"Says the girl whose legs are shakin'." She pointed at them. "Looks like you're in need of a little . . . relief. Hold on, I just got his number."

"I hate you," I spouted.

She waved me off. "You love me, and you know it. Just like you're gonna fall in love with him."

I huffed out in frustration. "Would you stop it?"

"Um, no, I already ordered my bridesmaid dress."

"Well, I do hope they have a return policy."

Mel sobered, seeming to catch onto my expression. That this was a bigger deal than she was making it. "Seriously, Em . . . I'm shocked you went for a guy like that. How the hell did that happen?"

I shrugged a helpless shoulder. "It was just one of those instant attraction things. That fuzzy feelin' you get when you look at someone." God, it'd been so long since I'd experienced it, I'd forgotten that it was real. "He came up to me when some jerk was gettin' handsy, and that was that."

"Love at first sight."

"Hardly. That guy is an asshole. Singled me out. Tried to get close to me to get his way. I'm not okay with that."

"Really? So, what, you're just . . . not attracted to him anymore? Poof. You're immune?" It was all disbelief.

"Maybe if he hadn't lied to me about who he was."

She flopped back on the bed and studied her nails. "Well, at least you know now why he walked out. Standing up for your honor and all."

"Honor? Hardly. He just figured I was easy prey and would fall all over him and do whatever he wanted. He should have thought twice about that."

I shoved my makeup case onto the top of my clothes with a little more force than necessary, flinging shut the lid and trying to zip it.

"Maybe he's a good guy," she said with a shrug.

I shot her a disbelieving look.

She grinned. "Okay, fine. That boy is as wicked as they come. He looks like he crawled right out of hell, nothing but a sexy, tattooed, fallen angel in a fitted suit. Yummy."

"What's gonna be hell is having him on that bus," I muttered, fighting the flutter of wings that scattered through my belly and managed to flap all the way into my chest at the thought.

Crap.

This wasn't good.

"Might be fun. Who knows?"

"And it might be a tragedy."

Didn't she get it? We were talking about the fate of our band. I was tryin' hard enough to figure this out. To come to grips. To be brave. Looking for a way to say yes, and not feel like I was selling my soul to the devil.

Guessed I was, after all.

"You're so dramatic."

"It's called realistic."

Unable to handle the force of it for a second longer, I flopped down on the edge of the bed and buried my face in my hands.

Mel edged forward and rubbed my back. "Hey . . . I'm just teasing you. I get it. You even kissing a man is a big deal, and now he's gonna be in your face nonstop for a while. But you did the right thing . . . giving this a chance. Maybe it's time to give your heart a chance, too. Forget that bastard Nile. Only thing he's ever done is cause you pain."

I wished it was that simple.

"Think about it . . . the worst thing that can come of this is a really great record deal for the band," she urged, prying my hands away so she could meet my eye. "From there? Who knows what else. It's time, Em. It's time to let go of what's holding you back."

But she was all wrong.

So wrong.

Because the worst thing was that signing with Mylton Records meant I'd be tied to Cory Douglas. Forced into his space.

And I couldn't imagine a worse fate.

I was right.

This was going to be hell.

Sheer, utter hell.

What had I gotten myself into?

I climbed the steps to the bus, holding onto the railing because my legs already felt weak. That feeling only increased tenfold when I made it up to the front living area. I froze at the top.

Everyone was there.

Rhys and Leif.

My brother, who looked at me with some kind of apology that I couldn't quite interpret.

And Royce.

Royce was sitting on the couch with his long legs stretched out in front of him, furiously tapping away at his phone and still wearing that suit like he didn't realize we were going to be on this grubby bus for the next six hours.

In my spot, of course.

Mel nudged me from behind. "Um, hello, Em . . . do you think you could keep moving a foot or two or ten? I do have two suitcases, and I'm teetering on a step. Help a girl out, would you?"

"Oh, sorry," I said, jolting forward a step to get out of her way. Last thing I wanted was to come across as self-absorbed. Not a pretty trait.

But I didn't get very far.

Because that dark gaze lifted to meet mine, sealing me to the spot. I felt like my feet were glued right there on that floor, unable to move or breathe or do anything but get lost in the raw command of his eyes.

Mel banged her way past me from behind.

"Thanks." There was no missing the mockery in her tone.

Rhys hopped up like the cavalier champion that he was. "Ahh, Mells Bells, let me help you with that, sweetheart."

She rolled her eyes. "I made it all the way over here with these, I think I can make it ten more steps."

"But why would you want to do that when I'm right here?"

"Because then I would owe you something."

He grinned one of his cocky grins. "Well, I could easily figure out a good solution for that. A three-easy-installment payment plan."

"In your dreams, cowboy."

"Cowboy? I'm the stallion, baby."

She sent me a look. "We are dumping him at the next stop."

Leif chuckled.

And I just stared as the ramble of voices continued in a haze around me.

I couldn't process a thing going on.

Not when I was completely caught up in the man who had taken possession of the entire bus, filling it with that energy I couldn't escape.

I tried to swallow around the feeling laying waste to my insides, and I lifted a defiant chin. "You're in my spot."

He quirked a dark brow. "Am I?"

"You are."

"Huh. Great minds?"

I kinda wanted to slap him. Was he really gonna go after the whole playful bit after what he'd done? I wasn't about to fall for that façade, either. I had his name.

Snake. Scoundrel. Schemer.

"I think you were just goin' after the best spot," I said.

"I'm sorry, I didn't know it was taken."

"Well, it is."

I would have been able to pull off the whole bitch thing a whole lot better if my voice hadn't been quivering.

But I was going with the whole "fake it until you make it" philosophy. Pretendin' as if he didn't affect me at all. That my heart wasn't somewhere in my throat, and my belly wasn't doing somersaults.

With a slow, wicked smile, he eased up to standing. So maybe I should have let him remain sitting. Because the man rose to his full, towering height, standing over me with a smirk pulling at one corner of his sexy mouth.

He dipped in lower, his voice only meant for me. "Pardon me, Precious."

If he called me that one more time, I was gonna snap.

He stepped out of my way so I could get to my spot.

It wasn't like we had a whole lot of space to keep separated.

We had the front sitting area where we usually hung out, a pocket-sized kitchen stocked with snacks and drinks at the ready. In the middle section were the rows of bunks that were stacked three high on each side, and there was a smaller sitting area at the very back that was usually reserved for writing music.

It was a quiet, private place for when we needed to let our creativity bleed free, unhindered by the movies and conversations and mayhem that was usually going down up front.

I should probably exile myself to my bunk. Hide out. It wasn't like it was that long of a drive. But I didn't want to give him the satisfaction of thinking that his presence was swaying me, either.

He needed to know if I made the decision to sign, it was going to be of my own accord. Not because he'd twisted my arm or filled my head with pretty words that I knew full well he didn't mean.

I flopped down into the spot he'd vacated.

The leather was warm.

Crap.

This was so not good. Because I was warring against the need that flooded my belly, pressing my thighs together when I was assailed with the scent of him.

Cedar and whiskey and the barest hint of lingering cigarettes.

I felt drugged by it, my mind going hazy, or maybe it was just the fuzzy feeling I was struck with when he sat down at the table across from where Richard was sitting.

His legs so long he had one tucked under the table and the other stretched out into the aisle, his body slung back.

Casual and fierce.

How did he manage that?

I fumbled in the messenger bag I'd dumped on the floor, grabbing a notebook and flipping it open to a scribbled-on page as the bus rumbled out of the parking lot.

I tried to get lost.

To stare out the window as we left the city behind, as the trees grew denser and the road narrowed into two-lanes.

Seemed I couldn't do anything but count the erratic beats of my heart as I felt those penetrating eyes continually flicker to me.

Invading.

Searching.

Penetrating.

Finally, I huffed out a breath and stood. "I'm going to go work on some music."

Wishful thinking.

But sometimes the only thing a girl could do was pretend, and I'd become a pro at it.

Thing was, lyrics had been flirting at the edges of my mind for weeks. The muted strains of a new song stalking me from the fringes of my consciousness.

Wisps of beauty I could almost taste.

Rhythmic.

Magical in its dance.

Evaporating into nothing the second I reached for it.

If I could just grab it, hold it, I was sure things would be okay. That I'd be on my way to healing. If only I could figure out a way to get there.

I guessed maybe because it felt like a secret. As if maybe I were cutting myself wide open and exposing something I wasn't quite yet ready to reveal.

"You want me to work with you?" Rich asked, glancing up from his phone.

"No, I'm good."

Worry passed through his expression. "Let me know if you change your mind."

"I will."

Grabbing my things, I headed for the back, stepping over Leif's legs where he was engrossed in a movie, headphones in his ears. Rhys and Mel were still shooting jabs at each other where they were sitting at the second table tucked behind the couch.

I fumbled down the narrow aisle of empty bunks, feeling grateful that we had two buses for this tour. The rest of the sound and stage crew were on the other, that bus pulling out late last night so they could be at the next city to set up for tonight's show.

There'd been no rest on the tours back when we'd had to share.

It was true—we'd come a long, long way. Our beginnings humble. Filled with hope and belief of who we might one day get to be.

Our heads in the clouds and our hearts in the stars.

I made it to the back room. The seating area was a horseshoe leather couch that ran along both sides and the back. The sitting surface was wider, big enough for someone to lounge and curl up or even sleep on when there was a need.

The curtains were drawn back, filling the space with natural light, the country going by in a blur of greens and browns and peace.

I went for my guitar case where it was always waiting for me in the closet. I took it out, flicked through the latches, and pulled out my baby. Climbing onto the couch in the corner, I drew up my legs and rested her across my lap.

Strummed my fingers over the strings and felt the chord resonate to my soul.

I listened for the words. For something to speak to me. Come to me. For my spirit to get lost in sound and feeling.

Strumming softly, I closed my eyes and drifted a bit.

Waiting on the piece that had always been most important to my soul to make itself known.

The music that lived inside of me.

I was hit with a line, and I thought it was shock that had me scrambling to grab my pen. I leaned over the top of my guitar so I could reach my notebook that was open on the seat in front of me, teeth tugging at my lip as I scratched out the messy words.

Come to me
I've been waiting for a break
Looking for something to save me from myself

My mouth hung open on a silent gasp. Caught in a stupor. Stunned by the impact.

It wasn't much, but they were the first words I'd gotten onto a page in three months.

I froze when I sensed the movement.

That energy blasted through the atmosphere even though it was coming at slow speed. Warily, I peeled my attention from the scribbled words and dared to look up, hugging my guitar to me as if it were a lifeline.

Royce stood in the doorway.

My mouth went dry, and a shiver raced across my flesh.

He'd lost his suit jacket, and his hands were planted on either side of the doorframe. The sleeves of his shirt were rolled up his forearms the way they'd been last night, the top two buttons of his shirt undone, giving a better glimpse of all that cryptic ink.

Black hair unruly, eyes hard and mouth soft.

Completely controlled and looking like he might bust apart.

"What are you doing back here?" I asked, hoping it came off as a demand, but it came out way too curious for that.

And maybe that was the problem.

He left me compelled.

He cocked his head, arrogant and sure. "I heard you playing."

I turned my attention out the window, trying to figure out how I was supposed to handle this man. "That's what I do. I play." I shifted my gaze back to him. "Isn't that why you want me? Because I play?"

I was referring to the contract, the deal, the band.

But the second I said it, I knew it'd come out all wrong.

His nostrils flared, the man a picture of power and sex, and he eased forward, sliding the door back into place, closing us in.

"I think you already know the answer to that."

Disbelief huffed from my nose, and I tried to turn away from him, but he just came closer. Closer and closer until he was leaning over me, one hand planted on the back of the couch as he angled down to get in my face. I tried to withdraw, to hide my face, to tamp down this craziness that I was feeling at his proximity.

He hooked my chin with a tatted knuckle, and I sucked in a staggered breath.

"Yes," he murmured, so low, so rough. "I want you because you play. I want you because you write the type of songs that have never been sung, and you sing them better than anyone else could."

Onyx eyes blazed that icy fire.

Chills and flames.

I didn't know which one I was feeling most.

"I want you because when you stand on a stage with the rest of your band, you become something that no one else can replace. You become brilliant. *A fucking star.*" The last he grated up close to my ear.

Trembles rolled, and I struggled to keep myself from reaching for him. From caressing the curve of his powerful jaw and from touching my fingertips to the thunder raging in his chest. Cautiously, I looked up to meet the brunt force of his gaze. "And what if I don't want to be a star?"

His teeth clenched. "Bullshit. You were made for this."

"And what if I don't want it anymore?" It came out softer than I wanted it to.

"Is that what you really believe? That you don't want it anymore? Or are you letting fear stand in your way?"

It felt like he was sifting around in my heart and mind. Searching through the rubble and debris.

"You don't know me."

He edged back, staring me down. "Don't I? You think it's not written on you? Fear? I'm here to take that away."

My frown was instant, a pulse of panic drumming at my ribs.

Apparently, he knew I'd gone running off that stage last night, the first mistake in a line of them that had sent me running to him.

"I wasn't feeling well last night . . . that was all."

A skeptical smirk pulled at one side of his mouth. "And your first thought was to drown your sickness in tequila?"

"Isn't that everyone's first thought?" I tried to go for light. That was a mistake, too.

Because he hit me with an offhanded smile. Oh, I really wished that he wouldn't, because it was all kinds of pretty, as if maybe he had a sliver of *nice guy* buried underneath.

"Only when what you're nursing is a sick heart." He said it as if he got me in a way he shouldn't.

Our gazes tangled, awareness thrumming between us as strong as the rhythm of a guitar.

I thought maybe he couldn't handle the force of the connection, either, the feeling too intense, and he ripped his eyes from mine.

His attention drifted to my notebook as if it were safer.

"What are you working on?"

I flipped it shut. "Nothin'."

"Nothing?"

"Just a song that won't come."

"And why's that?"

"Because sometimes life isn't fair and it steals the things that are most important to us."

His lips pressed into a thin line of regret, and he huffed a heavy breath as he turned away, as if he were warring with something inside himself.

Two seconds later, he quickly swiveled back, standing like a towering fortress in the middle of the small space.

A whole new intensity lit a fire in those eyes. A writhing of the blackest kind of storm.

Hatred and hostility and compassion.

"I want you to know I'm doing everything I can to make this right for you. That I want the best for you and for your band. I need you to know that. To remember that."

"I get you're doing your job, but don't you dare stand there and tell me it's not about the money. I'll be the first to admit it's a whole lot about that for us, too."

Weren't most people's dreams paved in gold?

My spirit rumbled in protest, knowing it was so much more than that. That we wanted our music to mean something. To touch people. To somehow let them know they weren't alone in this great big world.

My focus moved to the door where I knew the rest of my band was, their lives so committed to what we did, one-hundred-percent in. "If I do it, it will be for them."

"And what about you?"

"Maybe I just want something simpler. A home and a family."

"You think you're not made of song? You think your spirit doesn't ring with beauty? I can feel it, Emily, the burn of it coming from you. Don't sell yourself short."

"Sometimes the only path to peace is to settle." The words

were frail wisps.

He dipped down so close I could taste the words that rolled from his tongue. "Don't settle for anything less than *everything*. I will die before I watch you do that."

I felt his promise like an earthquake.

It rocked me.

Body and soul.

"Like this isn't about the money for you?"

I refused to believe it was anything else.

I had to remember the reason he was here. His cruel intentions from last night.

His jaw clenched, and he set both hands on the back of the couch on either side of me. It angled me back, the man hovering an inch away. "No, Emily. It's not. Not for a second."

Then he straightened and walked out, leaving me sitting there gasping for breath.

Royce

"Did you get them to agree?" I pressed my phone tight to my ear where I paced just offstage in the wings, voice lifted only high enough over the roar of the club for Pete to hear my growl.

"One, and we're making progress with the other."

Frustration squeezed my lungs, and I paced some more, trying not to yank out all my hair. "Goddamn it."

"Calm down, man, this shit takes time, and you have to know how delicate the situation is."

I blew out a breath. "I know. Fuck, I know. I just don't know how much time we have." My gaze moved out to the stage where the roadies were rushing to finish setting up for Carolina George. A DJ was playing old country music from the overhead speakers, and white strobes flashed over the crowd, rowdy and anxious for them to take to the stage after the local band had opened up.

"We're working as quickly as we can, and it's coming together as planned."

"It'd better."

Dry laughter rolled from him. "Dude, I am doing everything I can. If this backfires, whose ass do you think is on the line?"

"All of our asses are on the line," I grunted low, glancing around, making sure I was out of earshot. We were all riding a very thin line. Risking it all. "But I'm not letting that motherfucker get away with this for any longer. Not either of them."

"I know, man, I know," he conceded.

I blew out a breath. "No matter what happens, I've got you, Pete. You aren't going to take the fall for this. It's on me."

"However it goes down, I'll be standing beside you. I want this just as bad as you."

A sigh filtered out. "Thanks, brother. Keep me posted."

"You know I will."

He killed the call, and I immediately tapped out a text.

Me: Hey Mag-Pie, thinking about you. What are you up to tonight? Staying out of trouble?

I capped it with a winky face. You know, going for the cool big brother rather than the overprotective one that was itching to rip out a motherfucker's throat.

Two seconds later, my phone blipped with a response.

It was a picture of her smiling face in her room, hugging a stuffed animal to her chest.

My heart clutched.

Fuck, I loved this kid.

Maggie: Just hanging out.

Me: You're nineteen. You should be out.

Maggie: Thought you'd rather know that I'm safe at home.

Me: All I care about is that you are safe. And HAPPY.

Maggie: Hmm . . . funny how I feel the same way about you.

I rolled my eyes.

Me: I'm not the concern here. I'm good.

Maggie: Isn't that what all the girls say about you?

Light laughter seeped out.

Me: You're a pain in my ass, do you know that?

Maggie hit me up with a slew of kissing hearts.
I sent a text back with a bunch of alternating birds and pizzas.
She sent me a row of middle fingers.
Another text came in a second later.

Maggie: Seriously, Royce. I want you to be happy. Maybe it's time to let go and move on.

Images flashed, the memory of *her* face hitting me like a bulldozer.

In an instant, I was consumed by excruciating pain. Chest so goddamn tight I thought I would implode.

I just swallowed it down and let it fuel me. Used it as a reminder that I couldn't fail. That I couldn't get distracted by this insanity I was feeling.

I stuffed my phone into my pocket just as the stage manager was herding the band out from the back. Richard clapped me on the shoulder, dipped his head.

"Kill it out there. Prove to me why I'm here," I told him, attempting to cover the coarseness in my voice.

Rhys answered for him, whirling around and pointing both fingers at me. "Oh, you know we will. You don't have to worry about that. Watch how magic is made. Want to know the reason the place is packed?" He gestured around, his grin about as huge as his confidence. "Take a peek at us, and you've got your answer."

Leif tossed a drumstick high in the air, catching it without missing a beat as he casually passed by.

The three of them strutted out onto the stage. That was all it took for the crowd to go wild, for anticipation to thunder and roar. Shouts and stamps of feet and a barrage of applause echoed through the music hall, excitement rising up from the bottom, billowing and blooming and filling the space.

But it was the feeling that came over me from behind, crawling up my back and pricking like the delicious dig of fingernails into my flesh, that sent a clap of thunder rolling through my body.

Slowly, I turned to glance over my shoulder. Emily was walking up, the stage manager on one side and a sound technician messing with the speaker in her ear on the other.

Mel followed close behind, head dipped down as she quickly tapped something into the tablet that she carried.

Energy flashed.

A bolt of intensity.

A burst of light.

A fucking thunderstorm.

I knew she felt it, too.

Knew it in the way her footsteps faltered and her delicate shoulders stiffened, awareness riding over her silky flesh. Warily, she lifted her head to peek at me, like she thought she was going covert and I wouldn't notice.

Not even a chance.

A chord strummed through the middle of me when that jade gaze met with mine. Confusion widened her eyes and attraction parted her lips.

Tension swelled.

Binding and tugging.

God.

This girl was going to do me in.

I tried to shun it. To ignore the fact that she wielded this power. She'd already fucked it up once, the girl a roadblock that had thwarted my intentions.

Course changed.

Looking at this girl made it hard to remember the end game.

I lifted my chin at her as she got closer.

"Good luck," I told her.

Her face pinched, and she glanced out at the riot going down at the foot of the stage. The blip of the faces that flashed in the strobes of blinding light, the pound, pound, pound of need that clamored from her fans, each of them wanting to get closer, hungering to be a part of what she was.

Of what she became when she stepped out on that stage.

She returned the power of that gaze to me. Sheer terror lined her features. Nerves wringing her out.

My guts clenched, tied in knots. I wanted to go for her. Wrap her up and hold her and tell her that it would be okay.

That I would protect her.

Whatever it took.

Because I knew right then, that was exactly what she needed. For someone to see through the bullshit façade she wore like armor. Begging for someone to tear it down while holding onto it with all she had at the same time.

She inhaled a shaky breath and started for the curtains so she could make her entrance. Our shoulders brushed as she passed. A bolt of desire streaked through my body, her sweet intensity so thick it surrounded me in a cloud of overwhelming need.

Shocked, she jumped away.

Affected.

Prisoner to this craziness, too.

I couldn't give into it. Not again. It was wrong. Wrong on every level. But I was beginning to think there wasn't a thing in this world that could make it go away.

My mouth moved with silent words. "You're a star."

I wondered if it was possible for her to see herself the way the rest of the world did. If she had the first clue that everyone turned to face her when she walked in the room. The girl was allure and temptation.

A snare.

I thought maybe she was caught in one, too, because she seemed to have to rip herself away from our connection. Throwing back her shoulders and forcing on that brave exterior, Emily stepped out from the high, towering drapes. That was all it took for the zealous crowd to go mad, and screams filled the cavernous space.

"Hello, hello," Emily called through her mic as she slung her guitar strap over her shoulder. "We are Carolina George, and we are thrilled to be here in Alabama tonight."

A roar of energy exploded.

Leif drummed his sticks in the air, and Richard drove into the chords of one of their most popular songs. Rhys stepped forward into a blue spotlight as he played the bassline, and Emily stood in the middle of it all.

She wasn't just standing in a spotlight.

She was the light.

A motherfucking star.

This . . .

This was where music came alive.

Where it was breathed to life.

Where everyday people got the chance to touch on something extraordinary.

Where true talent was exposed.

I stood there watching.

Itching in belief and discomfort and the hatred that ran fast in my blood.

Knowing exactly what it was that I was missing.

Carolina George played. Their style was a cross of country and indie rock.

Sweet.

Sultry.

Soulful.

Richard, Rhys, and Leif entranced the audience.

But it was Emily who *owned* them.

Looking at her, it wasn't hard to see how obsessions were born.

Hatred bled free at the thought that anyone would seek to dim this light. Anger booming in my blood like a gunshot. Fast and furious. There before I knew what hit me.

Maybe it was right then that I knew I'd never allow anyone to hurt her.

Not ever again.

nine

Emily

$\mathcal{I}$ belted the lyrics to the crowd that was held in rapture.

My heart overflowing.

It was insane to think how thousands of strangers could gather in the same place and feel the same thing.

Music making us one.

Connecting us in a way that I was certain nothing else in the world could.

It was an upbeat song we were playing. One that shouldn't hold the power to bring tears to my eyes. But emotion was riding high. A feeling coming over me that I hadn't felt in so long as I sang into the mic.

My feet might be walking these city streets
I'm sure I've never been so alone

Catch Me When I Fall

I might be surrounded
But I'm wonderin' if it's ever gonna feel like home
Because baby . . . baby, I'll always be country at heart
Baby . . . baby, I'll always be country at heart

When I stepped back and started to clap to the beat, Richard drove into the guitar solo, his fingers flying across the frets. My brother had the entire crowd going wild. Riding a high unlike any other.

I stepped back up to the mic, and I gave the final lines my all.

Because, baby . . . baby I'll always be country at heart
And this country heart will always belong to you
I'll always belong to you

I held the last note, my chest tight as my voice soared to the ceiling.

Joy bloomed as bright as the flashes of lights that strobed in my eyes. The last of the song trailed off, and a roar of applause took its place.

An overwhelming thunder.

Shock blistered through my being.

I did it.

Oh my god, I did it.

I nearly slumped forward with the magnitude of the relief that I felt. It was the first show I'd played in three months that I didn't feel as if I might fall apart. Break down in front of the world with nothing left to give.

I dipped down in the deepest bow. Gratitude poured off me in waves.

The roar of the crowd only grew.

"Birmingham, you are beautiful. Thank you for welcoming us tonight. We will never forget you!" I was smiling as I issued the statement under the shimmer of stage lights, my breaths still short and choppy from the performance.

My brother moved to the edge of the stage, and he reached down to touch the hands that were lifted high, stretching out, as if they were begging for just a moment more.

He stepped back and tossed his guitar pick into the crowd. "I love you, Birmingham! Goodnight!"

His small token incited a scramble of flailing arms and diving bodies vying to catch it. It was funny how one little piece of plastic could almost cause a riot. But the real riot broke out when Rhys peeled off his sweaty tee, the way he did night after night, revealing his carved, chiseled body.

"You are the fuckin' best! Thanks for an amazing show!" Screams erupted from below, a slew of bleeding hearts begging for his attention. The boy was as sexy as they came, and he knew it, too, a showman all the way down to the marrow. He twirled the shirt above his head before he sent it sailing into the tumult roiling at the foot of the stage.

It was a crush of diving women and whipping hair.

Our own, personal pot stirrer. Always lookin' for trouble. If he couldn't find it, he was always happy to cause it.

He just grinned, chuckled into the mic attached to his ear, not saying another word as he sauntered off the stage.

The cockiest boy with the biggest heart.

I bit down on my bottom lip, almost surprised by the laughter I could feel bubbling up from inside.

I felt . . . good.

Better than good.

Amazing.

Free.

As if a little bit of myself had been unchained tonight.

Immediately, my attention was dragged to the wings of the stage.

Drawn.

Compelled.

As if I could sense the power of the potent, decadent gaze. But I guessed that I really could. Because Royce was there, barely concealed by the curtains, staring back at me.

Our gazes met in a tangle of confusion and need.

My heart stammered a reckless beat.

I wanted to refuse to believe his presence had any bearing on my holding it together during tonight's show. Wanted to dispute the idea that I'd somehow found the peace I'd been missing with the knowledge that he was standing nearby.

Watching.

Protecting.

But I didn't have time to contemplate all of that right then, so I handed my guitar to one of the stagehands and headed toward the wings with the intent to put him fully out of my mind.

Wishful thinking.

Every step that I took got slower and slower the closer I came to where he was standing, caught up in the gripping energy that pulsed and shivered and shook me to the core.

God, this was crazy.

Crazy that a single man could evoke this reaction in me.

Our shoulders touched as I passed.

A bolt of electricity streaked through my body.

I sucked in a staggered breath, my pulse thudding out of sync.

Oh God, what was he doin' to me?

Melanie was instantly at my side, and I ducked my head, trying to tear myself from the magnetism that pulled me in the opposite direction.

"Girl, you killed it tonight," Melanie gushed. "You are back on top, right where you belong. Goodness, the entire place was going mad over you. That last song . . . you are ridiculous." She waved her hand emphatically. "It shouldn't be legal to be able to sing like that."

She didn't even pause before she shifted gears, right back to business. "Let's get you to the green room. You have ten minutes before VIP ticket holders will start to be let in. Grab some water, pee if you need to, shine up your nose. Maybe wipe that ridiculous grin off your face."

With the last, she knocked her hip into mine, and I found myself giggling.

It felt so right.

"You want me to stop smilin' now?" I asked as we jostled through the chaos happening backstage.

"Hell, no. It's the first time I've seen you this happy in ages. I was getting worried about you."

"I told you I was fine."

Only now it actually felt like it might be true.

We ducked into the green room, and I went right for the bucket filled with ice and waters, cracked the lid off one and guzzled the entire thing.

Richard, Rhys, and Leif piled in behind us.

Rhys threw a fist in the air. "Yeah, baby girl, you killed it tonight! Did you feel that? Holy shit, energy was out of control. Our girl is unstoppable!"

Redness flushed my cheeks, and there was nothing I could do to stop my grin, hope brimming wide. Threatening to overflow. "I don't think I couldn't have felt that," I admitted with a disbelieving shake of my head. "I don't think there was a person out there tonight immune to it."

"That's because it was fuckin' brilliant. Off the hizzle. Hittin' 'em hard with the sizzle."

Yeah, Rhys actually rapped it, sliding his hands like he was skipping a record.

Leif shook his head. "Melanie was right. We're leaving you at the next city."

Richard chuckled a little, roughing a hand over his sweaty face, his attention sliding to me, casting me in a warm glance.

Affection.

Relief.

I knew my brother was as thankful as I was that I'd somehow managed to find my groove.

"Five minutes," Melanie called.

The guys were grabbing waters, so I popped into the small dressing room that really wasn't more than a closet and dug my phone out of my bag so I could snag my own pics with fans.

It was something that had always meant something to me, the scrapbooks I made with the pictures I took with fans. I loved capturing these moments of the band. Our faces and expressions after a show. The encounters with the people who supported us most.

Phone in hand, I dipped back out. Leif and Richard were

standing face-to-face, two of them enthralled in a conversation, Leif gesturing wildly. Richard nodded emphatically.

Clearly, they were discussing one of Leif's epiphanies. The guy was so creative. Hit with ideas that flowed from him like a handwritten story.

On the other side of the room, Rhys had Melanie tossed over a shoulder, throwing her around in some kind of celebration that I was pretty sure she was gonna make him pay for later.

I'd put down money that Rhys didn't mind paying the price.

I grinned at the scene.

It was so normal.

So right.

I did my best not to search for Royce. Like a fool, wondering where he had disappeared to. If he'd stayed. If he was thinking about me the way I was thinking about him.

A little worried I was gettin' obsessed.

But that's what crushes did. They mashed you up inside, twisting you in a knot of attraction. Heart, mind, and body tied.

Needing a distraction, I peeked at my phone. When I saw there was a text I'd missed, I swiped the screen and entered my passcode.

My brow pulled together as my gaze moved over the message.

Confusion quickly morphed to dread.

Freezing every cell in terror.

Unknown Number: Miss me? Don't worry, Emmy Love, it won't be long now.

To anyone else, the message would appear innocuous. Friendly, even. But I knew . . . I knew it was meant to be cruel. To insight fear. An outright threat.

My hands started to shake. A cold, clammy sweat gathered at my nape. A rush of dizziness almost canted me to the side.

I squeezed my phone.

Tight.

Maybe what I was really hoping to do was crush it. In the process, crush *him*.

I refused to let him taunt me. Not like this. I was stronger than this. Braver than this.

A hand landed on my shoulder.

Screeching, I jumped about ten feet in the air.

Rhys cracked up. "Emily Iris, you are the jumpiest little thing on the planet."

Turning around to face him, I forced the wobbliest, fakest smile. "You just caught me off guard, that's all."

He didn't need to know he'd almost sent me into a tailspin.

He gestured to himself. "It's all the ninja skills."

Melanie rolled her brown eyes, her ponytail swishing over her shoulders as she readjusted her shirt. "You're about as inconspicuous as a stampede of bulls."

"What are you talking about? I'm as light as a feather." He bounced around on his toes and threw some fake jabs.

"More like an avalanche of boulders."

"Boulders? What are you sayin'? I remind you of a set of big balls, Mells Bells? I know you love me. You can just come right out and say it. No need for innuendo."

"Gross. Clear enough for you?"

He barked out a laugh. "Ah, you are cruel, gorgeous. Lucky for you, I'm a man who likes punishment."

"You are incorrigible."

"Feel free to *encourage* me any time."

"Ugh," she groaned. "Case in point. Now go put on a damn shirt, it's about time to start letting people in."

"Believe me, baby, they want me just like this." Rhys rocked his hips, sweat dripping from his abdomen.

"Gross," she said again. "And there are children out there."

"Fine, fine." He was grinning like mad when he pulled a fresh tee over his head, and I was just standing there, trying to hold it together. To pretend as if I was with them.

Feeling their ease and joy.

Acting like that one stupid text message didn't have me close to falling apart.

I couldn't let myself. Not after we'd finally gotten a glimpse of normalcy.

"You good?" Melanie asked, stumbling a little when she noticed my expression.

"Totally."

Lies. Lies. Lies.

Maybe if I told myself enough of them, I would start to believe them myself.

She hesitated, searching my face. Finally, she conceded with a soft, concerned smile that told me she didn't fully believe me, either, before she turned back to the rest of the group and snapped her fingers in the air. "It's time."

She strode out the door to give the security guard the go, and I shuffled over to where Richard and Leif had gathered by the Carolina George banner, Rhys right on my heels.

Melanie led in the first group.

It was a mother and her two young daughters. Maybe six and eight. Both of them were holding poster boards, *I love you Carolina George* written in glitter and stars, as bright as the stars that were shining in their eyes.

This . . . this was what made it all worth it. What made me want to fight. To stand up and be brave and bold and take a stance rather than keeping this festering secret hidden for a second longer.

I just didn't know how I was ever going to be able to force it from my tongue.

The mother ushered her girls forward. "It's so nice to meet you, Emily. This is Saige and Becca. They're a little shy, but believe me, they are very excited to meet you."

She was hovering over them, her arms stretched out like a safety net. Caring and protective and full of excitement for her children just because she knew this would make them happy.

My heart pressed full at seeing such a sweet family.

Sorrow and joy.

Sorrow and joy.

I knelt down. "Hi, there. It's so nice to meet you."

The youngest one stepped forward. As cute as could be, her voice tiny and musical, and a slice of pain panged in the middle of me.

A little piece of my soul crying out for what it had lost.

"Hi, Emily," she drawled with the tiniest lisp. "I'm Saige. I'm your biggest fan in the whole world. You are so pretty. I like your eyes."

A tender smile pulled across my face. "Well, I like your eyes, too. Did you have fun at the show tonight?"

She nodded. "It was my favorite in the world, and my favorite song in the world is 'Heartstruck.' I can sing it good. You wanna hear?"

She belted out a line in her little girl drawl.

Right then, I was the one that was heartstruck.

"I'm glad I got to sing it for you tonight, but wow, I think you sing it way better than I do."

Her mouth dropped open. "Really?"

"Really."

I turned to her sister. "How about you? What's your favorite song?"

Her eyes went round as saucers, as if she couldn't believe I was talkin' to her, and I could feel the tension drain away. The fear I'd felt a moment ago was pushed down into the recesses because moments like these mattered too much.

I needed to be present. To be right and good. I wanted to give it all. To be my best. To be an example for young girls like this.

And how could I do that when I was running from everything? If I couldn't take a stance?

"I . . . I . . . all of them," she said.

Gratitude and hope pulsed through my veins.

They both passed me keepsake books they'd made with pictures of our album covers pasted on the pages inside. I grinned as I signed them, then grinned even wider when their mama took a picture of the three of us.

"Thank you so much," their mama said. "I don't think I can express what this means to them."

"We're just thankful for you supportin' us. We couldn't do this without you."

I glanced up at the guys who were getting no love.

Poor boys.

They didn't need to worry. I was pretty sure we could expect a fangirl or two.

Oh, and were there ever. Rhys got about fifteen marriage proposals, a slew of phone numbers, and a few keys to hotel rooms.

He accepted them all.

No surprise there.

Only question was who he'd actually grace with his presence tonight.

Richard and Leif got a whole lot of propositions, too.

Richard always refrained. A stab of sadness hit me. I still couldn't fathom why he'd given up what had meant most. Why he would walk away.

Leif was all too excited to show off the band he'd recently had tattooed on his ring finger.

A symbol of his forever.

We signed, and we smiled, and we posed until I was close to being spent and still feeling better than I thought I had in years.

"Only a few more," Melanie promised, leading out an older couple and letting in the next group.

It was four guys . . . barely men, really.

Raucous and rowdy.

The stench of beer came off them in nauseating waves, their movements a little unruly and their voices slurred.

My chest gave a little lurch. A vibration of a warning.

I swallowed it down.

This was all part of the game. They were just looking for a good time. I had no right to begrudge them that.

Still, I couldn't stop the small throb of panic as they came closer.

"Holy shit, it's Carolina George! Is this real life?" one of them shouted, throwing his arms in the air. "Day fuckin' made!"

Richard chuckled and reached for the shirt he wanted him to sign. "We're just thankful you're here, man. Songs don't mean anything if there isn't someone there to listen to them. We appreciate your support."

"Fuck yeah. We had to buy these tickets from a scalper, but it was worth every penny. Show was off the hook."

"Glad to hear you think we're worth it," Rhys said as he was signing a baseball cap.

"Best show this year. You guys nailed it. Way better than when you were opening for A Riot of Roses. Dickbags sucked."

My entire body flinched with the mention of that band. Time spun backward. Rushing to catch up to tonight's text. The two of them paired left my knees weak and my stomach turning.

Hold it together, Em. You can do this. A few minutes more. That's it, I silently told myself.

Besides, that's what that bastard wanted, anyway. He wanted me trembling with fear. Cowering. Giving in.

Screw him.

Still, I was having to paste on a smile when one of the guys came up to me while the other three were caught up in a conversation with the rest of the band.

He was smiling, too. Though something about his was all wrong.

Off.

Salacious and vile.

"You got the prettiest voice I ever heard," he slurred, his breath knocking me in the face. A clean shot of stale alcohol and depravity.

My smile slipped. I fought to maintain it.

"Thank you," I barely mumbled. I reached for the shirt he had so I could sign it and get him the heck out of there.

Pulling it back, he angled his head, eyes moving places they shouldn't. "Even prettier up close, too. Distance is a disservice."

I grimaced, words creaking, "You're too kind."

"Good thing I'm here . . . up real close where I can get a good look."

Unease rolled across my flesh. A flicker of panic.

What a creep.

I looked around for Melanie or the security guard. Melanie's head was poked outside the door, most likely talking to the security guard who was probably getting the next group. I prepared to give the signal, the one we used when someone was getting a little too *friendly.*

"How about you and I have a drink?" he asked.

The smile I forced was brittle. So fake I could feel it cracking. "I don't think that's a good idea."

"I think it's a great idea."

"No, thank you."

I started to tug at my ear the way that Melanie and I had agreed as our signal. But I didn't have time before he flew forward, a hand pawing at my hip, the man slurring through a laugh, "Ahh, come on, you don't have to be so shy."

The dam holding back my panic crumbled.

It surged free.

Hitting my bloodstream at warp speed.

Hot and ugly and despairing.

There was nothing I could do.

Nothing to stop it.

Memories assaulted me. Picture after revolting picture invading my mind.

A hand on my throat. Binds on my wrists. A plea on my mouth. "Don't. Please."

"Don't touch me," I shrieked at the man, ramming my fists to his chest as a full bout of horror took hold.

Fight or flight.

I intended on doing both.

But I didn't have the time to think another step through because the guy was being tossed to the side.

Cool rushed in to take his place, and I tried to get a breath, to remind myself I was just fine, that no one could hurt me, to clear the panic clouding sight and reason.

But the images kept coming.

Assaulting.

Bashing.

Ruining.

Tossing me back in their hole.

"Emmy Love. Begging doesn't change a thing. A debt's owed. Simple as that. Sorry your name came up when the debt came due. Though I can't say I'm complaining."

Air wheezed down my throat, and I was barely processing the menacing words that reverberated through the room. "Even think about looking at her again and you bleed, motherfucker."

"Hey, man, I was just trying to get my shirt signed. Bitch freaked the fuck out for no reason."

Another growl. This one low. "You really want to die tonight, don't you?"

Anxiety seized every cell in my body.

Knees went weak.

Legs gave out.

Then onyx eyes were flashing white violence in my blurry sight.

A storm of aggression.

A blaze of brutality.

Arms were around me before I could fall, and I was suddenly floating.

Cradled.

Held.

"I've got you, Emily. Shh. I've got you."

I loosely looped my arms around the back of his neck, pressing my face to the tattoo at the front, inhaling deep.

Safety and warmth.

"Royce," I whimpered. There was nothing I could do. It broke, a flood of tears seeping from my eyes and into his hot skin.

My spirit wept with the realization that this might never end.

I might always be a prisoner.

Trapped.

Unable to get free of *this*.

A sob burst up my throat, and I buried it in the tremor of his thick throat.

"I've got you, Precious. Nothing is going to happen to you. I promise you that." He murmured the words as he carried me out a door at the far end of the room and into a gloomy hall that ran the back of the club.

The door slammed behind us.

Voices seeped through the walls, shouts and a scuffle, and it only made me cry harder.

A big hand was rubbing my back, the man carrying me as if I

didn't weigh a thing, his strength wrapping me whole.

"It's okay. It's okay." He turned and slid down the wall, sitting on the floor and cradling me in his lap.

This massive, dangerous, intimidating man brushed tender fingers through my hair, whispered soothing words to the top of my head, "He can't hurt you. He's gone, Emily. He's gone. I won't let anyone hurt you. Not ever again. It's okay. It's okay."

Not ever again.

Not ever again.

But he didn't know what I'd been through. What I was dealing with now. And the last thing I wanted to be was some kind of damsel in distress. But sometimes the weight of the war you were fighting felt like too much.

I held tighter to his neck. "He touched me," I hiccupped.

"I know. I saw. He's lucky he's still breathing."

My eyes squeezed shut. "I hate this, Royce. I hate it so much. Someone even looks at me funny, and I'm fallin' apart. This isn't who I am."

Anger radiated from his massive body, and he tightened his huge arms around me. "He touched you without permission. You don't have to apologize for reacting."

The door suddenly banged open.

Our attention jumped that way.

Richard strode out, rage in his stance, his face twisted with worry and frustration. One look at us and it contorted with surprise and suspicion.

In a flash, Royce had us on our feet. He took a step in front of me as if he were a shield.

Richard stumbled to a stop, lines denting across his brow as he looked at Royce glowering back.

"I've got her, you can go," Richard told Royce offhandedly.

Dismissing him.

"I don't think so," Royce replied.

Richard frowned before he leaned around to get an eye on me. "You can come out, Em. That handsy fucker is out on his ass. We don't need any of that shit. You okay?"

"I'm fine," I said, wiping the tears from my cheeks with the back of my hand and trying to keep the quiverin' from my voice.

Richard scowled. "You're not fine. I mean, fuck, Emily . . ." He threw an exasperated hand back in the direction of the room Royce had just rescued me from. "You've dealt with a million guys like that, and never once have you had this kind of reaction."

Fury huffed from Royce's nose. "Back down, Ramsey. The last thing she needs right now is you coming out here tossing around accusations."

"How the fuck is this any of your business, Reilly?"

Royce lifted his chin. "You can't expect me to sign a band and not be concerned about the welfare of its members. It's my job to see to both their mental and physical well-being."

Richard looked as if he wanted to call bullshit.

Maybe I did, too.

Because I couldn't put my finger on this man. Only thing I did know was I wanted to sink every single one of mine into his skin.

Hold on for dear life.

"Well there's no fuckin' band if she can't stand on a stage," Richard spat. "If she can't stand in front of the fans. Even the assholes. You think chicks weren't climbing all over Rhys? You didn't see him losing his shit."

A low, forbidding sound rumbled from the man in front of me. "I think it'd be best if you went back in with the rest of the band."

"That's my sister."

"Who's obviously upset. I won't stand for you making it worse."

Richard huffed in disbelief, propping his hands on his waist, pacing a circle. "Fuck," he suddenly swore.

Anger and regret.

"Fuck, Emily." Richard's tone turned pleading. "I'm sorry, I shouldn't toss this shit in your face. Not when you're upset like this. But you've got to admit it . . . you're different. Fucking different and something has changed and it's killing me that you won't let the ones who care about you most in on it. You are *scaring* me."

Didn't he get that he was scaring me, too?

A fresh round of tears built in my eyes. I tried to hold the burn back, to stop from squeezing them closed.

No use.

Moisture spilled free.

Hot and fast.

"I'm here for you, Rich. Because of you. Don't you get it? That I would do absolutely anything for you? What I would sacrifice for you?"

He thought I was pushing him away, and I was begging him to breach the space.

Pain blanched my brother's face, and I wondered what was goin' through his mind. What would he do if he knew what I'd done for him?

My brother was rough and kind and passionate. Talented and beautiful to the eye. He had always been my hero. The one I'd looked up to.

I couldn't fathom how he could get involved in something so filthy. Something so wrong and depraved.

I guessed maybe I was the fool to think that I could derail it.

"I would never ask that of you," Richard said, shaking his head in misunderstanding. "And this isn't about me."

But it was.

It'd always been.

I sniffled, the words stifled, frozen on my tongue.

I wanted to release them. So badly. But they were bottled. A festering mess that I was sure one day would blow.

Richard fisted a hand in a frustrated appeal. "Nothing is going to change if you don't make that change, Emily. Nothing. It's time for you to come clean about what you really want, about what is really going on, before we run out of time. Ask Reilly here . . ." Richard gestured to him with his chin. "Opportunities like this don't come around more than once, and I want you to take it with us. Fuck . . . we need you to. Carolina George isn't Carolina George without you."

Sadness billowed, and I wanted to rush him. To hug him and hold him and beg him to open up to me, too. To confess.

"I'm almost there, Rich. I'll make up my mind soon. I promise."

In or out. Because I couldn't keep going on like this.

He just nodded, sent a questioning, confused glare at Royce before spinning around and heading back for the door.

"Ramsey," Royce grated just as my brother was getting ready to step back into the room.

My brother paused, looked over his shoulder.

"Just to be clear . . . from here on out? If someone touches her without her permission? They lose their hands. And if anyone pushes her before she's ready? That becomes my problem. Do you understand?"

Richard shook his head in disgust. "Fuck you, Royce, if you don't think I want what's best for my sister. What's best for this band."

The door slammed closed behind him, and I exhaled a heavy sound.

Unable to keep up with the events of the night.

Soaring to the highest high before I'd been sent crashing to the lowest low.

A free fall I wasn't sure I was ever gonna recover from.

"You don't have to get in the middle of me and my brother, Royce. I know you want me to sign as badly as Rich does."

For a beat, Royce stood with his back to me before he slowly turned around.

Eyes stared back as if he could see right into the heart of me.

Molten fire.

My soul on display.

I wanted to gather it up.

Cover it.

"I'm a big girl. I can handle it." The words shook loose of my tongue.

He swiveled the rest of the way around and slowly started my way.

One step.

Two.

The click of his dress shoes on the cement floor sent bursts of energy through the air.

They struck my body like little lightning pulses.

One of the first songs I'd ever written played in a slow drone that crawled in from the recesses of the dingy music hall.

As if maybe it were calling me back.

My voice barely distinct enough to touch our ears. It was a sad, sad love song. Edged in longing and painted in faith that things would one day be better.

Turn out the way they were always meant to be.

I just wished it were the truth.

"I'm not here for Richard." Royce's voice was a sharp barb.

I nodded quick, tongue darting out to wet my lips. "I know . . . you're here for the band."

He reached out and brushed a lock of hair from my face, those fingertips riding down my cheek in a coarse caress.

It buzzed all the way to my center. "No, I'm here for you."

My mouth dropped open. Attraction alive. No longer did I know where I was standing.

Flying. Falling. Hoping. Weeping.

"I . . . I don't understand what you mean."

The tattoo on his throat bobbed. "You changed everything," he murmured, like admitting it caused him physical distress.

"You don't even know me," I whispered.

"Are you sure about that?" he challenged.

My mouth trembled, and my tongue almost managed to form another lie, but instead the hint of a truth was breaking free. "I don't want to be afraid, anymore, Royce. I don't want to feel powerless."

"You are the strongest person I know," he grated hard.

My head shook. "No. I've been breaking apart for a long time now."

"No, Emily, you're searching for a way to be whole."

I blinked at him, unable to process, to understand how he could know that about me. "I'm trying. I really am."

"You have to be willing to destroy whatever it is that is holding you back." He gazed back at me as if he had a first-row seat to all my secrets. Like he knew them better than me.

My mouth flapped open, my senses going haywire, this feeling that he could really see to the vile stain in me. "I want to be.

Strong. Like you said."

A big hand stroked across my jaw.

Shivers raced. Heart stampeding.

But it was in a whole different way than with that jerk inside.

"You are, Precious. Brave. Strong. I see it in you. No one can stop you."

"I don't want to let wickedness reign." How was I admitting this to him, as vague as it was? But it felt natural.

Trusting him when I'd thought he was the last person that I could.

Felt so right after I'd been the brunt of such a lie.

"Then don't," he almost demanded.

"My standing up means knocking down someone powerful. It's not gonna be easy."

"But is it worth it?"

"Yes," I whispered so fast. I'd never heard a truth ring so loud. I couldn't allow Cory Douglas to remain free after what he'd done. Sickness tremored through my body when I thought about him doing it again. Hurting someone innocent. Someone who couldn't fight back.

Royce's eyes flashed. The blackest black. That white fire burning fury. "Then you take the motherfucker down."

"I . . . I'm almost ready. Almost there."

He blinked long, his lips twisting in something that looked like guilt. "We should get you out of here. I shouldn't be out here with you."

My teeth raked my bottom lip, not sure that I wanted to give up on the connection. The feeling that maybe someone got me on a level no one else could. As if he'd been sent to make me see myself in a different light.

To remind myself of who I wanted to be.

"What if I don't want to leave?"

He huffed out a rough chuckle. "It's a conflict of interest."

The way he said it made it sound like it was a whole lot more.

"Are you not . . . interested?" I wanted it to come off as sexy. Progress, you know.

Asking for what I wanted . . . for what I needed.

Too bad I was shaking under the ferocity powering from his body.

"Am I not interested?" He angled closer, cedar filling my nose, the threat of sex hitting my tongue. "Have been dying to touch you. Taste you. Take you. But we can't do this."

I blinked up at him. "I'm starting to wonder if us *doing this* is how it's supposed to be."

His thumb traced my cheek, and he slowly shook his head. "Grace always precedes beauty."

My eyes pinched. Confused.

"Belief always precedes strength. You are all those things. And I won't taint that."

"What if I want you to taint me?" It left me on a breathy plea.

Danger rumbled in his chest, and his mouth was at my ear. "You don't know what you're asking for."

He stepped back, straightened out his jacket. "Come on, let's get you back to the hotel. I'm going to walk you to your door, let you inside, and then leave you there and spend the rest of the night wishing that I didn't have to."

Royce

The next night, after yet another show, I was trailing twenty feet behind the rest of the band that walked the sidewalk.

Call me antisocial.

But I really couldn't risk getting in Emily's space. Not when she was calling to me like a goddamn drug, one so powerful it could never be kicked. And I'd barely even had a taste.

Laughter billowed through the humid night air, Rhys acting like the clown he was, telling some over-the-top story about Richard and him when they were teenagers. Dude never let the cloud hovering over his band rain on his parade.

The whole time, I watched Emily like a hawk.

Ready to swoop in if she so much as stumbled.

If Richard so much as looked at her wrong.

It wasn't his fault. I got it. He was at a loss as to what was wrong with her. Trying to help her, not even knowing he was partly to blame.

My cell buzzed in my pocket.

I dug it out, gritting my teeth when I saw who was calling.

Shit.

This was the last thing I needed.

The group was far enough ahead that they wouldn't have to be subjected to the conversation, but still, my voice lowered to a growl when I answered, "What?"

I doubted he expected some kind of pleasantry.

"I'd like a status update." Contention clawed through my stepfather's voice.

"Everything is progressing as planned." Didn't even try to keep the venom out of my voice. Animosity was our normal MO, anyway. Only difference was the bastard didn't know how far I was willing to take the hatred.

He scoffed through the line. "As planned? If this were coming along as planned, they would have been signed three months ago. If they think by holding out they're going to get more money out of me, they are seriously underestimating who I am."

My teeth ground so hard I didn't know how they weren't dust. Just like the pieces he'd stolen of me. Pieces I was taking back.

"Not everyone's choices are driven by greed," I returned.

He chuckled. "Ignorant boy. Until you figure out money is what makes the world go round, you won't be worthy to stand in my shoes. I never should have allowed your mother to talk me into bringing you on. Pathetic. Do I need to send someone else to finish this thing?"

I fought to keep my cool. To keep from exploding. To keep from telling him that I was nothing like him and I'd never be.

I'd rather die, and I completely meant that.

"As I said, it is under control. This band is about trust. Don't mess up the progress I've made by adding someone else to the mix. Believe me, they will not appreciate that."

A huff filtered through the line. "You have two days to get this finalized."

"That's not enough time."

"Two days," he repeated, and the line went dead before I had the chance to say anything else.

Bastard.

I bit down on a knuckle to keep from hurling a string of expletives into the air. I needed more time. More time to understand where Emily stood and what she needed. More time for her to trust me when I hadn't given her a reason to do it.

Real reason? I needed more time to figure out how to do this without hurting her more in the end. Closer I got to her, the more I realized I was walking a thin fucking line. Maybe it was me putting on the brakes.

The group headed up the walk toward the hotel where we were staying in Mobile. Emily had performed at tonight's show while I'd stood in the shadows offstage, watching the quivers rolling through her body and the tremors in her voice.

The girl hostage to fear.

She'd skipped out on the VIP meet and greet.

I didn't think anyone blamed her, all except for the grumble of disappointed fans who'd wanted to be in her space. Didn't think she quite got that she was the showstopper. The reason. Or maybe the fucked-up thing was that she was becoming mine.

We entered the luxurious lobby, the lights stark inside, gleaming on the polished white-and-gold floors. Off to the right, an elevator swept open, and the entire group rushed for it as a team.

Mel hauled Emily along, laughing and playful. Leif, Richard, and Rhys piled in behind them.

I slowed. Close spaces, Emily, and I did not mix. Or maybe they mixed too well.

Holding an arm out to keep the elevator door from sliding shut, Rhys popped out his head. "You coming, money man?"

I shoved my hands in my pockets, rocked back on my heels. "Go on, I'll catch the next."

"Ah, we can make room. You afraid we bite?" He grinned, flashing his teeth.

I almost laughed. "Nah . . . think I'm actually going to grab a drink."

Good excuse, right?

"You need a drinkin' partner, city boy? I'll gladly drink you under the table," Rhys shouted from the elevator door.

Mel's head popped out below his, angled up so she could catch his eye. "Uh-uh, Rhys. It's already after midnight. You're on the schedule to hit the hotel gym before we pull out tomorrow. No hangovers for you."

"You underestimate me, baby. I can totally swing an all-nighter and still put you all to shame in the gym in the morning. I'm a god amongst men!"

"What you are is the God of BS. Now get your butt back on this elevator," she demanded.

"How about a little compromise. You and I pull an all-nighter and get our workout in my bed. It's a win-win."

"In your dreams, cowboy."

"Stallion, baby. When are you going to get that through your pretty little head?"

She shoved at him, and he was howling with laughter as his arm dropped free and the elevator door started to close.

I caught only a glimpse of the side of Emily's face.

Jade eyes soft. Warm with an affection I didn't deserve.

The tether that tied us thrummed. A low-pitched frequency that hummed through my body.

The door fully closed, cutting off the connection.

Shit.

I had to end this. Scrape this feeling from my skin. Keep her from sinking into my bones.

I moved into the mostly empty bar in the hotel lobby, slipped onto a stool, ordered a whiskey. I took a sip from the tumbler, the thick, heady flavor hitting my tongue, and I exhaled a heavy breath, trying to erase all the thoughts and worries and bullshit that threatened to bury me.

Unable to sit still, I reached into my jacket and pulled out the small journal I carried with me. A tangible reminder of my purpose that sat in my breast pocket right over my bitter, ugly heart. It was what I used to hash out the bullshit decaying in the middle of me.

I opened it to a blank page, intent on letting my fingers free with some of the hate.

I let it flow, my hand moving quickly over the page.

Easily.

But the words that spilled out were ones I definitely shouldn't write.

Fuck.

I wanted to stop it, this familiar feeling that crested from within. A lure tugging me back into long-since-dead dreams.

I didn't know how much time had passed when I sensed it. Skin prickling in awareness. I shifted to look over my shoulder at the short hall that ran off to the side of the bar. It led outside to firepits that overlooked the river the hotel butted against.

Blonde hair was piled on her head in a messy twist, the girl wearing a sweatshirt that draped off one shoulder and yoga pants.

Casual.

Couldn't say so much about the punch of lust seeing her like that elicited in me.

The swell of protectiveness that crashed.

I should stay sitting right here. Same way as I should have done that first night I'd seen her at that bar back in Savannah. Instead, I was tucking the journal back into my pocket, digging out a twenty, and trapping it under the tumbler I'd emptied.

My shoes echoed on the stark floors, my heart rate catching time, everything slowing and speeding and warping when I pushed out the door.

My attention darted to the left, then to the right, relief hitting me when I saw she'd curled up on an outdoor couch tucked in the shadows at the far side of the empty patio.

Flames lapping up.

Illuminating the soft curve of her face, nose and chin and lips. I wanted to be the one tracing each of them.

I slowed as I approached.

I knew she felt me.

Could tell in the way she hugged her knees tighter to her chest.

In the energy that spilled to the ground. Rushing. Crashing between us. Her teeth raked anxiously at her bottom lip when I slipped down in the cushioned seat off to the side, her face scrubbed of makeup, everything about her fresh and soft.

Fuck me.

She was gorgeous.

"What are you doing out here?" I asked.

There was no accusation to it. Just interest.

"Needed to get out of that room. Get some fresh air." She huffed a little breath from her nose, fidgeted with her sweatshirt. "Couldn't sleep."

"No?"

She tipped her face to the night sky. A slight breeze blistered through, whipping the tiny strands of her hair, the soft wisps kissing her cheeks. "It's one of the things that's been eluding me the most lately. Sleep. Peace."

I barely nodded, not sure what to give, how far to push her, what she was ready for. "And you find it out here? Peace?"

My gaze drifted to the blackened river that snaked through the city, the hotel tucked up close to the river's edge. Moonlight glittered in the rippling water, and a few sparse lights from boats dotted the expanse.

She offered me a soft, wistful smile. "Isn't it, though? Peaceful? When you don't have a home, I guess you have to find it wherever you go."

I dragged a knuckle over my lips. Girl set me off kilter. "Is that what you're missing? A home?"

She was back to staring at the endless sky, hugging her knees to her chest. "The road gets hard, you know? Bein' alone all the time? Surrounded by thousands of people, and still so many times it feels like you're just . . . there. A prop. Something to be seen but not really heard."

"I get that."

I did.

More than she could imagine.

"Is that what's stopping you from signing? The road? Traveling? Being on the stage night after night rather than in the comfort of four walls?"

Is that what she was running toward?

She exhaled a heavy breath, and a lance of pain struck through her expression. "I want those things. So much. A home and a family. There's a huge piece of me that is achin', knowing what I'm missing."

I could hear the hesitation in her voice, the girl wavering, close to giving me more.

"But I want to play music, too," she added.

Exposed.

Vulnerable.

Beautiful.

"I want to play. Make it beautiful. Touch people's hearts even if it's just in passin'."

"You do it better than anyone I've met."

She forced a playful smile. "Are you tryin' to come onto me again, Hollywood? Trying to win your way so I'll finally sign that contract? Sell my soul and my songs to Mylton Records?"

Her voice hitched somewhere between a tease and a true question.

Chuckling low, I leaned forward and rested my forearms on my thighs, staring at her through the jumping flames. "Seems I don't know how not to come onto you, Emily Ramsey. You do something to me that you shouldn't. But in this case? No. I'm one-hundred-percent sincere. You have to be the most talented person I've ever met."

A blush colored her cheeks. Heated by the fire. Heated by my unrelenting gaze.

My fingers itched, wanting to reach out and feel the burn on her skin.

Her eyes traveled off to the side, the girl warring with something deep. Finally, she turned her attention back to me, her stare hard yet open. Baring herself. "How would Mr. Fitzgerald feel if he knew my songs had run dry? That I haven't been able to write in months?"

I had to keep myself from cringing at her statement.

Traumas did that.

Stole your inspiration.

Your faith.

If you let them, they would steal who you were meant to be.

I could feel the piece of paper I'd ripped out of the journal burning a hole in my pocket. Desperately, I wanted to comfort her. To just . . . fucking say it. Time was ticking, and still, it was far too soon.

"If he was smart, he would wait for them. He'd know they would be worth it," I told her.

She studied me, like she was trying to pry every single thought from my mind, all while placing her cares in my hands. "And what if they never come? What if that well has gone dry? What if I've already broken apart and there's nothing left to give?"

"Maybe it's Mylton Records that doesn't deserve you, Emily. Just like me."

Pain pinched her face. "I . . . I think I need to tell you somethin'."

She blinked a bunch of times.

My heart twisted into a thousand knots.

Thunder hammered in my chest.

I swallowed hard. "I'm listening."

She cringed, fidgeted, dropped her gaze. "It's nothin'."

I slipped forward, angling my head so I could capture her eye. "It's not nothing if it means something to you."

Warily, she peered up at me.

Two of us trapped.

Prisoners to whatever the fuck this feeling was. Something unfound. Bigger than I'd ever experienced.

Impossible.

She shifted that sexy body on the couch, letting her feet drop to the ground as she edged my way a fraction.

Intensity lit.

Banged in the bare space between us.

I had to stifle a groan. Had to fucking remind myself fifteen thousand times that I couldn't have her. Had to clench my fists to keep from driving my fingers into her hair and kissing her wild.

"Why's it like this between us?" she finally whispered, blinking like she'd just been imagining me doing the exact same thing. "Why is it that every time I get in your space, I feel like that's where I belong? You make me feel like I can spread my wings. Fly even when I'm fallin'. Like I can tell you anything."

There was nothing I could do, nothing but lean in closer and set my hand on her sweet face.

Felt like I was struck by a bolt of lightning.

A crackle of energy streaking up my arm.

"You will fly, Emily. Right now, you might have had your wings clipped, but I promise, you were meant to soar. You are a fucking star."

She pressed deeper into my hold, inhaling, eyes dropping closed as she relished in my touch. Slowly, those jade eyes fluttered back open. "How's it possible that you make me remember wanting to be that? How's it possible that you make me want at all?"

My heart clutched.

"Your happiness is the only thing that matters, Emily. And that's not something I can give you."

There I went, pushing her away when I needed her close. But I didn't know how to do this. How to fucking take what I needed without destroying another piece of her.

"Are you tryin' to wreck me a little more, Royce Reilly, because you sayin' things like that sure don't make me want you any less."

Sadness and need pulled through her expression.

A plea.

I wanted to drop to my knees and give her anything she asked for.

"No, Emily, I'm trying to be the man who comes up alongside you and reminds you of how amazing you are."

"I bet we'd be amazin' together."

Shit.

This woman was testing my willpower. A second away from putting it to shame.

Loved that she was brave. That she was asking for what she wanted.

"It would be wrong for me to touch you again. We got caught up that night. That's all. We can't do this."

Every fucking word felt like the cut of a knife.

Rejection moved through her features, and she sat back,

peeling herself away, girl fidgeting in unease as she fumbled to standing. "I think I better call it a night."

Her smile was as forged as the documents I'd found in my stepfather's office. Though hers was done with grace. Softness. As a way to protect rather than to destroy.

I eased up to standing, towering over her. Like a fool, I dragged my fingertips over her plush lips. "To sleepless nights."

A shiver rocked her, my actions tossing her in violent waters. Dragged forward before she was sent flailing back. Her lips trembled at one side, and she sidestepped out of the sitting area. The tether that bound us stretched tighter and tighter as she shuffled away.

Every step, she was taking a little bit more of me with her.

Like she couldn't take the pressure, either, she paused, and turned to look back at me from over her shoulder.

Face soft and hopeful.

Brave and scared.

"Are you sure you don't want to come up?" she asked.

Visions flashed. Me peeling those scraps of fabric off her body. Exposing all that sweet flesh. My dick pushing into all that tight, wet heat.

I had to get her away from me before I made another terrible, terrible mistake. Before I went for her. Took her. Fucked her fast and touched her slow.

She'd let me.

I knew she would.

But getting lost in her wasn't an option. It couldn't happen.

"That's a bad idea, Emily. I won't be another of your mistakes."

As it was, I was going to be nothing but a bad fucking memory.

Her gaze softened, emotion passing between us, something real that I needed to ignore.

She gave an awkward, fumbling nod. "Okay then."

She turned and slipped back through the double doors.

I watched her move through the hall running the edge of the bar, the girl glancing back once when she made it to the elevators.

Standing there, I watched her go, possession and my greed

filling me full.

I refused it.

I waited ten minutes before I finally blew out a strained breath, headed inside, and rode the elevator to the ninth floor where our rooms were. I took a left down one hall then a right down another, knowing I needed to lock myself in my room. To put as many barriers between us as possible.

But it didn't matter.

I paused outside her door.

So what if I'd made it my business to know her room number each night?

Wavering, I angled my ear, listening inside. Could hear her strumming aimlessly at the chords she'd been trying to play that day on the bus.

God, I was asking for all kinds of trouble, overstepping boundaries I shouldn't take. Still, I slipped the piece of paper under her door.

Before I did something stupid like knock, I made a beeline for my room. As soon as I stepped into the darkness, I shrugged out of my jacket and tossed it onto a chair. I went straight into the suite's bathroom and peeled off my clothes.

Revealing the scars that lined my body.

Not physical.

Could get beat to shit and I wouldn't give a damn.

It was all the rest that was torture. Making me question my sanity. This thirst to destroy becoming more than I could bear.

I stripped down to my boxers, panting by the time I had. I planted my hands on the vanity and stared at myself through the glow of the mirror.

I lifted my chin, exposing the ink imprinted on my skin. A black hawk tried to take flight on my chest, its wings rising up to wrap my neck in a vain attempt to soar. A shackle bound one foot. Chained. Unable to fly. Held down by the ghosts writhing across my stomach.

Ghosts that would haunt me forever.

My eyes took in the words written in the mix of it.

Love is the heart's greatest deceit.

It was instant, the way the room spun, the way hatred and turmoil and hurt squeezed my ribs to the point of shattering.

Suffocating.

In a blink, I was struck by the past.

Taken hostage to the pictures that invaded my mind.

I propped her on the bathroom counter. She giggled a sexy sound. "Royce. What do you think you're doing?"

I nuzzled into her neck, her dark hair falling across my face. I inhaled. "Loving my wife. I missed the hell out of you."

She tsked a coy sound. "How could you miss me when you were out chasing your dream?"

"Dreams don't mean a whole lot if you aren't there to share them with me."

She giggled more. "Sweet talker."

I was palming my hand across the huge swell of her belly. Joy rose, pressing full.

Was it even possible to feel like this?

Awe slammed me when I felt the little kick. "She's moving."

She pressed my hand closer to her stomach. "She hears you."

"Think she knows how much I love her?"

My wife looked back at me with adoration. "How could she not?"

I fought the memories, hands fisting on the cold granite. My jaw clenched so tight it pierced my head with a stake of pain.

My eyes slowly opened until I was staring back at my reflection.

I had to remember.

I had to remember.

Couldn't forget the goal.

My purpose.

So how, after everything, was the girl across the hall the only thing I wanted?

I guessed I really was a bastard.

eleven

Emily

The stench of evil filled the room. Wickedness abounding.

Smothering.
Gagging.
Darkness consumed, a blind over my eyes. I yanked at the bindings on my wrists. Desperate.
A hand clamped down on my chin. "Shh, Emmy Love. Careful. You don't want to go and hurt yourself."
A whimper bled free. "Please, let me go. I'll give you anything."
Hot breath hit my ear. "Promise?"

I jerked up to sitting, panting, skin drenched in sweat. My eyes jumped everywhere all at once, searching for a demon hiding in my room. Shadows leapt across the walls and danced on the floor, the silhouette of the two pygmy palm trees in planters on my balcony swaying through the silver rays of moonlight that poured in through the sliding doors.

I gasped in relief.

It was just a dream.

Just a dream.

A nightmare that I couldn't escape.

Hunting me down night after night.

Sleepless.

Exhaustion weighed down, but there was nothing I could do but slip from my bed, unwilling to lie in it for a second longer.

I couldn't take it.

I stood in the middle of my room. Once again, completely alone. Heart pressing so full at my chest, the hurt so big in the middle of the night that I was sure it might implode. I shuffled back over to the nightstand, flipping open my journal and gripping the piece of paper that I'd found this morning before we left Mobile for the next show.

It was a beige parchment, torn at one side, the strong handwriting denting the paper and making it look as if the words had been stamped there.

Emblazoned.

Have you been looking for someone
To fill up what you're missing?
Who is it who's gonna stop you
From the circle that keeps going 'round?

In the dim light, I set it under the three lines I had written on the bus the first day Royce had climbed onto it. The day he'd invaded my space. I'd thought I'd been quick enough to flip the page closed. It wasn't like it was earthshattering material, anyway.

But it was something.

And he'd remembered.

And—my nose curled in question—he'd written this. Written it and left it under my door.

Somehow, that made me feel like flyin', too.

Comforted.

A feeling coming over me that maybe I wasn't completely alone, after all.

Inhaling a deep breath, I padded around the bed and headed for the balcony doors. Sure I wasn't going to get another wink tonight.

Quietly, I edged open the sliding door and stepped out.

The night was late, the drone of the city quieted as most had given themselves to sleep. Finding rest in the deepest hours.

Hugging my arms over my chest, I edged farther outside and tipped my attention above to the heavens.

A canopy of stars stretched overhead, muted and dulled by the city lights that glowed from all around, threatening to snuff them out. Humidity held fast, a blanket of heat on my bare arms and legs, my nightgown wispy and thin, though it didn't do a whole lot to give relief from the heat.

Thing was, I'd always felt at home in this weather. Something about the weight of the mugginess made me feel grounded.

Familiar and right.

I trained my attention above, staring steadily into the endless sky.

Right into infinity. Deeper and deeper until a cascade of stars made themselves known.

That was the beauty of looking at the twilight.

It was always there.

Hidden but waiting to share its light.

There for anyone ready to witness its beauty. Wish upon it. Cast up their beliefs and ambitions and dreams, and hope like crazy that someone or something might actually be listening.

There were few things in this world that made you feel so small as looking upon the vastness of the heavens.

It didn't matter if you were rich or poor. Famous or inconspicuous. Royalty or pauper. Somewhere in between.

Everyone felt insignificant when gazing upon the infinite.

A strain of a guitar broke into my senses, and I craned my ear, drawn toward the subdued melody. Barefoot, I shuffled over to the edge of my balcony, feeling like a creeper, but unable to resist my curiosity.

Plucks of guitar strings climbed into the air.

It sounded of imprisoned passion.

Bottled suffering.

My senses were hit with the dampened scent of cigarettes.

Cedar and sex.

Chest heaving with awareness, I pressed my back to the wall that butted up against the next room, and I peeked through the wispy, dancing shadows that crawled through the vacant night.

I tried to muffle the gasp that raked up my throat when I finally made out the lone figure sitting at the far side of the balcony attached to mine. He had his face upturned to the sky, as if he'd been drawn to the vastness as well, although his eyes were pinched closed, his expression marred in a grief and despair so profound I felt it like a punch to my gut.

He was shirtless, all of that ambiguous ink exposed though hidden, the man with his hand wrapped around the neck of the guitar that rested on his lap. The fingertips of his right hand slowly plucked at the strings as he moved through the progression, the pawns tattooed on his fingers moving on the frets.

My heart shivered, and I was sure it was gonna leap right out of my chest.

The lyrics I'd found under my door spun through my mind.

He played.

Suddenly, it didn't seem like that much of a surprise.

Like it perfectly fit.

His melody shifted, the strains mournful, a rapturous cry I could feel winding around my body.

Morbidly alluring.

I felt fettered to it, my spirit in chains, and I carefully climbed onto the metal chair set up at the pony wall and started to crawl up so I could get to the other side.

Foolish and careless.

Reckless.

He'd kept turning me away, and somehow, I kept crawling right back.

I was halfway over when the chord fumbled and the guitar clanked. I jerked my attention up in time to catch the flash of inky eyes.

"Emily. What do you think you're doing? You shouldn't be out here."

Based on the greed that flashed and pulsed? The energy that licked like the kiss of a hot breeze?

I knew he was right.

But for the first time in my life, I didn't care.

I wanted to wade into his black waters.

I wanted to slip under.

Get swallowed whole.

Let him invade.

I was tired of playing it safe.

Look what that had gotten me.

Royce

$\mathcal{I}$ stared at where she froze halfway over the short wall that separated our balconies. Girl wearing a flimsy white nightgown that was just this side of see-through, thin straps on her delicate shoulders, fabric the barest caress over her tits, long legs a milky glow under the moon.

What the hell was she doing?

Every time I tried to push her away, she managed to get closer.

"You shouldn't be out here," I repeated over the landslide of jagged rocks scraping my throat. Nothing but a lie considering the only thing I wanted was for her to stay.

"Why is that?" she asked in that drawl, and fuck me, I couldn't come up with a good reason.

All except for the ones where I was about five seconds from going to her. Five seconds from throwing her over my shoulder.

Taking her inside and laying her on my bed and giving into this thing going on between us that was becoming impossible to resist.

"It seems we're both havin' trouble sleeping, and I don't know about you, but I'm tired of being alone."

She slipped the rest of the way over, hitting my balcony floor on her bare feet.

She pushed up to standing. Those waves of blonde were bound up in a messy knot on top of her head, and her face was clear, barren of makeup, just like last night. Somehow, that made her all the more appealing.

I went to set my guitar aside.

She lifted a hand. "Please . . . don't stop. I didn't know that you play. That was . . . beautiful. And sad."

Compassion filling her voice, she watched me through the hazy shadows. Looking for the truth.

Things she wasn't supposed to see.

Girl had the power to dig them out, anyway.

Reaching over to the small table beside me, I picked up the cigarette that was slowly burning in the ashtray. I flicked the ash and took a deep, long drag. I held it in, staring at her from across the space before I exhaled toward the sky, watching the smoke twirl and coil and climb, disappearing into the nothingness.

I leveled her with my gaze. "I wouldn't be a very good judge of talent if I didn't play, would I?"

I picked across my guitar, the sound of it lulling us into a peace that neither of us should feel.

Common ground.

But that's what music did—it reminded us that we weren't so different, after all.

Shrugging, she took a timid step forward. "Sometimes all it takes is listening from your heart to see where true talent grows."

A snort huffed through my nose. "That's appreciation, Precious, not knowledge."

She cocked her pretty head, fiddling with the hem of her nightgown, tugging it up to expose the top of her thighs. My mind was instantly back to when I'd had her propped on that table back in Savannah.

Knots of lust fisted my stomach.

My mind going haywire.

Shorting out.

How the fuck had this girl gained the power to ruin me like this?

"Honestly, Royce, do you believe in Carolina George? Or are we just another job? Do you really think we have what it takes to be somethin' great?"

She took a step toward me, watching me like she trusted me. Respected me. Like something had changed in the span of days.

I'd be a fool to deny it.

Could feel the shift happen along the way.

That connection growing.

Gaining in speed.

Pushing to my feet, I propped my guitar against the small table.

"You are great." It was gravel on my tongue. "That's knowledge. Truth. The question is, what are you going to do with it?"

Funny how I just kept pushing her and pushing her in a direction that hadn't been my original purpose. Not that I hadn't wanted her to succeed.

Flourish.

But seeing this girl fly had started to feel like a necessity.

She released a small, incredulous sound. "That seems to be the question, doesn't it?" Her face pinched, and her voice quieted. "I'm tryin' to hold it all together, you know?"

Honesty poured from her, and my heart kicked an extra beat.

The air surrounding us was dense and deep.

Small, disbelieving laughter filtered out of her mouth, and she turned her attention up to the blackened sky, like she was trying to see what was written in the stars.

"A year ago? It all made sense. Playing. Living this crazy life. We were gonna get a big deal, and we'd finally be a *big deal*. Play at big stadiums. Get invited to all the award shows. Be somethin'. The guys would be living their dream. Money and fame and power."

She said it like she'd decided it was dangerous.

She wouldn't be wrong.

"I would be livin' mine, though my dreams looked a bit different. Don't get me wrong, I'm not about to scoff at the money. I want it as much as them. But Richard and Rhys? I think they'd be content to be on the road for our entire lives. But I wanted more, Royce. I wanted it all. I was gonna get married and have a family, and they'd be there at my side, and I'd be writing music, singing it and playing it because I'm not sure I really know how to fully exist without that being a part of me. It's just natural."

She blinked my way.

Pleading.

Like maybe she thought I was the only one who would get this part of her.

"It's natural because it's what you were born to do. You are a star, Emily. And fame doesn't have a fucking thing to do with that."

A sad smile twitched at one corner of her lush mouth, and her head angled farther. "But it only takes one mistake to ruin everything, doesn't it? One misfortune, and everything starts fallin' apart? Piece by piece. Brick by brick. I'm not sure I have what it takes to climb out of the rubble."

Rage fisted my hands. "And what started that? Let's go back and fix it."

"If only it were that easy." Quiet horror weaved through the lines in her expression, grief and shame, like she was a prisoner forced to watch all those misfortunes play out time and again. I wanted to erase them.

Wipe the terror from her face and scrape the guilt from her soul.

"I . . ." Her words faltered.

I took a step closer.

A tremor rocked the ground.

Attraction and greed.

Her lips parted under the force of it before a frown took its place. "I just . . . I want you to know I would do anything for the boys. For the band. I love them, and I want the best for everyone, and I want you to know that I'm trying to get over this hurdle so

I can be what they need me to be."

"What about what's best for you?"

"What's best for the band is what's best for me. They're my family. I believe in what we're doing, and I don't want to lose sight of that. And now you're here." Her voice trembled. "I know we didn't meet under the best circumstances, but I want you to know that I am tryin'. I don't want you to think that I'm being difficult for the hell of it. Bratty and petulant and arrogant. You've been nothing but fair, and I know the offer is fair. More than fair."

Fair.

What bullshit.

Like she was the one who owed me an apology?

"You have a right to be skeptical. People get deceived all the time."

A half smile quirked at her mouth, worry threaded with all her glowing, outright hope. "Like that first night?"

There she went . . . offering an olive branch. A bridge for us to cross to meet in the middle. Giving me the opportunity to explain myself.

Emitting forgiveness like it was a sweet fragrance.

I couldn't remain standing still for a second longer.

Tension swelled.

Rising between us.

I moved that way, stalking slow, my bare feet on the hard ground. I came right up to where she stood, my shadow covering her whole.

Like there was any chance of me standing anywhere else.

She rasped a shocked, needy breath, and her hands flew up to steady herself on my bare chest.

Fire flashed.

Fuck.

That was a mistake.

But I couldn't move. Couldn't do anything but dip down lower to ensure she was listening.

"I would never take advantage of you. Never."

The words were rough.

Scourges of a promise.

I prayed they were the truth. That I could fucking pull this off without hurting her more.

But looking down at her? I knew that I already was. That my thirst for vengeance was crushing sound reason.

I shouldn't be doing *this*.

Wanting her in a way that I didn't deserve.

Feasting on pure, innocent beauty.

Still, I was stuck, unable to move away from the face that stared up at me, her scent invading my mind and my senses.

Her short fingernails scraped my flesh.

They moved over the ink imprinted on my chest, tracing over the hawk wings that fluttered in sync with the ragged rhythm of my breaths, right over the raging thunder that battered at my ribs to the words inscribed there.

I'd purposefully placed them there so I'd see them every morning when I looked in the mirror.

A warning not to fall.

Love is the heart's greatest deceit.

"Do you feel that?" she asked. So quiet. So unsure.

"What?" I growled, wrapping an arm around her waist to tuck her closer.

"This feelin' like I know you in a way that I shouldn't. Like we're connected in some way that we can't see. Like we've been tied somewhere in the past. I felt it that first night, and I've felt it every night since."

Like the selfish fucker I was, I let my nose travel across her temple, inhaling her delicate scent.

Cherries and the sky.

"I think you're searching for something that isn't there." It came off my tongue like a demand, hard and praying that she would think better of this and get the fuck out of there before I lost my mind.

Did more damage.

"And maybe what I've been lookin' for is standing right here."

"You don't know what you're asking for, Precious," I murmured at her ear. I trailed my lips across her skin, tracing down her neck and scrolling over her delicate shoulders.

Kissing across the soft, seductive flesh.

Emily whimpered and dropped her head back to grant me better access. "I think what I'm askin' for is you. Can you hear it? The way my body is calling out for you? It shouldn't be possible. It shouldn't. But I can't stop the way I'm feelin'. I couldn't stop it then, and no matter how hard I've tried, there is no stopping it now."

A little piece of me died right there.

Maybe it was one of the threads that hung onto *her* so fucking tight.

Snip, snip, snip.

Like maybe there was a chance of my getting free.

I shuttered my heart against the thought.

"I want you so fucking bad it hurts, sweet girl. You have me so spun up, I'm forgetting who I am."

"Or maybe you are just discoverin' something new."

There she went with all that belief. Seeing something brilliant and good buried in the bad.

She should be terrified. But she was holding onto me like I might be able to offer her something better.

I hoisted her from her feet. She wrapped those sleek legs around my waist about as tightly as she wrapped her arms around my neck.

"I want to feel somethin' good." She whispered the words along the pulse point that thrummed in my neck, her lips so soft as she kissed along the flesh. "I need you to remind me that there is somethin' good out there for me. I need to feel. To feel alive."

Flames leapt, and my stomach fisted with need.

Greed taking me over.

"I'm the last person you want to show you that."

"You're wrong. You're the only person I want to show me that."

I'd left the sliding door open to my room, the lights completely cut, the only illumination coming from the bare lights that shone from the balcony wall that became a hazy mesh with the moon.

I carried her to the lounge chair that sat immediately inside, set her onto her feet, and swiveled her away from me just as fast.

There was a large mirror hanging from the wall right in front of her.

I needed her to see herself the way that I did.

A gasp raked from her throat, surprise and heat exploding in the atmosphere.

I bent her over so her hands were planted on the arm rests of the fabric chair.

The back of her neck was exposed to me, her firm ass angling toward me in its own plea.

Jade eyes glittered where they met mine in the shadowy reflection, and tendrils of blonde that had gotten loose brushed her shoulders, her chest heaving like a song that had gone out of sync.

I smoothed my hands over the curve of her ass, my cock jumping in my jeans, need winding me so tight I couldn't breathe. "You are so fucking perfect, Emily Ramsey. This body."

I nudged my painfully hard erection against her bottom.

She whimpered and pressed back, welcoming the heat, her eyes never leaving mine as pants jutted from her mouth.

The sound was like gasoline to the charged, dense air.

I eased her back, running my hands up the outside of her ribs until I was cupping the front of her neck in my hand, the other pressing down on her quaking, quivering belly.

Blood thundered beneath my palm, a blustering storm ravaging the night sky.

Frantic and erratic and freed.

No fear.

I wanted to get lost in the sensation. Drunk on something that was pure and right.

From behind, my mouth caressed up the angle of her jaw and moved across her cheek. "This face that is unlike anything or anyone else. Priceless. Precious."

She leaned back into me, the caress of her body ravaging my senses, her head resting on my shoulder.

The girl fully entrusting herself to my hands.

Fuck. This little thing was more than I could handle. A bigger temptation than I could endure.

Hands spread wide, I rode them down her slender arms until I was threading my fingers with hers. "These fingers that paint art. A picture written in song."

She shuddered, her exhale sharp. "Royce," she begged.

Guilt streaked.

What am I doing?

What am I doing?

I knew better than this. I needed to put an end to this before it completely spun out of control.

Before I couldn't take it back.

But there was no stopping this moment.

I gathered our weaved hands and pulled them to the trigger point of her heart, holding her close. "But this? This is so much more than all of that. Better than anything I've ever witnessed. You want to see something good, Emily? Look right here."

I pressed tighter against the drumbeat of her heart, and my voice lowered to a grunt. "And I refuse to taint that. Refuse to mar it with depravity. I've fucked up in more ways than I could ever count, and I won't fuck this up, too. You're worth too much, and I'm not talking dollars and cents."

"You think we're not all made of mistakes?" she murmured into the night.

Slowly, she turned around to face me. Her eyes glimmered in the muted light. "You think all of our days aren't missteps and accomplishments? Joys and sorrows? Victories and failures? Not one of us is perfect, Royce, not one. Either we choose to remain captives to our mistakes or we choose to rise above them. Learn from them and become better."

I held her by one side of the face. "And is this you rising above them? Or is this you making a mistake you're going to regret forever?"

It was nothing but a warning.

Desire flashed through her expression, and she raked her fingers across my chest.

Hooks in my soul.

Shit.

She fluttered them all the way down my abdomen, my muscles

flexing and ticking and jumping in need.

"This is me deciding what *I* want." Her words were coarse and real. "What *I* need. What feels right. That is, unless you don't want it? Tell me you don't want this."

She eased down.

The girl a queen who'd gotten to her knees.

Shit. Shit. Shit.

This was bad. So fucking bad.

She planted her hands on the outside of my thighs.

My dick jumped.

"I don't." It was gravel.

Her voice turned vulnerable. "Don't lie to me, Royce. It's the one thing I'll ask of you. The one thing that would break me."

Goddamn it.

Cupping her face, I let my thumb trace along the defined angle of her cheek. "You want the truth? The real truth? It fucking pisses me off how goddamn bad I want you, Emily. Want you in a way that isn't right."

She exhaled a quivering breath, and her tongue darted out to wet her lips, nerves shaking her down. She flicked the button of my black jeans, her expression going shy and sweet.

I fucking loved that, too, need coursing fast, riding high, threatening to consume.

I was worried about wrecking her, but I was pretty sure it was this girl who was going to wreck me.

Leave me undone.

Unhinged.

Because I raked out a sound of compulsion when she edged my pants down my thighs and my cock sprang free, need so intense I couldn't see.

Blinded.

Completely shattered when she wrapped a trembling hand around my length.

"Fuck," I grunted.

"I can't believe how gorgeous you are. You make me shake, Royce. Most nights I can't sleep . . . and I lie there tossin'. You want to know what's given me comfort? Thinking about this.

Touchin' you and you touchin' me."

She stroked me once, from base to tip.

Tiny thunderbolts of pleasure streaked.

My hips jutted forward without permission.

My thumb stroked her plump lips, and she sucked it into her mouth, and everything shifted. My spirit and my heart and my dick lunged forward, like the girl had a cord harnessed to my soul.

Possession took over.

"You gonna suck me, sweet girl? Take me with that sweet, sweet mouth? Sing me like one of your songs?"

She bit down on my thumb, just enough for me to feel the pressure, and I pulled it free with a pop, smearing her saliva that I'd gathered across her lips. They shone in the glint of moonlight.

She pressed a kiss to the head of my cock.

I jerked.

Fuck.

Little mind-wrecker.

All purpose failed to make sense.

"So beautiful. Every part of you," she whispered like praise, her expression severe and intense and awed. "I bet I could write a million songs about you."

I understood the urge.

Then she stroked her tongue across the top, down the side, back up and down again.

Licking me into a frenzy.

By the time she wrapped her mouth around me, sucked me down deep, I was already ready to blow.

"Fuck, shit, yes," I grunted as she took me whole, both of her hands wrapped tight at the base of my dick. Stroking in sync.

My hands fumbled to get ahold of her face. To guide this dangerous rhythm. Worried if I let her take control, she was going to own it forever.

"You're wrong, Emily. Fucking wrong. You're perfect. Fucking perfect." It all fell in an incoherent ramble from my mouth as she fucked me with hers, those eyes never leaving mine, communicating something I didn't want to read.

The girl pure and hopeful and brave.

My hips jutted, pressing deeper, taking more when I knew it never should have been mine. Guilt constricting, filling me up in the same second as pleasure was taking me over.

Her soft tongue drove me into a frenzy, her mouth working me over and her spirit stealing into the cracks. Making space where I didn't have any.

She moaned.

Taking what I would give. The tip of my cock hitting the back of her throat, the girl doing her best not to gag, the vibration of it hitting me like a bomb.

My thighs shook and my balls tightened.

And I was splitting.

Shattering.

Overcome as she swallowed me down while I gasped and shuddered, my mind leaving the space, floating out somewhere where it had no right to be.

Somewhere where I experienced her like a new song that burst in my mind.

Came to life in the same second a piece of myself did, too.

Emily swallowed as I pulsed, her eyes closed like she was relishing in the feel. In the experience. Like she wanted this every goddamn bit as much as me.

"So fucking perfect. So fucking perfect." I could barely get it out over the heaving of my breaths, shallow and short, my heart stampeding, beating a path outward, like the bastard thought it would be a fine idea to meet with hers.

Reckless.

So goddamn reckless.

I pulled out of her mouth, slumping forward a bit, and Emily pressed her thighs together where she remained kneeling. I reached down and swept her up, setting her in the chair as I dropped to my knees.

My own offering.

Wishing it could ever be enough.

I spread my hands up the outside of her thighs, and she arched back in the chair, that flimsy material concealing next to nothing and leaving everything to the imagination.

Imagination that was running wild.

Wondering what it might be like if I really got to have *this*. A connection that was real. Something good.

"Please," she begged.

"I wish I could give you everything," I murmured, kissing up the inside of one thigh as I pressed my hands under the thin material, gathering the panties that covered that delicious heat.

I edged back to peel them down, watched her pant and shiver and moan.

"What do you need, sweet girl?"

"You. Everything. Anything," she said as those hands spread down her body.

Fuck.

She shouldn't be saying things like that to me.

I tugged her to the edge of the fabric chair, and I spread her by the knees, perfect, pink pussy on display, just like the rest of her.

"Perfect," I rumbled again before I was diving in for a taste.

Surprise jetted from her lungs. "Oh god."

I devoured the girl.

Devine.

Delicious.

Everything.

Fingers found my hair, digging in and tugging tight as she murmured her madness into the air.

"Yes. Royce. God. I shouldn't feel like this. It's not possible. You feel so good. So right."

I wanted to beg her to stop, but it only incited me further.

Drove me to a ledge where I was so close to jumping.

Tongue lapping at her clit, I let my fingers explore, riding down her thighs, brushing her ass, sweeping through her engorged lips.

She bucked. "Please."

I pushed two inside her tight pussy.

I nearly went off again, mind running wild. Desperate to know what my cock would feel like to be taking my fingers' place. To feel the clutch of her body. To fuck her into oblivion.

Right where she was driving me.

I sucked and licked at her clit, driving my fingers fast and deep and hard.

She writhed and jerked, and I could feel her winding up.

Pleasure gathering to a pinpoint.

My assault increased, and I was touching her everywhere, laving with my tongue, sucking her into my mouth and scraping with my teeth.

Two seconds later, she fractured, the girl a million pieces I held in the palms of my hands. She cried out my name. A prayer. Like I could make an impact that would build something rather than destroy.

And I wished and I wished and I wished that it could be. That I could have a fucking do-over.

I slowed, led her through the aftershocks, the little pinpricks that buzzed through her body.

I edged back, looked up at this gorgeous woman who was spread out for me.

Skin covered in sweat, the smell of her sex on my tongue, need filling our air.

Her nightgown had gotten pushed up high around her waist, and that's when I saw the scar etched on her side.

A jagged X carved right over her hip.

That was all it took to make me feel like I was going to vomit.

Quickly, I tucked myself back into my jeans and scrambled to find her underwear that I'd tossed to the ground, averting my gaze as I helped her back into them.

Those eyes kept peeking at me.

Searching for me.

To latch back onto the connection.

"Royce?" Her voice quivered, and I knew I was the biggest bastard that had ever lived.

thirteen

Emily

"Royce?" I asked again.

I could feel his heart shuttering. Shutting down in fear. Closing over in something that looked like terror.

Avoiding my eyes, he urged me to stand while the man remained kneeling as he helped me into my underwear.

There was something about it that felt so utterly intimate even though I could tell he was tryin' with all his might not to be affected.

Not to feel what had taken us over.

But it was his firm yet trembling hands that gave him away. The soft surety of his movements. The care in his regard.

The man was crouched down with all that black hair flopping over to one side, the tattoos scrolled over his shoulders and down his muscled back exposed to me for the first time.

A huge fallen cross that lie broken on the side of a deserted hill, weeds and thorns growing up to cover it, words that I couldn't make out scratched out in crooked lines on his side.

Fingers clawed out from a pit in the ground.

Clearly condemned.

Looking for a way to be saved.

Maybe I was crazy that I had the urge to do some of that saving, wondering if in turn, he could do a little of that saving, too.

That maybe, somehow, we were two fragmented pieces that fit together.

But it was the words I saw he had imprinted just under his collarbone that made my spirit ache in agony.

Love is the heart's greatest deceit.

My stomach tangled in another rush of want.

And maybe, maybe, I was just a fool.

Keeping his head down, he eased the lacy fabric all the way up my legs. Shivers streaked across my flesh as his forearms disappeared under my nightgown.

My hands darted out, fingers digging into his shoulders for support.

To keep from falling.

Tripping headfirst right into this dangerous, mysterious man.

"Royce." This time I was begging.

Praying he wouldn't stamp out this little part of me that he had sparked to life.

Reluctantly, he lifted his gaze. Hammering me with all that intensity.

Potent and wicked, though it was the flickers of grief shimmering in those onyx eyes that threatened to annihilate.

Totally wipe me out.

He kept me pinned with that unwavering stare as he eased the fabric of my nightgown up a fraction, his thumb just caressing over the scar that had been left to devastate. One I wished he wouldn't have noticed. One I was doing my best to ignore.

"I don't deserve to be touching you," he murmured, voice a rough abrasion in the night.

"Aren't I the one who gets to make that choice?"

For a beat, his eyes slammed closed, and then he was on his feet, stealing my breath as he swept me off mine, gathering me into his arms. He carried me across his room and into the attached bathroom. Setting me on the counter, he grabbed a washcloth and wet it under the water.

Softly, carefully, he ran it over my lips, like he was trying to erase the mark of him from my body.

Not a chance of that.

One of those big hands came up to tenderly cup one side of my face, thumb sweeping along the hollow of my eye, the action completely at odds with the weight of his words.

"I want to protect you, Emily. I want to take every fucking bad thing that has ever happened to you and delete it. Purge it from your body and rip it from your spirit. I want to stand in the way of every goddamn thing that might hurt you in the future. Including myself."

"Is that what you see when you look at me? Someone who needs to be protected? Saved?"

"I see someone who's holding onto so much pain."

A huff of remorse and defiance left me. "I don't want anyone to pity me. That's not what I'm lookin' for."

"Doesn't everyone need someone to fight for them? To stand up for what's right? To take care of them?" It looked as if he was the one in pain when he said it. As if maybe he was desperate for someone to come alongside him.

His expression shifted through a million different emotions.

I fought to keep up.

To understand.

"I don't want to hurt you," he murmured, so tight and hard that I wanted to reach out and ask who it was that had hurt him.

To hold him the same way he wanted to hold me.

"That's good because I don't think I've ever felt so safe as when I'm with you," I whispered, sure I'd never known a greater truth.

I felt as if I might crumble and break apart and, when he picked me back up, I might be whole.

Which was insane.

I hadn't known him for more than a handful of days, and the man was written in errors. Abrasive and curt and asking me to do the one thing that I was having the most difficult time forcing myself to do.

But there was something in his eyes that I believed.

Something about him that made me want to dig for more.

Seek and discover.

"That's because you're reckless." His response was a caress.

A lash.

I let my fingertips fumble across his jaw. "I'm not a fool. You think I don't know you're hiding something underneath all that brash exterior, too? Maybe that's what's calling out for me. Maybe you need me the way I need you. Don't pretend like you don't feel this."

A smirk tweaked at one corner of his mouth. "You are asking for it, aren't you?"

"I think I made that plenty clear."

Affection flitted across his features as he stared at me through the vapors of dull, muted light, gone before I could be sure that it was real. "You should go. We have to be up in a few hours."

Wow.

So that was how it was gonna be.

That hollow space that screamed of abandonment flared in the middle of me, but I locked it down and tried to make sense of what he was really saying.

I raked my nails across his chest, right over the black hawk he had tattooed there, the wings spread and trying to take flight. But one of its feet was shackled, locked by a manacle that dragged him down and kept him from soaring, chained him to faces and snapshots of memories I didn't understand, a morbid story written in mystery across his ripped, packed abdomen.

"Is that what you want, Royce? For me to leave?"

He laughed out a disbelieving sound. "You really love to test me, don't you, Precious?"

"Isn't that what life is . . . one big test?" It almost came out a tease.

He scruffed a hand over his face. "Pretty sure I'm about to fail this one. Strike that. Clearly, I already did."

My belly twisted.

"Didn't feel like a failure to me," I murmured in a low voice.

I was trying to seduce him, and I didn't have the first clue what I was doing.

Being reckless, that was what.

He shocked me by dragging me to the very edge of the counter, wedging his delicious body between my thighs, his hot hands cupping me by the bottom. "If I passed, then you got an A+."

A giggle slipped free, shyness breaking way. "You think so?"

"Told me not to tell you lies, didn't you?" It was a grunt, those fierce eyes aglow. "You just rocked my fucking world."

My heart expanded. I wanted to do it over and over again. "I'm glad." I studied him, voice sincere. "And you made me feel alive in a way I haven't in a long, long time."

Royce sighed and dropped his forehead to my chest. "You're killing me, Emily. Fucking killing me. I shouldn't be doing this. I shouldn't be touching you at all, and I'm not sure I know how to stop."

"Then don't."

My stomach took that very inopportune time to growl.

Awesome.

Royce looked up at me with a grin. "Hungry?"

"Starving."

Starving for him and this feeling and this insatiable need, but I guessed I could eat, too.

He went right into protective mode. Demanding and brash.

"Let me feed you."

It wasn't a request.

Still, I agreed, whispering, "I'd like that," as I swiped my tongue over my bottom lip, wishing it was his doing the honors.

He groaned again. "Little mind-wrecker."

I frowned at the unintelligible ramble that fell from his mouth, but he ignored that he'd said anything at all and helped me down. He gestured for me to use his things that were set out on the counter.

"I'll order us something."

"Thank you."

He started out the door, his bare back so delicious and on display, wearing tight ripped-up jeans, something I'd never seen him in before that made me wonder about the persona he fronted. But then I realized it didn't matter what he was wearing. There wasn't a thing that was fake about him.

The man raw.

Real.

A little bit terrifying.

Pausing at the doorway, he shifted his attention back to me, expression written in stone. "I shouldn't be doing this."

"You keep sayin' that."

"It keeps being the truth."

Then he turned back around and pulled the door shut behind him.

I rinsed my mouth with his mouthwash, scrubbed my face under a cold spray from the faucet, and retied my hair up on my head considering it was looking like a rat or two had taken up residence in the locks.

AKA Royce's desperate hands.

Sucking down a shiver, I stepped back out.

He was at the hotel room door, the man so obscenely hot as he let in room service.

The server rolled in the cart, and Royce dug out his wallet and gave him a tip, the man thanking him profusely.

Following him back to the door, Royce shut it, then slowly turned around and eased out into the middle of the room.

Everything trembled.

God, I didn't think I was ever gonna get used to the sight of him.

"Come here," he commanded, and I shuffled forward on bare feet, fiddling with the hem of my nightgown, all of a sudden feeling unsure.

He pulled the lid off the tray to reveal a board of cheeses and meats. Crackers and jams. Berries and fruit.

Grabbing the bottle of champagne from the ice bucket, he expertly freed the cork. It popped, and my nerves leapt, my legs shaking as I stood there with the weight of those dark eyes watching me as he tipped the bottle over to fill a flute.

He handed me the first one and then filled another.

"Sit," he said, gesturing to his unmade, rumpled bed.

God, he could be bossy, but I was all too happy to oblige.

I climbed up on the edge near the end and tucked one leg under my body. He moved forward, lingering an inch over my face, noses close to touching.

He tipped his glass to mine, his voice a rasp. "To sleepless nights."

Our glasses clinked, and my heart shivered.

I took a sip, letting the cool, bubbling sweetness glide down my throat, not knowing exactly what to do with myself as he climbed onto the bed in front of me.

My attention moved to the expanse of his bed where he'd clearly been tossing, just like I had been.

I had to wonder if I hadn't heard him in some sense. That feeling like I understood him on a different level. In some unfound way that should be impossible but somehow felt like the only thing that made any sense right then.

"You couldn't sleep?" I asked carefully.

He took a sip of his champagne, those hawk's wings flitting in distress as he swallowed heavily. "Me and the night aren't the best of friends."

"And why's that?"

He grinned, though it was bleak. "Don't you know that's when the demons come out to play?"

Didn't I know it.

"And why are they torturin' you?" I asked.

"Told you I've made more mistakes than I can count."

"Isn't that what forgiveness is for?"

He chuckled a menacing sound. "Not when you don't deserve it."

"I don't believe that."

"That's because you don't know the things I've done."

"Try me," I challenged.

He laughed low. "You looking for a reason for me to send you running tonight?"

"No, Royce, I'm lookin' for you to give me a reason to stay."

His throat bobbed again, his voice so hard and low I felt the words like a rough blade. "Fine. You want to know? I let someone hurt my baby sister. Hurt her so badly that I'm not sure she will ever recover."

"It couldn't have been your fault."

"It was."

My face pinched. "I don't believe that."

His laughter was dark. "Well, you should."

I chewed at my lip, averting my gaze before I warily looked back at him. "I'm sorry that she got hurt. It's the worst feeling in the world when the ones we love are in pain."

He looked away, too, shaking his head. "Goddamn it, Emily. Why are you so sweet?"

"I hate that you're hurtin', too, you know."

Need rumbled in his throat, and he set his flute aside and climbed to his hands and knees, crawling toward me.

Predatory.

Possessive.

It pressed me onto my back, the man hovering a foot over me, my heart thundering as I struggled to breathe. I reached up and touched his face, fingertips moving across his full lips.

"I have to admit, I'm happy you were havin' trouble sleeping tonight."

He kissed across my fingertips, soft nibbles at the flesh. "Me, too. And I have to wonder what that makes me."

"A man."

A smirk took to his sexy mouth. "Oh, Precious, I'm all man."

Tingles spread, butterflies flapping up a storm.

"I'm getting that, though I think I might need to experience it all to make a final judgement call."

Good lord.

Did that just come out of my mouth?

Power ripped across his flesh, and he let out a short laugh. "You really do love to test me, don't you?"

Biting down on my bottom lip, I nodded my head against the

mattress. "I . . . I want to live, Royce. Without the fears that have been chasing me. You've reminded me that I can."

He reached out and grabbed a raspberry from the tray. He slipped it between my lips. The sweet tartness hit my senses, and I moaned a little with the flavor of it and the champagne on my tongue.

Royce growled and buried his face in my neck. "Kill me now."

When he pushed back up onto his hands, he was grinning. "Tempt me all you want, woman. You have no power over me."

A giggle broke free at the same time as I was slipping my free hand up to the side of his neck so I could hoist myself to sitting. "Is that so?"

"It's so." He dipped down and pecked his lips to mine.

So sweet.

I hadn't even thought it was possible.

"Very so. Now come on, let's eat."

He smacked me on the thigh, a love tap that had me gasping. "Bossy."

He quirked an eye at me as he moved to rest against the headboard. "You have no idea."

"I think I'm gettin' one."

"Eat."

"See." I widened my eyes at him. Playfully.

He took a sip of his champagne and popped a blueberry into his mouth.

"Tell me why you weren't sleeping." He cut me a glance as he reached for a slice of cheese.

I peeked over at him, nibbling at a cracker. "Sleeping isn't the problem. It's the dreams that are waiting for me when I do fall asleep that are."

A frisson of rage sizzled across his skin. Every muscle in his glorious body flexed. "How long?"

I shifted in unease, but I couldn't help but open up a little more. "I guess you could say my life has been a spiral for the last six months."

Loss after loss.

One tragedy piled on top of the other.

Pain lanced through my being, and I tried to hold it back, the visible effects. But Royce saw it. He shifted, angling around to set a big hand on my face. "If I could take part of it away, would you let me?"

Intensity blazed.

I struggled to inhale.

"I feel like you already are."

His head shook. "No. I mean more, Emily. Would you let me go after whoever it was that hurt you? The one who put this look on your face?"

Panic flooded me. The idea of him knowing. Of my having to step up and step out. The words vibrated on my tongue, vying for release. But I wasn't ready.

I blinked at him. "I think you know what I need, Royce. Know what I'm missing. The lyrics I can't find. I found your offering under my door when I got up this last morning."

Emotion raced across his face. "It was nothing. I was just scribbling words."

"Then how is it that they fit so perfectly?"

My mind immediately went back to finding him strumming his guitar, the mournful, wistful strains that had permeated the sky.

"I guess you inspire me."

Soft laughter rippled out. "Maybe it's you who's inspiring me. I hadn't written a single word in three months, Royce. Three months. It was like . . ." I struggled to find the right explanation. "It was like there was a void inside of me where nothing lived. Nothing breathed. And one minute of you, and there was a flicker of life. A spark."

He grabbed my hand and splayed it over the phrase inscribed on his chest. "Like you sparked something here. Shouldn't be possible, Emily."

He said it as if it caused him regret. That he truly believed he shouldn't be allowed to feel a thing for me.

I rolled over, making him angle farther back. I pressed my hand harder against the pounding that raged. Over the statement that made me want to weep. "Who is she? Who does this belong to?"

Torment seized his expression, and the name that groaned

from his mouth came on a torrent of pain. "Anna."

Anna.

I tried to picture her face. Wondered if she was anything like me. Why she would leave this beautiful man broken and scarred. My heart felt as if it'd become a hundred-mile-wide crater. "You told me last night that the only thing that mattered was my happiness. I want you to know that yours matters, too. It matters to me."

He threaded his fingers loosely in the fall of my hair. "I shouldn't want you, Emily."

It was a warning. This boy's heart was unavailable.

I wanted it anyway.

"Sometimes we need the very thing we think we shouldn't."

"Emily," he groaned.

Heat lapped in the bare space that separated us.

No words needed for this understanding.

He just watched me with those eyes.

Learned me while I learned him.

And I was lost.

Lost to this man who was sucking me under.

I got the distinct sense that I was falling. That whooshing feeling when your heart got unstable, cracking open to make room for something that hadn't been there before.

I knew I shouldn't welcome him there, in that patchy, uneven ground that still hadn't healed, especially when his seemed to be fortified by bricks and chains.

But I couldn't seem to stop it.

There was something about him that made me want to fade right into him.

Melt under those hands and come alive under those eyes.

"I think you're wonderful," I whispered down at him.

For a beat, everything felt too heavy. The moment too intense.

Then he grinned, like he was shaking the severity off, and he tossed me onto my back on his bed. I bounced, my face breaking into a tender smile when he climbed over me.

Warmth spreading wide.

"You're the best thing I've ever seen," he said, a hand tucking into my hair.

That was right before he dipped down and pressed his mouth to mine.

Magic.

Kissing Royce Reilly was nothing short of magic.

The soft pull of his lips. The decadent caress of his tongue. The drug of his scent.

I whimpered, then sighed when he pulled back far too soon.

"Tell me, Emily Ramsey . . . did you know it the second you were born that you were a star?"

Light laughter pulled up my throat. "My mama said I was a diva from day one. Throwing tantrums like nobody's business."

He grinned down at me. "I don't believe it. You? Throwing tantrums?"

I swatted at his shoulder. "Are you mocking me?"

A tease widened his eyes. "Never."

"I don't believe you."

His grin widened. "You're all fire, Precious, but the best kind. A star bursting on the stage."

My teeth clamped down on my lip to stop the blush. "You're just trying to sucker me in." It was soft and full of ribbing.

He rolled to his side, taking me with him, tucking my body close to his. "Is it working?"

"I'm pretty sure you could ask me to do anything right about now, and I'd be game."

He laughed. "You should never say things like that to a man. I could come up with some pretty ingenious things."

"You act like that scares me."

A grumble rumbled around below my ear, the man's heart beating an erratic thrum, thrum, thrum.

"Reckless girl," he murmured at the top of my head.

"I'm just looking for what I want."

"And what's that? What is it you really want?"

I flinched a little, letting my thoughts wander. "You know, I was supposed to get married."

I wondered if he knew anything of my past. If he'd researched who we were or if he'd simply been given a task.

He froze, and I lifted my head so I could meet the hatred that disfigured his expression.

Wow.

Not what I was expecting.

"No," he grated. "I didn't know that. You're not . . ." He trailed off like he couldn't bring himself to say it, though his attention was darting to the bare spot on my ring finger.

"No," I rushed on a pulse of disgust. "He cheated on me."

It hit the air like a hollow arrow.

Vacant space in the middle.

It's the way he'd left me feeling.

Abandoned and alone.

"Fucking moron."

"Yeah."

"Want me to kill him?" It was all a mischievous gleam, Royce going for light when I could see his muscles twitching in restraint.

"Um . . . I think that would be a very bad idea. I think I like you outside of jail, thank you very much."

Low laughter rumbled from him, the words filled with an undercurrent that I couldn't quite sort out. "It'd be worth it. Fighting for what matters is always worth it. No matter the cost or the consequence."

I let my fingertips play across the horrid face that screamed out from the valley on his abdomen, wondering what it meant, a little terrified to know the answer. Wondering just what lengths this man might go to. "Well, believe me, *he's* not worth it. Not in the least."

"Have half a mind to break him limb by limb just for ever touching you."

"Jealous?" I teased.

"Very." He didn't seem to be joking.

"I'm just . . . I'm just sad that I trusted him. That I'd planned on starting a family with him."

Grief throbbed from deep within, and I pushed it down, not ready to share all the ugly details with him, not sure I even trusted myself with them right then.

"Sad that he let me down so far when I needed him most," I

continued, the words cracking as they were expelled. "That's what hurts more than anything else."

Royce pulled me close and exhaled into my hair, his warmth spreading over me. "I hate him for hurting you. Hate any bastard who would touch something so precious in the wrong way." He held me close, his arms so strong, the churn of his heart stronger. "Kills me, sweet girl. Kills me."

He buried his nose in my hair, inhaled deep. "What are you doing to me?"

I wrapped my arms around him and held on tight. "I hope it's the same thing that you're doin' to me."

He sighed. "It's never going to work, Emily. We are nothing but a conflict of interest."

Emotion gripped me by the throat, everything thick and heavy and tremoring, and I just gave him everything I had.

Knowing I didn't have anything to lose. This moment might be fleeting, but it was ours.

"I'm so lonely, Royce. So lonely, and for the first time in so long you make me feel like maybe I don't have to be. Like maybe there might be someone who fits me, after all. Like you just said, I want to fight for what matters most. No matter the cost or the consequence."

There I went.

Cutting myself open wide.

Offering this man things I'd never offered anyone else.

Hoping when all of it came gushing out, he might be strong enough to hold it. He might be the only one who could.

"Damn it, Emily. You're not alone. You're not."

He wrapped me tight, and I pushed out a shuddering sigh.

"Sleep, sweet girl. Sleep."

And for the first night in months, I did.

fourteen

Emily

*T*hrough hazy morning light, I stood at the nightstand next to the bed and gazed down at the man who was sleeping facedown, covers tossed aside, the strength of his back on display.

Wide, wide shoulders tapering down to his narrow waist, half of his firm ass peeking out from below the sheets.

My stomach tumbled.

God, he was gorgeous.

Last night had been close to a miracle. I'd slept for hours wrapped up in his warmth.

Safe.

Secure.

Somehow, I'd managed to only let my heart get broken a little bit when I'd heard him whimpering *Anna* in his sleep just as the day was dawning. I'd peppered a bunch of kisses to that spot on his chest, wishing I could be the one to hold some of his pain the way he was holding mine.

When he'd seemed to settle, I'd slipped out of his bed with the faint strains of a melody playing in my mind. In them had been the intonation of lyrics, and I'd grabbed a piece of scratch paper and scribbled them out.

My life's a spiral
But I think it's you who sent me spinnin'
Now we're reeling out of control

I tucked the ripped sheet under his watch on the nightstand.

I gasped when a hand reached out and snatched me by the wrist, and Royce flipped over onto his back and dragged me on top of him.

Giggles burst free.

All mixed up with the desire that boomed.

His hot body against mine.

Chest bare.

His cock eager and hard where it was pressing at my belly.

Oh my, was this ever the best way to start off the day.

"Mornin'," he rumbled against my forehead.

"Good mornin'," I whispered back.

Wrapping those massive arms around me, he heaved out a sound of relief. "Where do you think you're sneaking off to?"

I rested one side of my face on the hammering going down in his chest. "Bus pulls out in two hours. I need to get a shower before we leave."

He angled up so he could press his nose into my neck. "I think I like you just fine smelling like me."

Another giggle.

Electricity skimmed my skin. Pinpricks of growing need.

If I could have, I thought I might have stayed there forever.

"Well, you might like it just fine, but I'm pretty sure the rest of the band might have something else to say about it."

He leaned back, hitting me with a grin.

Affection bloomed in my spirit.

I thought there was a chance I liked this bad boy far too much.

"Not sure I give a shit what anyone has to say about us." His gaze was tender. Playful, even.

My heart expanded.

It was the first time he was even talking like this.

Like . . . like maybe we were a possibility.

"I don't so much, either."

Then his fingers were winding in my hair, and he was kissing me.

Deeply.

Hands exploring. Palming my bottom, urging me closer, riding up my back until he was framing my face in his firm, sure hold. Angling me just where he wanted me.

My heart stampeded, pressing full at my chest, my stomach coiled in exquisite threads that I was pretty sure were stitching me together.

Keeping me from splintering apart in his hands.

Breaking the kiss, Royce dropped back to the pillow, pants ripping from his chest and something that looked like a satisfied smirk riding his delicious mouth.

I peeked up at him, biting my swollen lip. "I really need to go." It was loaded with reluctance.

"That's a terrible idea," he murmured.

"We'll be on the bus soon. You don't have to wait that long."

He sighed a rough, needy sound, softness mixed in the middle of it. "Is it wrong I'm afraid this moment is going to cease to exist? That I'm going to be stepping back into an old reality the second you disappear back over that wall?"

"And why would you think that?"

"Because I can't have you."

I reached up and traced the scruff of his jaw. "You already do."

A frown pulled across his brow, and I kissed it, trying to ease the pressure.

I got it.

He was supposed to be representing us. Bringing us into the Mylton Records fold. Right then, I was his *job*. But after last night, I was certain our hearts rose so far above all of that. We could figure it out.

"I think . . . I think I might be ready." The words creaked with uncertainty when I released them.

His scowl came at me with full force. "For what?"

"To sign." My tongue darted out to wet my lips. "I'm tired of letting my past hold me back from what I want. Tired of letting the people who've hurt me be the rulers of my life."

Worry flew through his expression, remorse and regret. "And are you sure this is what you want? To sign this record deal?"

Why was he looking at me as if maybe he thought I shouldn't take the jump?

"You're the one who told me I'm a star. That I'm meant for this."

Confusion raced through my senses, and he tightened his hold on my face. "You are. And I want you to be sure you're teaming with the right people to get you there."

"I want you on my side," I whispered close to his lips.

Strain blew out on a sigh, and he curled an arm around my waist. "I am. I want everything for you. Everything that you want in this life. You deserve it all."

I was pretty sure it was too soon to tell him that was fast becoming him.

Giving in, he loosened his hold, mischief moving across his face. "Go on, gorgeous girl. You need to get back to your room before Melanie comes looking for you, and that is a shitstorm I can do without."

"She's not so bad."

He arched a disbelieving brow. "I think the girl carries around a machete for the sole purpose of protecting your virtue. Every time she walks into the room, my dick shrivels up, sure it's in mortal danger."

More laughter, everything feeling so easy. "She likes you . . . I think you're okay, big man. That pretty cock of yours is just fine."

A teasing grimace paraded across his face, and oh man, did I like this side of him, too. "Uh . . . Mells Bells earned her name from somewhere. Think Rhys might be missing a vital part or two." A defined brow arched. "And did you call my cock pretty?"

This time, my laughter rolled, and my head was spinning with a rush of dizziness.

Like streaks of sunlight blazing through the breaks in the trees. Disorienting and beautiful.

"If it fits," I muttered, doing my best to flirt and not trip into self-consciousness.

He growled and rocked his hips into mine, the hot, hard length of him pressing at my belly. "I'll show you where it fits." Need poured through me like a waterfall, and Royce chuckled low. "Go to your room before I keep you here all day."

"I like that idea better."

He went soft, touching my cheek. "If you really want me, Precious? You need to wait. Wait until you're sure. Until you really know who I am. That I won't be a mistake." The last was stern. Laced with bitterness.

I pushed my mouth up under his jaw, inhaling his scent, cedar and smoke and a vestige of me. "I don't think that's possible," I murmured, "I don't think I could regret experiencing a single thing with you."

Tearing myself from him, I eased off the bed and forced myself to head for his balcony door.

Before I stepped out, I glanced back, my sight full of that sinful, mysterious man lying across his bed with a flare of morning light striking across his body.

Exquisite.

Devastating.

Before I ran back to him, I forced myself to step out into the rising day, shuffling on my bare feet back over to our shared wall.

I hoisted myself up so I could slide over it. The second my feet touched down on the other side, Royce was there faster than I could process it, leaning over the wall, a big hand splayed around the back of my head to tug me in for a mind-bending kiss.

That's what being kissed by Royce Reilly felt like.

As if I'd been altered.

No longer the same.

Everything shifted around inside, shuffled in an outright disorder to settle into a newness where everything fit.

I pulled back with a smile, heat on my cheeks and hope in my belly. "I'll see you in a little bit."

"I can't wait," he said, watching me edge back across my balcony to the sliding door.

Finally, I tore myself away, spinning on my heel and racing into my room. I didn't even take the time to look at my phone that still sat on the nightstand connected to the charger. I went right for the shower, turning it to hot, letting steam fill the room as I lifted my nightgown over my head.

For a second, I pressed it to my nose, relishing in his distinct smell that lingered there, wondering what direction we were heading.

I stepped under the spray, knowing wherever it was, I couldn't wait to get there.

Thirty minutes later, I was showered and dressed. I didn't wait for Melanie to pick out my outfit.

I was feeling too good and too free and too right, so I pulled on my favorite white dress and slipped on some strappy wedge heels.

I dried my hair and applied a small amount of makeup. I leaned away from my reflection to crane my ear when my phone started to go off with a string of messages from the other room.

Then it dinged with more.

I sped up a little to finish getting ready. Once I did, I moved into the main room, which was a junior suite this time, just like Royce's next door. A couch and table were in the front portion and the bed was in the back without a wall to separate them.

Going for the nightstand, I grabbed my phone and swiped across the screen to find the group text.

Richard: Did everyone hear?

Rhys: No, man. What's up?

Leif: ???

Richard: Got some good fucking news.

Rhys: Yeah?

Rhys: Let's hear it.

Rhys: Don't leave us hanging, asshole.

Richard: Everyone meet in my room in two.

By that time, five minutes had already passed, and there was a battering at my door before I heard a card sliding into the lock and the door unlatching. Melanie pushed her way through without an invitation.

"Oh my god," she gushed as she flew inside.

Holding my phone in my hand, I turned my attention to her. "What's going on? Richard said there's good news."

She skidded to a stop in the middle of the room. My best friend vibrated with excitement. "Richard got a call from Karl Fitzgerald this morning. He's procured a spot for Carolina George to perform at the ACB Awards this weekend if you sign! Oh my god . . . the ACB Awards!" she shrieked. "Can you believe it?! I guess something happened with one of the bands that were supposed to be performing, Fitzgerald called, and boom. He's making good on his promises to make y'all superstars."

The ACB Awards were the premiere country music awards. Marrying country and pop and rock. It gave the Super Bowl audience a run for its money.

She took a surging step toward me and grabbed me by both hands, giving them a fierce tug. "This is big, Em. So big. Everything y'all have been dreamin' of. Can you imagine it? Up on that stage. God, I have to find you something amazin' to wear. Oh crap. Crap, crap, crap. We don't have a lot of time."

Her voice went faraway while anxiety clawed beneath the

surface of my skin. Like little fire ants going on a crusade. It was muddled by the rush of euphoria that hit.

I felt as if I were being pulled in two different directions.

Split down the middle.

But Mel was right. This was big. Something that had seemed like an impossibility. For years, it had been so far out of reach that it had felt like a fantasy.

Now, the only thing I needed to do was jump.

The one thing standing in my way was finally getting the courage to stand up and hold that bastard accountable.

But what would that do to Richard?

A tremor of fear rolled down my spine.

And what would putting it out in the open do to me?

But I couldn't go on allowing that man to exist as if nothing had happened.

Dread and belief staged a tug-of-war inside of me.

I could do this.

I could do this for the band.

I could do this for Royce.

Most of all, I could do this for me.

The door banged open.

Rhys and Leif barged in. Rhys tossed his arms into the air as if he were calling a goal.

"Holy shit, baby girl! Did you hear?" He was all burly grins and country twang and dollar signs in his eyes, which was just fine, considering the guy managed to do it without a lick of pretension.

He rushed me, wrapped his arms around my waist, and spun me around.

Joy bounded from him.

"We did it! Fuck yeah!" he shouted. "We did it!"

Then he froze, hugging me too tight. I thought he just then remembered that I'd thrown a wrench into our plans about three months ago.

Stalling.

Digging in my heels.

Freaking out in some small way every time I got on the stage, until it'd all come to a head over a week ago when I'd run from the stage having that anxiety attack.

Slowly, Rhys set me onto my feet, the man holding me on the outside of the arms as if he were offering to stay right there and be my support, though there was no missing the outright dread he wore on his handsome face.

I gave him a reassuring smile, glancing around in time to catch Richard walk through the door.

His green eyes flashed, my brother watching me so carefully, with so much hope, that my heart physically panged.

I knew right then that I was ready.

I looked back to Rhys, who waited with eager apprehension.

"We did it." The words rushed from my mouth on a wisp. Pride and faith and hope. "I can't believe it. We did it."

Rhys hooted and spun me around again.

Laughter bubbled up from my spirit. Spilling out as I dropped my head back and let glee rush free.

The only thing I could feel in that moment was the joy spread out in front of me.

In front of us.

It was only amplified when I felt my brother's relief pour into the room like a flood.

Leif's relief.

Melanie's relief.

It all surged and brimmed and overflowed.

"Yeah, baby!" Rhys shouted. "Carolina George is gonna go down in the record books. Month from now, every person on this planet is gonna know our names."

My heart went soaring a little higher when I caught sight of Royce slowly making his way in.

In an instant, the man had shifted the air.

Caused my heart to go into overdrive with a glimpse of him.

His strong brow pinched in confusion as his attention bounced around, obviously trying to catch up to the meaning of the scene he was walking in on.

Freshly showered, black hair sleek and damp, the man wearing another one of his suits that made my insides go funny.

I was a puddle at the sight, though he was standing back,

tucking his hands into his pants pockets and watching the moment unfold.

Skepticism riding high.

I tried not to wonder why he hadn't told me this was coming last night.

Warned me.

Prepped me.

Or maybe he just wanted to offer me this moment.

For me to experience it for myself so I could realize how much I truly wanted it.

Because I did.

I did.

Melanie threw her arms around Rhys as he continued to bounce me, my best friend joining in. She hugged us tight as the two of them jumped around, the movement jostling more uncontained laughter out of me.

Leif joined them right before Richard did, too.

The whole group of us hugged so hard that I no longer held onto any questions or fears.

The four of them squeezing so tightly, the reservations and dismay no longer had any space within me.

Support staunch.

When someone knocked at the door, Rhys set me onto my feet, all of us sharing small smiles as we stood in the glow.

Royce opened the door.

A delivery person stood there with a huge bouquet of flowers.

All pinks and purples and golds.

Roses and lilacs and irises.

Royce signed for it and carried it over to the table, his energy invading the space.

The card fitted on the little stick had my name scrawled on it in a pretty script.

"Must be from Fitzgerald," Rhys said with nothing short of triumph. "Here on out, I bet we are royalty, baby. Let the prezzies come rollin' in."

I couldn't help but notice the way Royce flinched where he backed away to lean against the wall with one ankle crossed over the other. For a second, I met that fierce gaze, the man too quiet.

Shifting in barely contained fury.

Why was he so upset?

This was what he wanted, wasn't it?

What he'd been sent to do?

Under the weight of it, I inched for the vase he'd left on the table.

Knowing this was it.

Fitzgerald was welcoming me into the Mylton Records family. I either had to sign or walk away, but I had no time left.

With a shaky hand, I pulled the card from the stick and fumbled into the envelope, eager to see what the inscription read.

My eyes moved over the words, shock stalling my heart before horror crushed down.

So heavy my knees went weak. My soul screaming out. Or maybe it was the silent one I could feel fisted in my throat.

Obliterating the joy I'd felt. The spark of hope I'd needed.

Emmy Love,

I hear congrats are in order. Smart girl. I'm so glad to hear you came to your senses. I can't wait to see you at the ACBs. What do you say you and I pick up where we left off? Sounds good, yeah? You and me? Tell your brother I said hi.

X

X.

X.

X.

The scar burned like it'd just been branded on me with a hot poker, and I crumpled in two, holding myself over the spot.

The walls spun. So fast I was sure I was gonna faint.

Whirling and whirling.

I gasped and choked, unable to see through the torrent of tears that instantly blurred my eyes and soaked my face.

"Emily . . . what the fuck is going on? Who is that from?" Richard demanded as he rushed for me.

Melanie was shouting from the side, "Oh shit, she's havin' a panic attack. A bad one. Someone get her some water and a cool washcloth. Hurry."

But I knew there wasn't a single thing any of them could do to make this better.

Royce

*M*otherfucker.

I swore, I watched it all play out in slow-motion while violence screamed through my muscles, my hands pulling into fists of rage.

Emily taking the card. Pulling it free. The confusion that quickly morphed to terror.

I was already fucking pissed, wondering what fucking game *Daddy Dearest* was playing this time. What shady angle had set off the celebration I'd walked in on two minutes ago.

Fucker kept me in the dark like he thought I wasn't capable of doing my job.

If he only knew.

Or maybe the greedy bastard had finally realized that I was coming for him.

Took half a second for me to come to terms that she was really going to sign.

Before I was ready.

Before I had everything I needed.

I stood by the wall with my spirit thrashing, heart clattering at my ribs, anger stoking my blood into molten fire.

I struggled to hold it back.

To get myself under control before I said or did something that would ruin it all.

But she was breaking.

Richard hovered over her, roughing his hands through his hair and bending around to try to get in her line of sight while still holding back, at a loss for what to do. "Emily, fuck . . . what's going on? Please . . . you're scaring us."

The rest of them danced around her, hands not quite touching, like she was cracked glass that was going to shatter.

Wondered how close that was to the truth.

"Em . . . what happened? What did the card say?" Melanie coaxed.

Yeah.

I really wanted to know the damn answer to that, too.

Protectiveness rose up in the middle of me. A black cloud that obliterated reason. Everything ceasing to matter except for the fact that this sweet girl was crumbling. I tried to remain standing in the corner. To mind my business like I wasn't the fool who was getting so wrapped up in this girl that he could no longer see straight.

In a way I shouldn't. Couldn't.

Emily bent over, gripping the table, gasping through a sob.

The cord holding me back snapped.

Pushing around Richard, I plucked the card she had crushed in her hand.

I scanned the inscription.

My sight turned red.

The edges black and bleak.

Death stroked in bright, vivid colors.

X.

Didn't know if I wanted to puke or go on a rampage.

"Get out," I grated, barely able to bridle the wrath that

consumed me.

To stop from putting my fucking fist through a wall.

From hopping a plane and finishing what I should have finished years ago.

Richard's attention jerked to me, worry and confusion twisting in his eyes.

"What?" he barely muttered.

"I said, get out."

His entire face pinched. "Excuse me? I don't know who you think you are, but she is my fuckin' sister. You don't get to start tossing around demands just because you are part of the label."

"Out." It was a growl. He was lucky I didn't spew fire with it. My gaze jumped around the room. "All of you, out. Now. It wasn't an invitation."

It reverberated around the room. Hard. Rough.

I knew I was a second from completely losing it in front of them. From sweeping her up and holding her and wiping all those fucking tears from that gorgeous face.

"I've got her, Reilly. Back off," Richard said, anger riding out the confusion.

"I'm not fighting with you right now, Richard. Get out. We'll deal with this later."

He wanted to throw blows.

Fucking fine.

As far as I was concerned, the asshole deserved to get his ass beat.

But not right then. Not when Emily needed me.

Suspicion oozed from him as he glared at me. I glared right back, pretty sure my teeth were grinding to powder with the amount of restraint it took me not to physically toss him out.

Finally, he let his focus drift to Emily. "Em?" he softly asked.

"Please . . . go," she whimpered, still holding herself around her middle, and there wasn't a fucking thing I could do but wrap an arm around that same place like I could hold her together.

Support her.

Keep her from dropping to her knees.

Relief.

It exploded in the middle of me at the barest contact. Hers and mine. Hers and mine.

I stood at her side, guarding, watching everyone as they slowly backed away. Each of them watched us like they had no clue what was going down.

All of them except for Melanie, who looked like she didn't know whether to thank me or go find that machete.

Finally, they relented, reluctance in their demeanors as they filtered out the door. Richard cast one long glance over his shoulder before he gave in and stepped out, letting the door slam closed behind him.

In a beat, I had Emily in both my arms, hugging her tight against my chest.

A sob burst from her throat.

"Royce."

"Shh . . . baby . . . shh." My hand was in her hair, the other wrapped around her as I carried her over to the couch. I sat her down on the edge of it. She crumpled forward, and I knelt in front of her, pressing my mouth to her forehead. "It's okay. It's okay. I've got you. I'm not going to let anything bad happen to you."

He would die before he ever touched her again.

Emily hiccupped, gasping for breath. "I thought I could do this, Royce. I want to. But I can't. I can't."

I brushed back her hair, trying to get her to look at me. "It's okay. It's okay. You don't have to do anything you don't want to do."

Maybe I was signing it all away. My own efforts. The end game.

Right then, I didn't fucking care.

A frown tugged so hard across her face, her features distorted with pain. "Why didn't you tell me? Why didn't you tell me Mr. Fitzgerald was gonna spring this on us? He said I had a month. A month to decide."

"I didn't know, baby. I didn't know."

"Isn't it your job to know?"

"I didn't. I swear to you."

I edged her back, holding her by either side of the face, forcing her to look at me. "I won't let anything bad happen to you. I promise you that."

She looked over at the flowers, expression grim when she turned her gaze back to me, her entire face soaked with the tears that wouldn't stop streaming down her face. "Do you know Cory Douglas?"

Terror ridged her question, and I knew she was opening up to me in a way that she hadn't opened up to anyone.

She was offering a piece of herself.

Asking me to hold it.

Not to crush it.

My soul raged, my chest close to caving, hatred carved into my response. "Yes. His band is signed with Mylton Records."

I left out the rest.

A shudder ripped through her body. "We . . . we toured with them at the end of last year. Opened for them in a few cities."

She stumbled over the words. Sheer terror blazed in her green eyes.

I wanted to commit murder.

Wished that I had.

My nod was cutting. "I was aware of that."

Blinking through her tears, she averted her gaze, and I couldn't do anything but take her by the chin, my voice so soft when I whispered, "Emily."

For a moment, we stared, tied in this intrinsic way that I didn't come close to understanding.

"He's not a good man, Royce," she rasped, the words barely there but so loud I heard them bang in my soul.

"I know, sweet girl, I know."

He was a sick, twisted bastard.

"I . . ." she started.

"You can tell me," I told her.

Terror ridged through her features, and she gave a small shake of her head. "I'm not sure that I can."

It burned on my tongue. The confession. But where would that leave any of us?

Still, I was asking. Pushing. "He hurt you."

Wasn't so much a question as a hate-filled assertion.

"He . . ." She trailed off, unable to finish the thought.

I searched for something that wasn't a lie. Something that wasn't my own manipulation. "Don't ever let someone back you into a corner, sweet girl. Don't ever let them force you into something you don't want. Manipulate or coerce you. But also, don't ever let them hold you back. You are the one who's in control. You are the one who has the power to end this."

"I . . . I want to. I just don't know if I can."

"You can, Emily. But when you're ready. On your terms."

Fuck.

What was I doing?

"But the band," she whimpered.

I stroked my thumb across the hollow of her eye, gathering the moisture. "Your band is good. More than good. Incredible. There will always be opportunities for you. You will succeed, no matter what. Don't let one person make that decision for you."

Chaos pulled her features into a thousand knots. "I thought our band signing is what you wanted? I don't understand what you want from me."

"For you to be happy. For you to feel safe. And he will be there at the awards show."

Wasn't like either of us didn't know who those flowers were from. She just didn't have the first clue how I knew.

Her nod was full of grief. "And if I say no, that I can't do it? Then I'm letting my band down. My family. The people who mean the most to me. They would be devastated."

I got as close to her as I could, my hands spreading out around her head like I could get inside, embed my hope and fear and fucking regrets into her. Let her know it would be okay. That I would do anything I had to in order to make this right. "But what about you, Emily? Will it devastate you to be in the same building with him?"

Would I be able to stand there and allow it?

Allow him to breathe her air?

Allow him to breathe any air at all?

A fresh round of tears streaked down her face. "Not if you're there with me. You . . . you are what makes me feel safe." She locked her hands around my wrists as I held her face in both hands "How is that possible? I've only known you for a short time, and when you step into the room, all the darkness falls away."

I pulled her closer, our noses brushing, my voice shards. "I'm terrified the only thing I'm going to do is bring more darkness into your life. There's so much ugliness inside of me, Emily. Things you can't see. Things I don't want you to."

My heart belonged to violence.

To hatred.

To the commitment I'd made to take back what had been stolen from me.

To set things right.

Problem was, I no longer knew what that meant.

Girl clouding my judgement.

Rearranging all the brittle, broken pieces of my heart.

She tightened her hold. "And the only thing I want is to see you better, and for you to see me for who I really am."

My baby sister's face flashed through my mind. Nadia's came skidding in right behind it.

Clutching my heart and lighting a fire in my spirit.

"You told me not to lie to you, Emily, and the truth I'm giving you right now is I'm terrified of falling for you. Terrified of the way you make me feel. This wasn't supposed to happen."

"What if it's unstoppable?" she asked, those green eyes racing over my face like she could see right through me, hooks sinking in, staking claim.

A pained breath heaved out of my lungs, and I dropped my forehead to hers. "Then we're fucked. I'm already wrecked, baby. And when this ends, I'm pretty sure I'm going down in flames."

"I don't understand what you're sayin'. What's ending?"

"I'm going to fix this." It was the only explanation I could give her.

"What I need to fix is me, Royce. The lies I've been telling myself." She pressed her hands over her heart. "I have to. I can't keep goin' on like this. Cory . . ."

My teeth gritted.

Cory was going down.

Hard.

"Won't touch you again," I interjected

Shock marred her face as she stared at me. Like maybe she was worried she'd given me too much, the girl trying to cover, not quite ready, but wanting to offer it at the exact same time.

Energy spiraled. A vortex sucking me in. I wanted to fully give in. Just fucking stop fighting it.

Wasn't sure I knew how.

"I don't want to cause any trouble between you and Mr. Fitzgerald . . ."

Oh, there was gonna be trouble all right.

"But . . ." She hesitated, fidgeting with her fingers. "I can't remain silent anymore. After I sign, I'm going to have to make a stand. Do something. And I'm not sure right now exactly what that looks like. It could get messy. I think . . . maybe you should stay away from me until it dies down. I don't want you to get in the middle."

Affection pushed and pulsed.

I could barely see.

My hold on her face tightened in emphasis. "I'm the last person you should be worried about, Emily. The last. But you're right. It's better if we stop whatever this is before it's too late. Before I hurt you in a way that I can't take back. But promise me, Precious, promise me. You do what's right for you. When you're ready—to tell me, to tell Melanie, to tell anyone? Whoever it is? You do it. Just . . . do me a favor. If you're going to agree to do that show? Know that I will be there for you, Emily. I will protect you. Tell them yes, but under the stipulation that you don't sign the contract until after. Until you play and you're sure. Do you understand what I'm telling you?"

That piece of shit couldn't have any power over her before this ended.

"But what about Mr. Fitzgerald? I don't know the details, but I'm guessin' he's not gonna be pleased with that."

Hatred rolled out on dark laughter. "I'll handle Karl Fitzgerald. Don't give that bastard a thought."

Her eyes pinched, her pulse thudding so fast and hard and

erratic. The beat of it calling for me.

It was fucking brutal.

"I . . . thank you, Royce. Thank you for all you've done for us. For me." She pressed her hand over the thunder raging in my chest. "You are the best thing that has happened to me in so long."

I pressed a kiss to her forehead.

Relishing.

"No, baby, you are the best thing that has happened to me."

Then I stood, went to the door, and pushed out into the hall.

The second I stepped out, Melanie darted in, cutting me a glance of worry and speculation as she passed. The door slammed behind her, and I heaved out a strained sigh and started for my door only to freeze when I felt the presence behind me.

"What the fuck is your game?"

I slowly swiveled around to find Richard glaring at me from ten feet down the hallway.

He moved for me, advancing until he brought us head to head.

Toe to toe.

I lifted my chin. "I needed to have a word with your sister."

A strobe of anger flashed through his eyes, and he lowered his voice. "I asked you to come here to help convince her to sign. Show her the reasons that she should. Not for you to go thinking she's a good place to dip your dirty dick. She doesn't come with the package."

Rage flared, and I pushed him by the chest.

Hard.

He stumbled back into a door across the hall.

"The fuck?" he shouted low, the words barely contained in the hotel hallway.

I got in his face, voice grating and hard, dripping venom. "You have no fucking clue what your sister will do for you, do you? Have no idea what she's been through, what she's going through, to keep your name clean?"

Bewilderment bounced through his expression, and the redness coloring his cheeks quickly drained, his flesh turning a pasty white.

"What the hell are you implying?" he shot back, eyes

narrowing.

"Playing ignorant isn't a cute look on you, Ramsey."

He shoved me back an inch.

"You think you know a fucking thing about me? Don't you dare come in here trying to toss around some bullshit you don't know shit about. And if my sister has issues with something in my life? She'll come to me. *Me.*" He slammed a fist on his chest. "The last thing we need is some ex-con sniffing around, thinkin' he's gonna get a bigger bite out of the pie."

I blanched.

He let go of a menacing laugh. "You forgettin' I know who you are, asshole?"

My jaw clenched, and it was taking my all not to lunge for him. To keep from pounding that fucking knowing smirk from his face.

Only thing saving him was it was clear he thought he was standing up for his sister's honor. Protecting her.

He took a step closer. "You think I don't see you salivating over her? Sick bastard wanting to take a little more? She's a *good girl*, has been through a ton of shit, and she sure as hell doesn't need more. So why don't you do what you do best and sign this fucking deal, and then step the fuck back?"

Eyes shooting daggers, he pointed at her door. "If I catch you even looking at her again, I'm going to ruin your ass, starting with me telling her who you are."

"You were the one who wanted me to come here, Richard." My voice lowered, nothing but gravel. "The one who wanted to sign with Mylton Records so badly that you were willing to go behind your sister's back."

He scoffed out a laugh. "I was doing it for the band."

"And the deal was you didn't mention my past if I came here. You want me to walk, keep making threats."

It was bullshit.

I wasn't going anywhere.

But Richard didn't need to know that.

What he needed was to keep his fucking mouth shut.

He scrubbed a frustrated palm over his face, backing away and shaking his head. "Just, don't touch my sister, man, and we're cool."

He didn't need to worry about that.

I wasn't going to touch her again.

But not because I was doing him any favors.

This? I was doing it for her.

Because she was quickly becoming the only thing that mattered.

sixteen

Emily

"Can we talk?"

My brother's voice hit me from behind, and I flinched where I stood at the edge of the pond outside the hotel, arms crossed over my chest, hugging myself beneath the sun that shone from above.

I was wearing the warmth like a blanket of security.

Warily, I turned to look at Richard, who was under a shade tree about thirty feet away, hands stuffed in the pockets of his holey jeans. Dark blond hair flapped in the wind and those green eyes watched me with worry, as if he wasn't sure the two of us understood each other anymore.

Close yet detached.

Loyal forever but the connections that had bound us slippin' away.

My heart ached at the thought.

"Of course," I gently called, though I really wasn't sure it was such a good time, considering I was fighting tears.

Not even sure where they were coming from anymore.

Tears of horror at the thought of having to see Cory Douglas again all mixed up with this confidence building in me, making me ready to fight. Because I wasn't gonna allow that vile man to hold me back from what I'd dedicated my entire life to.

I'd come to acceptance.

It was okay to feel fear, but it wasn't okay to let it dictate my life.

Or they could have been tears of gratitude. Gratitude for being invited to play at the awards show that'd felt like nothing but a pipe dream.

The reality of it was overwhelming.

The pride and the joy and the hope for the future.

Most worrisome of all, I was pretty sure these tears had everything to do with Royce.

Maybe I was wrong to push him away.

Derail us before we had the chance to get started.

But I couldn't put him in that position. It was gonna be a firestorm when I made the accusation against Cory. Carolina George up against A Riot of Roses, Mylton Records smack dab in the middle.

I couldn't ask Royce to get mixed up in it any more than he already was.

We really were a conflict of interest.

Richard took an apprehensive step my direction. "Hey," he said.

"Hey," I returned, softer, hating that he was watching me like I was gonna break. Considering that was precisely what I'd done back in the hotel room, I couldn't blame him.

He took a few more steps. "You okay?"

My teeth clamped down on the inside of my cheek, and I warred with what to tell him. "Yeah," I whispered.

"That's what you keep saying, Em. Again and again. I can't keep accepting that every time you freak out. This is serious. Guts are all twisted up, worryin' about you."

My ribs clamped down on my heart. Squeezing so hard. Affection and grief. "I'm tryin' to get better."

"When did you get sick? What did I miss? I keep thinking this is about Nile, but there's this spot inside of me that's insisting that it's bigger."

I could feel my expression pinching up. "And what about you, Rich? You think I'm not scared for you? You think I don't know something's going on? That you're into somethin' you shouldn't be?"

Agitated, he drove a hand through his hair, tone deflecting. "I don't know what you're talking about. And this isn't about me, Em."

"Isn't it? We're all tied, Rich. All of us. And if one of us is hurting? In trouble? That means the rest of us are, too."

Alarm shook his head, and he put his hands out in front of him. "No, Em. This is something you cannot get involved in. Can't. You need to stay out of this."

I stepped toward him, a plea in my voice. "What if I'm already in it?"

Fear streaked through his features, and he shook his head harder. "Not possible."

"Secrets don't stay secrets forever, Rich. They don't. People find out about them, and they come back to haunt us."

"Shit," he wheezed, looking off into the distance. Panic rolled through his body. A second later, he jerked his attention back to me. "Whatever you think you know isn't the truth, Em. I don't know what the hell you think you saw or what someone told you, but I promise you that I'm fine."

"And what if I saw it for myself? What if I'm tryin' to protect you, and I don't know how much longer I can keep on doing it?"

Richard erased the last bit of space between us, jolting forward and grabbing me by the shoulders. "I would never ask you to do that, Emily. Never. Stay out of it . . . it's dangerous."

A tear slipped free. "It's way too late for that."

Dread filled his expression. "What are you saying?"

"I . . . I'm just . . ." The confession lodged itself in my throat.

Richard pulled me into his arms, hugging me tight. I could feel the frenzy buzzing to his bones, his voice so hard that it sent a rush of terror zinging through my blood. "Tell me, Emily. Fucking tell me who hurt you . . . for what? Because of me? They're dead."

And that was the thing. Without question, he was telling the truth. That was a consequence I couldn't swallow.

I wrapped my arms around his waist, and the refusal was out before I could stop it. "No one hurt me, Richard."

I wondered if he could taste the lie the way I did.

Perverted and vile.

How was I ever gonna get this out when one atrocity was hinged on another?

"I'm just . . . I'm worried about you." I pulled myself back to look up at him. "Who is she, Rich?"

Maybe if he could give me something, I could give him something back.

Instead, he went rigid.

Chills raked down his spine, freezing him cold. He pressed his mouth to the side of my head, words so hard I could feel them penetrate to my soul. "No one."

Then he peeled himself away and strode for the bus that was waiting to haul us to the next city, his big body rushing across the lawn as if he were trying to run away.

Escape.

I knew in that second that his lie was as big as mine. And I didn't know how many more we could tell before everything came toppling down.

"I'll see you and raise you a hundred." Rhys slammed a hundred-dollar bill down on the table as if he was some kind of high-roller. He, Leif, and Richard were playing Texas Hold'em on the tour bus.

Darkness pressed in on all sides as we traveled through the night, the low rumble of the big engine humming as we barreled down the road.

"Ah, come on, dude, that shit is not fair. You really gotta go there?" Richard moaned, a forced smile perched on his face as he glanced between his hand and Rhys and back again, scratching at his chin as he contemplated his next move.

Trying to act as if all of this was normal.

As if things hadn't busted up between us four days ago, walls coming down for a flash before we'd both shoved the barriers between us back into place.

"Pussy," Rhys goaded, flapping his hand of cards toward his face without giving him a peek.

Richard swatted them away. "Uh, yeah, you're on to me . . . I do love me some pussy."

"Ha. If only you could get some." Rhys smirked.

Leif laughed and threw a wadded-up napkin at Rhys. "Stop projecting, asshole, and play."

"Projectin'?" A scowl the size of Canada took over Rhys's face. "Come now. Who do you think you're talkin' to? I could have had any lady in the house tonight, and I only took two. I am the picture of self-restraint."

He gave a bow where he was stuffed behind the small table.

Melanie looked up from her tablet where she sat next to me on the couch, voice wry. "You are actin' like you deserve some kind of dignitarian award."

"With the way those two were grinnin' when they walked out, I think it's safe to say I do. Just doing my part at makin' the world a happier place, one woman at a time."

"Sounds like someone needs a big ol' slice of humble pie to me," I sing-songed under my breath, my knees curled under me as I doodled in my notebook.

Trying to act normal, too.

Three hours ago, we'd wrapped a show at Olive's, a trendy bar in Gingham Lakes, Alabama.

We'd had to leave there right after the show in order to get to the next venue in South Carolina in time, the wheels grinding and eatin' away at the miles to get us where we needed to be.

It was gonna be a long night.

I jolted when a flying card impaled me in the chest. I jerked my head up to glare at the culprit, Rhys, who was just smirking.

"Who needs humility when you look like this?"

Mel rolled her eyes. "If your head gets any bigger, there won't be any room left on the bus for us."

He tapped at his chin as if he were contemplating curing world hunger. "Huh. You know, I haven't really had any complaints about the size of my *head*."

"You are disgusting," she told him.

I grabbed the card and flung it back. I had to stick up for my best friend and all. "I second that."

Of course I had to go and miss him by about a mile.

"So dangerous, Em," he ribbed. "You should watch yourself with sharp objects."

"Speaking of sharp objects, one more pervy comment and you'll need to watch yourself while you're sleeping tonight," I tossed back.

I was actually smiling for what felt like the first time in days.

That was until my heart suddenly took off at a sprint, all my senses tilting to the right the second the door separating the sleeping quarters and the main area slid open.

Royce slowly stepped in, his jacket discarded and the sleeves of his white dress shirt rolled up those sinewy, muscled arms, the man radiating power and greed and everything that dropped my stomach right to my toes.

One second of him and I could barely breathe.

I tried to keep my head lowered.

Appear as if I were buried in seriously important business. You know, like drawing a stick figure of a decapitated Rhys I had planned to deliver on the wings of a paper plane.

But not looking was impossible.

This faking thing was getting old.

Four days had passed since the incident at the hotel.

Four days since I'd told the band that I was in. That I would sign as soon as the show was over.

Royce had kept his promise—I wasn't sure what he'd told Fitzgerald to smooth things over, but we were slated to play. Our manager had the contract—the contract that was scheduled to be signed after the show.

"Yo, Royce, my man," Rhys hollered. "What the hell have you been up to for the last hour? Tell me someone explained to you that you gotta hold the code browns for the next stop. Tour bus etiquette, brother. Bus can't take it."

A smile actually ridged Royce's plush mouth as he slipped by.

My heart fluttered.

"No need to worry. Had a call I had to take."

"Ah, I see . . . some more of that secret, covert shit you seem so keen about." Rhys was all easy smiles.

Leif kicked Rhys under the table. "Dude, why always such an asshole?"

Rhys hiked his shoulders as if he didn't have a clue what Leif was talking about.

Royce slipped down onto the leather coach chair that was swiveled around to face the table and couch. It might as well have been a throne with the way the man owned it.

Possessed it.

The same way he had possessed me.

Infiltrated every thought and dream. Made me feel brave and confident and beautiful when I stood on that stage night after night, singing my heart out and wondering if a piece of me was actually doing it for him.

He rocked forward and rested his tattooed forearms on his knees, flashing the pawns stamped on his knuckles, as if they were being ruled by the intricate king inked on the back of his hand.

The resolve I was trying to cling to went fuzzy.

"Talking to my mom, actually," he said in his low voice.

My chest fisted. It was the first time I'd heard him mention her.

I could feel it—the unbearable shift of energy that shivered through the dense air.

Bitterness and unease and regrets.

My ribs constricted around my heart, stalling out the flow of blood. I had to bite down on my lip to keep myself from looking up, drawn that direction.

Out of the corner of my eye, I saw Leif nudge at Rhys with the toe of his shoe again. "See, asshole. Think before you speak."

I was pretty sure that was Leif's mantra. Motto. The way he lived his life.

Royce shook his head.

I didn't see it. I felt it.

Crap. Now I was sensing his every movement. I was so screwed.

"It's fine." A rough chuckle left him. I almost drowned in it. "Might have a few mommy issues. Nothing new. No need to tiptoe around it."

Richard cleared his throat to break up the tension. "You want to deal in, Reilly? Asshole here is about to steal the shirt right off my back. Don't want to be the only sucker getting swindled. Tell me you've got some cash to throw down."

I knew some words had been said between them.

Hell, no one could miss the outright animosity that had been ricocheting between them for the last four days.

Surely Richard wasn't happy that Royce had kicked everyone out.

Taken charge.

Clearly lettin' on that things had been brewing between us, standing firm at my side when I'd needed him in a way I hadn't anticipated.

And still, I needed him just as bad. Was aching for him to touch me. For him to whisper his comfort into my spirit.

But how could I ask him to stand in the flames for me?

Cory Douglas was a rich man. A famous man loved by millions of fans that he'd blinded with the bling of his smile and the dimple in his cheek.

The devil's dimple.

He was the kind of guy who dripped slime and scum and sleaze but always got away with it.

"Ah, he'll have plenty of dough as soon as we finally sign, yeah?" Rhys issued it like a cheer, grinning in Royce's direction as if they were the best of friends. "Bet there's a big ol' bonus when we sign on that dotted line, isn't there, Reilly? No wonder you don't mind climbing this bus night after night, slummin' it with the entertainment."

Rhys's deep brown eyes twinkled with mirth. The guy couldn't be serious to save his life.

Leif kicked him again. This time hard. "God, man. Do you have no tact?"

Rhys hiked his shoulders again. "What? I was born in a barn. Remember?"

"You wish, Cowboy," Melanie said, rollin' her eyes.

"Stallion, Mells Bells, stallion. How many times do I have to tell you?"

"That's it. You're getting your ass left in Dalton, Rhys," she said. "I can't be on this bus with you for another day."

We were playing a show in South Carolina and then had a couple days off to stay in Dalton, South Carolina.

Our hometown.

My chest swelled with the thought of being in my mama's kitchen, the smell of freshly baked biscuits and love in the air.

I couldn't wait.

I needed a breather.

A break from all of this pressure.

"Not about the money," Royce said, gaze falling on me as if I were the ultimate target.

An exotic destination.

Shivers raced. Temperature rising to 150 degrees. If I stayed in his space for a second longer, I was going to combust.

I shot to standing. "I'm gonna go work on some music in the back. Goodnight, everyone."

Waving an awkward hand, I scrambled for the back like my tail was on fire.

Good thing I was going for subtle. But it wasn't like I hadn't been all sorts of neurotic lately. At this point, I was pretty sure they expected it.

Heart in my throat, I fumbled down the narrow aisle of bunks, almost gasping out for the fresh air when I made it to the back room. At least in there, there was only the vague, lingering scent of Royce coating the room.

I didn't bother flipping on the light switch. I went right for my guitar, pulled her out of her case, and cradled her on my lap in the wafting darkness that slashed in through the windows.

Blinks of light and miles of shadows.

There was something comforting about it. The stars drooping low, as if I could reach out and brush my fingertips through them. Stir them up and twirl them around. Maybe become a part of them if I could somehow manage to get close enough.

I flipped open my notebook to where I'd been working.

Shock raked from my lungs when I saw the scraps of ripped paper that had been tucked inside. I picked them up, my eyes adjusting to the dim light, rereading the lyrics that had begun to weave, the hum of a tune infiltrating my mind.

Come to me
I've been waiting for a break.
Looking for something to save me from myself

I moved to the first sheet he'd tucked under my door.

Have you been looking for someone
To fill up what you're missing
Who is it who's gonna stop you
From the circle that keeps going 'round

I shifted that one behind to find the one I'd left on his nightstand four mornings ago.

My life a spiral
You sent me spinning
I've lost control
Now I'm questioning everything I think I know

My heart raced like mad when I shifted that one behind the others to find a new one waiting, again written in that bold, masculine script.

I already hit rock bottom
Waiting to catch you now

It's you, little mind-wrecker
Trippin' me up long before you could know

Everything squeezed, my heart and my belly and the hold that I had on my guitar.

The glue that melded us together.

Breaths heaving from my lungs, I spread the pieces of paper out on the seat, and I strummed that low, echoing chord, humming beneath my breath as I let my spirit chase down the song.

Threads of the obscure melody encircled me.

Comforting and right.

Even quieter, I began to piece together the lyrics as I picked through the progression of the patchwork song.

My fingers fumbled on the strings when I felt the presence overpower the room.

That lingering scent was no longer just a hint.

It was an inundation. A torrent of longing that hit the air.

Cedar and a dark, decadent promise of sex.

Shivers raced across the surface of my skin.

Slowly, I opened my eyes to find him standing in the small doorway, so much like he'd been the first day he'd stepped onto the bus. Only now, everything felt different.

Ominous and bleak and foreboding.

Hopeful and bright and burning.

The man a dichotomy I wanted to discover.

"What are you doin' back here?" I asked.

Tension bound.

Pushing at him.

Pulling at me.

A tremble of irrevocable desire that banded us like a tether.

Royce stepped forward and slowly slid the door closed behind him. His massive shadow towered over me. A wraith I wanted to disappear into.

"Was worried about you," he grunted.

I tried to focus on him through the muted flashes of light that strobed through the trees whipping by at the side of the narrow, winding country road.

His sharp jaw and his defined cheeks and his powerful brow.

But it was those onyx eyes that had me pinned. Intensity brimming from their depths.

"You don't need to worry about me," I whispered into the passing night.

"I don't think I could stop. It's getting harder and harder to stay away from you."

"Don't you think it's for the best?" My argument felt weak. "You're the one who's been tellin' me from the beginning that we are nothing but conflict."

"Maybe it's a war I want to fight."

A sizzle of need blistered the air. The song still playing through my mind. This man standing across the space and still touching my soul.

I gripped my guitar like a security blanket.

"I don't want you to go down for me," I told him.

His nostrils flared, his body rigid as he took a step forward. "You are everything that is good in this world, Emily Ramsey. Everything that is right. Going down for you would be a fucking honor. But you aren't the only person I owe a debt to. The only one I'm fighting for."

The words inscribed on his chest blazed through my mind.

The name he begged in his dreams.

My heart shuttered and flailed.

Maybe ending this now was for the best, because I had to wonder right then if he could ever love me.

The way I could feel myself falling for him.

"Your heart isn't yours to give away," I murmured, a soft admission.

His big body moved across the tiny room. Filling it full. Overpowering.

Blood crashed through my veins, my heart hitting a jagged boom, boom, boom.

He planted his hands on the back of the couch on either side of my head.

Hovering.

Towering.

Making me squirm in my seat.

He angled his head, his nose brushing mine. "And somehow you managed to steal a piece of it, anyway."

His gaze wandered to the scraps of paper I had laid out in order on the cushion.

Could feel the energy rumble from his spirit.

"Do you hear it, Emily? Do you feel it yet?"

"It's right there, waiting for me to grab it, just out of reach."

Just like him.

He traced his fingertips over the scraps without looking down. As if the lyrics might seep into his bones.

Liquid.

"Sing it to me," he murmured.

Emotion knotted my throat. So tight I was sure I was choking. The feeling trying to break free.

He angled closer, his face caught in the blinking, glittering light. Those full lips moved, barely brushing mine.

Inviting.

Coaxing.

"Hum it," he demanded.

Our eyes locked.

I thought maybe I could feel it crawling out of my spirit. The broken melody vibrated up my throat and spilled out of my mouth.

The words began to bleed free.

Come to me
I've been waiting for a break
Looking for something to save me from myself

I swore, he inhaled them.

Lived them.

His jaw clenched, those eyes fierce, but he began to sing the part of the first verse he'd left for me, voice raw and filled with that same mournful intonation.

Have you been looking for someone
To fill up what you're missing
Who is it who's gonna stop you
From the circle that keeps going 'round

He touched my cheek.

My phone went off in a slew of blips.

I jerked back, blinking off the stupor, the spell the man had me under.

My phone blipped again.

Royce swore under his breath. Frustrated, he raked his fingers through his hair. "Seems someone has something important to tell you."

Flustered, I dug into my pocket to pull it out, and I thumbed into the screen.

I wished I hadn't.

Wished I would have just changed my number.

Erase who he was and who he'd been.

Nile: I heard you're coming back to Dalton.

Nile: I can't wait to see you.

Nile: Things aren't right without you in my life.

Nile: I'm going to fix this, baby. You're going to see why you're making a huge mistake.

Nile: I promise you.

I cringed as I read through his messages.

As if he had a right or a say.

Royce's expression flashed possession.

I wondered what he saw written on me. I was beginning to think the man had his own special view. A vantage no one else possessed.

"Who is that?" This time, the demand resounded with a low

undercurrent of anger.

I blinked through the annoyance. "My ex," I said, futility oozing out with it.

Lost dreams and lost causes.

How was it possible Royce's expression darkened?

An eclipse.

"I take it you didn't like what he had to say?"

I fiddled with my phone, glancing down at it. "Not so much." I peeked up at Royce. "It's funny how someone can be the one to let you down, and they suddenly think you're the one who's holdin' them back. That you're the one who ruined things. Convenient, isn't it?"

"That's what cheaters do, Emily. They make excuses. Pin you with the blame."

"Unfair, isn't it?"

Royce gave a tight nod. "What did he say?"

Bitterness tumbled out in a rush of words. "He thinks he's gonna win me back. Like I could possibly forgive him for what he did."

Royce angled down, getting in my line of sight. "Do you want to? To find a reason to forgive him?"

A stake of light cut across his face right at that moment, that face illuminated in a blast of red.

He looked like a man on fire.

Consumed alive.

Or maybe it was him who was consuming me.

"There are some scars that can't be undone," I whispered. "And there's nothing he could say or do that would change what he left inside of me. I needed him, Royce. Needed him more than anything, and he wasn't there."

"You're not doing that great of a job convincing me not to end this asshole." A charge of violence streaked just under the surface of his skin. The ghastly faces on his arms coming to life.

Screaming out for vengeance.

But this wasn't his debt or due.

"No . . . though you could hog-tie him for me while I'm there. Might make my stay a little easier. He is a pig, after all." With a tiny smile, I shrugged a single shoulder, thinking maybe I should go for light before Royce really lost control.

Royce managed to grin around the hostility vibrating his big body.

God, it was pretty.

Punching me with a shot of affection so big I felt it like a chemical explosion.

He took the phone from my hand, watching me as he did.

Carefully.

As if he were asking me for his trust.

I trembled. Quivers of excitement and unease.

"What are you doin'?" I asked, all breathy as I sat forward.

Royce smirked. "You won't let me take him out in the traditional sense, I have to get creative."

He stretched out his arm and snapped a picture, typed a bunch of words before he pressed send and tossed the phone to the other end of the couch without letting me see what he'd said.

Then he stood, taking me with him, shocking me by wrapping me in his arms.

What in the world?

With Royce, I never knew if I was coming or going.

Warmth raced. Flames and need. A combustion sparking right in the middle of me.

Royce hugged me tighter, rocking me into a slow sway. Then he began to hum. Humming that song that had somehow become ours.

I got lost in it, in the rough scrape of the melody that reverberated up his throat.

I exhaled a shaky sound, falling into his embrace as he hugged me tighter. He pressed his mouth to my temple and murmured, "Finish the song, Emily Ramsey. Write it and live it. Find someone who's good enough to live it with you."

Then he turned and left me standing there as he disappeared out into the main cabin. Taking another piece of me with him.

If I'd really managed to steal a piece of his heart, then I was pretty sure he'd stolen all of mine.

Chewing my bottom lip, I glanced at where the door had slid

closed behind him before I rushed back for where he'd tossed my phone.

The image was still there, glowing on the screen, vague and brilliant. He was glaring at the camera, ominous and dark, and I was looking at him from the side as if he were the light.

You thought you could hold her back.
Dim her light.
Belittle her existence.
She's a star that can't be extinguished.
Soulshine.
Her flame is too bright.
Look too close? I'll personally see to it that you get burned.

And suddenly, that's where it felt like I was. Flying. In the stars. Soaring above the earth. Wishing there was some way that I could take this beautiful man with me.

seventeen

Royce

"He's here, Royce. Oh God, he's here." Whimpering echoed from the other end of the line.

I pressed my phone harder to my ear, trying to make out the secreted words that were laced with hysteria. So quiet I could barely hear them. Only thing I could process was the hiccupped terror that was coming out of my baby sister's mouth as she pleaded with me from across the fucking country.

Rage pulsed beneath my ribs, and I gritted my teeth as I started to pace along the alleyway behind the club where the band had just played.

Music throbbed through the dingy walls and rippled in shockwaves across the muddy puddles gathered in the pitted pavement. A siren wailed as it sped down the street, car engines accelerating, the sounds of the filthy city crawling through the muggy atmosphere.

I dropped my head, gritting the words, trying to sound rational when I was two seconds from hopping on a plane so I could go on a rampage. "Calm down, Maggie. Tell me what's happening."

"Cory Douglas is here. Downstairs."

Motherfucker.

Was that bastard serious?

That goddamn callous and cold?

I tried to keep my voice calm when I was a beat from coming unhinged. "Take a deep breath, sweetheart, take a deep breath. I'm right here with you. I'm right here. Do you hear me?"

She sucked for air. "Yes," she whispered, sniffling, trying to contain her sobs.

Hatred clutched my heart. So tight, I was pretty sure all the blood was being squeezed out. What was left was nothing but a hollowed, thudding pulp of destruction.

My baby sister was nineteen and still acted so young.

Naïve and innocent and completely violated.

Locked in that time. Forever a prisoner to the age when she'd been savaged.

Fifteen.

"Okay . . . okay," I coaxed. Or maybe I was only trying to talk myself down from the ledge. To keep from coming unglued and destroying my purpose. Ruining it all before I got the chance to take that piece of shit down.

"Tell me where you are."

She whimpered. "I'm in my closet."

"Okay, good girl. Is your door locked?"

"Y-y-yes," she stumbled. Wanted to ask her if she had a knife or a gun or a fucking rocket launcher. Girl deserved to blow that shit into the fucking sky and let the bullshit rain down around her.

"Good. Very good." I raked a hand through my hair, pacing some more, trying to figure out what the hell I was going to do. How I could make this right when I was on the opposite side of the country.

Hours and a few documents and one beautiful girl away from ending this once and for all.

"But I'm scared." It was a wheeze of shame.

"I know, sweetheart, I know. But you did exactly what we talked about. You did good. So good. What I need you to do is stay there until I call you back, okay? I'll give you the go when it's safe to come out."

"Okay." The word was nothing but a hitched sob, but in it, I knew she was giving me her trust.

"I'm going to hang up right now, and then I'm going to call you right back. I want you to plug 9-1-1 into your phone and be ready to call it if you need to. If anyone comes into your room before I call you back, call it. Don't hesitate or question it. Do you understand?"

"Yes."

"Okay. I'm hanging up. I love you, Maggie."

"I love you, too."

I ended the call and immediately dialed the number.

Two rings later, *Daddy Dearest* answered.

"Ah, Royce, to what do I owe the pleasure?" he answered.

"Tell me you didn't invite that twisted fuck into your house."

Pretentious laughter rippled out. "I assume you're talking about our friend Cory."

My teeth grated so hard I could feel my jaw crack. "Don't act like a fucking prick. Tell me that cocksucker is not in your house."

He tsked. "Such a chip on your shoulder, Royce. Green is such an ugly color on you."

He thought this was about me being jealous? Thought it was about money?

Like any of that bullshit counted. But I knew well enough that it was the only thing that mattered to him.

"Tell me if he's there, because your *daughter* is locked upstairs having a panic attack, not that you'd notice or care. I'd just like to let her know when it's safe for her to come out."

I could almost see him rolling his beady eyes. "Always so dramatic, isn't she? Just like her big, bad brother. Making things a bigger deal than they really are."

It took everything I had to stop myself from putting my fist through a wall, wishing it was his face. Still, I was pressing my knuckles against the pitted, jagged brick, sucking in cleansing breaths before I totally blacked out.

Before rage took over and I said or did something I couldn't take back.

"Tell me if he is there." The demand flew off my tongue. Daggers and knives. Sharp enough to kill. I only wished.

"You can cool the overreaction. He's gone. And before you start making accusations, he showed up at my door. What kind of person would I be if I was so rude not to invite him in? He's one of our biggest names. The best talent we have. He is the face of our label, Royce, don't you agree? Besides, Anna was with him. You don't expect me to be some kind of coldhearted bastard, do you?"

Agony clutched my chest.

Her face flashed through my mind.

The memory a jagged knife twisted in my guts. I slumped forward, my hand pressed to the wall to keep me standing.

Breaths nonexistent.

Lungs caving.

He laughed. The asshole knew exactly how to bring me to my knees.

"He's gone?"

"As of five minutes ago."

It was the only relief I could find. That my sister was safe. But that didn't mean Anna was.

I had to push the thought out of my head. Shun it. It'd been the only way I could stay sane for the last four years.

"And I'm not sure why you're the one making demands when I don't have my contract in my hands."

I was still reeling from Maggie's scare, but I knew what was important to Karl Fitzgerald. It was my duty to play the part. See it through to the end.

I wasn't going to mess it up now.

"I told you what it would take for them to sign."

"The deal was they had the spot at the ACB Awards if they signed. It wasn't your place to renegotiate."

"And the one thing they need to see is you'll actually come

through for them. They want to see you're not talking out of your ass. That this isn't bullshit. You make a big promise? They want evidence you're going to deliver. You do this? Get them on that stage? They will sign. I guarantee that."

Part of me wanted to derail the awards show.

Last thing I wanted was Emily there. In the same room with that bastard. Hell, I didn't want her in the same state. But I got the distinct sense she needed this. To see she was stronger than she gave herself credit for. That she was going to rise above it all.

"You guarantee it?" It was a challenge. A gauntlet thrown.

"Yes," I told him, sure, though I wasn't sure at all. Wasn't sure if they should go through with it. If I should just come out and ask her to do this for me.

The only thing I knew was I was doing what was right for my sister.

For Anna.

For this motherfucking world.

"Fine. But if I don't get that contract? Your ass is done. You won't work in Hollywood again. Not in music. Hell, I'll see to it that McDonald's has you blacklisted."

I wanted to tell him to fuck off. To bring it on. Only solace I had was knowing this asshole would soon have what was coming to him.

"Perfect."

He laughed. "So cocky and sure of yourself."

"You seem to forget who I am."

I ended the call without another word and called my sister back. She answered on the first ring.

Hated that I'd even left her waiting for a second.

"He's gone."

She gasped out a cry of relief. "Are you sure?"

"I talked with your dad. He said he left five minutes ago."

I could almost see her nodding frantically from across the miles, like she was trying to convince herself of her safety.

Ripped my fucking black heart out of my chest. Wanted to give it to her for collateral, but who I was failed to matter. Only thing left of me was the debt. A reckoning that was coming.

"Are you okay?" I grated, barely able to control the hatred in the words.

"I think so."

"You are strong, Maggie. The strongest person I know."

"I don't feel like it."

"The fact you called me? That you did what you did? That makes you a survivor. A fighter. That is what makes you strong. And I promise you I'm going to take this threat away from you. Make sure you don't have to live your life in fear."

"And what if you get hurt in the process?"

"I'd die for you." It flew out of my mouth like a bullet. So fast it cracked in the air.

"And what if I want you to live, too?"

"Everything I do is for you."

She gulped for air. "Then do this for me, Royce. Live for me. End this, but don't be stupid. You think I can't see the hatred in your eyes? You think I don't feel your desperation? Don't do something that ruins you. He already ruined me."

She might have been naïve. Stuck in that time. But she was wise beyond her years.

"You aren't ruined." I refused for her to even think it.

I might have been ruined.

Irredeemable.

A sad, pathetic Hollywood cliché.

But not her. I refused to let it happen.

"Then let's thrive together," she whispered.

"I'm going to get you out of there, Maggie. Get you out of that house forever. Soon. So soon."

"I'm ready."

When she said it, I could picture her hugging her knees to her chest where she sat on the floor of her huge walk-in closet, buried in the deepest corner, hidden by draping clothes hanging from above, wiping the tears from her face with the heel of her hand.

Relief bounded through my chest.

It was the first time she'd said it. Always so frail and fearful and agreeing with every bit of gnarled, distorted BS that bastard spewed. Scared to deny the lies he fed her.

He expected her to swallow it down and purge it right back out.

"I'll talk to you soon."

"I love you so much, Royce."

"I love you, too. Mag-Pie. We're almost there. Just . . . hang on for a few more days."

Ending the call, I pressed the top of my phone to my forehead, wondering if the pressure could force out the disgust and hurt and savagery that spun through my mind.

This feeling that I was on the edge of something severe. No footing remaining underneath. I was about to slip. When I hit the bottom, there would be nothing left.

Only thing I knew was I was taking both of those bastards down with me.

Finally, I forced myself out of the alleyway, but I found I couldn't go back to the hotel where the band was staying. Couldn't bring myself to step into another vacant room, the blackness from within swallowing me whole, night after night taking another piece of me.

Knowing Emily would be close.

So fucking close.

So far out of reach.

I hit the sidewalk. The night was alive, neon signs flashing from where they hung outside bars and clubs, beacons for those out looking for a good time.

A way to forget.

To let go.

A lighthouse for the hopeless who had nowhere left to go.

Pretty fucking sure I fell into the latter.

I passed by a couple larger clubs, opting for the first dive I came to.

They were easy to spot.

Grungy and bleak.

The sound of live music seeping out from within, tendrils that swirled and wafted, crawling along the ground until they found someone to sink their claws into and sucker inside.

At the door, I paid the five-dollar cover and moved inside the crowded space.

It was drab, as expected. Muted, hazy lights glowed from the lamps that hung from the rafters, extended by metal ropes from the ceiling, set to a slow sway by the beat of the bass from the band that played tonight.

For the last year since I'd taken this position, these had been the types of dives I'd sought out.

Fitzgerald called it dumpster diving.

Thing was, you found the best talent in the lowest places. Bands made of grit and determination and raw genius. They were just waiting for someone who knew what the fuck they were doing to sculpt them into something great.

It was my job to chase greatness.

Not that any of that was even a concern now.

That title nothing but a way to swindle myself in.

Didn't mean I wasn't good at it.

I'd had the honor of discovering some fucking awesome bands that had earned their right in the spotlight.

Like instinct, my attention moved to the two-foot riser stage where three guys performed beneath a fog of yellowed, dingy lights.

I pegged them as local.

Twangy country boys who were slinging covers.

Good but not great.

I found a secluded booth in the back, slipped into the scarred wooden bench. A second later, a waitress appeared. "What can I get for you?"

"Woodford, neat."

"Be right back."

She disappeared back into the fray, and I slung myself back in the booth, fingers tapping at the tabletop.

Itchy.

Antsy in a way I hadn't been in forever. Could feel this slowly brewing storm coming to a head.

In a flash, the waitress was back, sliding the glittering tumbler down in front of me.

"Thank you."

"You're welcome. Let me know if you need anything else."

She walked away, and I brought the glass to my lips, taking a big gulp, hoping it might calm my raging nerves. That it might soothe some of the hatred that roiled and disgust that distorted.

I cringed when I felt movement at the side, cringed even harder when I felt the hand on my shoulder.

"You look lonely."

I lifted my attention to the voice. Flirty and high and not close to being the sultry voice I'd come to crave.

"I'm not looking for company."

I turned away and took a sip of my drink.

Giggling, she slipped into the booth beside me.

"Maybe I could change your mind."

I swiveled a hard glare her way. "I don't think so."

Her blue gaze swept over me, the girl gorgeous in that overly done way, dressed up for a night out, to dip her fingers into something salacious and sinful.

I couldn't blame her.

But not with me.

Not tonight.

She leaned closer. "You sure about that? You look like you're nursing a broken heart. Nothing like a little distraction to make you forget."

I almost laughed, looking over at her when I asked, "You think I'm suffering from a broken heart, huh?"

I had news for her. This heart had been broken a million years ago. No chance of healing it.

Angling her head, she smiled something sad. "Isn't everyone?"

Couldn't help but return a smile. "Seems so."

"What could it hurt to be broken together?"

"I don't think that's a good idea."

Had no fucking clue what was holding me back. Probably was exactly what I should have done. Put a wedge so thick between me and Emily that neither of us would attempt to cross it.

Sever the bonds my heart had been so foolish to forge.

Fucking impossible.

Knew it with the tremble of my insides that came with a lash of awareness.

Need and this deluge of devotion that engulfed me.

My gaze drifted, and it immediately snagged on the silhouette of the girl who'd been haunting me since the moment she'd stumbled into my life. Eyes piercing me from across the cramped bar, bodies shifting around her while the girl stood stagnant in the middle of them.

The eye of a storm.

A spotlight.

Soulshine.

My guts twisted.

Need consuming.

Dick instantly hard.

But it was the way my spirit shivered that was the problem. The way possessiveness bounded.

She wore that fucking white dress that damn near dropped me to my knees every time it was draped over that gorgeous body.

Nashville written all over it.

Cute and sexy.

Blonde waves cascading down her back.

Old, scuffed brown cowgirl boots accentuating a mile of legs.

What the fuck was she doing here?

Alone.

Immediately, it sent me spiraling back to the first night in Savannah. When she'd been out by herself, searching for a way to erase the agony that clung to her like a disease.

Tonight—with the way she looked—I had to wonder if she wasn't looking for me.

Drawn the same way I was.

Magnets pulling through time and space.

I leaned toward the woman whose name I hadn't bothered catching, gesturing with my chin. "That's why."

Her attention moved to where Emily stared at us.

The girl winced. "Sorry . . . I didn't realize."

She quickly slipped out of the booth, but not before Emily had whirled around and started to push through the crowd.

Fleeing.

Motherfucker.

My guts tangled in regret.

What I needed to do was let her go.

Not feel as if I'd committed a wrong.

She wasn't mine and I wasn't hers.

As soon as I thought it, I knew it was a blatant lie.

Sliding out of the booth, I tossed a twenty onto the table and shouldered through the crowd in the direction she had gone.

Something frantic rose up. Clutching and strangling.

People glared as I shoved through, but I couldn't seem to find it in myself to give a fuck.

One thing on my mind.

One destination.

I caught up to her close to the front door. Knew she sensed me there, the way her footsteps faltered for a beat before she increased her pace.

Hated that she was running from me.

Couldn't stomach the idea even though I knew it was for the best.

I grabbed her by the wrist. Flames swept up my arm, so intense I was pretty certain my chest seized. She whirled around. Distress twisted her face into a knot of pain. "Please . . . just let me go."

My hold intensified. "Is that what you want?"

Confusion pinched her face. "I thought that's what we decided was for the best."

"It is. Doesn't mean it's what either of us want."

She squeezed her eyes closed. "Why's this so hard?"

I took her hand, trying to get her to see me. To look at me. Slowly, she opened that mossy gaze to me, looked back in the direction of the booth where I'd been sitting.

"Did you want that girl?" Pain leached into the question.

"No. Not for a second."

Sadness pulled across her face, and she gently tapped her fingertips over the words stamped across my chest. "Maybe someone else deceived you . . . hurt you . . . but I'm not her. And I'm not sure I can keep deceiving myself about what I feel for you."

Then she pulled away. So close but out of my reach.

And I was terrified that was exactly where she was always going to be.

eighteen

Emily

"Load 'em up and move 'em out." Rhys held open the back door of the Escalade that was waiting at the curb.

"Cool your jets . . . since when are you the one trying to wrangle the band?" Melanie arched a brow at him as she handed her duffle bag to the driver, who was loading our luggage into the back.

"Um . . . hello, Mells Bells. Every second we stay standing out here is one second I don't get to spend with my mama, and that's just uncool. So why don't you get that sexy ass of yours into the SUV so we can get out of here."

"Mama's boy."

Rhys touched his chest. "You say that like I'm gonna take offense to it. I think it just might be the best compliment you ever gave me. I'd go down in a blaze of glory when it comes to my mama."

Melanie chuckled. "I think you might be right, cowboy."

Rhys narrowed his eyes.

She patted him on the chest as she edged past him. "I know, I know—stallion."

Rhys gasped and clutched her hand, holding it closer to his chest. "Holy shit. I think the sky might be fallin'. Did y'all hear that? Mells Bells just complimented me and acknowledged what a thoroughbred I am in the same breath. I think it's gonna be a damned good day."

"It will be a good day when we finally get to Dalton," Richard grumbled.

"Then let's do this shit," Rhys said, smacking his hands together as the last bag was placed inside and the driver lowered the hatch.

A tremble of nerves rumbled through my body. I glanced over at Royce, who was standing on the sidewalk, hands shoved in his pockets, wearing another of his suits.

Sunshine poured over him. Lighting him up even though I wasn't sure I'd ever seen him appear so dark.

Beautiful and raw and rippling with that energy that grew stronger every day.

"You ready to check out our hometown, Money Man?" Rhys asked. "You should probably know you don't need to be wearing that suit."

Somehow, Rhys had convinced Royce to come with us to "check out the old hood."

The hint of a smile played around Royce's mouth. "I figured if I am going to meet your mom, I'd better dress to impress."

With the way his eyes cut to me, I wondered exactly whose mom he was talking about.

He was staying with us since my mama had an extra room.

Need twisted my belly.

Last night, everything had finally shattered when I saw him with that woman at the bar.

For a split second, I'd thought he was with her. I'd been struck frozen while visions of him taking her back to his room had assaulted me. Stripping her of her clothes. Touching her the way I was desperate for him to touch me.

And I knew it then—in the way my heart had completely clutched in my chest. Stalling out before it'd jumped into a sprint when he'd looked at me as if he'd been watching for me.

Waiting for me.

As if he needed me every bit as much as I needed him.

I was falling and there was zero hope of being caught.

Swept away by a current that was stronger than my reservations.

That current only intensified when Royce edged up behind me right then, his breath caressing the shell of my ear.

"In you go, Precious," he murmured just for me, voice rough as he guided me toward the third-row seat.

The very backseat that the two of us had been relegated to. Melanie had claimed she'd put all our names in a basket and pulled them out at random.

I called BS, although there was a bigger part of me that wasn't complaining at all. The part that shivered with needy nerves as I climbed into the backseat.

It was my heart sure it was getting ready to get crushed all over again that was doing the worrying.

Royce guided his massive body in beside me.

I did my best not to breathe him in.

Useless.

I was inhaling all things Royce Reilly.

Cedar and sex and that lingering scent of cigarettes. I had the urge to burrow my nose to his throat.

In the cramped confines, the outside of his thigh pressed up against mine.

My heart stuttered and heaved.

This was going to be a very long trip.

Everyone else piled in, Rhys in the front, Richard and Melanie in the middle.

Leif had flown home to spend the few days off with his wife and their kids.

The driver pulled out of the hotel and headed in the direction of my hometown.

"Here we go," Rhys called. "Dalton, South Carolina. Best fucking town on the planet. Basically because I was bred and born there." Rhys shifted around to toss an exaggerated wink to Royce.

Royce just grinned with a small shake of his head.

Looked like Rhys was winning him over, too. Adding an easiness to the air that wouldn't be there if it wasn't for his casual smiles and friendly gestures and over-the-top ridiculousness.

It was hard not to love Rhys Manning. I just wondered if he'd ever completely love someone back.

Well, other than his mama, of course.

The car sped down the road, the city disappearing behind us as we began the two-hour trip that would take us deep into the country.

My gaze drifted out the window, taking in the increasingly familiar scenery. God, I hadn't realized how much I'd missed it. How I'd been longin' for something familiar. Something that reminded me at the end of the day, after the lights went down and the glitz faded away, that this . . . this was what was important.

Family.

Above, blue skies seemed to go on forever. It was dotted by a few flawlessly puffed white clouds that looked as if they'd been drawn on a child's coloring page, one perfectly hewn at the bottom edge of a blazing sun so distinct you could almost make out the little triangular rays.

I'd have been lulled into the deepest comfort if it hadn't have been for the tension that bottled in the space between Royce and me.

Awareness thick.

Our breaths shallow. Time spinning in a way that felt as if it were knitting us together all while forcing us apart.

Two worlds shoved together that couldn't possibly fit.

And somehow . . . somehow, I was getting to the point that I was willing to risk it all to give it a try.

Would he be willin', too?

Because I was pretty sure a risk was the only thing we were.

The SUV slowed as we made our way into a town that could

barely be considered a city.

Royce leaned over, eyes watching me as he whispered, "Are you happy to be going home?"

There was almost pain in the question.

I pulled his hand into my lap for the briefest second, squeezed it in sincerity. "Yes. So happy. I have to admit I'm glad you're goin' to be there with me. That you can see where we're from."

Regret and something that looked like guilt traipsed across his face. "I hope you can always say that about me—that you're happy I was here. A part of your life . . ."

He didn't add the rest, even though I heard it plain as day— *before I am gone.*

A stake of the grief I could already feel coming sliced through my heart.

Agony.

I forced myself to ignore it, gave him a smile as the driver pulled up in front of Melanie's childhood home. She hopped out almost before the car came to a complete stop. Apparently, Rhys wasn't the only anxious one. "See you all tomorrow!" she said, rushing to the back and grabbing her bag.

In less than a beat, we were back on the road, driving through the tiny town and even farther into the country.

Here, it was nothing but a dirt two-lane road. The driver slowed and made a right-hand turn onto the narrow lane that led to our properties. Rhys's family lived on the left, and ours was off to the right. Both homes were set on three acres of rolling fields, though ours had a corral and a barn to shelter the horses.

"Go left," Rhys instructed.

The SUV rolled to a stop at a clearing in front of the small white house. A single-story three-bedroom with a porch on the front. Rhys hopped out and popped his head back into the cab. "See you in a bit, suckers."

"No rush," Richard ribbed.

"Don't act like you won't be missing me," he told him, reaching in to pat him on the cheek.

Richard grabbed his hand and squeezed.

Rhys jerked away, laughing and shaking out his hand, though

he was still leaning in. "Ow, you asshole. You overcompensatin' for something with that grip? Or are you just trying to get rid of me so you can stand in the limelight? Don't be fucking with my hand. Next stop Nashville, baby. The big time. Don't go and fuck that up. Y'all would suck ass without me."

"You wish, dude," Rich taunted, smiling wide.

"No wishin' about it." Rhys winked.

Nerves roiled through my spirit with the mention of Nashville.

It was coming up fast. Faster than I anticipated. Here before I could make sense of it.

Royce glanced at me.

As if he'd felt it.

That powerful gaze met mine. A hard whisper in my ear that I felt like a caress. *You can do this.*

Rhys pointed at each of us. "Y'all don't have too much fun without me. See you tonight for dinner. Tell your mom to make double the mashed potatoes. This boy here is hungry."

He patted at his ridiculously flat, muscled abs.

"Like she forgot who you are," Richard grunted. He glanced at Royce. "Asshole would eat all the food at his house and then come raid our fridge."

"How could I not when your mom loves me more than you? That'd be rude. She even stocked extra Oreos in spots that only I could find them."

"That was me trying to hide them from you, jackass," Rich deadpanned.

"Liar!" Rhys sang, laughing loud, slamming the door shut and slinging his duffle over his shoulder as he headed for the porch. The Escalade was backing up when his mama came flying out and threw her arms around his neck.

Dropping his bag, he lifted her up and spun her around.

So sweet. But it felt even sweeter when Royce hooked his pinky finger with mine, our hands hidden between our legs where they rested on the seat. The smallest embrace. A tiny reminder that he was here, with me, at least for a little while.

The hardest part was knowing the only thing I wanted was for him to stay.

"What can I do to help?" I asked as I stepped down into my mama's old kitchen from the narrow second set of stairs.

The scent of a chicken roasting in the oven held fast to the air, and warm sunshine slanted down through the window, spraying spikes of light onto the worn linoleum floor.

I was hit with a burst of longing.

A nostalgia so fierce I could feel it hugging my spirit like an old friend.

My mama was wearing shorts and a tee, her graying hair tied up in a tight bun, her middle expanding in time with the lines that deepened on her face.

She glanced over her shoulder at me from where she was at the counter snapping the ends off the fresh green beans that no doubt had come from her garden.

Her smile so wide, her green eyes sparkling with an outpouring of love.

She would always be the most beautiful woman I'd ever seen. The picture of who I wanted to be.

"I thought you were nappin'?" she said with one of her small, curious smiles.

I huffed out a sound. "Couldn't sleep," I admitted as I waded farther into the kitchen, coming up to her side so I could help her with the chore.

From the side, she took a long look at me, studying hard, her voice lowered when she asked, "This have something to do with that man who came following you in this afternoon?"

I flinched a little. Was I that obvious?

"Mmmm," she mused, looking at the job she was doing as if it wasn't anything at all when I could feel her toiling with something big. "He is somethin' to look at, isn't he? Little scary, actually."

She cut a glance my way, watching for my reaction. Ready to catch my true feelings. The woman had always been able to read me like an open book. One that had pictures painted in just to be sure you actually picked up on the meaning. Hell, I was pretty sure that book even had cliff notes.

"I'm a little scared of the way he makes me feel, honestly."

She gave a tight nod, as if she totally got it. "So . . . are you two a thing?"

"No," I mumbled, snapping the end of a bean and tossing it into the colander.

She laughed a light, knowing sound. "Well, there may not be any labels you have placed on each other, but you definitely are something. I felt you two coming on like a sonic boom. Think I felt the rumble of it an hour before you hit town."

"No, Mama. I think we might be too complicated for each other. Too messed up. Besides, we don't exactly match, do we? I think I might be a little simple for him."

She pushed out a small sigh. "Too simple? I don't think so, sweet girl. But there is no doubt that man is carrying around a burden. You can see it written all over him. Holds his shoulders too high to keep the weight from crushing him."

I blinked through the confusion. "He's a fortress, Mama."

She bumped her hip into mine. "One you wanna climb."

"Mama," I chastised.

She laughed. "What? You're a grown woman, and that is one fine looking man."

"Mama," I hissed quickly again, though I was laughing a little, too.

"I might be old, but I'm not blind."

"You're not old."

"You're the blind one," she told me softly, as softly as she was looking at me. She reached out and touched my cheek. "And I see the burden you're carrying, too, Em." She grimaced. "I hate that Nile hurt you. I nearly chased that boy out of town with a stick when I found out what he'd done."

My head slowly shook. "It's okay."

"No, it's not."

I fumbled a smile, and she frowned. "What is it, sweet girl? It's more, isn't it? There's something there that wasn't there before. Something that's dimming those trusting eyes, and I hate to see that."

I scrambled around for an explanation, for something to give her because I didn't want to give her a lie. If she knew about Richard, about what I'd done to protect him, what it'd done to me, she would be devastated.

But I knew if I was goin' to take a stand, neither of those things would remain a secret for long.

Dread curled through my body.

A bridge I was going to have to burn was coming up fast.

Would I be brave enough to light the match?

My tongue darted out to wet my dried lips as I struggled for the right words. "All my life growing up, you told me that life is full of choices. Ones we don't always want to have to make but we're forced into. That sometimes life takes us directions we never planned on goin'."

"It's never too late to turn back."

"But what if we get there and there's no way of leaving? What if we have a dead-end coming up, and there is no way to stop before we collide with it?"

Worry sped across her features, and she set her hand on my cheek. "You can trust me with anything, Emily. You know that, don't you?"

I pressed her hand closer. "I do. But there are some things we have to stand up and do for ourselves."

"I will always be here if you need me. But the one thing I want you to remember is if you're in the middle of something, dealing with a stronghold in your life? Know you have the power to crush it. Make the choice never to go back. Or if you are stuck? In a place you can't leave no matter what? You make that place your own. Conquer the cruelty. Own the oppression." Her voice deepened with emphasis. "You, Emily Ramsey, are stronger than you think."

I started to respond, but I fumbled, words dying on my tongue when I felt the presence invade.

A quiet power that infiltrated the room.

I glanced up to find Royce standing in the kitchen entryway, shifting in discomfort, roughing one of those inked hands through his black hair.

God, the man was staggering.

Stunning where he stood.

He'd changed into ripped jeans and an old band tee, his attire so different than what I'd grown accustomed to seeing him wear, though it somehow seemed to fit him perfectly.

He looked like he'd been plucked from a stage. A rocker who played hard and fast and a little wicked. Or maybe like one of those tatted Instagram boys with a gazillion followers, tossing one of those sinful, brooding smiles at the camera.

So sexy he wasn't real.

So appealing he sent my tummy quivering and my knees knocking right there.

My mama sent me a glance, as if she were worried the entire place was gonna go *kaboom.*

"Hi," I whispered, the word trembling like my heart.

"Hey, sorry to interrupt. I was just looking for a glass of water."

My mama jumped into action. "Oh, goodness, I'm so sorry. And here I pride myself on being a good host, and I didn't even offer you anything to drink." She grabbed a glass from the cupboard. "I have fresh-brewed iced tea if you'd prefer?"

"Water is fine, thank you, ma'am."

Why did his being polite instead of bossy and demanding get me all hot and bothered, too?

This boy was a danger to my mind. To my sanity. Who was I kidding? He'd already stolen it. Left me reeling and unsure and wanting things that were going to leave me scarred and banged up more than I already was.

Why did we always go chasing after pain?

Ice clanked as she dropped it in the glass, my mama moving quick as she filled it the rest of the way with water from the dispenser on the fridge.

While Royce just stood there watching me.

Pinning me.

Owning me.

It was true.

This bad boy?

He had my heart.

And I knew he was going to leave it mangled.

She handed him the glass.

"Thank you," he said, bringing it to his plush lips.

"Make yourself at home," she said, glancing at me. She looked back at him. "I trust you got settled in the guest room?"

"I did. I appreciate you letting me stay."

"Well, any friend of my daughter's is a friend of mine."

Something flashed through his expression, gone before I could make sense of it.

"Of course, all of her enemies are my enemies, too." She said it as if she was trying to be funny, but we both heard the threat.

Apparently, my mama had gone badass.

God, I was going to have to see to it that she wasn't hanging out with Melanie so much.

He looked directly at me. "If she were mine, I'd fight for her, too.".

Royce

"Holy crapballs. That dinner was delicious, Mabel." Rhys mumbled it as he was shoveling fresh apple pie into his piehole.

No doubt, someone had gotten a good look at him and the phrase was coined.

Dude never shut up, which only made him more likable, which kind of annoyed me, too.

My entire being was riding on a razor-sharp edge.

Agitation burning a path through my body as I tried to sit there like a normal human being and not some squatter who was stealing space.

If I was being honest, this whole damn scene was a little hard to stomach.

Hanging out in this quaint home, sitting at an antique oblong dining table that was covered in a white embroidered tablecloth that had probably been in their family for generations, the dishes we were eating the most delicious meal I'd ever tasted surely hailing from the same time.

Mr. and Mrs. Ramsey were sitting to my right at the far end. Their youngest son, Lincoln, who was twenty-five and lived on a smaller house to the back of their property, sat between Mrs. Ramsey and Richard, who sat directly next to me.

Rhys and his mother sat to my left, and Emily rounded out the circle where she sat on the other side next to her father.

The entire dinner had been spent with the group chatting and visiting and catching up, and doing it because they actually fucking cared.

A family.

The real kind.

The right kind.

I glanced at Emily.

Screw the fucking apple pie.

She was the most delicious thing I'd tasted. This wanting more was getting excruciating.

Feeling the weight of my stare, she peeked across at me and gave me a tender, shy smile.

Girl fucking stole my breath. Ripped it right out of my lungs. I shifted in the turbulence. In this unending need.

Richard and Emily's father cleared his throat. "So, Mr. Reilly, we're glad to have you in our home. Rich here has been telling me about the opportunity you've brought about for the band. I always knew these two would make it, but it's good to see someone coming along beside them who believes in them the way that me and their mama always have. Rare thing to find someone so committed to their job that they actually take the time to see it through right, the way you're doing."

Lenny Ramsey basically looked like the image of what I'd expect Richard to look like in thirty years.

Tall and strong, a lean body that had barely thickened with age, face wrinkled like a map from years of manual labor and squinting beneath the sun.

A man who was not to be fucked with but who you could come

to with anything.

Loyal to the bone.

"Nice, Dad, nice. Here I am, working my tail off day after day for you, and the only people you believe in around here are these two jerks who took off and left us in their stardust."

Lincoln was all grins when he looked at his family around the table, pride shining in his eyes, the tone of his words wholly playful.

Like this was the only way he could say he was happy for them, too.

Mr. Ramsey chuckled. "Don't worry, son. Wouldn't trust these two to run the family business. They'd be off in the back fiddling with some instrument or another, totally forgetting there are phones to be answered and orders to be filled. We'd be bankrupt in no time."

His words didn't hold an ounce of displeasure.

"If you're so spun up over it, I'll trade you." Richard elbowed Lincoln with the tease.

Lincoln's eyes went round in feigned horror. "More money than I could ever spend and women throwing themselves at me night after night? No thanks. Sounds miserable."

The faked frown on Richard's face was just as grim. "It's terrible. Let me tell you, little brother, you would not want to have to stand a day in my shoes. You'd never make it."

Mrs. Ramsey tsked. "Now, you all stop making light. There is a whole lot of work that goes into this music business. Emily, Rich, and Rhys work just as hard as the rest of us, just different."

"Yeah!" Rhys shouted around another bite.

"We work long hours, and the road gets really lonely," Emily added.

Lincoln lifted his hands and pretended to play the world's tiniest violin. "Keep singin' it, sister. I feel terrible for you."

He winked at her. Pure affection.

I had the urge to rub at the raw spot on my chest.

Mr. Ramsey returned his attention to me, lifting his brow, drawing the topic back to his original question.

I cleared my throat. "I only want the best for them."

214

He smiled and rocked back in his chair. "And you believe your record label is the best? Mylton Records?"

He wasn't testing me. He was legit a straight-shooter. Asking me man-to-man.

Guilt thickened my throat.

"In the end, it will be." I gave him the most honest answer that I could.

Still, it drew tension, something unsettled moving around the table while all eyes landed on me.

"In the end . . . meaning when we finally sign," Richard jumped in, like he was doing me a solid and saving my ass.

I glanced at him.

Hard trust blazed back, though it was inscribed with a demand. Like he was telling me I'd better not do anything to betray that trust.

Anxiety clawed, and I took a drink of my water to try to swallow it down.

"I know that it will be," Emily added in a low voice.

The sudden banging on the front door jolted everyone from the conversation. Mr. Ramsey stood, wiping his mouth with his napkin and tossing it to the table. "I'll get that."

The dining room was in a nook off the living room, and only the edge of the front door was visible from where I sat. He moved that way, his long legs taking the room in an easy stride. I could see his entire demeanor shift when he opened the door.

His voice was lowered, but still it traveled through the space, anger lining the question like a rod of steel. "What do you want?"

"I want to talk to Emily." The voice was pissed and hard, fueled by indignation.

My entire being ignited, a flaming fury, immediately uncontained. Even though I couldn't see him, didn't have a clue what he looked like, it didn't even take a second for me to realize who the bastard was.

My gaze instantly jumped to the girl. The girl who was practically seizing, every muscle in her delicate body knotting in disdain and disgust and hurt.

The entire room fell silent.

Eyes darting everywhere, not sure what to do.

My hands fisted under the table, rage when I took in the expression on her face as she fumbled to stand, shaking so hard she could barely find her footing.

"Emily," Richard questioned with dread and his own brand of anger. She settled those green eyes on him. Whatever passed between the two of them made Richard sink back down into his seat.

Couldn't look away as the girl slowly inched toward the door, her spine rigid and her spirit spilling out all over the place.

"Emily," the prick said like he had the right to claim her when she came into sight.

"Em." Her father's voice was caution, telling her she didn't have to do anything she didn't want to do. She had a ton of people there to back her up if she wanted us to toss the prick from the property.

Hell, I was about to build a ten-foot wall around her and paint it with signs that read *No Trespassing*.

"It's okay, we probably need to talk a few things out," she whispered, her voice tight and laced with caution, though I could see her giving her father a reassuring nod. It only stoked the fire that lapped and surged inside me.

Warily, her father seemed to give, and she touched his arm as she passed and stepped out into the darkness, shutting the door behind her.

Nerves fucking raced, so goddamn hard I could feel the beat of my blood through every inch of my body.

I gripped onto the edge of the table like it could be the anchor that kept me pinned in that chair.

Trying not to spin out of control.

To do something that I couldn't take back.

Mr. Ramsey stood at the closed door in outright reluctance before he finally heaved out a sigh, roughing a hand over the spot balding on the top of his head as he headed back into the dining room.

Rhys swore under his breath, and Richard bounced his knee, while Lincoln looked at their father like he was waiting for him to give the cue to attack.

Hostility seethed in all of them.

It only fed my aggression.

Mrs. Ramsey and Rhys's mother tried to strike up a conversation to cover the bleak mood that descended on the room.

Directly to the side of the dining room, the intimation of voices echoed through the thin walls of the house, gnarled and distorted.

Through the side window, I could barely make out the shape of the girl, her shoulders slouched and her arms crossed over her chest.

A guard.

Security.

Comfort.

Heat blanketed my skin, and I could feel the beads of sweat gathering on my forehead.

Swore I felt a piece of myself crack. Splinter away. Slammed with the need to be that for her.

Her protector.

Her shield.

The one she could rely on when the people she'd relied on most had left her high and dry.

To carry her and let her carry a little bit of me.

Stupid.

So fucking stupid.

I fisted my hands tighter and tried not to blow.

The prick's voice got louder, elevated in anger. Emily's response was a string of words that I couldn't understand, though I could tell she was upset.

"This is bullshit," Richard grumbled.

There was a scuffle of sounds. Footsteps and shouts and a small crash.

That was it.

All I could take.

Mr. Ramsey was starting to stand, but I was already on my feet. Violence streaked through my muscles and aggression slicked across my flesh.

Fire heating me to the core.

Mr. Ramsey frowned in surprise, hovering between sitting and standing. Richard stuck out his hand, his gaze slanting to me for a beat, a warning and a buoy. "Think Royce has this one, Dad."

Confusion and speculation crowded the lines on their father's brow, but I couldn't find it in myself to stop. Didn't care what anyone else thought in that moment because the only thing that mattered was I needed to be there for Emily.

"I'm just going to make sure she's okay." The words cracked, a blatant lie and the outright truth.

Their voices continued to carry, their argument a muffle of quickened words and old hurt and new wounds that were bleeding through the atmosphere. Could feel the entire table watching me as I moved through the living room, opened the door, and stepped out onto the porch.

Heatwaves instantly clawed at my overheated skin, sticky and thick.

From the side of the house, Emily's heaving words became clear, agony threaded through every one. "No, Nile, you don't get to make accusations about my life. It's none of your concern. Not anymore."

"Are you fuckin' kidding me?" His voice was hard. Riddled with scorn. I wanted to skin the flesh from his bones.

I took a silent step in the direction of their voices, trying to hold onto my quickly dwindling control. To remind myself I was only out there in case she needed me. That this wasn't about me needing to enact a little piece of revenge for that piece of shit hurting her.

"Is this about that freak who was in that picture? Writing you up like some kind of pathetic poet? Seriously, what the fuck is wrong with you, Emily? Don't even know you anymore, running around with some goth boy who looks like a junkie or some shit . . . what is he, some kind of wannabe rocker?" His voice was pure disgust. "I thought you were better than that."

"You're gonna judge him when you're the one who cheated on me?"

"You were gone for three fuckin' months."

"And that makes it okay?"

"A man has needs, Emily."

"Glad to know I didn't fill them. And guess what, Nile, I have needs, too. And I needed you to be there for me. For you to be waitin', just like you'd promised you would be."

"Right . . . you wanted me waiting around for when it was convenient for you."

"You have no idea what you're even sayin'. I *loved* you. And I came back because I needed you more than I'd ever needed you . . . and I found you with someone else. You destroyed me. Ruined the last piece of true belief I was clinging to."

He surged into her space. "Let me fix it then."

She tried to step away. "It's too late for that."

"This is ridiculous, Emily. Just . . . get over it. We need to move on with our lives."

"I already am," she told him.

No doubt, the asshole took that as her admission that she was with someone else because he grabbed her by the arm. She squeaked a sound of surprise.

Destruction screamed through my veins.

I eased off the side of the porch.

"You think you're going to walk away from me? After I sat around here waiting for you to get over this stupid fantasy world of yours for twelve fucking years? I don't think so, Emily."

"Let her go." I pressed the demand through clenched teeth, hard as stones that pummeled him from behind.

The prick froze. He was still gripping Emily's wrist as he turned to look at me. He was lucky I didn't rip his arm from his body.

A sneer twisted up his face. "You think this is any of your business?"

Aggression curled.

Tension mounting.

I forced myself to remain planted. Forced myself not to give in to the insanity I could feel blanketing my brain, covering me in a cloud of madness.

"Yes," I told him.

Simply.

Wholly.

He cracked a menacing smile. "Move on, fuckboy. She's my fiancée, so do yourself a favor and take your city ass back in that house before you get yourself introduced to the kind of country welcome you don't want."

"I told you to let the girl go." I could almost taste the venom on my tongue.

Emily yanked her arm, trying to free it from his hold. "Just . . . let me go, Nile. It's over."

He squeezed harder, derangement spilling out. "It's over when I goddamn say it's over."

Emily gasped in pain, and I watched those green eyes go wide with fear and surprise and more of that hurt that kept getting dealt her way.

Jerking harder, she managed to break free, but with the momentum, she stumbled back, losing her footing.

She tripped backward and slammed to the ground.

He turned to go for her, and Emily was backpedaling, scooting on her butt away from the bastard who actually thought I was going to stand there and allow him to violate her all over again.

There was nothing left.

That insanity that had been building for years came to a head.

Breaking.

Logic shot.

Rationale gone.

I flew for him, feet pounding the ground like a war drum. Soon as I got close enough, I threw an arm around his neck and got him in a chokehold from behind.

I cinched down tight.

A sound of shocked aggression shot up his throat, and his hands instantly came up to my arm that was locked tight. Fucker kicked and scratched and struggled to break free.

The prick was one of those brawny, meaty fucks, asshole trying to toss me like I was just going to let go.

I squeezed tighter, cutting off his airflow, my voice a threat in his ear. "I won't think twice to end you."

Could feel the panic ripple through his body. He threw an

elbow backward and caught me in the rib. Pain splintered, punching the air from my lungs. I only held on tighter, throwing a fist into his side from behind. He howled, shouting in pain, and he lurched forward.

The movement set me off-balance. He managed to break free and whirled around before I could process it. A fist came at me and hooked me on the jaw.

Hard.

I grunted through the explosion of fire that burst across my face.

"You like that?" he taunted, jumping around and lifting his fists.

I just swallowed it down, let it feed the fury, the violence that erupted in my blood. I moved for him, faster than he could prepare himself, and I threw a jab to the right side of his face, another to the left.

Skin split and blood splattered.

I could feel Emily's torment rolling along the ground, her cries filling the night.

Nile bellowed in pain, swiping the blood dripping from the gash on his cheek and lunging for me. He got his arms around my waist, his weight taking both of us to the ground.

We hit it with a thud. In an instant, we were a tangle of scrambling, toiling bodies, both of us vying to pin the other. Fists flew, grunts and hits and curses filling the air. He clocked me on the right ear. Pain split through my head like the pierce of a knife.

Rage and bloodshed. A disturbance that glowed and amplified.

A flash of red.

A strobe of dark.

I tossed him off and had him pinned before I even realized I'd done it. Fists pounded his face.

Relentless.

Unforgiving.

He deserved no forgiveness.

Bones cracked, blood splattering as I struck him.

Again and again.

Consumed by this madness.

By this rage.

Hands grabbed me from behind, trying to drag me off. I only fought harder to get to him.

"Royce, stop! Dude, fucking stop! It's done. It's done."

Air raking my throat, Richard hauled me off the bloodied heap of the prick who lay moaning on the ground. Face mangled and unrecognizable.

I thrashed, needing to get in one more hit.

"Cool it, dude," Richard demanded. "Calm the fuck down."

"Oh my god." Emily's mother rushed around the side of the house. "What happened?"

Her gaze moved around the scene, calculating, adding it up, and she dropped down to kneel at the side of the bastard like he deserved any grace or good.

Not when he was trying to wreck it.

Except she gripped him by the jaw, leaning over him, spitting the words, "I do not ever want to see you on my property again. Do you understand me, Nile?"

She stood. "Someone get this garbage off my lawn."

Richard kept my arms pinned behind me as she moved for Emily, who was huddled with Rhys's mother over by the side of the house.

Horror etched on her gorgeous face, fear in her eyes.

I wanted to feel it.

Regret.

Remorse for doing what I'd done.

But I couldn't will it to come.

Because I was a monster. Just like I'd warned her from the beginning.

Retribution was coming.

And I'd only just begun.

Royce

Blood-tinged water swirled in the tub where I stood under the steaming spray of the shower, the color fading to clear as I scrubbed away the evidence. Every inch of my body was on fucking fire, skin covered in bruises and scrapes and cuts that I was happy to wear like a brand.

One sleazebag down. Only a couple more to go.

After rinsing the last of the residue from my flesh, I turned off the shower, stepped out onto the rug, and grabbed the fresh towel Mrs. Ramsey had left me with when she'd told me I should get cleaned up. That was right before the woman had whispered a quiet, "Thank you," under her breath and shut the door, leaving me alone with the disorder still rioting in my spirit.

I dried myself off, the steam of the room sticky on my skin, a clammy sensation coming up from the inside.

How the fuck had I let everything get so far out of control?

Slipping.

Royce Reilly was known for his discipline and restraint.

His ability to get a job done.

Which was why my stepfather had put so much trust and faith in me when I knew it was about the last thing he'd wanted to do.

I was valuable.

An asset.

And now I was one mistake away from blowing the whole thing. From missing the purpose.

Fuck.

I could still get my ass hauled away to jail for what just went down. With my record? I'd probably land back in prison for years.

But how could I not stand up for her?

A light tapping sounded at the door.

Heaving out a strained breath, I wrapped the towel around my waist, completely on edge when I cracked open the door to the darkened hallway, not sure who or what was going to be waiting for me on the other side.

Richard.

He narrowed his eyes and leaned up against the open doorway, eyes making a quick sweep to see what damage had been done. Taking in the cuts and the blossoming patches of blue and purple and red.

Letting loose a low whistle, he looked up to meet my face, arching a brow. "You good, man?"

I laughed out an incredulous sound. "Just perfect."

He gave a tight nod. "You caused some mad destruction out there."

"Fucker deserved it."

"Yeah, he did." I wasn't sure if I was surprised by his response or not. "Kind of wished it was me who got to do the honors. But looking at you now? Have to say I'm glad I let you step up and take the fall."

He had the nerve to grin.

Short laughter rumbled out. "Pussy."

He chuckled. "Hey, just speaking the truth. You look a little rough for the wear."

I raked a hand through my wet hair. "Feel a little rough, honestly."

The second of lightness morphed, his brow knitting with worry.

"Don't know you all that well, but it seems to me you short-circuited out there."

Discomfort had me fidgeting, muscles rigid. "Some things are worth losing your mind over."

Contemplation moved through his expression before he leaned back to glance both ways down the empty hall where we were on the second floor, making sure it was clear before he turned his focus back on me. "I'm not going to ask you why you went ballistic. I think it's plenty obvious. Only thing I'm going to say is don't play fucking games, man. My sister has been played enough."

"Last thing I want to do is hurt her."

Remorse drew his brow together. "And the last thing I want is to see her hurt." He hesitated, casting his attention to the ground before he looked back at me, some kind of worried confession in his tone. "Listen . . . my sister . . . she implied she knows about some shit goin' down in my life right now. Pretty sure you were implying it, too."

He searched my face.

Rage banged against my ribs. I tamped it down. "Shit goes down in Hollywood all the time, Ramsey. Sex, drugs, and rock & roll. Isn't that what they say?"

Wasn't sure I could give him anything. He couldn't be trusted if he was involved in anything with Cory Douglas.

His lips pursed in remorse. "Yeah, well, I stumbled into that bullshit on accident, Royce. Not sure what you know, but I need you to understand I never wanted to get mixed up in it. Tryin' to get out. Make sure this band remains unscathed. Just . . . can you find out what she knows? How involved she is? Need to make sure she's safe."

"Maybe you should actually talk to your sister."

"Have tried a thousand times, man. She shuts me down. Tells

me she's fine. Know she's putting on a front, and I don't know how to help her if she won't let me see. Need to make sure she's good. I can't risk her."

My own guilt pulsed. "Like I told you, the last thing I want is to see her hurt."

He stepped back, pinned me to the spot with a hard gaze. "Then don't let her."

"I only want to do what is best for her."

"You gonna tell her who you are? What your history is?"

If only he knew the half of it.

Trying to hold it together, I attempted to scrape the misery from my voice. "It's more complicated than that."

"You care about my sister? Then uncomplicate it."

"Life's not always that cut and dry."

He staked his fingers through his hair, looking to the ground before looking back up at me. "No. But when we care about someone? We give all we have. All it takes. No matter the cost."

With that, he left me standing there without the chance to respond. Like I'd have a good response, anyway. Like I could change any of this. Go back and erase it and be something better.

Huffing out a breath, I finished drying off and dressed in a clean pair of jeans and a tee. No sign of another clean-cut suit.

Guessed my life really was coming to a head.

Finally, I forced myself out into the dimly lit hall. Most of the lights in the house had been cut, everything silent and stilled, like all the spirits locked up behind closed bedroom doors were being held hostage by the uneasy buzz that remained in the atmosphere.

I started for the guest room at the end of the hall.

I made it halfway past Emily's door before I fumbled to a stop. Held.

Tugged back by the need to go to her.

To touch her face and whisper her name.

Muted light glowed from under her door, like her soul was spilled across the floor.

I looked to the empty guest room at the end of the hall, trying to convince myself to take the fifteen steps to get there.

But no.

There I was—rapping my knuckles lightly at the wood that separated us, my forehead pressed to it, sure she could feel me the exact same way I felt her.

Pulled.

Drawn.

Hooked.

Movement stirred from the other side, and the door creaked open an inch.

One of those green eyes peered out through the crack, soft and sad and eager.

Like she had been expecting me.

Waiting for me.

"Royce." My name sounded like honey on her tongue.

Need twisted in my guts.

Delirium.

Lust.

"Hey," I grunted low, looking away before I dragged my gaze back to the one who had the power to change everything. "Wanted to check on you."

Those eyes moved over me as she edged the door open farther.

I got hit with a wave of her.

A swell that nearly knocked me off my feet. Cherries and the sky and all things good. She'd showered and changed, that hair tied loosely on her head, wearing black sleep shorts and a draping cream-colored sweatshirt that hung off one shoulder, that delicate flesh glowing like moonshine.

"You wanted to check on me?" she whispered so low, with so much disbelief that I felt my heart clutch, my spirit trying to prepare itself for the rejection. For the moment when this girl finally realized that I was no good.

Her teeth raked at her bottom lip, and her chest heaved before her hand was coming out to lightly brush across the small cut on my cheek. "Look at you. I can't believe you got yourself in the middle of that for me."

Could feel my face pinch up in my own disbelief. "I'd do it a million times over if it meant protecting you. The only thing I regret is that you had to witness it. That I lost control like that in front of you."

Her head shook. "That was on him, Royce. He was the instigator of hate. Of violence. You were just protectin' me. Why's it feel like that's what you have to keep doing?"

"Maybe that's what I'm meant to do."

There I went. Spouting the things I shouldn't say.

"I hate that you feel like you need to take care of me. That I'm helpless."

A hiss of refusal pushed between my clenched teeth, and I edged a step into her room, backing her inside. I snapped the door shut behind us.

Instantly, I felt the walls close in. The air grew dense and deep, so thick it was hard to move.

She stood in the middle of it like an anchor.

A beacon.

Soulshine.

So stunning, she was the only thing I could see.

"You think I think you're helpless?" My head shook as I took another step toward her. "You think I don't see how hard it is for you to walk out on that stage night after night? That I don't feel your fear? Your struggles? And you do it, anyway. Because you're a fighter."

With shaky fingers, she reached out and traced along the angle of my face. "You are the fighter, Royce. A defender and a guard. It's becoming harder and harder to stand without you."

A grimace pulled to my mouth, and Emily turned away and slowly moved over to her window. Tendrils of blonde cascaded down her back, falling free of the twist. She crossed her arms over her chest, the girl's shoulders heaving as she stared out into the night.

"We all deserve to have someone stand beside us. All of us, Emily. I'm here for you . . . because I want to be. Because there's nothing I want to see more than you becoming every single thing you were meant to be. You are a star."

Fuck.

I wanted to be that person for her.

Wanted to be good enough.

Right enough.

"Royce . . . there is something I need to tell you, and I need to start from the beginning."

She peeked back at me before she continued, "Nile and I?"

The thought of the two of them together sent possession streaking through my bloodstream.

She froze as if she felt the force of it. She hugged herself tighter, her confession so quiet as she murmured it into the shadows lapping in the room.

"We were gonna have a baby."

Pain flooded from her when she made the confession.

Every cell in my body cringed.

Twisted and gnarled.

At the same time, her entire body seized for a single moment.

The two of us tied in that second.

Sharing grief.

Thing was, I wasn't sure which of us the torment was coming from.

Visions assaulted me—so severe I felt them like bullets. *An infant in my arms. Her tiny cries. Her sweet face.* My hand darted out to the wall to keep myself standing.

When Emily looked back at me again, tears soaked her face.

"You don't have to explain anything to me." Panic had me loosing the words. A coward who didn't know if he could handle hearing her truth. The girl was fully offering her trust to me, and I wasn't sure I trusted myself with it any longer.

No longer sure I could see this through.

My intentions blurry.

Fading into the background of this girl who'd become the light inside of me.

She shifted to face me. "After tonight? I need to tell you this, Royce. I need you to listen. I need you to hear me. I need you to know all the pieces of me."

My spirit lurched.

Making a play to meet with her. I forced myself to remain rooted by the door when she shifted around to face me.

"We were together for years, Royce. Years. Having a family

was the one thing I knew for certain I wanted for my life. I always wanted to play. To sing and bring songs to life. To whisper hope into people's ears when maybe they needed to hear it most. Is it wrong that the one thing I needed to hear the most was someone callin' me *Mama*?"

She pressed her hands to her chest like she was trying to hold that broken part of her heart inside.

I had to stop myself from dropping to my knees.

I wanted to rush her. Wrap her up and promise her I would fix it.

Moisture clouded those jade eyes, the girl chewing at her bottom lip like she was praying I could understand even a small amount of her grief.

She didn't get that I felt it like a punch to the gut.

That I got it on a level that had sent me spiraling for years.

"I was so happy, Royce." Emily whispered it. A choked confession as she turned that gorgeous gaze up to me. "But when I lost the baby?"

Her expression wrenched and grief stalled her words. "It was like there was a bolt that no longer fit. A piece that was no longer holding us together."

There wasn't anything I could do but move her way.

Drawn.

The girl a flame.

A light I couldn't turn away from.

I brushed back a lock of hair matted to her cheek.

"I get it, Emily. I get it." The words were razors raking my throat. "Losing a child is the worst thing that can happen to anyone."

Emily's gaze moved over me. Need and hope and everything I was terrified of shining back. "That's why I'm telling you, Royce . . . because I know you get me. You're not gonna make light of something that was so important to me." She swallowed hard. "A part of me hated Nile for not being there for me, for drifting away, but there's a bigger part that knows I pushed him away."

She pressed both her hands to her flat stomach. "Afterward, I felt so empty. My heart no longer felt right. No longer beat right. I couldn't even conjure up an 'I miss you' when I talked with him on the phone."

Desperate, I cradled her face in my hands. Night wrapped us in shadows.

Angling my head, I dipped down, my nose brushing hers. "That's not your fault. You don't have to feel guilty for mourning. Not ever."

I tried to sound reasonable. To cover up the misery cutting me to shreds.

She reached up and gripped me by the wrists.

Hanging on like I was a lifeline.

A buoy.

"I was pretty sure I'd hit rock bottom. Depression took me over. The spark I'd felt to sing and play dimmed so far that I thought it might have been extinguished. But I had no idea how bad it was goin' to get."

Emily's eyes pleaded with me to see.

Like she wanted me to reach inside and see all that she had suffered.

Hold it.

Fuck, I wanted to.

I increased my hold. "You can tell me anything, Emily. You can trust me."

Fear traipsed across her face. The same fear she'd been wearing since I met her. "Rich . . . h-h-he got himself into trouble. Into something that I can't even process or understand."

My chest fisted. Knew well enough where she was going with this. "Tell me, sweet girl."

Agony pulsed through her expression. "Cory Douglas . . . he's involved in something wicked, Royce. Something so bad that it hurts just thinking about it. And my brother . . . I . . . I think he might be wrapped up in the middle of it." Her voice lowered in dread.

To a hurt I could feel cutting her wide open.

"Cory . . . after one of the shows we opened for his band, he lured me to his hotel room. He said he needed to talk with me."

Fury raced. This overwhelming need to annihilate taking me over. Completely.

Fuck justice.

Fuck my freedom.

I'd gladly spend my life rotting behind bars if it meant it would keep this look off Emily's face.

"I should have known, Royce . . . I should have known. There was this . . . chill in the air. Evil. I could feel it crawling over my skin. Lifting the hairs at the nape of my neck."

She blinked a bunch of times, like she was trying to see but wanted to block the memories at the same time.

"The second I stepped through the door, he had me pinned against the wall. He grabbed me by the jaw and he . . . he said my brother had taken what was his and he'd chosen me to pay off his debt."

A shudder rolled down Emily's spine.

I gathered her closer. Wanting to bear some of it. Wanting to shoulder it.

All the while my mind was slammed with a memory carved so deep in my brain I could never forget it.

"What are you doing here? I said you were out," I'd grated, barely containing my fury as I backed him toward the door.

He laughed.

A maniacal, unhinged sound.

"You took the one thing that meant anything to me . . . now I'm going to take everything from you. You should have known better than to fuck with me, Royce. Now I'm going to fuck with you. Don't say I didn't warn you."

Rage burned through my blood. It took all I had to remain standing in front of Emily.

She inhaled a shaky breath. "He grabbed me by the arm and dragged me over to the table. Pictures of Richard were spread all over it. Pictures of Richard with a woman who wasn't dressed. She was kneeling with her arms tied behind her back. Some of them were of her on his lap. One had them leaving a hotel room."

Emily dropped her attention to the ground, unable to look at me when she said it. "I think . . . I think she was being forced to be there."

My insides curled in aggression.

In my own disgust.

I hooked my index finger under her chin, coaxing her to look at me. "Emily. Precious."

That energy sifted around us. Taking a different shape.

Her tongue darted out, swiping across her quivering bottom lip. "Cory had pointed at the picture . . . said that woman belonged to him. That he'd *marked* her. At first, I was confused . . . I knew Cory was married—"

That word sent a stake of pain slicing through my being.

Refusing to feel the impact of it, I pulled Emily closer as she continued through a rush of quieted words. "—and that woman, she wasn't his wife. It all hit me in an instant . . . the disgusting mess they were involved in."

The words heaved from her throat, and I couldn't do anything but gather her up. "Fuck, Emily."

I pressed a frantic kiss to the top of her head, and she clung to me, her face buried in my throat. "I wanted to run, Royce. I wanted to scream and beg for help, but I was frozen. Frozen in fear and shock."

Her entire body rocked like an earthquake, and she dug her fingers into my chest. Words nothing but whimpers. "He forced me onto my knees like that girl, tied my wrists behind my back, and blindfolded me. Then . . . then he kissed me. Soft. Like I was an old lover."

Revulsion blazed across her skin.

Rancid and foul.

"Next thing I knew, he had me on a bed and was pushing up my skirt. I was begging him . . . begging him not to hurt me. To let me go. That I would give him anything."

She hiccupped for a breath, burrowing her face deeper into my throat, the words barely heard though I felt them to my soul. "He *marked* me, Royce. He carved an X on my hip. Just like he'd done to that girl. The pain—it was excruciating—I screamed even when he was threatening me not to make a sound. He told me I belonged to him, told me if I said a word, he was gonna expose my brother. Ruin us all."

"Jesus, Emily." My hands palmed the back of her head, her back, trying to give her comfort when I felt her completely coming apart.

Guilt clutched me in a vice.

Suffocating.

Those nails scraped deeper into my skin, like she was carving me with her grief. "When he took that knife and cut off my panties, I knew he was goin' to do terrible, terrible things to me, Royce. I knew it. He had me blindfolded, which I was only half grateful for, because then maybe it wouldn't seem so real."

I wrapped her tight.

No space between us.

That connection no longer pulling.

It was tying.

Binding us in a way there was no chance either of us would come back from.

She laughed a confused sound through her tears. "I got so lucky, Royce. Not ten seconds after I screamed, someone was knocking on the door, calling out, 'Room Service.' Cory had shouted that he hadn't ordered anything, but they kept pounding. Cory had leaned up and put his disgusting mouth by my ear and whispered that he'd be right back, warned me not to make a peep."

Her fingers curled in deeper, voice haggard. "It all happened so fast—the sound of Cory answering the door before it burst open. A fight broke out . . . all this banging and crashing. I started screaming, begging for help, and a second later, the room service guy was ripping at the ties on my wrists and picking me up from the bed. I was weeping when he carried me running across the room. He set me on my feet and whispered for me to run. So, I did, Royce. Three steps down the hall, I tore off that blindfold and didn't look back."

Destruction lined my muscles, and my bones creaked under the pressure.

Emily's grief banged against the walls. Banged against my spirit. She edged back, turning that unyielding gaze up to me, regret racing through her face. "Instead of calling the police to report what happened, I just . . . ran. Ran scared. Terrified for my brother and what he was involved in. Terrified for myself. I ran and ran until I got back here to Dalton. I up and left the band without a word. I didn't even check on that guy . . . don't even know what happened to him. I'm sure the second he saw it was Cory, he'd been too scared to say a word."

Her words hitched. Like she was begging for me to see. To get it. Not to judge her.

As if this girl could hold any of the blame.

"When I got to Dalton, I went to the house Nile and I shared. Things were already bad between us, but I needed someone to confide in. To stand beside me. I guess I was hardly surprised to find him with another woman. Still, I'd never felt so alone. So lost as that night, standing out there in the road. No home. No one to call. Terrified to tell someone and terrified not to. So, I kept it bottled, let it fester."

She splayed her hands out over her sweet heart. "I let it fester and fester until it started coming out as these anxiety attacks that I couldn't control. So much guilt for letting that man roam free, so much worry over Richard, hiding something like that, for being involved in the first place. And then Cory started sending me messages . . . saying he would be back to take what was his and do it soon. It all became too much to handle."

With the pads of my thumbs, I swiped the tears from under her eyes.

"I'm going to end him, Emily. I promise you, I'm going to end him."

She brushed her fingers across my mouth, hope breaking across her gorgeous face. "I didn't tell you because I wanted you to enact revenge for me, Royce. I told you because you need to know what I have to come out and say. What this is going to mean for your job."

"Fuck my job."

Her voice softened, those fingers tracing my lips, their own brand of comfort. "But I told you for more than that, Royce. I told you because you are the only person I can trust. Because you're the first person in forever who I feel like understands me. Because you? You are the person I want standing by my side."

I wanted to be him.

Fuck, I wanted to be.

I wanted to be the guy she thought she was talking to.

"You're the reason I want to get on that stage each night, Royce, because I want you to *see* me. I want you to *hear* my songs because I think you might be the only person in this world who can understand them. I want to sing them with you." On the last, her voice dipped with need.

With outright desperation.

"Emily." It was both a plea and a warning.

"Royce," she whispered back. "Don't you see it? I found you when I needed you most."

That feeling rose in the middle of us. Intense and deep and bigger than I ever should have let it grow.

I gathered up one of her hands and pressed her fingers to my lips. "I'm not sure I'm strong enough for that. I wish that I was," I murmured, searching for strength. For a reason to keep this charade up.

Guilt crushed me under a million pounds of stone.

Obliterating.

Too much.

I had to get out of there before I made this worse. Before I hurt this girl any more than she'd already been.

"You are that person," she almost begged. "I see it. I *feel* it."

She traced her fingertips over the battering going down in my chest.

My head shook. "No. I'm not, Emily. You are too precious for me to allow myself to be another man to do you wrong. But I promise you, Cory Douglas will pay for what he did."

It took everything I had to straighten and head for the door, my stomach somewhere in my throat and my heart on the floor. Her voice stopped me halfway out.

"Before you walk out that door, Royce, I need you to know something." She slowly pushed to standing. Her presence slammed me from across the space.

Wholly consuming.

She took a step forward. "Before we sign after the show on Sunday night, before I stand up and take a stance against Cory and risk losing it all, before I put my brother's future on the line, I need you to know."

Energy hummed, as powerful as her words. "I love you. I love you in a way I've never loved anyone before. I know you don't feel it back, but I need you to know."

Love is the heart's greatest deceit.

It screamed in my mind.

A lump grew in my throat, my tongue so thick that I couldn't speak.

Couldn't answer.

Couldn't process what she'd said.

I stepped out and snapped the door quietly behind me.

Darkness consumed me out in the hall.

I stood frozen in it.

Unable to move.

Stuck by the sound of her heart crying out. The girl the loudest song.

Truth.

Truth.

Truth.

And I realized I had nothing left.

Only her.

Without thinking it through, I swung the door back open and pushed back inside.

twenty-one

Emily

*S*hock ripped up my throat when the door banged back open without any warning.

Energy raced, Royce's presence surging back into the room.

A storm that'd hit land.

Overpowering.

As terrifying as it was beautiful.

I guessed that's what I felt when he wrapped one of those strong arms around my waist and tucked me tight against the erratic beat of his heart.

Terrified by the intensity of what I felt.

The stunning relief.

The overwhelming joy.

By the realization that I felt more for this man in the weeks that I'd known him than what I'd felt in all the years I'd been with

Nile.

He splayed his other hand across my face. Onyx eyes flashed like strikes of lightning in the muted light. "You think I don't feel it back? Fuck. I love you, Emily. I love you so goddamn much I can't think. Can't see. Can't feel anything but this need I feel for you."

My heart pressed and pulled and thudded, growing so big inside of me I was sure it was gonna rupture where it pressed against my ribs.

"I love you," I rushed to whisper back.

"Fuck." Royce dropped his forehead to mine, his eyes squeezed tight. "Say it again."

"I love you, Royce. I love you so much more than I've ever loved anyone or anything. You've ruined me."

That was it.

His aura gasoline.

My confession a match.

We struck.

Our mouths and bodies collided in a frenzy of greed.

Hands ripping and touching and raking. Impassioned kisses of warring teeth and lips and tongues.

We bit and licked and stroked in a desperate play to consume.

The rhythm of our hearts an erratic thunder that rumbled in the air and rippled across our skin. We spun and spun as we fought to get closer, me fumbling to get the shirt over his head, my palms pressing flat over the hot planes of his magnificent body.

His cut abs shook and flexed beneath my touch, his hands diving under the fabric of my sweatshirt, dragging it up as he trailed his hands up my back. The man's fingers reached all the way around to run up my sides as he pulled the sweatshirt over my head.

My chest heaved, chills streaking as my bare flesh was hit with the cool air that pumped through the vents. My nipples puckered, and my small breasts ached for his touch, this unending need gushing through my body, wringing me in a fist of lust.

His touch chased away the chill, his mouth following suit, crazed as his lips ran the line of my shoulder, caressing down across my collarbone as he cupped my breasts in his hands. "Shit . . . fuck . . . Emily. You are perfect. You are perfect."

We were spinning, frantic. The two of us banged into the dresser as we moved deeper into my room, lost to this delirious dance.

I peppered a million kisses across his chest, across the tattoo that shattered a piece of my heart.

Love is the heart's greatest deceit.

"I love you, I love you, I love you," I murmured across the inked flesh. Like I could heal whatever wound had written it there. I prayed he'd understand that piece that broke off belonged to him. That I was giving it to him. An offering to make him whole if he would let me.

And if those words were true, then I wanted to be his only lie.

He groaned, twisting a hand up in my hair, palming my bottom and tucking me against the rock-hard length begging from his pants as he kissed me mad.

Dizziness swept through my mind, desire so fierce it was blinding. My eyes only accustomed to him.

That face and this body and his mesmerizing soul. He backed me toward the bed. His fingers found the elastic band of my shorts, and he shoved them down as we went. I twisted them off my ankles, whimpering with need when he tossed me onto the bed.

Totally naked.

Bare.

Exposed in a way that I'd never been.

I pushed up onto my hands, heart screaming at my chest, as if it were trying to break out and find a way to get back closer to him.

"Look at you," he murmured, so rough, I felt it scrape across my flesh.

Chills spiraled down my spine, getting lost with the need shimmering on my skin.

"First time I saw you, you knocked the breath out of me, Emily Ramsey. Prettiest thing I'd ever seen. But it was this I felt."

He climbed onto the bed, splaying one of those big hands over the thunder banging in my chest.

Everything heaved, my breath and my soul.

"I felt you, too."

Something staked through his expression, grief and guilt, more of that shadowy darkness that howled with his harsh, raw beauty. I wanted to traipse into the savagery of it.

I pressed his hand closer, refusing to let him go. "Something has always been missing inside of me, Royce. Something I didn't understand. It was you. It was you."

A space carved out in the middle of me that hummed like a song. A plea that whispered to be filled.

"I didn't think I'd ever feel again. Wasn't supposed to. You changed everything." His words were coarse. Gravel. As rugged as his muscles that flexed and bowed, the man so big where he hovered over me.

"That's what fallin' does, Royce. It changes everything. Because when you fall, you don't know where you're going to land. This . . . this was where I wanted to be. To fall and land in the safety of your arms."

A growl reverberated up his throat, and he was raining a frenzy of kisses down my throat.

A downpour of devotion.

"I won't let anyone hurt you. Not ever again."

He kept exploring my body with his mouth, kissing over the swell of my breast before he was pulling a nipple into his mouth. He lapped at the sensitive flesh with his tongue.

Flames shot through the middle of me, lighting up every cell. My hips bucked, seeking friction. "Please. Royce. I need you."

I was starting to beg, little pleas filling my childhood room as he traveled down my quivering belly.

I lost my breath as he kissed over the scar on my hip, the mark Cory had left when he tried to violate me. I'd worn it like shame. But I knew better now. Knew I had to stand, that holding my tongue and burying my pain wasn't going to help anyone.

"You are the most courageous person I know. So goddamn gorgeous. Inside and out. Wanna get lost, Precious. Give you everything you deserve." He rumbled the words in a maddening puzzle across my trembling belly.

"Royce, I need you."

He lifted his head. The man so beautiful my lungs faltered at the sight.

Every time.

But this time . . . this time he was mine.

He edged back off the bed and shucked the jeans from his hips, pushing them down his muscular legs and stepping out of them.

He stood at the side of the bed, completely naked, him looking at me, me looking at him.

Two of us devouring the other with our eyes.

My mouth watered and my throat went dry.

The man was covered in a canvas of ink, his skin swelling in spots from the battle he'd fought.

The man standing for me.

And I knew right then that I would always stand for him.

My gaze traced over chiseled muscle and sinister innuendo, the man a song written of scars and tragedy.

I was so ready for him to let me see. To let me bear some of what he held.

His thick penis bobbed against his stomach, hard and engorged, dripping from the tip. I scooted up my bed, planting my feet on the mattress and spreading my knees, asking for what I wanted.

Him.

All of him.

Everything.

A growl echoed through my room. Bouncing from the walls. Amplifying the feeling.

"You have any idea how sexy you are? Voice the sweetest sound and body the greatest temptation?" he grated.

"Funny, how I could say the exact same thing about you. But how is it temptation when two souls belong?"

I swore, there was a low hum in the room. A call. A rhythm that sped out of time.

"Do you hear that, Royce? Do you hear me calling for you? I think I have been my whole life."

He climbed onto the bed and crawled over me. My breaths

came shorter and shorter as he nestled his body between my thighs, hands planted on either side of my head to hold himself up.

"Your voice is the only song I hear." He leaned down and plucked my earlobe between his teeth before he whispered at the flesh, "Soulshine."

My spirit shivered.

He kept me pinned with those eyes as he reached down, guiding himself, the blunt head of him pressing at my center.

A breathless whimper left my lips. A breath that Royce swallowed as he filled me in a quick, possessive thrust. Sensation blistered, the man so big, stretching me wide and filling me full.

I could barely breathe, my breath gone and my heart lost.

"Fuck . . . you are perfect. So perfect," he grated through the softest kiss, the man always an enigma, dark and light, tender and raw.

He searched for his own air, only finding me.

My fingers sank into his shoulders, holding on tight as he began to move. Hard and deep and a little rough.

Just like I knew he would be.

Bliss. Bliss. Bliss.

Every second.

Every touch and nip of teeth. Every stroke and kiss.

This man who consumed me whole, took me prisoner, freed my soul.

I knew it as he watched down over me, his cock driving us both into madness, his eyes on me as our ragged pants filled the heated space between us.

I'd never felt so alive.

So right or whole.

He reached up and gripped the headboard as his pace increased, hips slapping as he took me hard, the other hand winding down to stroke me into oblivion.

Nothing left but this.

This moment.

Him and me. Me and him.

That moment when you felt something searing together.

A fusion.

Forged by fire.

Melted liquid that washed and spun and blended until it solidified into a different shape.

Something better than it'd been.

Us.

His lips parted and his fingers strummed and his hips slammed.

I felt him like a landslide. The sweeping of every cell. A gathering that shattered until I knew nothing but the pleasure I'd only found in this man.

An orgasm ripped through my body. My head rocked back, ecstasy a desperate moan that bled up my throat, every nerve ending alive, shivering with a pleasure so intense we'd gone off the Richter scale.

"Shh," he murmured, kissing the sound away, muffling it as I moaned and writhed and floated away into some faraway place that only existed to us.

"I've got you, Em. I've got you," he mumbled through his kiss. "I've got you. I'm not going to let you go."

My body tremored and my walls clutched, and Royce was trying to subdue a groan as he drove faster. His thrusts became erratic and fierce, so deep and desperate that they sent pleasure rebounding for a second time.

His hips jerked and snapped, and he clutched me like a lifeline. I felt the two of us falling.

The air whipping around us as we tumbled to a sacred place.

The man clinging to me as we plunged into the nothingness. Sped through the darkness.

I could feel everything breaking apart.

The foundation I'd known rocked.

Obliterated.

But I wasn't afraid.

I knew when we hit the bottom, he would be right there to catch me.

Darkness wisped like pale threads through the room, the night long, the quiet lulling us into a deeper peace.

Royce's arms were curled around my body, and I was tucked into the den of his chest. Secure and held.

Our hearts thrummed at a hushed pace, contentment covering me in a blanket of euphoria.

Royce hugged me closer and pressed a tender kiss to the side of my face. He exhaled. It sent a river of that energy rippling through the air. "I think we just defiled your childhood bed."

A smile pulled across my mouth as I snuggled down deeper into the well of his warmth. "I think it was worth it."

I could feel the force of his grin. "Yeah? Well the rest of the house might not be so agreeable." Amusement blustered through his quieted tone, the man the lightest I'd ever felt him be. I wanted to hold onto that, too.

His joy.

Wanted to be partner to it.

To feed it. Nourish it. Watch it grow.

"You think they heard us?" I whispered. Redness bloomed on my cheeks, and I trailed my fingers over the intricate king tattooed on the back of his hand, knowing he was mine. Realizing I was right there. Waiting for his next play.

"Nah." It was a short, muted laugh. A complete lie.

I cringed. "Oh my god. . . that is so embarrassing. My daddy is gonna kill me."

Those strong arms flexed as he pulled me tighter, so close I didn't know where he started and I ended, our legs bare and tangled, our hearts synced. A beat in time that only belonged to us. He nuzzled his face into my hair, his words a slight, growling murmur. "You still think it was worth it?"

I rolled around to face him, staring into those onyx eyes glinting in the threads of light that poured in through the window.

I touched his face. "You are worth everything."

He gathered my hand, kissed across my knuckles before he twined our fingers together. "I want to be. I want to be worthy of you. Want to give you everything in this life."

"What if the only thing I want is you?"

A grin played over his lush mouth, though there was something sad about it. "You have me, Emily. For the first time in years, I feel real. Like maybe I could be whole again." Somberness stole through his expression. "You were the last person I should have fallen for. It shouldn't have been possible for me to fall at all."

"Because you're a representative of Mylton Records?"

"Because my life is so much more complicated than you know." Guilt spilled out with the words. "Have a history, Emily. Baggage."

I shifted, and he rolled onto his back. I angled up on my side so I could look down on this man who I still couldn't really believe was lying in my bed. "What if I want to carry some of that baggage for you? Hold you the way you've been holding me? That's what love is, Royce." I traced my fingers over the inscription on his chest. "Maybe you forgot what love is or maybe you stopped believing that it was real. But you found it in me, just like I found it in you. We belong."

"I'm afraid you're going to hate me when you find out who I really am."

"That's not possible," I rushed through a whisper. My hand spread over the pounding in his chest. "I know you."

He brushed his fingers through my hair, dark eyes fierce. "We're going to take him down together."

"I don't want you to get in trouble with your job when I do it."

Coming out was going to put two of the men I loved the most on the line.

Royce and Richard.

Hard, low laughter rolled out of Royce. "Don't you worry about me."

"How can I not worry about you? I love you, remember?" An adoring smile tugged at my mouth.

Royce pulled me to straddle him, that unyielding gaze on me. Though it'd gone tender. Soft, unrelenting affection that filled me to overflowing. He reached up and cupped my face in one of those massive hands. "I want to live for you."

I leaned down, my lips a whisper against his. "And I want to sing for you."

I could feel his smile beneath the softest kiss.

"What song is it you want to hear, Royce? What can I give you?"

He gripped me by both sides of the face. "Peace."

He looked up at me, awareness spinning through the space, energy alive.

Want went slip-sliding across my flesh, as intoxicating as his hands that slid over my shoulders and down my sides to grip me by my waist. Royce lifted me, lining up his massive length with my center, and he slowly guided me onto his erection, the man hard and ready for me again.

It pressed the breath from my lungs, a frenzy of need that cascaded through my body.

Eclipsing all thought.

All reason.

It chased out everything but the sensation of this man.

Every cell aware.

Every nerve alive.

All of it burning for him.

Morning light spilled into my room. I stretched, my body so blissfully wrung out that I could have curled back up in my bed and stayed there forever.

The sheets smelled like him. His powerful aura still hung in the room.

Cedar and sex. Nothing but sweet, dominant man.

A smile took to my face, and I pulled the covers to my chest, relishing in the memories of last night.

He'd slipped out just before dawn, planting a kiss to my temple and a whisper of forever.

"Soulshine."

Gnawing at my bottom lip, I tried not to dig too deeply into what that meant, and instead just focused on the fact that we had made it here. That we'd toppled our obstacles.

Decided *we* were worth the risk.

Fears trampled in a stampede of hope.

For the first time in so long, it was the biggest thing I felt.

Hope.

A future waited out ahead of me.

Lessons that had prepared me. Wounds that had fortified me. Moments that had added up to teach me what really mattered.

What I really wanted.

With that realization, I sat up. A piece of paper crinkled on the bed next to me.

My heart skittered in a race of anxious nerves, and I reached for the ripped scrap of paper, my eyes moving over the words that had been added to our song, the strains of the chorus becoming a melody in my head.

I'm in a free fall
Don't let me drown
Years spent wasted
Waiting on you to catch up to me
Catching up to you

I clutched the sheet of paper to my chest. Cherishing the words.

Cherishing the man I'd never expected.

Had never seen coming but had come at the perfect time.

Bursting with emotion, I reached over to my notepad and tucked the slip inside before I tossed off the thin covers, pulled on a pair of shorts and a tee, and twisted my sexed-up hair into a loose knot on top of my head.

I padded out into the hallway. Voices lifted from below, the smell of bacon and biscuits rising up to fill my senses with the most intense form of familiarity.

Home.

And I knew . . . I knew that's what I wanted.

To build one.

Something beautiful and strong. Carved out of the cracks of

both of our lives. Constructed by our deepest scars and our innermost desires. Fortified when given to the other.

I went into the bathroom at the end of the hall, brushed my teeth, and for a second, I stared at my reflection in the mirror.

Bright pink cheeks, eyes wide, lips swollen.

My chest squeezed with affection

I unlatched the door so I could head downstairs. Halfway out, I tripped over my feet.

Royce was right outside the door.

The man wore a sleepy grin and no shirt, and my tummy was doing crazy, needy things, shivers racing and that pink on my cheeks heating to an inferno.

With a smile ticking up at the corner of his mouth, he edged forward, stealing my breath, filling my lungs, those eyes knowing and playful when he murmured, "Morning, gorgeous."

My teeth clamped down on my bottom lip to keep myself from going giddy. "Good mornin'."

"You sleep okay?" Affection, all mixed up with a dose of amusement, danced across his face. I figured I'd better play along.

"Oh yes . . . the best sleep I've had in a long, long time." I drew it out, acting as innocent as I could.

"Hmm. Something must have worn you out."

I lifted my chin, gave him a smile. "No, actually, I was resting up because I figured I was just gettin' started."

A smirk took hold of his face. So decadent. A promise of the most delicious sort of sin. His voice dropped an octave, so deep and slow. "Is that so?"

I nodded erratically.

He angled down, faster than I could make sense of it, pinning me to the wall. He rocked his hips forward, his hard, massive erection straining behind his jeans.

I gasped at the sensation.

"Don't say you didn't ask for it," he warned.

Need blazed a path through my body. This was so not good for first thing in the morning, right out in the open in my parents' house.

Still, I couldn't help but pitch my head back to meet his eyes, to taunt him a little in the way he was taunting me. "I'm not asking for it. I'm beggin' for it."

Dropping his forehead to mine, he groaned a needy sound, though I could feel the force of the smile that was splitting his face. "What I'm going to do to you, sweet girl."

"I can't wait," I murmured back.

When a door slammed from somewhere downstairs, I jumped, then grinned, figuring it was best to detangle myself from him before I let the moment get carried away. "I'll see you downstairs."

I started to walk off.

He smacked my bottom.

Jumping in surprise, a high-pitched squeak flew from my mouth.

Without slowing down, I whirled around to glare at him from over my shoulder. Totally feigned of course.

He just cocked a smirk, the man never letting me free of the clutches of that gaze as I headed to the first floor using the main set of stairs. I hit the landing at the living room.

Laughter bubbled into the air, loud and a little obnoxious, and there was no stopping my smile as I pushed through the swinging doorway into my mama's kitchen.

Melanie was there, sitting on the counter, swinging her legs over the side. She grabbed an apple from the fruit dish and started tossing it into the air. "Well, well, well, look who's awake. Sleeping Beauty in the flesh. I heard things got interestin' around here last night."

Oh yeah, they got interesting, all right.

My mama looked over at me from where she was scrambling a big skillet of eggs on the stove. The lifted scowl knitting her brow emphasized the river of wrinkles mapping her face. "Good mornin'."

I couldn't tell if she was watching me with worry or speculation or because she was itching to give me another one of those talks about safe sex she'd brutalized me with when I was twelve.

Turned out, sex with Royce was anything but safe.

All concerns tossed right out the window. Consequences be damned.

I was pretty sure I'd be content to live out my years in his aftermath.

"Mornin'," I managed, shuffling into the kitchen and trying to pretend as if my entire world hadn't just gotten tipped upside down.

Set to right.

Nothing the same but somehow feeling as if it was exactly how it was supposed to be.

"Coffee's ready." Mama pointed at the pot as if I might have forgotten where she'd kept it for the last thirty years.

I beat a path for it. "Thank you."

I grabbed my favorite mug and filled it with the steaming brew, bringing it to my mouth to take a sip.

Melanie grabbed the almost-empty container of vanilla creamer. "You want some of this, or did you get enough cream last night?"

I spewed out the coffee I had in my mouth, spilling half the cup onto the floor in the process. I swiped at my mouth with the back of my hand, flustered, heat racing to my cheeks and horror filling my belly.

"Melanie, what is wrong with you?" I demanded beneath my breath, glancing to the swinging door and praying my daddy hadn't overheard.

She rolled her eyes. "What, you think you're going to keep that news under the covers? Because we all know that's exactly where you were rolling around with Royce last night."

My mouth dropped open. "That's it. Your BFF status has been revoked."

She rolled her eyes again. "Sorry, but you seem to be missin' the *forever* part. You're stuck with me."

"Not if I kick you to the curb."

"No thanks . . . I'm fine right here." She crossed her legs and lifted her cup to her mouth as if she didn't have a care in the world.

Warily, I let my attention slide to my mama. It wasn't like I was a child, but this was her house and yesterday was the first introduction she'd even had of the man. And things had been . . . rough.

Mama arched a brow. "Well, if you want to keep secrets, you should probably do things in secret. You think I didn't hear him sneaking out of your room at the crack of dawn this morning? You forget your old mama is up to welcome the sun."

I cringed. By the way she was looking at me, I was pretty sure she'd heard him go sneaking in there, too. "I'm sorry."

A soft smile graced her mouth. "What are you apologizing for? It was a rough night last night. You aren't the only one who needed comfort."

"Yeah, like poor Nile," Mel piped in, feigned concern in her voice. "I bet he was wishing for someone to kiss his boo-boos. Poor thing."

"You heard about that?" I asked.

She scoffed. "Whole town has heard about it. Nile gettin' his ass handed to him by some city boy. Guy will probably never show his face again. Especially considering he got his nose busted good."

Mama tsked a disappointed sound. "Well, Nile has been spoutin' enough nonsense that he should have known he was eventually going to get what was coming to him. That boy has always had a sweet tooth . . . wanted his cake and to eat it, too. Think he can mess around on my daughter, and when he doesn't get her back with a snap of his fingers, get aggressive? Oh no. I'm not about to stand for that."

"Seems someone else wasn't about to, either." Melanie cocked a brow toward the ceiling where there was some light banging on the floor. I could almost see him, dressing in front of the mirror, pulling on one of those tailored suits.

Or maybe fitted jeans and a tight tee.

I couldn't decide which way I liked him best.

I guessed love blotted out those sort of lines. It was the whole sight of him that left me undone.

Melanie shot me a wry grin. "Look at her, Mabel. She has literal hearts in her eyes."

My mama smiled slow, looking at me with question and worry and hope.

I glanced between the two of them.

"I love him," I whispered the declaration into the air.

It was the easiest one to confess.

I turned my attention to my mother, having the compulsion to give her the admission. To let her know that this meant something. To let her know that this meant something.

She gave a slow nod. "Oh, sweetheart, I could have told you that."

"Is it that obvious?"

"It was written all over you the second the two of you walked through the door yesterday. You've always worn your heart on your sleeve, and it was bleeding all over the place."

I nibbled at my lip, trying to quell the emotion I could feel rising up, the questions that came in waves.

Reminding me that I wasn't close to having all of this sorted.

That I was still a mess.

That I still had to face Cory tomorrow night.

Maybe that would be the biggest obstacle of all.

"It scares me . . . to let myself feel this way again. I hardly know Royce," I said, unable to stop some of the worry from oozing out.

My mama held my face in one of her hands as she angled her head to meet my eye. "All that matters is that your heart is listening to *who* he is, sweet girl. Time has no bearing. Circumstances no relevance. The only thing that matters is that you've looked to the inside."

"I worry I keep missing the important parts."

Mama frowned. "You can't judge yourself over Nile. You two fell in love young . . . and it was always an innocent love. Easy. The two of you didn't know anything different, and you grew apart rather than growing together."

"I know that. I know what I feel for Royce is real, and I know what he's feelin' is real, too. There's no mistaking that." I hesitated before I let another flicker of worry climb free. "There's a tiny part of me worried that Royce might have gotten swept up into the craziness of the band. That maybe he sees me onstage, and that's the woman he wants."

The girl who hungered to stand in the spotlight.

Soulshine.

Is that what that meant?

What he saw in me?

Because the man was so much larger than life. A force that commanded a room. Money dripping from his pores.

But I felt it—something so much deeper. That dark creativity that billowed and shook and shivered through me every time I was in his space.

"I just want him to want me for me. For the simple girl from South Carolina and not the girl who is gettin' ready to sign with his record label."

Mama frowned. "You think he wants you for your money? For what the band can bring to the label?"

My frown was deeper, contemplation and worry and questions winding through. Rejection of the idea hit me hard. "No . . . I . . . don't think so. I mean . . . I'm sure he's worth so much more than I will ever be."

At least, I thought so. Another thing I didn't know about him. The only thing I knew was we had been his purpose, Carolina George's name on that dotted line.

I guessed the real problem was I felt something lurking way down deep in Royce's spirit.

The ugliness he'd warned me about.

The baggage he hadn't given me insight into.

It was the part that made me tremble in fear.

Question everything. If I was racing into all of this far too fast.

"God, I'm a mess right now." I let go of a self-deprecating chuckle.

Light laughter tinkled from my mama. "Right now? That's called life, sweet girl. It's always messy. And believe me . . . the best things in life are forged in the fire."

"And that man is flames." Melanie ticked up a smirk.

Shoving all the concerns down, I swatted at her. "I swear, you are gettin' your status revoked."

She gasped and turned her phone out at me. "Not a chance. Then I wouldn't be able to wear this."

There was a dress on the screen. Cream-colored, made of a wispy material, plunging at the neckline with a slit running up one side. The bridesmaid dress as gorgeous as could be.

I scowled at her. "Don't get ahead of yourself," I told her.

But it was that feeling balling up in my chest, a want unlike anything other, that warned me I was already there. So far ahead of myself that I no longer knew what direction I was going.

I was a fool if I thought I could slow this down.

The kitchen door banged open, and Richard strode in. "Good mornin'." He went right for our mama, dipped down to kiss her on the cheek. "How's my favorite girl?"

Mama blushed, then clucked her tongue. "She's just fine with all her babies under the same roof. But don't you think it's about time you found yourself a different favorite girl?"

There was movement at the door, and this time it was Royce carefully pushing through, as if he were treading water, not sure what he was going to be walking in on.

A suit.

He'd opted for one of those perfectly fitted suits, dark just like the man.

I thought maybe my mama whimpered under her breath.

Apparently, he had that effect on people.

Melanie hummed the wedding march under her breath.

Those stormy eyes met mine.

And I knew . . . knew I was ready. That I was gonna get on that stage tomorrow night. I was gonna sing proud and loud and with all of me, and then, at the right time, I would tell Royce I was ready.

I'd make it known.

I was going to take Cory down. I just prayed he wouldn't take Richard down with him when he went.

Mama smacked her hands together to break up the intensity. "Breakfast is ready. Let's gather at the table. Call your brother and your daddy and tell them to come in. They're out at the barn tending to the horses."

Melanie and I helped Mama fill bowls full of bacon and eggs, a basket full of biscuits, and a boat full of white gravy.

We set the overflowing dishes on the table, while Richard and Royce grabbed plates and silverware and situated a place setting at each spot.

God, that was cute, and Royce Reilly pulling off something cute was nothing but a crime. A danger to my senses.

Because having him rough and raw and soft and sweet meant he was everything.

Linc and Daddy came in, stomping off their boots in the mudroom and washing their hands at the sink. When they made their way inside to take their seats, Daddy clapped Royce on the shoulder in a clear show of support.

Assuring him he backed his actions.

Everyone gathered around the table.

Though this time—this time Royce pulled out the chair next to mine and settled into it. When he pulled my hand into his lap under the table and threaded his fingers with mine, I blew out a contented, satisfied sigh.

And when my daddy bowed his head to say grace, I squeezed Royce's hand, giving thanks that Royce was the man meant to stand at my side.

Royce

*I*t's funny how when you spent years of your life hungering for one thing, entirely focused on one objective, you were still kind of shocked by the anxious disturbance that roiled through your spirit when you realized all that work and effort and hate was getting ready to culminate.

The soul-wrenching thirst to see it through.

To finish it.

Defeat had never been an option.

I sat on the couch on the bus with my attention wrapped up in my phone, on the message that my stepfather had sent, biting at the inside of my cheek and trying to see through the rage that clouded my sight. Distorted my senses.

Loathing thicker than it'd ever been.

Fitzgerald: You're off. I'm coming to Nashville to see to it that Carolina George signs.

Bitterness spun through the deepest part of me, a vat of venom and a moat of hostility. My teeth clenched as I tapped out a response.

Me: They don't trust you.

His return was almost instant.

Fitzgerald: And I don't trust you. I want you out of this equation. The plane will be waiting for you in Nashville at five to bring you back to L.A.

Me: I'm sorry, but it's too late now. There is no going back.

It was no apology. It was a warning of what was to come. The storm that had been howling and building, assembled like an army, was getting ready to touch down.

It struck me.

That flash of energy.

A bolt of intensity.

A burst of light.

Emily.

Emily.

She'd become the thunderstorm.

I lifted my head so I could watch her climbing the tour bus steps, a river of blonde, curled locks that billowed and bounced around her shoulders, the girl in a flowy tank and fitted jeans and a mile of long legs.

Lust fisted my guts, all coiled up with the mess that she'd made of my heart. Cracking it right down the center.

Taking all the parts she shouldn't have been allowed to have.

She stopped in front of me, wearing these strappy heels, girl standing over me like a teenaged boy's wet dream.

A perfect fantasy.

Smooth skin and perky tits and a waist that perfectly fit the span of my hands.

She lifted a coy grin. "You're in my seat," she said in that sweet drawl.

It was the same accusation she'd made the first day I'd climbed onto the bus, when I'd had no clue where it was taking me, though there'd been a part of me then that had already known I was diverting paths.

Shifting gears.

Or maybe I'd just been on the wrong road all along, and I was finally finding my way.

"Is that so?" I let the rough tease wind out of my mouth, and I shifted back on the couch, draping an arm over the back of it as I looked up at her.

Playfulness ridged her mouth. "That's so."

Faster than she could brace herself, I reached out and snagged her around the waist. Emily squealed as I pulled her down onto my lap and wrapped my arms around her.

Tight.

Giggles ripped free, she threw her arms around my neck, her legs draped across my lap, the girl sitting sideways all tucked up to my chest. She smiled at me with one of those smiles that hit me like a landslide.

My heart raced a frantic beat.

It was the first time I'd touched her like this. Right out in the open.

I let my gaze trip around the band sitting around the bus. Every single one of them was staring back. I met their stares, tugged her tighter, knowing I was making a statement.

Mine.

This girl was mine.

And I wasn't going to let her go.

Didn't give a fuck what anyone had to say about it.

From where he sat opposite us at the table, Richard lifted his chin, acceptance and a warning.

Rhys turned to Leif and smacked his open hand onto the table.

"Told you, man. Pay up. One hundred bucks."

"Shit," Leif grumbled, digging into his wallet.

"Pssh." Melanie huffed and waved an indulgent hand. "You deserve to lose all your money if you didn't see that one coming, Leif."

I hugged Emily closer as the bus rumbled out of the hotel parking lot.

Couldn't even be pissed at Rhys.

He was right.

This girl was worth betting on.

"This is it." I squeezed Emily's hand when I felt the nerves rustle through her delicious body where she sat beside me in the limousine that was filled with all the members of her band, plus Melanie and Leif's wife, Mia.

Thrill and dread vied for predominance in Emily's spirit, and I leaned in, murmuring in her ear, "Are you ready?"

Emily squeezed my hand back, trying to breathe through the agitation. "As ready as I'm ever going to be," she whispered, peering out the windows at the crush of people who were gathered behind the ropes, holding signs and hoping to catch sight of their favorite celebrities.

Musicians and actors and the famous for being famous.

But tonight?

One of their most loved was going down in a blaze of infamy.

"Holy shit," Rhys muttered under his breath. "Do you see all those people? Think all of Nashville is out there. Probably half of Hollywood, too."

Richard roughed a palm over his face to break up the stress.

The pressure intense.

Tonight, there was no room for mistakes.

I knew that better than anyone.

Leif pounded his fingertips onto the tops of his thighs, drumming an out-of-control beat I was pretty sure was in sync with the racing of his heart. "We've got this, guys. Just . . . take a deep breath."

"Hell yeah, we do. World's about to know how awesome we are." Rhys proclaimed it, but his voice was subdued.

Awed.

Like maybe he was just then accepting the reality of it.

Sure, Carolina George had amassed a dedicated following.

But this?

I knew it was unlike anything any of them had ever witnessed other than through the screen of a TV.

Performing at the ACB Awards was considered the pinnacle of success.

The height of achievement.

A stage for the most sought after. The one with the most smash hits and the most dollar signs.

And Carolina George had been invited to play before they'd even signed a major record deal.

The one coveted spot for up-and-coming talent was hard to score.

Carolina George deserved it.

No doubt.

I just wondered what that prick had manipulated to get them there.

Richard cleared his throat.

"Want to say something before we go out there. We have given our entire lives for this. Given years to fighting for this. We've been broke. Destitute. Close to homeless. It's cost us relationships. It's taken a toll on our minds and our bodies. I know it hasn't been easy. But I want you all to know . . ."

His gaze bounced around to each of them. "I want you to know I wouldn't want to do it with anyone else. Couldn't. Carolina George is the four of us. Together, we're magic. Remove one of us, and we wouldn't have a leg to stand on. You all make this band what it is, and I'm goddamn grateful for that."

Rhys lifted a fist in the air before he stretched it out toward Richard. "No one else I would have gone along for this wild ride with, brother. You led us to something great. Now we get to revel in this awesomeness together."

Blowing out an emotional sigh, Richard leaned forward and pressed his fist to Rhys's. Leif leaned in and did the same, his eyes jumping around at the band. "And we're just getting started."

Their attention shifted to Emily. She cast me a tender smile before she eased forward.

"I can't wait to share this with you all. You . . . you are my family. The ones I can trust. The ones I'd give anything for. I'm so proud to be a part of this band. So proud to be Carolina George. So proud I get to stand up there and share this with you."

"Thank you for doing this, baby sister," Richard said, his voice thick. "I know you weren't sure this was the direction you wanted for your life. But I'm going to do everything in my power to make sure this is the life you want to live. To right anything I've made wrong. I promise you that."

Her smile turned somber, and she glanced back at me for a beat. "I don't think I'd want to be anywhere else."

My insides clanged. A fucking fierce urge to make those promises, too.

She pressed her little fist to theirs.

A four-pronged star.

My chest clutched, this girl shining the brightest to me.

Joy and pride lit up their faces.

Wholly deserved.

I just prayed it fucking worked out in the end. That I hadn't made the wrong choice. Ended them before they ever had the chance to really begin.

Rhys jerked his head at Melanie. "Mells Bells, get your ass over here. You think we coulda done any of this without you nagging our asses all day long?"

"Asshole," she mumbled.

"You know it." He grinned.

She scooted forward just as the limo was rolling to a stop at the curb. The next in line.

They all looked out the window, knowing things were about to get real, before they all looked back to each other, their fists united. "A song is nothing but a dream. And we dream out loud," Emily told them like it were their mantra.

The limo door swung open, and Richard stepped out to cheers that were no doubt going to grow after the world got a taste of them tonight.

Like Richard had said, they made magic.

It was no lie.

Rhys was all cocky arrogance as he slid out, already a rock star in his mind, celebrity to the bone, tossing out his dimple and his smile as he swaggered down the carpet. Leif ducked out, quiet the way he was, stretching out his hand to help his wife climb out.

I slipped out and then reached back in to extend my hand to Emily, who accepted it.

Lush legs exposed, tanned and shined up for the night, she stepped out in her super short dress. A dress that was a black sequined swath that hugged every curve of her body. Showed her off like the star she was.

Stunning.

Staggering.

Could feel the crowd take note. Certain she was someone remarkable even if they didn't know her name yet.

They didn't get yet that she was everything.

I clutched her hand as we stared down the crowd that made their way to the massive music theater.

Emily shivered, nerves making her back go ramrod straight, her spirit swamped in hope and apprehension.

"You look amazing. Fucking incredible, Emily. Talented beyond measure. Beautiful and kind. You are stopping the entire world in its tracks right now. You have this. But if you need me? I am right here, baby. I won't let anything happen to you. You don't have to be afraid." I whispered the words into her ear as she struggled to find her footing, her courage where she stood at my side, staring down the red carpet like it contained a field of land mines.

A treasure buried at the other end.

"I'm so glad you're here with me." A weak smile pulled at her mouth, like I was the only person she could see right then. Not the flash of the cameras or the shouts of excitement or the thrill of the A-list celebrities who would be taking up the front rows. "Actually, we wouldn't be here at all if it weren't for you, would we?"

I turned to her, cupped her face, my voice hard, low with emphasis. "You would be, Emily. One way or another, today or in a year or ten years, you would be here. There is no stopping something as incredible as what comes out of you. I know it. Believe it."

She caught her bottom lip between her teeth. Swore, I could feel her spirit reaching for me. Twining and twisting and making me into something I wasn't before she came into my life.

Something better.

"And sometimes we need someone to believe in us for us to finally believe in ourselves." The second she said it, she dropped her head to mine and pressed her lips to my mouth. Two of us were caught. Hovering around the other. Breathing the other in. Nothing else existing except for the connection that tethered us.

Kept us from floating away.

Magnets.

The limo drove away behind us and another pulled into its spot.

I straightened, readjusted my tie, and took in a steeling breath. "Let's go make you a star, Emily Ramsey."

"As long as you don't let me fall when I get there."

"If you do, I will be there to catch you," I murmured.

Placing my hand on the small of her back, I began to lead her down the aisle.

I played it as I always did, a straitlaced businessman. There wasn't a chance anyone would recognize me as Royce Reed.

Too many years gone.

A quick name change and who I was in the past no longer seemed to count.

If anyone did find my face familiar, they would pin me as a Mylton Records exec.

Still, I was on edge, not knowing when that rat bastard Cory was going to make his appearance, but I was certain he was already there. Pompous fuck parading as a star when he was nothing but a hack who'd stepped in to steal the limelight. On top of that, I was waiting for my stepfather to show his greedy face.

That piece of shit nothing but an insult to this injury. Salt in a bitter, putrefying wound.

"Emily Ramsey?" A photog called Emily's name, and she jumped, like she was shocked that in the midst of the flood of famous faces he knew her name.

Gathering herself, she pinned on her gorgeous smile and moved that way. I stepped away so he could photograph her, the man hitting her with a slew of clicks and flashes as she approached.

Seemed fitting considering the girl could be working a runway.

"You look gorgeous tonight. Are you excited for your first live telecasted performance?" he asked from behind the rope.

"Definitely," she answered. "It's a dream come true."

"And who are you with tonight?" Brow arched, he glanced at me.

I shifted on my feet, anxious as I looked her way. She stretched her hand out for me, and I moved to her side. I angled my head, answering for her, "I'm with the record label who got lucky enough to discover the true talent of Carolina George before someone else had the chance to snatch them up."

Emily flinched at the description.

It was a dick move.

I knew it.

But the last thing we needed when this all went down tonight was for the media to be looking deeper into it. Fodder for a frenzy.

Digging for dirt.

If they dug deep enough, they were going to find bodies buried all over the place.

Enough fuel to set the tabloids on fire.

Make no mistake.

This house was going up in flames.

But I was a firm believer acts of arson should be kept discrete.

Still, I wound my arm around her waist.

Possessively.

Could almost feel her breathe a sigh of relief.

Fuck. I wished I could go back, tell her before we'd stepped out tonight. Confess it. But everything had lined up exactly as it was supposed to.

I had to see it through.

Finally, we made it all the way to the theater doors where the guests made their way in. Right inside, the rest of the band was waiting, accepting flutes of champagne, toasting each other again.

My phone vibrated in my pocket. I pulled it out.

Pete.

Thank fuck.

I'd been waiting all day for his call. Pins and fucking needles that were knitting me into a cluster of anxiety.

I leaned into Emily's ear. "I have to take this."

Curiosity filled her expression, but then she nodded, not pushing it. I dropped a kiss to her temple since I couldn't seem to walk away without doing it.

I paced into a secluded corner, voices and music loud, so I was lifting my voice when I answered, "Pete."

"Royce, man. We are a go. With Fitzgerald putting a wrench in things and demanding he be in Nashville to see through the signing, we had to scramble to get everything set in place to go down there rather than here. But it's done. His plane is in route . . . he's going straight to Reuben Carmichael's house where the meeting is set rather than going to the awards. Everyone will be ready and in place for when you get there."

A lump lodged itself in my throat. My sister's face flashed. Anna's right behind it. "You got the two girls to testify?"

"Statements are signed. And Càrolina George's manager rolled. Took a bit, but it's done."

Relief blistered through my body.

Singeing.

Scorching.

Vindication taunting me. So close I could taste the victory on my tongue. Feel the destruction of it vibrating through my fingertips.

"Where are you?" I looked around, attention jumping faces as I searched for the only ones that I cared about.

"On my way to the airport. Flight is in an hour. Don't worry, brother, I wouldn't miss this for all the money in that piece of shit's offshore bank accounts."

"We can't fuck this up."

"There's no way for it to get fucked, man. It's done. Alarms are already sounding. This is it."

"I know."

"Okay. I'll be there soon. Board will start receiving emails and faxes soon."

This was it.

This was retribution.

Mutiny.

This was the war he'd never seen coming.

twenty-three

Emily

I stood in front of the mirror in the dressing room, fidgeting and shifting and trying to control the shallow, jagged breaths heaving in and out of my lungs. The stylist had just left after dressing me for the performance because apparently it was sacrilegious to go onstage in the same dress you'd walked the red carpet in.

Now, Melanie fretted around me, readjusting the dangly, sparkling beads that hung from the super short dress, the whole thing glitter and gold and gorgeous. The V neckline plunged so low I was pretty sure the whole world was getting ready to get a peek at my belly button, the back completely bare save for the few strings of beads that danced down to kiss the small of my back from where they hung from the thin strap where the dress clasped together.

They'd done up my makeup in the same brilliant golds, every

inch of me shimmering.

Stomach in knots, I stood there feeling a million miles out of my league and somehow exactly where I was supposed to be.

"Is this really happening?" I whispered to my reflection, unsure of the girl who was staring back.

"I do hope that's a rhetorical question, because your hot ass is due out on that stage in fifteen minutes," Melanie mumbled from behind me, shifting the fabric over my butt as if it might stand the chance of covering any more of it.

Nerves scrambled around inside of me, butterflies traded in for a scatter of birds flapping their wings.

I sucked in a staggered breath.

"I mean, seriously, this dress is out of control. You're going to be smeared all over the best-dressed features in my favorite magazines, and believe me, there won't be a question of who wore it better. I won't even have to make fun of you . . . question what you were thinking for wearing something so awful."

She peeked around my side to hit me with the tease through the mirror. Though there was something soft about it . . . pride glinting in my best friend's eyes.

There was something especially amazing about getting to chase down a dream with the people you loved most.

Then she smirked. "Unless you flash me a tit. Then we're going to have a problem."

My hands flew up to my barely covered breasts. I frowned at her. "If I have a boob pop out, I'm totally blamin' it on you. You were the one who insisted this dress was the one."

"I guess I can handle that considering the rest of the world would be thanking me."

"I hate you," I told her with a pout.

"You love me, and you know it."

"Barely," I razzed then sobered. "I love you to pieces, Mel. I'm so glad you're here."

"I know, Em. I know. I'm so glad I'm here, too. Now let's go out and show the world what you're made of."

I pulled in a steadying breath and followed her to the door. She pulled it open and stepped out into the chaos going down in the hall. People rushed and shouted, the distant roar of the speakers from the main stage rumbling through the walls and sending tremors underfoot, everything so loud that I could feel the beat of it in my pulse.

Or maybe it was the thunder that boomed through my being when I caught sight of Royce outside the door. He was leaned up against the wall with his hands stuffed in his pockets.

Black hair perfectly mussed.

Demeanor fierce.

Provocative in that dangerous, reckless way.

So sexy in that suit it was a wonder he didn't get mistaken for a model.

I was beginning to think he belonged in the spotlight. The way he sang so deep and raspy, like he could hardly bring himself to do it but couldn't stop himself. The way it seemed to have a direct connection to my soul. The way those fingers strummed across his guitar. The words he whispered in my ear.

My heart.

My haven.

My dark star.

He turned his attention on me. I couldn't move. Glued to the spot. Pinned by that stare.

He came my way.

Melanie started humming the wedding march again.

This time I didn't try to stop it.

I wanted it—everything he had to give, and then I was going to beg for more.

Those eyes raked me. Head to toe and back up again.

I was pretty sure I could reach out and dip my fingers into the lust pouring from him.

Flames licking into the space, kicking my heart rate into overdrive.

He leaned in to murmur with that rough voice against my ear, "You are a vision. The most stunning creature I have ever seen. You are the sunrise and the sunset and every second in between. Have half a mind to throw you over my shoulder and hide you away from the rest of the world. I'm not the sharing type."

Desire curled through my stomach. "That's good because I don't share either, and I think you already know who I belong to."

A growl reverberated up his throat, and he pressed his face into the sensitive flesh of my neck. "Mine," he grated.

Shivers rushed and raced, and I tried to remain steady.

"Come on, you two," Melanie cut in from where she waited behind. She pointed at Royce when he swiveled to look at her. "You can dirty her up later, but if you mess up her makeup right now, I'm gonna drop-kick your ass right out of here."

He raised both hands in surrender. "I didn't even touch her."

"Liar. You have glitter on your face."

Royce chuckled. God, I loved that sound.

Melanie snapped her fingers in the air. "Let's roll."

Royce wrapped an arm around my waist, protectively guiding me down the packed hall, shouldering through the throng of people who bustled one direction or another, through the disorder that blustered and spun, the chaos only adding to the thrill.

We hooked a right at one passageway, taking it before we made a left into another. I nearly stumbled in my tracks when I heard the voice on the microphone echoing through the theater as the year's best video was awarded.

Cory Douglas.

I sucked in a lurching breath. My heart leapt into a rebellious sprint. As if it were making a bid to escape. To hide. To flee.

Fear blanketed my mind. Despair sinking in my spirit. Panic a stampede in my veins.

I can't do this.

I can't do this.

"Yes, you can." Big hands were on my face, trying to get into my blackened vision, to find me in the storm. I didn't even realize I'd said the words aloud. Didn't know how I remained standing as alarms blared in the ugliest recesses of my head.

Mind back in his room.

Prisoner to the depravity of his voice.

"Do you hear me?" Royce demanded, words razors, none of his fury directed at me. "You can."

"I don't . . ." I hiccupped over the crash of fear. Legs weak.

How could one moment in time become my greatest stumbling block? But I hadn't dealt. Hadn't let it go. Hadn't healed.

Kept it secreted for so long that right then, in that moment, the truth of it was overwhelming.

In the flash of a second, I was whirled around and whisked into a private spot where the only thing I could feel was Royce.

The man a tower over me.

His presence thick and severe and daunting.

"I won't let him hurt you, Emily. Never. You are safe. Listen to me. You are safe. I will never let anything happen to you. I'll die first. Other than getting on that stage, don't leave my side. Remember, we are taking him down. Together."

Royce tightened his hold. "Don't let him steal this moment from you. Don't let him steal another second. He's going to pay. That bastard is enjoying his last few minutes of freedom. I promise you that."

Struggling to see through the terror, I lifted my head to meet the murderous expression etched on his face. The savagery in his eyes.

"I want to be strong. I don't want to be powerless."

"You aren't. Not even close. I can feel your spirit from a hundred miles away. You have the strength. The courage. It shines . . . burns from you . . . so fiercely that it's blinding. You can't let him dim it. Strength isn't just physical, Emily. It's what's in you, down deep inside. Show him you're unstoppable. Show him why he's the one who should be afraid."

I thought maybe he heard me trying to convince myself because he was murmuring, "I believe in you. I've never believed in anyone the way I believe in you."

He pressed his lips to my forehead, and he murmured the word against my skin as if he wanted to write it on my heart and mind, "Soulshine."

But the truth of it was that he was mine.

What made me burn.

I nodded frantically against the soft embrace. Gulped back the panic. Tried to bind the fear. "Okay," I rushed.

Relief blasted across Royce's expression. "Good girl. Are you ready?"

"Yes."

Royce led me back to the edge of the stage where the rest of the band was gathered, waiting for our cue.

Richard shot me a look of worry, and Royce shot him one back, standing staunch at my side, a barrier from the rest of the world.

Terror quivered in a wave under my skin when Cory Douglas started to exit the stage with the members of the popular country band that had just received their award.

From where he stood next to me, a palpable rush of anxiety rolled through Richard. His own apprehensive awareness skittering through his spirit.

But I could barely contemplate it. Not with the tremor of sickness that rolled through my body.

A tumble of dread.

Blond hair unkempt the way he always wore it, the disgusting man smiling his outrageous smile, knowing people were fawning over him. Wanting to touch him and have a piece of him, while I wanted to rush out, grab a mic, and shout what he'd done.

Let it carry to the heavens, to the airwaves, go on forever until there wasn't anything left for him.

Rage bristled from Royce's flesh, as if sharp barbs had spiked from his skin, the ghastly images he'd etched there roiling and shouting their hate. I had to wonder if it somehow went as deep as mine. If he felt that much for me that he couldn't breathe.

He tightened his hold on my side, his glare enough to decimate the opulent theater.

Cory made it to the wings, and he was immediately surrounded by his entourage. But he stumbled a bit when he saw me, a grin splitting his face, depravity in his eye as his stare hit my body.

Vomit churned in my guts, threatened to rise.

Royce moved to stand in front of me. A living fortress protecting me from the repugnant and corrupt.

Cory's expression shifted, his chin lifting in a challenge, and I was sure it was costing Royce everything to remain standing there while the violence lapped and surged and screamed.

Every muscle in Royce's body was held taut.

Cory quirked a grin.

Malicious. Reeking of victorious greed.

The crush of bodies pushed him forward, and he disappeared in the midst, and I sucked in the first real breath I'd had since I'd heard him onstage. The air was thick, barely breaching my lungs, shallow as I fought to gain control.

To remember.

To remember why I was doing this.

My little-girl dreams. My brother's ambitions. The work of this family.

I couldn't let him take that, too.

Royce squeezed my hand, his voice gravel. "Show him who you are."

A woman wearing a microphone on her head waved frantically at us as the lights in the theater went dim, our cue to take our spots during the two-minute commercial break.

Someone ushered me forward, breaking me from Royce's hold. I looked back at him from over my shoulder as we were herded forward, a frenzy of lowered voices shouting their last instructions.

Onyx eyes met mine. A wild disorder. The perfect sin.

My life.

I ripped my gaze from him and rushed out onto the darkened stage. I fumbled to get hold of myself as a stagehand helped to situate my guitar over my head. He pointed at the black X where I was supposed to stand, a sea of faceless shadows sitting out in the audience beyond.

Anxiety blazed through my blood. Seeped all the way to my bones. I was unable to breathe. Unable to see. I could feel the pressure radiating from all around, the members of my band held on this moment.

Terrified by the thrill.

Enraptured by the charge of energy that zinged through the atmosphere.

My family's future was in my hands, which were shaking so out of control I wasn't sure I was going to be able to make my fingers cooperate to play.

A countdown blinked on a hidden screen that only we could

see, and my heart thundered in my chest, so hard I was sure the microphone had to be picking it up.

Boom. Boom. Boom.

A spotlight came on to light the smaller, elevated stage to the right. Angelica Leon stood on it, wearing a blue satin dress with a billowing train, delivering her choreographed welcome.

Introducing us to the world.

A superstar in her own right.

A country singer who'd gone pop and then had landed herself in five blockbuster movies.

". . . playing their first live televised performance right here at the ACBs, it's my pleasure to introduce you to Carolina George." Her voice lifted on the last as she swept her arm in our direction.

A furor rippled through the theater, an energy unlike anything I had experienced anywhere else.

Brilliant and bold.

A shock to the senses.

I trembled, staring out into the silhouetted faces that took up the endless rows, the balconies filled, stretching all the way out to the televisions people were glued to across the nation.

The lights came up.

Blinding.

Disorienting.

Strobes of lights flashed, the stage consumed in a blue haze of smoke that lifted in vapors around us, as if we'd just appeared from out of nowhere.

Summoned by the magic of the music we made.

Leif lifted his drumsticks in the air, beat them together as he gave us our count.

Richard drove into the intricate introduction of the song we were set to play, his fingers fast and precise as they moved up and down the neck of the electric guitar.

Our most popular.

My favorite.

One that had always been closest to my heart.

Still, I felt frozen, my tongue thick, my heart beating somewhere out of time, out in a place where I didn't know how to catch up to it.

Where it was lost in the thorns and the briar.

And I knew this was it.

I was going to ruin it all.

I was going to let him steal it.

I couldn't bear the thought, and my attention slowly drifted to the wings.

Drawn.

Royce was there, hidden in the massive maroon drapes that hung from the rafters.

But I found him.

My spirit immediately knowing where to go.

My beautiful stranger.

Dark and deadly and dangerous.

An enigma that completed me.

The second before my part, I gripped my acoustic guitar, strummed a chord, and breathed her to life.

I moved up to the mic.

And I sang—I sang with all of me.

Twenty-four

Royce

A roar of applause filled the theater, the pounding thunder ascending to the soaring ceilings and flooding across the floors, spilling into the wings.

Emily stood at the microphone as she belted out the last line. The power of her sultry, mesmerizing voice echoed against the walls, filling hearts, the awe of it ricocheting through the audience to make a rebound. She stood in the glow of it, her head tilted back and her chest jutting forward, the girl giving it everything she had.

And God, had she given it everything.

My chest tightened, my spirit racing with the same admiration that blew every person in the place away.

Awestruck.

Carolina George had just become a household name.

A grand slam. Every fucking base loaded, and Emily had just busted that shit into the stratosphere.

She stepped away from the mic.

Blinking.

Stunned.

Like maybe she hadn't had the first clue what she was capable of until right then.

A stampede of shouts and cheers exploded in the air, and she gave a little wave before the lights went dim and shifted to the other stage so the next award could be presented. Immediately, the stage crew hustled to get the next act ready as Carolina George was quickly led off the stage.

Staggered, her spirit racing out ahead of her, Emily came right for me, wearing that dress and those heels and watching me with those green eyes.

Mind-wrecker.

I no longer knew myself.

The second she made it to the edge of the curtains, she threw herself at me.

"I did it. Oh my god, I did it."

I wrapped my arms around her waist, lifting her off her feet and holding her close. My voice was a low rumble at her ear. "You did it. Of course you did it. You are unstoppable."

Joy blew from her like a warm spring breeze. The kind that made you feel like you'd found yourself in paradise. "I can't believe it. I can't believe it. I thought . . . I thought I wasn't gonna make it. I almost froze . . . but I . . . I couldn't let him hold me back for a second more. Wouldn't let him steal that moment from me or the band."

"You were spectacular," I murmured, voice clogged and overcome.

By the performance.

By her voice.

By this woman I didn't deserve to be holding in my arms, but who I wasn't going to let go.

"No one was prepared for you, Emily Ramsey. You are the most breathtaking thing to ever hit that stage. It's where you belong. You are a star."

She curled her arms tighter, her confession a gush against my soul. "I don't want to do it with anyone else, Royce. I want this, and I want it with you."

Bodies bustled around us, and the only thing that mattered right then was this girl.

I needed her.

Needed her in a way that I had never needed anyone in my life.

Overwhelming.

Stunning.

Devastating.

"Come with me." Setting her onto her feet, I grabbed her hand, frantic as I started to pull her through the crush of people backstage.

"Where are we going?" she rushed to ask behind me, her voice barely breaching the rumble of voices around us, though I could taste her thrill.

The anticipation that streaked through that gorgeous body.

"Where I can have you in private."

We made it down one hall, then another. We wound down the packed hall to her dressing room. I didn't slow to glance around at who was watching.

Didn't give a fuck.

I needed her.

Right that second.

I opened the door, ushering her inside. I shut it behind us, closing us in.

Energy crackled.

A fire that lit.

I clicked the lock.

It resonated like a gunshot. Added fuel to the crash of need beating the blood through my veins.

Emily stood in the middle of the room facing me, the lights framing the mirror on the wall behind her still glowing bright, the rest of the room dim. That gold dress glinted and shimmered in the glow, her skin just as bright, eyes a vortex that sucked me under.

A supernova.

My insides clutched and pulsed, my dick hard and hungry. I moved right for her, hands gripping her by the face as I took her mouth.

Possessive and rough.

Tongues a tangle of need and fire. Lips greedy and desperate. As greedy and desperate as her little hands that started gripping at me. Ripping at my jacket like if she didn't have me, she'd go mad right along with me.

Tripping.

Tumbling.

No return.

I was already gone.

Lust boomed in the enclosed space.

Bounding against the walls. Growing in severity with each frenzied beat. She tore the jacket from my shoulders, her breaths hard as she went right back for me.

Our chests pressed tight.

Hearts crashing in time.

A frenzy that lit.

I grabbed her by the waist and spun her around, molding my body to her from behind, against that gorgeous back and her perfect ass.

I kissed along her bare shoulder, wanting to devour every inch.

"Royce." Her voice was a plea as her hands darted out to hold herself up on the back of the sofa couch that faced the small sitting area. I gripped her by the waist.

"That's right . . . you said you were going to be begging for it, didn't you?"

"Yes." It was a whimper.

I ran my hands up the front of her dress, pressing hard as I trailed up over her quivering belly, hands cupping those perfect tits. "Tell me you want me."

She moaned. "I want you, Royce. I want you more than I've ever wanted anything."

"What do you want?" It was a heated demand, hands getting impatient, gliding back down her sides until they were riding over the curve of her hips, splaying over her shaking thighs, until I was gathering up the material of her dress at the hem and slipping it up.

The flesh of her sweet, sweet ass was exposed, just a thin slip of material covering her drenched core. I traced my fingertips over the silk, subduing a groan.

Emily didn't. She mewled and pressed back. "This. For you to touch me. To take me. To stay with me."

My spirit thrashed.

Her words winding through the vengeance and hate.

I shoved the material aside, dragging a single finger through her tight slit.

"Oh, God, Royce. Please."

"Tell me," I demanded. I needed to hear it. All of it. "What do you want?"

Still, I gave her a little, dipping a single finger into her needy pussy.

I swore, she heard the fullness of my question because a tiny cry jutted out of her mouth. "I want it all, Royce. I want to sing. I want to play. I want a family. I want to be a wife. I want it all. I want it with you. Wherever you go, I want to go with you."

She squirmed, the girl's throaty voice filling the air, wrapping me in knots when she gave me her heart.

This time, I was groaning, and I edged back to peel her underwear down those long legs, kneeling as I went. The sight of her bent over like that was enough to knock the wind out of me.

Foundation rocked.

This girl a buoy when I'd been content to float away and drown. Sure I'd never feel again. Die in this destruction. I kissed a path back up her legs, teeth grazing her bottom, sliding my hands up the sides before I was jerking my belt loose, ripping the button and dragging down the zipper, freeing my cock that was harder than stone.

Grabbing myself, I dragged the tip through the crease of her ass, spreading her with one hand, lining myself up with her throbbing pussy.

I drove home.

A grunt tore out of my chest.

Heaven.

Motherfucking heaven when I thought I'd been condemned to hell.

Emily gasped and bowed forward, curling her fists into the couch as I filled her full. Girl so tight around me, squeezing my dick in the delicious clutch of her body.

My ultimate perfection.

"Good?" I asked her as I took two handfuls of her lush ass, kneading her flesh, trying to keep myself in check while I waited for her to adjust.

She turned her head and took in our reflection in the bright lights of the mirror. The two of us close to shadows.

Silhouettes.

"There is no better feeling than you taking me."

I pulled almost all the way out, watching the act, dick soaked with the girl. Lust and greed and this love she'd found in me pulsed. Tightening my chest and knotting my stomach in this need I knew would never end.

I'd never get enough.

I surged forward in a possessive thrust. "Mine. You're mine, Emily. You and me, Precious. It's you and me."

"I'm yours," she murmured. The girl's chest was pressed to the top of the couch as she struggled to breathe around the intrusion of me, as her pussy throbbed and clenched and begged for more, that dress hiked up around her hips, our bodies one.

One.

There would never be a better moment than this.

When I knew she was my all.

Life.

Death.

She was the fight.

She was the victory.

Fingers sinking into her flesh, I clutched her tight. I picked up a quick, hard pace. Fucking her with all the desperation I felt. Loving her with everything I had.

I spread her ass, taking her deeper, ran my thumbs along the seam where we were joined. I gripped her by the back of the knee and opened her wider, slipped a hand around to her clit as she leaned her back on my chest.

I took her ruthlessly, our pants filling the air, our hearts running wild.

Emotion surged into the room.

And she was whimpering, her cries tiny whispers, "I love you, Royce. I love you so much. You kept me from falling apart. Caught up to me at exactly the right time."

I pressed a hand to her chest, my mouth at her ear. "You are everything."

She spread her hand over mine as I stroked her, and I turned her a fraction so I could look at her all spread out in the mirror.

The picture of everything I'd wanted and never thought I'd have.

Her pants increased, her little body winding tight, and she was clamping down on me. I thrust deeper, harder as she rode out her orgasm that I could feel racing across my flesh. Her pleasure mine.

Pricks of it scraping my flesh, arrows that impaled, the barbs of her spirit sinking into mine.

Forever.

My balls tightened, shivers of ecstasy gathering at the base of my spine.

Fierce.

Powerful.

It burst.

Bliss sped through my veins, so intense the only thing I saw was this girl's light.

I grunted as I came, clutching her sides as I poured into her body, her walls clutching, sucking me deeper.

Sweat slicked our skin, our breaths shallow and fast, as fast as our thundering hearts. I hugged her close, pressed my face into the thrumming pulse of her neck. "I love you, Emily."

She turned her head, nuzzling her cheek into my face. "I love you, Royce."

Heaving out a sigh, I pulled out of her, tugged up my pants, and moved over to the sink. Wetting a cloth, I cleaned myself before I grabbed a fresh towel, ran it under the water, and moved back over to her. I pressed it between her thighs, cleaning her, hoping she'd know I'd always take care of her.

She braced herself on my shoulders, casting a nervous glance up at me. "Are you ready for this?" she whispered, her voice sounding of cautious excitement.

Not even fucking close.

A roll of anxiety slipped beneath the surface of my skin. A shudder of unease. "Are you?" I asked her.

"Yes," she said with a tiny smile, trust filling her green eyes. "I'm ready to do this. With you. Because of you. Because you reminded me of who I want to be. And tomorrow . . . I'm going to the police."

Everything clutched. My heart and my spirit and my mind.

My love for her up against my love for Anna. How could I separate the two?

The words pooled on my tongue, the confession that going to the police tomorrow was already going to be too late.

Instead of releasing them, I touched her chin. The most adoring caress. "You are the warrior, Emily Ramsey."

Held, she gazed at me through the leaping shadows before she shook herself out of it. "I should change. I think you might have ruined my dress."

That time, her tone went coy, low with playful seduction.

She grabbed a simple white floral dress that hung from her wardrobe rack.

"Let me help you with that," I murmured. I took her by the shoulders and turned her around, slowly unzipped the golden dress, and let it drop to her feet.

She breathed out a sigh.

Turning her back around to face me, I slipped the dress over her head, situated it on her sweet body. Reaching out, I brushed my thumb across her cheek, gazing at this girl who I would do anything for. "Before we step out that door, I need you to know one thing, Emily. Know that everything I do, I do it for the people I love. Whatever you do, don't forget it. And second? Don't leave my side."

twenty-five

Emily

The limo eased down the long driveway that led to Reuben Carmichael's home. If that's what you wanted to call it. The massive estate was spread out at the back of a sprawling lawn that seemed to go on forever, tucked behind a ten-foot gated wrought-iron fence. Abundant, flourishing trees surrounded the perimeter of the opulent residence.

Nerves rattled me to the bones.

Reuben Carmichael was one of the most successful country singers of all time.

A legend.

And we'd been invited to his house for the afterparty.

Richard let out a low whistle as the car eased around the colossal fountain with a statue of an angel in full flight. It appeared to be hovering over the gush of water spurting from the cascading pool, streaming arches lit up in hues of pinks and blues and greens.

"So this is how the other half lives," Richard mused as he peered out, my brother as anxious as could be, his knee bouncing at warp speed as we came to a stop.

This was it.

We all knew that it was.

After tonight's performance, we had reached a pinnacle. The peak we'd been climbing toward for years. It was time to sign away our souls in the hopes that we were appointing them to something better.

One way or another, our lives were about to change.

"All of you are about to be on the other side." Royce was leaned casually back in the leather seat, the man obviously no stranger to luxury, one elbow propped on the armrest, the other sure and firm around my waist. "Are you ready for that? Last chance."

I sucked in a deep breath.

Karl Fitzgerald would be waiting inside. We'd gotten word that we'd be having a formal meeting at 9:30 in one of the house offices. Apparently, Reuben didn't mind opening his house to Mr. Fitzgerald in the middle of a party, considering Mylton Records had plucked him up when he was young and shot him to the top.

He'd been hanging out there ever since.

"After tonight, where we belong couldn't be clearer," Rhys raved.

Leif scrubbed a hand over his face, still trying to break up the shock that we'd actually performed at the ACB Awards. That this was now his life. "That was some kind of spiritual shit," he agreed, looking around. "Not sure we've ever played like that before. There was just . . . something in the air. Something that hasn't ever been there before."

"It was all those lights shining on your face." Melanie grinned, unable to stop herself from getting in the tease.

Rhys chuckled. "Blinded by the light. Rest assured, if that's the case, then I don't want to see."

"No turning back now," Richard said, looking at me.

Royce tightened his hold around my waist, as if he were telling me that he would stand beside me, either way. That even if I walked now, he would still defend me, even when I knew he had so much to gain by us signing, that this was the mission that he'd been sent to do.

I sucked in a breath. "Let's do this."

"Let's do it," they all agreed.

Rhys tossed open the door, not waiting for the driver to come around to let us out. He slipped out and stood, accepting the flute of champagne a server waiting on the curb offered, waltzing up the stoned walkway that led to the front door as if he'd walked it a million times.

Richard, Leif, and Mia followed. Melanie slid out behind them. I waited for a second, until we were alone, so I could turn around and grab Royce by the face. "Thank you for this, Royce. For believin' in me when I didn't. I'm not sure we would be here today if you hadn't come when you did. You unlocked something inside of me that was holding me back, and I will forever be grateful for that."

Onyx eyes flashed. He reached out, took me by the chin. "You are a star."

My teeth clamped down on my bottom lip to stop the blush. "We should go."

"I'm right here with you, Emily. Right here."

I scooted out, trying to keep my dress smoothed down as I stood, and Royce slipped out after me, the man covering me in a towering shadow from behind.

An ominous protector.

I'd never felt so safe.

He moved up to my side and threaded his fingers through mine, brought my hand to his lips and pressed a kiss to the back. The man seemed to tremble. His aura agitated.

Distressed.

His jaw clenched tight.

"Are you okay?" I asked, glancing up at him.

I could have sworn his smile was a grimace. "Give me an hour, and I will be."

A frown pulled between my brows, and I started to ask him

what that meant, why he was worried, but he tugged at my hand and started up the walk. "We should get inside."

Clinging to his arm, I rushed to keep up with his strong stride, my heels clacking on the stones.

We took the three curved steps that fronted the entrance to the massive house. At the landing, the door was opened, another server there with his offering of hors d'oeuvres. Everything about this party was swanky, upscale, sent my nerves shivering through my body as we stepped inside the lavish mansion.

"Oh, my goodness," I muttered under my breath. I mean, we'd splurged a bit over the last year or two, feeling as if we'd finally made it, but I didn't think we had the first clue what *making it* really meant in the music world.

Because this was over-the-top.

Extravagant on a level that I wasn't sure I'd ever aspire to.

A simple life with a comfortable house and a horse and maybe a baby or two sounded about right.

Royce leaned in. "You're nervous."

A shiver curled down my spine. "I think I might be in over my head."

"You deserve all of this and more."

"And what if I don't want that, Royce? What if I want something humbler than this for my life? Would you be okay with that?"

I shifted my gaze to him, searching the lines of his mesmerizing face, wondering how it was that I felt as if I knew this man better than anyone and somehow knew so few of the details about his life.

About what *he* wanted.

Royce backed me up to a wall to get out of the bustle of servers and the slew of guests that rambled down the hall. The smile that curved his full lips was almost sad. "You're worried about the kind of lifestyle I want to lead?"

I gave an erratic nod. "I know so little about what you want in this life, Royce. I know your job is important to you. So important. That you're good at it. I also know you're based in L.A. And not that I wouldn't want to live there or couldn't live there, but

God . . ." I trailed off, realizing I was rambling, that I was getting so far out ahead of myself, and I didn't know how to stop.

Thinking about a future we'd only hinted at.

Wincing, he reached out and twirled a lock of my hair with a tattooed finger, his nose close to brushing mine. "Lifestyle doesn't matter to me, Emily. I'll live in a shack if it means my sister is safe. If it means you're safe. The only thing I care about is you accepting me, loving me, when you figure out who I am."

With a shaky hand, I reached out and cupped his face. "I know who you are, Royce Reilly. I see you, feel your beautiful heart that is beating behind that menacing exterior."

Those eyes flashed, and he cleared his throat, taking me by the hand. He led me deeper into the house. Royce grabbed two glasses of champagne from a passing server since we had fifteen minutes until we needed to meet with Mr. Fitzgerald. Royce drained his while I sipped at mine, watching the mingling groups.

The rich and the famous.

The view totally surreal, me standing there, ill at ease and trying to play it cool while Royce watched on like some kind of soldier.

Hard and brash.

A furor rippled through as a group made their way inside, showing at the end of the hall, shaking hands and returning the enthusiastic hellos as people vied to get a chance to meet them.

Sunder.

What had to be the hottest band in the world.

It appeared as if they stood in a spotlight, stealing the attention from every other celebrity in the space.

I was no fangirl, but my belly knotted. I'd met them a couple of times through the years, but always from afar. That and the fact that Leif and Mia felt like an extension of them. A part of their world that had been tied to ours.

But that didn't mean it lessened the impact of being at the same party as them.

Royce squeezed my hand. "We should go say hi."

I remained frozen to the spot. "Are you crazy? That is Sunder."

Okay, so maybe I was a little bit of a fangirl.

He chuckled low, cutting me a glance from the side. "Are you starstruck, Emily Ramsey?"

Redness flushed.

"They're the most down-to-earth people you'll ever meet."

"You know them?"

"Yeah," he said, though it seemed like admitting it almost bothered him.

As if it were some kind of sin.

"We go way back."

He hauled me by the hand across the posh living room to the group that had gotten accosted at the end of the hall. One of the guys lifted his hand when he saw Royce approaching.

Lyrik West.

Oh my god.

"Royce, my man, how are you, dude? It's been forever." He went in for one of those man-hugs while I awkwardly shifted on my feet.

Royce hugged him back as if they were the oldest of friends. "I know it. Too long. How are things in your world?"

Lyrik wrapped his arm around the waist of the woman at his side, hugging her close and stealing her attention. "World is perfect, man. Fucking perfect. Only because I get to call this one wife. This is my girl, Tamar."

She reached out to shake Royce's hand.

The woman was stunning, wearing a black leather and lace dress that few others could pull off. Sleek black hair and covered in tattoos, she was the perfect match to the devastatingly wicked man who stood at her side. The lead guitarist of Sunder was imposingly tall, nothing but lean muscle covered in a canvas of ink.

I peeked between Royce and Lyrik.

I guessed they kind of matched, too. The vibe they threw. The two of them larger than life. Commanding all the attention in the room.

"It's nice to finally meet you, Tamar. I heard someone finally lassoed this asshole." Royce seemed sincere, but still, he kept looking around.

On edge.

I wanted to reassure him that we were a done deal.

He could relax.

It was the rest of us that were suffering from rampant nerves.

Tamar canted a sultry grin up to her husband, who was looking down on her as if she were the brightest sun. "Someone had to do it."

He smirked down at her. "Think the real answer to that is there was only one person who *could* do it. Only you, Baby Blue."

I swooned.

Was it hot in here?

I almost had to fan myself.

Royce wrapped one of those strong arms around my waist.

A belt of possession.

Energy flashed.

"This is Emily."

I swooned a little harder.

At this rate, someone was gonna have to carry me out of there.

"Miss Carolina George." Lyrik chewed at his lip as he said it, appraising, and oh god, I was pretty sure I needed to find a closet where I could hide. "Great to meet you," he told me.

"It's an honor to meet you."

Tamar waved an indulgent, tattooed hand in the air, the huge black diamonds she wore on her fingers flashing under the light. "I'm pretty sure the honor is ours. I nearly wept when I heard you sing up there. God . . . that was just . . . amazing. Straight-up amazing. I heard you sing several times back in Savannah when I used to work at Charlie's. . . but you were some kind of spectacular tonight."

The blush I'd been fighting swept across my face, rushing like a wildfire down my neck and across my chest. "Thank you."

Tamar smiled. "I can't wait to see what you do."

"She's going to do amazing things. That you can count on." Royce squeezed my side.

"Holy shit . . . Royce Reilly. The motherfucking king."

I jerked my attention to find Ash Evans pushing through the crowd so he could get to Royce. Ash didn't shake his hand. Oh no. He threw his arms around him, lifted him off his feet, and bounced him all over the place. "I missed the fuck outta ya. Where the hell have you been my whole life, man?"

Royce laughed, though it was with a bit of discomfort. "Working."

"Wrong line if you're asking me."

"I wasn't," Royce answered, a little harder than I thought necessary. Confusion pulled through my senses, and I was trying to keep up, put the pieces together.

It took me a second to remember that Sunder had once been under the Mylton Records label before they'd branched off and their original lead singer, Sebastian, had started his own production company when he'd decided to retire from the road.

Still wanting to dabble his fingers in music but wanting it in a different way. I fully understood that.

Ash laughed a loud, raucous laugh, the guy so easygoing that he could put a raging bull at ease. "Gotcha, man. Gotcha. No sweat."

He turned his blue eyes on me, a big smirk lighting his face. "Hey there, darlin'. I'm Ash."

Right, because I didn't know who he was.

"I'm—"

"Emily fucking Ramsey. You think I could forget your name after that little stunt you pulled onstage tonight? You might as well get over that because you are unforgettable." He swiveled his attention to Royce, flapping his index finger in my direction. "This one . . . don't let her go."

Royce slanted those eyes to me. Pinning me to the spot. Expression as hard as his words. "Don't plan to."

Ash smacked a hand on his shoulder. "That's my man. You find something good? You wrap your hands around it, protect it with all you have, and well . . . yeah . . . you got it . . . don't fucking let it go."

Ash snagged a woman from around the shoulders and planted a sloppy kiss to her cheek. "Like this one."

She swatted at his chest, though she snuggled in to rest her head on it, all too willing to get swamped in his overbearing hug. "Hi, I'm Willow. Ignore this brute."

He gasped in feigned horror. "Now why would someone want to ignore me? I'm the best around, baby. A superstar. Best bassist in the land."

A giggle slipped from my mouth. "Well, don't tell that to our bassist, Rhys. He's been trying to give you a run for your money for years."

"Tell him to bring it."

"I'd gladly throw down some Benjamins for a friendly wager. And where the hell is Leif? Dude needs to get his ass whipped for sneaking in and snagging our Mia right out from under our noses."

Willow frowned through a laugh. "No betting for you, big boy. No ass kickin', either. Leave poor Leif alone. I think he got plenty enough crap from Lyrik."

"Are you trying to wreck my fun?"

"Totally, babe, totally. Goal of my entire life is to strip you of any joy." She rolled playful eyes.

I couldn't stop my smile.

They were adorable.

"Is Baz here?" Royce asked, looking through the group, antsy and anxious.

Royce let his gaze move over Austin and Zee, Sunder's lead singer and drummer, who were chatting with a group that had gathered around them.

"Be here in twenty. He was videoing with the kids before Shea tucked them in for the night," Lyrik answered.

Royce nodded his head, rubbing his hand over his mouth, looking around the growing crowd. "All right, tell him I'm here when you see him, yeah?"

"Sure thing, man."

They fist-bumped each other.

Then Royce gathered my hand again. Squeezing it hard. "It's time."

Nerves scattered, a bluster of energy, excitement and worry and dread. "It was nice to meet you all," I said with a little wave.

"Great to meet you," went up in a small chorus, and I let Royce lead me through the throng of toiling bodies.

Laughter and conversations were getting louder and louder as drinks were poured freely from the open bar. The mood growing rowdy.

Royce shouldered through, edging deeper into the crowd before taking two steps up out of the sunken room to a higher level.

As soon as we got to the top, Royce stopped in his tracks. Though there was no missing the way his spirit lurched out ahead. Hatred blazed from him, so acute I could feel it blasting through the air.

I froze at his side, my focus moving to where his attention was fixed.

Cory Douglas.

Nausea sloshed in my stomach, and bile rose in my throat.

Suffocating sickness.

I was again hit with the urge to run.

Royce squeezed my hand in a vice grip. Tucking me close while we watched Cory move through the crowd in all his cocky arrogance. Smiling his fake smile, dimples denting his carved cheeks.

Was it wrong I was almost relieved when I saw he was with a woman, her hand twined with his as they strutted through the group?

The woman I knew from pictures as his wife.

She was super tall, brown hair so dark it was almost black, cut in a sharp, long bob that swung around her slender, toned shoulders. She wore a red dress that was cut at different angles, a dipping neckline that lanced to the side, one side of the dress shorter than the other, a trapezoid cutout revealing her ribs on the right.

I was pretty sure he'd plucked her out of a magazine because she looked like a supermodel.

Part of me wanted to rush her. Grab her by the arm and shake it, warn her of who was lurking under that charisma and charm. The other part felt trapped. As if I'd gotten stuck in a tragedy, and I didn't know how to get out.

Royce's nostrils flared, and his hand clamped down on mine, so hard I winced. Or maybe I was just wincing because Cory was slowing, too, his attention raking over the two of us. His attention locked on where our hands were woven.

I swore I saw it.

Something flashing through his eyes.

Something sinister.

That was the blip of a second before a smirk was pulling to his perverted face, and he wrapped an arm around the woman in the sort of scornfulness that wasn't hard to decipher.

The woman's dark eyes dragged over Royce in a flicker of familiarity before she was turning her face.

My attention jerked to him, just in time to catch it, just in time to know.

Agony written on him. Deep gashes of turmoil.

Murderous animosity.

Anguish squeezed my heart, and my knees went weak.

But I couldn't look away. Couldn't help from searching the woman who shifted in discomfort. I nearly puked on her shoes when I saw the X that barely peeked out from the cutout in her dress. Her scar faded to just a shade lighter than her skin.

Oh my god.

My hand went to my mouth, and Royce must have felt me getting ready to splinter because he towed me down the hall without saying anything. His dress shoes and my heels clicked on the marble, echoing in our haste, my pulse stampeding in a slosh of trepidation.

So loud I was hearing a dull hum start up in the back of my head.

"He won't touch you," Royce growled beneath his breath.

Shards of broken glass.

Razors and knives that impaled the air.

"Just do not leave my side," he commanded.

"Is he . . . does . . .? Is she?" I tried to catch up to the question, to force some sort of coherency out. Fighting the feeling that was sinking to the pits of my spirit.

This feeling that there was something bigger—uglier—than I'd understood pushing up from the gaps. Winding in and invading.

I refused it. Didn't want to give it any credence. I wouldn't allow Cory Douglas to steal any more of my joy.

"He won't touch you," Royce reiterated.

Low and hard.

I got the feeling he was making the promise to himself.

Royce's hand squeezed down on my fingers, breaths turning shallow and haggard as we reached the doorway. Elevated voices echoed out, a buzz and a thrill spilling out through the cracks.

Royce straightened, steeling himself with all that power he exuded like a forcefield, and he tossed open the double doors to the massive office.

Inside, it was decorated in deep browns, ornate mahogany wood, a cow-print sofa, the floor-to-ceiling windows that spanned two stories edged in thick upholstered drapes.

The entire space gave off the vibe of pretension and authority—Nashville style.

All the members of my band had already gathered, the guys sipping from tumblers of scotch, toasting our good fortune, while I was suddenly feeling as if I were coming up on a catastrophe.

Melanie was tucked on a couch in the far corner, and our manager, Angela, sat in one of the upholstered high-backed chairs in front of the imposing desk.

Behind it was Karl Fitzgerald.

The man who'd been hunting us for close to a year. Someone who commanded respect, but there was just something slimy and seedy about him that had immediately made me refuse it.

But he was the money man.

And sometimes you couldn't ignore or pass that up.

Not when they were offering so much of it. Not when it would change everything. Not when this contract was written in the blood of my band.

Tonight had already been proof of that.

"Ah, I see you decided to show up," Mr. Fitzgerald said, rocking back in the leather chair that he helmed, his beady eyes immediately latching onto Royce.

Another burst of hatred sizzled through Royce's being. So violent I felt it punch the atmosphere.

A crack of lightning.

"I'm not here to argue with you, Mr. Fitzgerald. I'm here to sign the band you sent me to acquire."

Royce had gone all business. The same man he'd been that morning when he'd walked into Richard's hotel room the first time.

Mr. Fitzgerald's scrutiny landed on our entwined hands. An incredulous smirk played around his pompous mouth. "I see you've acquired a little something for yourself."

"What I do with my personal life is none of your concern."

"No?" he challenged.

"No," Royce returned, so cold, I was pretty sure everyone felt an ice age descend. Angela shifted in discomfort, her eyes wide and almost in shock.

Each of the guys took note of the malice that shivered through the air.

Shoulders straightening and spines stiffening.

Mr. Fitzgerald chuckled a low sound and then gestured to the contract that was spread on the desk in front of him. Angela had scoured it and given it her stamp of approval.

There was nothing left standing in the way except for this terror I could feel rising from my spirit and spilling into my bloodstream.

A warning.

Hostility that had smoldered and seethed and festered until it'd fermented into something toxic. So thick I was certain I was choking on it.

"Shall we finish this thing?" Mr. Fitzgerald asked, craning his head.

"That's what we're here for," Richard said.

My brother stepped up to take the fancy pen that Mr. Fitzgerald offered him.

He was a force. Powerful and proud and persuasive. Though I knew him well enough to see the way his muscles quivered with strain.

Thinking he had to hold the entirety of the weight of this decision on his shoulders.

He hesitated before the tip of the pen hit the paper, and he let the ink flow across the signature line.

He seemed to freeze on the last letter before he finished on a heavy exhale, relief entering his posture when he passed the pen over to Rhys. "This is it, man."

Richard clapped Rhys on the shoulder as he stepped up to take Richard's place. He leaned over the desk and signed with a grin and a flourishing sweep of his hand.

"It's done, baby. Big time, here we come. You're up, Leif."

Leif accepted the pen and leaned over the contract. He nodded his head along to some drumbeat that only he knew, as if he were ascribing this moment its own song.

A rhythm to this momentous memory.

He looked up at me. Passing the baton.

"Set it in stone, Em."

Nerves clawed across my chest. Everything tight. A pinpoint of anxiety.

Royce released my hand, and I felt the power of his gaze hit the side of my face. I looked that way.

You are a star, he mouthed.

I slowly eased the rest of the way up to the desk. Richard shifted the contract around my direction where I stood on the opposite side. Our eyes met, and I sent him a soft smile.

This was it.

I lifted the pen and set it to the line, my hand shaking out of control as I signed, the curly letters of my name blooming to life on the paper.

Done.

Finished.

Like Leif had said—our fate set in stone.

Carved into the paper that promised so many things.

I heaved out something that sounded of relief and shock, realizing just makin' the decision was the hardest part.

That lasted all of a second before a tremor of dismay curled through my senses when Karl Fitzgerald's quietly controlled voice hit my ear. "Good girl. Now it's time to start acting like the superstar I'm going to make you. Ditching my stepson should be the first move. The only thing he will bring you is disappointment."

Confusion clouded my mind, thoughts distorted, twisting with the dread I'd felt rising since the second we'd stepped into this house.

Stepson.

Royce was Karl Fitzgerald's stepson?

I stumbled back a step.

The information hittin' me like a slap of betrayal.

Why wouldn't Royce tell me he was related to him? After everything we'd shared, I would have thought that would have been simple information he would have given me.

Something about it felt . . . off.

Way off, the tidal wave of unease that had been gathering since we'd gotten to this house gaining speed.

Confused and taken aback, my gaze drifted to Royce.

He slowly shook his head in a silent apology before he tore his attention away and pinned it on Mr. Fitzgerald. Instantly, his expression turned savage, deadly as he stood there clearly trying to keep from throwing himself over the desk to enact his rage on the man who was glowering back.

Smug satisfaction on his face.

As if he'd just put Royce in his place.

Hostility raged in the confines of the room, and the rest of the band was shifting in the disorder. Not sure what was going down. But I think each of us knew it was bad.

"You are dismissed," Karl Fitzgerald told Royce, rocking back in the executive chair like he was the commander and the executioner. "Permanently."

My heart clutched, gaze swinging to Royce, expecting him to be devastated.

Instead, a vengeful smirk pulled to his face. "I'm afraid you don't get to make those decisions anymore, *Father.*" He spit it like a curse.

"Excuse me? Who do you think you're talking to?"

Royce just lifted his chin. That was right before the door behind us banged open, and two men in suits followed by about ten uniformed officers barged in.

A stampede of aggression.

One of the men held a huge file folder, and the other flashed his badge.

Stunned, I looked back at Royce.

Those dark eyes flashed.

Remorse and destruction.

And I got the sinking feeling he was about to destroy me.

twenty-six

Royce

A ripple of confusion and fear and betrayal bounded against the walls the second the office doors banged open and Pete, Detective Casile, and an army of armed officers stormed in.

I held fast, needing to see the bewilderment shift to ire in my stepfather's expression. I wanted to witness the second he realized I'd been coming for him the whole time.

The moment he knew he was going down in flames.

Couldn't stand it for long, the pull too great, and my gaze was getting drawn to Emily.

The girl a magnet.

Jade eyes darkened, swimming with distrust. The girl watched me like she was begging me to give her a good reason for my treachery. For not preparing her for what was coming when it was plain as day I'd known this was going down.

That this had been a setup.

To answer all the questions spiraling through that sweet, tender gaze.

It was bad enough when she found out I was Fitzgerald's stepson. Info I hadn't let her in on because it'd seemed too risky. Like if I let her get too close this would all fall apart.

I knew what was coming next would be a breaking point.

She'd never forgive me.

My guts tangled in regret. In another bout of loss.

I wished I could have done it differently.

But it had to come to *this*.

I needed that contract signed.

"What the fuck is this?" the bastard demanded, pushing to stand, shuffling the contract together on the desk.

I slammed my hand down on the papers, sneered his direction. "Not so fast. I think we're going to need these."

He struggled to rip the contract out from under my hand.

I snagged it up before he could get a chance.

All the men of Carolina George stood, trying to prepare themselves for the unexpected, confused and agitated.

Their manager, Angela, dropped her face into her hands and started to sob. She knew what was in that contract. The contract that had been altered since the last time the band had reviewed it.

But she was cooperating, knew not to say a word that would possibly tip Fitzgerald off to what was getting ready to go down. Willing to testify to save her ass.

Greedy bitch.

She probably wouldn't even see a jail cell.

Couldn't say the same for my stepfather.

Pete and Detective Casile moved deeper into the room.

The asshole glared. "Peter . . . what the hell are you doing here?"

"Sorry to interrupt," Pete said, quirking a smirk that promised he wasn't sorry at all. He was lanky and thin, in his forties, held down by Karl Fitzgerald's thumb for so many years that it was about time he finally came out from under it.

A dissenter.

Standing with me in this objection. He'd borne witness to more shady shit than any of us. He'd worked for Fitzgerald for the last ten years as his personal assistant. Once he realized how the company was really run, he'd started collecting evidence and feeding it to Detective Casile. We'd waited until we'd been certain we had enough proof to make sure Karl and Cory went down for a long, long time.

Enraged, Karl's beady eyes jumped between me and Pete and the detective, his throat bobbing thickly when it passed over the armed officers. He went for innocence when blame was written all over him. "What is the meaning of this? We're in the middle of a meeting here."

I tried to ignore the dread spilling from Emily who kept backing farther away. Tried to focus on my purpose.

I cocked my head. "The meaning of this is you're finished. You thought I was just going to stand aside and let you and Cory get away with what you've done? You are more delusional than I thought."

Fury knocked the calm façade he was wearing from his demeanor. His face turned so red I was pretty sure he was going to blow.

That was the plan.

"What are you talking about? This is nonsense."

I planted my hands on the desk. "What I'm talking about are the women you've extorted. The women you convinced to smuggle drugs in from other countries, promising them a better life, a home, and then turning around and forcing them into being your personal escorts once they get here. I'm talking about the money you've laundered through Cory Douglas, filtering it through A Riot of Roses' royalties. I'm talking about the deranged acts you covered for him in order to keep up the charade."

I angled down closer and spit the words in his face. "*I'm talking about what you allowed to happen to my sister.* What that bastard Cory did to her and you turned a blind eye because you are nothing but a greedy, motherfucking monster. I'm talking about every-*fucking*-thing you stole from me."

It was a growl.

Pure venom.

A bustle of energy shocked through the atmosphere.

Cracking and stirring.

"The fuck?" Rhys muttered.

Richard inhaled a sharp breath. Still wasn't sure how much he had been involved. If he'd been a willing partner or if he'd just stumbled on one of Karl Fitzgerald's seedy parties that gave a whole new meaning to sex, drugs, and rock 'n' roll.

Wrong place at the wrong time.

Underground parties that Karl threw.

Drugs and women and men at your disposal. It was always free, but oh, did it come at a cost. None knew they were being photographed. The pictures Karl used to manipulate his artists. What he held over them so he could siphon their royalties, keeping more of the pot for himself.

It was the devastated whimper coming from Emily that told me everything.

What made my spirit cringe and my heart flail. Urges hit me to turn to her and beg her to listen. To explain.

But I had to see this moment through.

"Are you joking? These accusations are nothing but lies. You have no proof." The bastard shook his head, dismissive. Like he thought this was another hiccup he could sweep under the rug.

Toss some money on it to cover it.

Pete laughed a sarcastic sound and tossed the thick folder to the desk. Picture after picture slid out.

Evidence that couldn't be contradicted.

Sex slavery and extortion and a mountain of depravity.

"Beg to differ," he said. "This has been coming a long, long time."

Fitzgerald's face turned beet red when he saw the contents of the files, panic rising up before he started tossing his gaze between Pete and me. "Fucking traitors. I was the one who took care of you." Detective Casile stepped forward. Karl rocked back in disbelief. In fear and the slowly sinking reality that this was happening.

His attention jumped around, like the asshole was actually

considering running.

I'd gladly take him down in a second flat.

"Karl Fitzgerald, I have a warrant for your arrest."

"This is bullshit. Complete fabrication. I want to speak to my attorney." Karl leveled me with a look that could decimate an entire village.

The detective moved around the desk. "I was just getting to that. You have the right to remain silent. Anything you say can and will be used against you in a court of law. You have the right to an attorney." He drew out that part like a taunt as he pulled out cuffs.

My stepfather sneered at me as the detective moved behind him, wrenching his arms behind his back. "You think you have the upper hand?" he spat. "I will destroy you, you piece of shit. I should have ended you a long time ago. What purpose does this serve? You just tossed the silver spoon I've been feeding you with in the trash."

Asshole was forgetting one very important thing—I was next in line. Not because he wanted me there. But because that was the one demand my mother had made when I'd been let out of prison.

I set the contract Carolina George had just signed on the desk, trapping it beneath the tip of my index finger. The contract in which Fitzgerald had altered the fine print without the band's knowledge.

Their manager had been in on it.

Paid off by Fitzgerald.

He wanted Emily, but none of the rest.

They'd just signed away their rights as a band.

I'd known he'd done it before but had never had the direct proof until now, the original and the altered contracts in my possession.

"If you remember clause 17.B3 of the Mylton Records bylaws, any fraudulent modifications or alterations of contracts is cause for immediate removal of Chair. Second-in-line is to assume that position. And guess who that is?"

My stepfather's current position gave him ninety-five percent of the votes, and he'd just ousted himself and placed me as the head of the company.

He struggled as Casile slapped the cuffs on his wrists. "No. I'll never let you take this company, you little fucker."

I lifted my chin, adjusted the cuffs on my suit jacket, finding some kind of sick calm in the midst of this.

Years of hatred.

Years of planning.

Years to bring this to fruition.

"You took everything in my life that was important to me. There is nothing left for you to take. This . . . this is for my sister, for my family, for all those women, you pile of shit. Get ready because I'm about to drop a match on it."

He roared. "This is my company."

Casile jerked him back. "Let's go."

"Fuck you. Release me."

Casile tugged him back, trying to wrangle him when he thrashed. "No. This isn't over. Not even close."

Satisfaction hit me as I watched them start to move him around the desk, all while I was getting smacked with an entirely different dread.

A river of disbelief and hurt flooded my system.

A deluge of her.

My attention jerked through the bodies surging forward to find her standing frozen in the middle of the chaos.

Hurt bleeding from that green gaze.

That energy tethering us shivered with sparks of unrelenting pain.

I started to go for her when Richard was suddenly in my face, forcing me to look at him as he yanked at his hair. "What the fuck was that?" he hissed, his voice lowered.

"I think it was clear enough."

"Yeah, it sounds like you just fucked us."

I laughed a low sound. "What I just did was save you."

In the background, my stepfather was still fighting. Thinking he had control of this. Control I'd taken from him.

Dropping his attention to the ground, Richard gave his head a harsh shake. When he looked back at me, fear blazed in his eyes. "Who is in those pictures?"

My teeth gritted. "Not you."

Didn't know if he was guilty or not.

But I hadn't come for him.

"This is bullshit. I want my attorney . . . now." My stepfather was shouting his demands while the officers pushed forward in a frenzy of activity. It jostled me back, out of the way, and a furor hit the room as the police officers tried to wrangle him through the crowd that was growing. People catching on to the fact that a shakedown was taking place in the middle of a celebrity fest.

Could only imagine what was going to be plastered across the tabloids tomorrow.

My bastard stepfather would be taken to the county jail where he would be extradited to Los Angeles. Originally, this was supposed to go down at his home. So my sister could witness it.

Since he'd demanded to come here for the signing, things had to be shifted last minute.

Pete and Detective Casile had come through like they promised.

He writhed, trying to break free, like he thought maybe he wasn't going to have to make this walk of shame through the guests of this party.

Another blow to his crumbling regime.

Through the chaos, my eyes raced to find the *one*.

Searching for the one thing left that mattered.

My sight landed on Melanie, who glared at me with outright disgust.

A roll of disappointment.

I jerked my eyes away, attention jumping across the faces as their manager was being led away by an officer, although without any cuffs.

Right then, I knew one more seedy fucker was being shackled and hauled away. Another group of officers sent to apprehend him during the meeting to ensure he'd be caught unaware.

His world shattered the way he'd shattered mine.

Hatred burned in my blood with the thought of the prick. At the reaction evoked in Emily when she'd seen him here.

Fear and shock and questions rolling from her.

I hated that she'd been subject to it.

I finally caught sight of her just as she raced out the door ahead of the mayhem.

Running.

And I knew exactly who she was running from.

twenty-seven

Emily

h God.

Oh God.

What just happened?

Rushing down the hall ahead of the chaos going down behind me, I struggled to make my feet carry me under the weight of the realization of what Royce had done.

He'd used me.

Used me to take over his stepfather's company.

A stepping-stone.

The memory of his warning tumbled through my mind.

"I'm afraid you're going to hate me when you find out who I really am."

I'd thought it was impossible.

Tears blurred my eyes, and I nearly bent in two, gasping for a breath as my mind reeled and my heart threatened to crack.

How could he do this?

My heels echoed in a panicked rhythm on the marble floor, and I hurried toward the end of the hall, coming up short when I saw the people swarming the entire place.

Packed wall to wall.

Bodies thick.

My eyes darted everywhere, landing on a small stairway to my left. I took it, stumbling up the steps as the chaos continued to grow from below.

When I made it to the landing, I fumbled down the hall to the left, ducking into the first empty room that I could find.

Desperate for seclusion.

For a way to clear the torment beating a path through my spirit and mind.

I slammed the door shut behind me, and I leaned against it as I struggled to remain standing, hugging my arms over my chest and trying to keep myself from splintering apart.

It was dim inside the sitting room, a couple lamps glowing their warmth that gave me no comfort. Walls decorated with large hand-painted family portraits, a big sectional leather sofa in the middle facing a large television on the far end, a few wing-backed chairs situated around the space.

Ragged pants heaved from my lungs, and I stumbled forward so I could sink down onto the couch.

Unable to remain upright when I felt the foundation getting ripped out from under me.

Everything I'd told Royce . . . everything I'd confided? Had every second of it been a ploy?

I dropped my head, trying to piece it together when the door creaked and the hairs at the nape of my neck lifted.

A sizzle of dread.

A prickle of alarm.

The door clicked shut again. Though this time, the lock rang out.

My legs wobbled when I forced myself to stand, when I forced myself to find the courage to turn around and face the evil I could feel filling the room like a sinister cloud.

"Get out," I rasped around the emotion that was already trying to bring me to my knees.

Cory Douglas laughed from where he stood at the door.

His blond hair appeared as crazed as the look in his eye. He shot me a condescending tsk, clucking his tongue as he drifted farther into the room. "Always so unwelcoming, Emily Ramsey. And here I'd heard it said that southern girls are the friendliest."

A shiver tumbled down my spine. Spread across my flesh. Pricking like barbed wire that snagged.

Little wounds that bled like the scar that he'd left on my body.

"Everyone's comin' for you."

It was probably the wrong thing to say, but I couldn't help but find some kind of justice in it.

I might have hated that Royce had used me to enact it.

It didn't matter.

I understood why.

A shudder ripped through me as I remembered the vengeance that had flashed in Royce's eyes when he'd told me someone had hurt his sister. The same agonized look he'd worn tonight when we'd come face-to-face with Cory and his wife.

Without a doubt, I wasn't the only person Cory Douglas had hurt.

From just inside the room, Cory cracked a menacing smile. "Seems so, doesn't it? Which is why I had to find you before it was too late."

A lump of fear lodged itself at the base of my throat. I tried to swallow around it. "It's already too late."

Cory moved in closer. The atmosphere went cold with the wickedness. "Nah . . . not quite."

He craned his head to the side, his own vengeance shining in his eyes. "You know . . . it's almost a little sad, isn't it? The way Royce is always trying to take what is mine?"

Disgust shivered across my flesh, and I took a fumbling step back farther into the room when he took one closer. "It was his fault to begin with, you know. First it was our band. Our band that was just getting ready to make it, on the cusp of greatness, and that bastard tried to take it from me."

311

Confusion twisted my brow. Mind spinning.

Cory must have seen it because he let go of a condescending laugh. "You didn't know that? Royce Reilly used to go by Royce Reed. Lead singer of A Riot of Roses. He always viewed me as a threat. Knew I was better than him. More talented. He tried to kick me out the minute before we got famous. Had to let him know who was really in control. Could anyone blame me?"

He was edging forward the entire time he was spewing the appalling words, and I was inching the opposite direction, out around the couch, trying to keep him as far away and as much furniture between us as possible. All the while trying not to crumble with the blatant admission he was making.

Cory dragged his fingers over his mouth. Maybe he couldn't stand the taste of his own depravity. "He learned real fast that he didn't have a say. I was far more valuable than him or any of the pathetic complaints that he had. Had to teach him a lesson, you know?"

Cory's voice shifted, drifting into this cold, distant malice. "Took his sister. Bitch deserved it, anyway."

Disgust prickled across my skin, the words a horrified tumble from my mouth, "Like you did me? Like you did that girl in the picture with my brother? Like you did with your wife? She was Royce's, wasn't she? His girlfriend?" I was backing up as I made the accusation. Sickness clawed through my being as I added it all up.

As it all came to a boil.

Cory was a sociopath.

A psychopath.

And Royce had used me to take him down.

Cory grinned. "Actually, she was his wife."

His statement hit me like a punch to the gut, the words inscribed on Royce's chest impaling me like a knife.

Love is the heart's greatest deceit.

Oh God, his heart belonged to his wife.

Anna. Anna. Anna.

"Asshole came after me when he found out about his sister," he continued. "He should have known he would be the one to go down. Fucker went to prison for three years for assault after he nearly killed me when I was simply paying back a debt."

He cocked his head. "See how that works, Emmy Love? An eye for an eye. You take something from me, and I take it back. Just like your brother tried to take Leah from me. Just like Royce tried to take my band from me. And now . . . now he's trying to take *you* from me. Well, I can hardly stand for that to happen since I haven't even had you yet."

God, he didn't even care that he was married. That his wife was somewhere in this house. Sickness rolled. He'd marked her. I could only imagine he viewed her as another possession.

Fear sliced through me. A dull, bitter blade dragging through my center. Cutting me open wide. Nothing there but more heartbreak and loss.

Trembling wracked my body, and I backed closer to the wall, trying to inch my way around the room toward the door. I was getting out of there before the monster snapped.

No one was touching me again. No one was going to hurt me again.

He kept coming closer, evil oozing from his pores and gushing into the room. "Get on your knees."

"I don't belong to you." It was a rasp of defiance.

Shouts echoed from somewhere downstairs, a commotion growing louder.

"They're comin'," I warned, trying to remain firm. To stay strong.

He laughed. "You really think I'm going down for this? You and Royce need to learn that I don't pay for anything. I take what I want. The world is mine, Emmy Love. Isn't that what they say? Cory Douglas is the king of the music scene?"

My mind flashed to the king etched on the back of Royce's hand. The pawns written on the knuckles of his fingers.

I had to wonder which was which.

Who was playing who.

Nausea curled in my stomach, and vomit crawled up my throat.

He slipped forward, closer and closer until he was two feet away. Until the only thing I could taste was his foul presence.

"Stay away from me. I'm warnin' you."

Cory cocked an insolent grin. "Or what, Emmy? What exactly do you think you're going to do?"

Exactly what I should have done all along.

Fight.

Royce

A flurry of activity buzzed around me, people scrambling through the room. Right as I was going after Emily, one of the officers had dragged me into a corner, asking me a bunch of questions. The whole time, I was searching over his shoulder, a hundred pounds pressing on my chest as I looked for her in the crowd.

Nerves racing.

This feeling taking me over.

Something different than coming to a boiling point with my stepfather.

Something sinister.

"We appreciate your cooperation."

I almost laughed.

I'd been plotting this for years. I was all too happy to

cooperate.

"Anything I can do. If you need me, you can get in touch with me through Detective Casile."

The second I said it, I dipped away, making my way through the bodies blocking the way to get out of the room.

Word had spread quickly that police officers were on the premises. A ton of people had scattered, not wanting their names in the press, while others were eager to get a front-row seat.

This was supposed to go down quick.

In and out.

And I hadn't seen Detective Casile in five minutes.

This already should have wrapped.

I pushed out into the hall, that feeling amping when I saw him walking toward me, frustration on his face. "Did you get him?" I demanded as soon as he was in earshot.

He gave a harsh shake of his head.

Dread spiraled.

Fuck.

Cory should have already been hauled away in chains. A fucking millstone around his neck.

"No. The team we sent to apprehend him was unable to locate him. Are you sure he was here?"

"Positive."

A low-sounding alarm started to thrum in the back of my mind, growing louder by the second. I sucked it down, tried to ignore the fear that dripped, a slow filter that trickled trepidation into my bloodstream.

"Fuck . . . he might have caught wind and slipped out while we were arresting Fitzgerald."

My head shook. "No, he's here."

I could feel it.

"Spread out. We need to get him. Now."

Shoving away, I rushed out into the main part of the house. Here, the house was packed. A throng that had missed the memo that cops were on the scene. Bodies pulsed and throbbed to the rhythm of the DJ that had set up outside by the pool. The accordion glass walls at the back of the massive house had been drawn back to create one huge free-flowing space.

My attention darted around the faces. Over the outright famous and semi-celebrities. Others that had snagged VIP tickets, so much awe in their eyes that I was pretty sure they thought they were floating on actual clouds.

But the two faces I was desperate to see were nowhere to be found.

I started to shove through the crowd, growing more frantic by the second.

My chest tightened.

Emily.

Fuck.

Emily.

I had to get to her.

Heart rate ratcheting up a few thousand notches, a fear unlike anything I'd ever felt crashed over me.

Wave after wave.

Surging higher and growing darker.

I nearly jumped out of my skin when a hand landed on my forearm. My attention jerked that way.

Acid pooled in my mouth.

Nadia.

Hatred and disgust billowed free, and my spirit seized in a clutch of pain. In old memories and old hopes and a lifetime of injury. She looked at me with those dark eyes that I thought I'd known. Looked at me like she still knew me. Like we still meant something to the other and she hadn't been a part of my demise.

"What do you want, Nadia? Aren't you terrified of me? Scared I might come unglued? Pose a threat?" I couldn't keep the venom from my tone, the hurt that bled and blistered. "You have a restraining order against me, remember?"

Regret passed through her eyes. "Royce." My name was a petition.

I ignored it.

Shocked by the fact that I didn't want to wrap her up. Hold her. My goal. My destination. Yeah, I wanted her safe. But the end game had shifted. The love I'd had for her a pale, pathetic

317

comparison to what I felt for Emily.

"Where is he?" I gritted out.

Worry moved through her expression. "I . . . I don't know. I've been looking for him for the last twenty minutes. He was acting strange."

Like that fucker acted like a normal human being?

Was real?

Whole?

My mouth twisted in a sneer. "Where the fuck is he, Nadia? I'm not fucking around. If you're covering for him——"

"I . . . I told you I don't know." The words trembled from the woman's lips—this woman I'd once committed everything to.

Her face pinched. "I'm scared, Royce. I . . . I made a huge mistake."

Anger blistered, but I shoved it down. "You don't need to worry. He won't hurt you again."

"I'm sorry," she whimpered.

I couldn't take the time to listen to her apology.

I tossed my attention across the roiling crowd. Knew how to pinpoint the action. The hotspots.

Sunder was out on the left side of the patio, surrounded by a horde of people who were vying to get a touch. To brush up against greatness.

Reuben Carmichael and his entourage were just inside.

Cory wasn't in the midst of either of them, and I knew well enough that he was powerful enough to create his own. That where he was, something wild would be going down.

Nothing.

On a silent roar, I roughed a hand over my face to break up the sickness I could feel taking over.

Panic racing.

Terror clotting the flow of blood through my body.

I pushed back through the crowd. When I broke free at the edge, I pointed at Detective Casile, who was giving some sort of instruction to one of the officers in a secluded area of the hall. "Spread out. He's somewhere here. His wife confirmed it."

Had the sinking feeling that he wasn't alone.

Without slowing, I burst through the doors of the kitchen. Blinding lights shone from the huge chandeliers dangling over the massive island, this room completely lit.

My eyes hunted through the faces.

Only one in mind.

Emily.

Soulshine.

Knew immediately that she wouldn't have sought refuge in the riot. Unless she was onstage, she was always on the sidelines. Slinking through the shadows. Feasting on the beauty of others, of music and hearts and hope, quietly adding her own into the mix.

Pushing out of the kitchen, I raced back down the hall toward the room where she'd left me. When she'd turned her back and walked away because she couldn't remain standing in the same room.

I started to search the rooms running the length of that hall, but the second I saw the desolated set of stairs that led to the second floor, I knew that was where she would have been drawn.

I bounded up them, taking them two at a time, my pulse a hammer that slammed at my chest and thundered through my veins.

At the landing, I started to take a right down the hall, but I stumbled.

Awareness crawled up my spine.

I angled my attention back over my shoulder.

Drawn.

Caught.

Hooked.

Could feel the terror ricocheting through the air. Trembling and shivering and cloying in my mind.

It was struck with the grave, dire need to protect.

The purpose I'd originally striven for was no longer certain.

Reason no longer real.

Mind-wrecker.

Spinning around, I rushed in the direction of her call, a fetter leashing me, pulling me closer and closer. I didn't even have to start searching the umpteen rooms.

I knew.

I grabbed the knob of the double doors to the right.

The knob rattled, the door locked.

Rage bristled beneath my skin, and I banged at the door, something between a shout and scream ripping from my throat. "Emily! Emily!"

Glass crashed behind the door, a scuffle, and then a bang on the floor.

I moved back a foot and rammed the door with my shoulder.

It shook but didn't give.

I did it again and again.

Ramming the wood.

Frantic.

Frenzied.

Shouting her name. Screams seeped through the walls.

I promised her I wasn't going to let this happen. That he would never touch her again. And I'd let it. Put her in the line of fire in order to fulfill my purpose.

Guilt and regret squeezed all the air from my lungs.

I couldn't . . . I couldn't let this happen.

Pain speared through my shoulder when I slammed the door again, but I felt the wood give. I moved all the way across the hall and threw myself at it.

Momentum splitting the wood at the lock.

The door banged against the inside of the wall.

Emily was on her stomach, fingernails scratching the wood floors as she tried to crawl away from the monster who was gripping one of her ankles. That shoe missing.

Blood was smeared across his face, his claws sinking into her flesh. Emily shifted around and kicked him in the face.

He roared and climbed over her, pinning her to the floor as he backhanded her.

It was the moment my hatred finally took over.

Stole my sanity and turned my sight black.

twenty-nine

Emily

A clatter of wood sounded from somewhere behind me, my heart racing in terror and hope.

Oh god. Someone was here.

But I was fearing they might already be too late when Cory climbed over me, his hand smacking across my face.

Pain fragmented across my cheek, sending my head rocking back.

I cried out beneath the fury that Cory succumbed to.

Perversion taking over.

He wrapped both hands around my throat and squeezed.

My fear was so thick it was blinding. Lungs failing in my chest.

I squirmed and flailed, the blood running off his chin dripping onto my face.

I'd gotten him good with a swing of a glass lamp that had nailed him. It'd stunned him, blood bursting from a gash on his cheek, sending him toppling to the floor. I'd tried to jump over him so I could get to the door, but he'd snagged me by the ankle.

Yanked me to the floor where he had me now.

"You fucking bitch. I'm going to end you. You think I'm going to let you get away with this?" Cory's words were a slur, hinged on his ragged breaths.

A blur flew into the room.

A wraith.

A shadow.

My dark, vengeful stranger.

He knocked Cory from me faster than I could process I was free. I choked and gasped for air while the two of them tumbled. They crashed into an end table. Wood splintered beneath their weight.

They tumbled, fighting to gain the upper hand. Bodies banging. Royce pinned Cory. "You piece of shit. You disgusting motherfucker."

Cory spit blood in his face. "Fuck you . . . just like I fucked your sister and your wife."

I saw it snap.

Royce's sanity.

Violence spilled out in a barrage of fists that pummeled against Cory's broken face.

Splitting.

Cracking.

Different than the night that he'd been protecting me from Nile.

This was vengeance.

Retaliation.

The man an avenger who was sent to destroy.

His hands flew. Unrelenting fury. Blood splattering across the floor.

I staggered to my feet, shuffling with one heel in their direction.

Shocked.

Lost to the stupor of what was happening.

Cory laughed a maniacal sound, his teeth white against the

blood covering his face. And I saw it, his hand wrapping around a jagged piece of wood. He lifted it and smashed it against the side of Royce's head.

Royce toppled over, dazed, and Cory was on him in a flash, lifting the jagged part of the wood, pointed like a spear, over his head.

Horror slammed me. The realization of what he was going to do.

There was no consideration. I rushed him.

Arms wrapping around Cory's waist, catching him by surprise. He flung his arm out to stop me.

The piercing agony in my shoulder sent me falling face-first to the ground, the wood impaling my flesh.

I screamed, holding onto the wound. Then I whimpered, trying to shove myself away with my heels when Cory started to climb to his feet.

Sure this was the end.

"Freeze." The voice banged through the room, and I cried out in relief.

A clamor of heavy footsteps pounded into the room, and Cory was pushed facedown onto the floor, arms wrenched behind his back while he laughed like the madman that he was.

From where I lay on the cold, hard floor, my eyes sought out the one who'd stolen my heart.

Royce was on the ground five feet from me, those onyx eyes wide with regret and affection, a gash on the side of his head matting his hair and running with blood.

I'd thought he was meant to be the one standing at my side.

My partner.

My soul ached.

Maybe sometimes the ones who were supposed to stand with us were only meant to stand with us for a moment in time.

There to serve a purpose.

Just like I'd been Royce's.

A scream tore from the doorway, and high heels clicked across the floor as the woman who'd been with Cory dropped to her knees at his side.

She wailed. "Cory, oh god, what happened? What did you do?"

She sank to her bottom when the officers hauled him up with his arms shackled behind his back. Cory's legs were slack beneath him, the man refusing to stand as the officers dragged him toward the door.

Tears streamed down the woman's face as she watched them take him away. Then she looked to Royce and slowly crawled on her hands and knees in his direction. "Royce, what have I done? I'm so sorry. I'm sorry."

She buried her face in his throat, and he threaded his fingers in her hair and slumped all the way back.

Love is the heart's greatest deceit.

Maybe he was right, after all.

Grief crushed down.

So heavy.

Too much.

A paramedic was suddenly there, a hand on my back. "Stay still. Don't move. Tell me where you're injured."

"My shoulder."

Gloved fingers moved over the wound that was excruciating, but it was the wound deep within my soul that was truly agonizing.

What left me battered and bruised.

Broken.

But the truth was, it was worth the sacrifice.

Cory gone. No longer a threat. Those women saved.

Royce's sister safe.

Just like me.

My spirit churned with a deep-seated relief.

I dropped my head, cut wide open by this double-edged sword.

The paramedic shifted me around to sitting and wrapped a blanket around my shoulders. "We need to transfer you to the emergency room for sutures."

"Okay," I whispered, though I was looking at Royce, who was in a similar position across the room. Being examined while the woman remained a ball at his feet.

Remorse thrummed in the distance between us.

That energy fierce.

Tormented and wrong.

His expression was grim. Confirmation that this had been his intention all along.

I was being placed on a stretcher as a precaution when Richard broke through the crowd gathered in the room. He ran to me.

Hands fisted in his hair. "Shit . . . Em . . . are you hurt? Oh my god."

Part of me wanted to go to him. To drop to my knees in front of him and wrap my arms around his fierce, warm, powerful body. Beg him to explain it to me. But the bigger part of me was terrified of what he would say.

What he would admit.

Richard gripped my hand. "I'm so sorry, Em. I'm so sorry. This is all my fault. I should have known from the start that Royce was up to something. He called me a week before he joined the tour and suggested that he come. He said he would make sure you signed if I agreed to bring him on, but he made me promise not to say anything. I thought he just wanted to sign the band. That we were working together to make that happen."

"It's okay," I mumbled.

None of that mattered anymore. This whole thing was much bigger than us. My worry for Richard still great, unable to believe he would be involved in any of the accusations Royce had made against Karl Fitzgerald.

With the things Cory had done to me, I had no question they were true.

Richard brushed back the hair matted to my face. "You know who he is?"

Royce Reilly.

Liar.

Lover.

My heart.

My biggest mistake.

Now head of Mylton Records.

Previous lead of A Riot of Roses.

No, I hadn't known.

But maybe I should have all along. The signs written in the

stars that I'd dipped my fingers into, unable to stop from giving into the temptation.

He'd warned me I'd regret it. From the beginning, he'd told me not to forget that I would.

But the heart had a mind of its own. Wayward and unruly. Reaching for the dangerous, sure it would be worth the risk.

My spirit shook.

I guessed maybe it was. Maybe I would have given anything to experience those few stolen moments. But I hadn't been prepared that it could hurt so much.

"A fallen star," I whispered.

Richard tightened his hold. "I should have told you."

My head shook. "It wouldn't have mattered."

Those confessions were on Royce.

The crimes on Cory.

"It's Cory who's to blame. Let's not forget that," I found myself saying.

Richard squeezed his eyes together, his expression morphing through a hundred different emotions as he came to a realization. "It was him? Cory was the one who hurt you? The one who had been causing you all that anxiety? Because of me?" The last was a guttural rasp.

My eyes squeezed shut, too, and instead of answering, I asked my own. "Who is she, Richard? Who is that woman in the picture? Please . . . tell me you aren't involved in something so cruel."

He pressed his lips to my temple, whispered, "Never. Never." It was a plea. "And because of you, she is free. That's the only thing that matters."

I choked over the emotion that surged.

The detective who'd first entered the office approached me, his eyes moving over me like he was looking for injuries. Sympathy filled his expression when he met my gaze. "I'm sorry this happened to you on our watch. That wasn't supposed to be how it went down."

I could barely nod.

"I'm going to ask that you make a formal statement tomorrow. Testify if you're willing."

My soul throbbed.

More of the pieces sliding together. What Royce had wanted all along. I'd been a target. A calculated casualty.

"If it means Cory will go away for longer, then yes, I will agree to testify."

He gave a somber dip of his head. "Go on, get checked out. I'll be in contact with you tomorrow so we can get your statement."

He stepped back, and Richard returned to my side as they started to wheel me away.

My spirit thrashed when I felt the presence consume.

That connection pulling at me in a way I couldn't let it.

The paramedics paused, and Royce was suddenly there, towering over me to the side.

"Emily." My name was grit.

Gravel.

Dirt.

Dust.

Floating away into nothing at the end.

My entire being winced at the familiarity.

This man I'd fallen so desperately for.

"I need you to answer something for me, and I want the truth," I said, trying to steel myself, not sure I was ready for what I was asking.

He lifted his chin, flashing the tattoo imprinted on his throat.

"The first night at that bar in Savannah . . . is that why you sought me out? Because you knew Cory had gotten to me? Because you needed me to testify to put him away? Because you knew Carolina George was the way to steal your stepfather's company?"

Regret blistered across his flesh, but his eyes . . . they no longer held any mystery.

No reason left to keep any secrets.

"Yes."

The word speared me like an arrow.

Tears slipped free at the corners of my eyes and dripped into my hair.

Royce reached for me.

"Don't touch me," I whimpered, angling away.

I couldn't handle it.

His remorse.

His hurt.

He'd hurt me enough.

My tongue darted out to wet my lips, and I forced out the one thing I needed to say. "I don't know how you knew, and I don't want to, but I want you to know, I would have done it for you. For your sister. For your wife. For those women. Freely. You just needed to ask."

Grief slashed across his face. "Emily."

I squeezed my eyes closed. "Please, don't . . . the one thing I asked of you was not to lie to me, and I'm pretty sure that's the only thing you've done."

Blanching, he stepped back, out of the way of the paramedics.

As they wheeled me out, I felt as if I was leaving a piece of myself behind.

Shredded.

Slayed.

Nothing left but fragments and mist.

Following along at my side, Richard dipped down to press a kiss to my temple. "I'm so sorry."

"It's not your fault."

He tightened his hold on my hand. "Yes, it is."

Royce

"Are you sure this is what you want?" Sebastian Stone sat at the table opposite of me in his kitchen in Savannah, Georgia. He slowly shuffled through the piles of paperwork set out in front of him. It wasn't that he didn't know every detail. Both our attorneys had spent hours hashing them out.

Sunlight poured in through the window of the close to two-century-old house that was nothing but southern charm.

The kitchen as country as his wife, Shea.

As country as Emily.

Emily.

Slanting a hand through my hair, I paced, shoved down the errant thought.

I didn't want to think about her.

Couldn't.

Not without breaking apart.

"You know that it is," I told him, grinding my teeth.

He sighed, and the guy rocked back in the white wooden dining chair and studied me where I was carving out a path in the floor.

Unable to sit still.

Unable to settle.

Children's laughter seeped through the walls. His children, Kallie and Connor, were playing upstairs, their carefree voices echoing down into the house.

Shea's voice was drifting down, the melody she sang mixing with the tenor of her daughter's.

Torment pulsed.

God.

This was too much.

"Royce, man, you've got to know what Mylton Records is worth." Baz gestured to the contract, dragging my attention away from his family.

I looked out the window over the side yard of the historic house, voice firm. "The artists represented under the label are worth more than any dollar amount."

He sighed. "Yeah. You're right. They are. Have to be a hundred companies who would gladly make you a very rich man in order to get their hands on this company."

I shifted around to meet his eye. "And that would mean they wouldn't have you to represent them."

He nodded slow, hand rubbing his chin, contemplation in his eyes. "Then let's do it together. Merge. You can work alongside me to make sure these bands are given the best chance. You and I know this business better than anyone else."

Resting my hand on the wall, I dropped my head, appreciating his belief. His support. Friendship he'd given me since the day A Riot of Roses had opened for a Sunder show in a seedy dive bar in Hollywood more than ten years before.

I glanced over at him. "Not the life I want, man."

Producing.

It'd never been in my blood.

It'd been nothing but an angle.

A way to infiltrate Mylton Records.

A frown pulled across Baz's brow. "And what life is it that you want?"

Regret pulsed out on a slow breath.

Emily.

Anna.

Emily.

Anna.

Their names ran through me on a downward spiral.

"Don't know."

Only I did. Knew it better than anything. Problem was, six months ago, before Emily had stumbled into my life, that picture had looked completely different.

Taking my family back.

Baz nudged the contract my direction. "You've got to at least take more money for this. Take a cut. A fucking percentage. Something."

Pursing my lips, I shook my head. "Don't want the money, Baz. You know what to do with it."

He scrubbed both palms over his face before he dropped them, the smirk on his face turning wry. "Then what? You don't want the money? At least tell me you want the goddamn band."

It was close to midnight when my driver pulled up to the circular drive in front of Karl Fitzgerald's mansion.

Pretension oozed from the white stone walls, all the windows lit up like the estate was some kind of beacon hovering over the city, a guiding light, though there was something about it tonight that appeared sad and pathetic.

I opened the door. "I won't be long."

He offered a curt nod, and I climbed out, striding up the walkway and bounding up the ten steps that led to the grand entry.

I didn't bother to knock or ring.

I let myself in.

My mother stumbled to a stop at the end of the hall when she saw me enter, wearing a silk nightgown and matching robe, clutching an empty wine glass, eyes red and blotchy.

"What did you do?" she demanded.

"What should have been done years ago," I tossed out, not even slowing as I headed for the set of curved stairs that led to the second floor.

"Royce . . . how could you? You've destroyed this family," she shouted behind me.

I ignored her and continued to climb, heading down to the end of the hall on the right. Quietly, I rapped at the door.

Maggie immediately opened it, like she'd been waiting for my return. Watching out the window for my arrival. She threw herself at me, hugging my waist, burying her face in my chest.

I wrapped my arms around her.

Hugged her tight.

"You're back," she whispered, clinging to me. "You're back."

My heart clenched. So fiercely I couldn't make sense of what it was that I felt anymore. "I'm here. I'm here. Not going anywhere, Mag-Pie."

Edging back, she stared up at me like she was almost scared to hope. "Is it done?"

I gripped her by the outside of the shoulders, rubbing my thumbs over her arms. "It's done."

Relief gusted out on a small cry that she tried to bury in my chest. I held her, rocked her and whispered, "I've got you. It's going to be alright. No one is going to hurt you."

She was nodding frantically at my words, trying to latch onto them, to take them on as truth.

"You still want to leave?" I asked quietly to the top of her head.

"Yes. More than anything."

"Okay, let's go."

She didn't hesitate. She stepped back, swiped a hand across her bleary face, and moved to the double doors of her closet. She grabbed a giant duffle bag that was already packed from the floor.

"Someone's anxious." I cocked her a teasing brow, going for light as I could when the weight of this reality had followed me all the way back to Los Angeles.

Four days since everything had gone down in Nashville.

Four days since Emily had looked at me with the hatred I knew I was going to leave behind in her eyes.

Four days of feeling like I was slowly bleeding out.

Four days since the fire she'd lit went dim.

Maggie choked out a laugh. "I've been desperate to get out of this house for four years. I almost ran down to meet you at the end of the drive."

She handed me her bag, and I slung the strap over my shoulder, slowing when her expression turned serious.

"I just want to start over, Royce. I want a life. A real one. And I can't do that here. Not after everything. I'm finished being scared."

I took her by the chin. "And that's what you're going to have."

Her smile was small and sad. "And now you get one, too. A restart. A new chance."

I tried to smile back. Was pretty sure it was a grimace. "Think it's too late for me, Mag-Pie."

thirty-one

Emily

*T*he harsh blaze of the summer sun beat down from the bluest sky.

Blinding rays glinted in golden streaks against my eyes, the air shimmering with the fever of it. Sweat gathered along my hairline, dribbling down my back and chest, soaking my tank top.

A swell of dizziness spun my head as I stood in the swamp of unbearable heat. But I forced myself to keep going, to keep plucking at the ocean of weeds that had grown up in my mama's vegetable garden.

It was all I could do.

Keep moving.

Keep busy.

Don't stop.

Because if I did, I knew I was goin' to crumble.

Fully succumb to this broken heart that just kept growing wider and deeper. A crevice that had cracked right down the middle of me.

Splitting me in two.

An abyss.

Infinite.

The weeks had passed in a blur of speeding days that dragged on forever.

Future never so uncertain.

Not mine or the band's or Mylton Records'.

Sorrow clawed through my being, and I blinked my eyes frantically, trying to see past the blinding pain that seared.

Gripping me in a fist of hopelessness.

"Would you come inside before you have yourself a heat stroke?"

My mama's voice hit me from behind, and I raked my forearm across my face, swiping up the moisture, not sure if it was sweat or tears. Gathering myself, I swung around to face her, pinning on the fakest smile I could find.

She just about stumbled in her tracks when she got a good look at me. "Oh, Emily."

Sympathy rolled out.

Sympathy I didn't have the power to stand up under.

"Don't, Mama. I'm just fine."

A frown dented her forehead. "*Just fine* you are not."

She kept coming closer. With every step, I could feel the exterior I'd been fronting crumbling. The faked smiles and the shallow conversations I'd been giving the last four weeks drying up.

We'd labeled Carolina George's break a vacation. A celebration of being signed. A commemoration of the huge influx of followers we'd gained and spike in sales after the performance we'd made at the ACB Awards.

We didn't let on that we'd been crushed. Had the rug ripped out from under us.

Neither Richard nor I able to stand.

He'd been . . . devastated when he found out what Cory had done to me.

Taking on the blame but unwilling to confess to me why he was hiding what he was.

He refused to explain what those pictures meant, even when I promised I'd still keep his secret. That I had no place to judge.

While I'd walked around like a zombie. Unable to feel and feeling far too much.

Watching the tabloids go wild with the speculation over Mylton Records, a barrage of pictures of Royce that had surfaced from years before, when he'd been a rising star.

Streaking and shining and so gloriously bright in all his desperate darkness.

Before he'd fallen.

Bound behind bars in a tiny cell for three years—something he'd never once mentioned—before he'd been released and found himself as Mylton Records second-in-line.

Now at the helm since Karl Fitzgerald had been dethroned.

God, it hurt.

Finding out that I didn't know him at all.

That his intentions might not have been wicked, but had still been wrong.

That he'd used me up and spit me out.

Now I was left unable to wipe the picture of his wife's face from my mind.

His fingers in her hair as he'd sagged with clear relief.

Like he'd been overcome with joy that she was free and safe, too.

And how could I bemoan that?

I just wished he wouldn't have made me fall in love with him along the way.

Just another one of those pawns on his fingers that had been played.

"I'm barely holding it together, Mama," I said in a rush.

Suddenly weak, I stumbled forward and slumped down onto the lawn that stretched between the garden and the back of my childhood home.

I blinked through the inner chaos, through the searing heat that I could feel burning me alive from the inside out.

A blistering torment that I wasn't sure I would ever escape.

A knot grew thick in my throat, emotion racing up from where I'd been trying to keep it buried for weeks.

Pretending as if I was goin' to be just fine.

My mama settled beside me on the lawn. The two of us stared off into the sagging heatwaves that glimmered across the rolling planes.

"I'm so sorry, Emily, about what happened to you. I . . . I still can't fathom it. The horror of it. There is no worse feeling for a mother than to know one of your children has been hurt and you weren't there to stop it. That there's nothing I can say or do now to fix it. Erase it. And God, that is the only thing I want to do. I want to take that pain from you."

I let my attention drift over to my mama, who was wearing her own heartbreak. "You know that it's not your fault. I'm a grown woman."

"But you'll always be my baby," she told me, her brow twisting, trying to get me to see.

I got it.

I got it so much.

"The only thing that matters is he can't hurt anyone anymore," I whispered.

"Is it? Is it the only thing that matters?" she asked, angling her head to the side in a bid to take in my response, to watch for my truth, because we both knew this was so much more than the trauma from Cory.

I sucked a heaving breath into my aching lungs. It trembled back out in an undulating wave of misery. "I couldn't sing, Mama. I couldn't write. All the songs that had burned inside of me dried up."

Gathering my fingertips to a pinpoint, I pressed them to the vacant spot in the middle of my chest. "It'd been that way since I was assaulted . . . a part of me that got locked up. Lost."

I let my gaze drift out over the property, to the branches of the trees that rustled in the hot summer breeze.

A tremor ripped across my chest. "And then he found me, Mama . . . this man who I knew so much better than to fall for found me, and for the first time in my life, I felt like I truly belonged. Like someone got me for me. Like a part of me that hadn't been there before had come alive. But I was wrong. So wrong. The only thing he did was leave me wandering. Adrift. Falling."

I struggled for air. "Now, I'm lost. So lost, and I don't know if I'm ever goin' to find my way back."

She reached over and threaded her fingers in mine.

Silent support.

Quiet encouragement.

Rocked with a spear of pain, I dropped my head, squeezed my eyes about as tightly as I squeezed her hand. "I'm pregnant, Mama."

She squeezed back. "I know, sweet girl. I know."

I lifted my gaze to hers. She sent me a secret, sorrowful smile. "You think I haven't noticed you running to the bathroom every morning the last week?"

My lips trembled in something between a smile and devastation. "You know when you wish for something so badly, with all of your might for so many years, and then it's given to you but it looks so much different than you ever imagined? You've got to wonder if you're being taunted. Given a curse."

A frown tipped her mouth down at the side. "Is that what you really think?"

A bluster of wind blew through, whipping my hair into disorder and rushing across my heated flesh. That cavern in the middle of me throbbed, suffering intense. But I welcomed it. Let myself feel. Maybe fully for the first time in weeks.

I shifted my gaze to my mother. This woman who had stood by me in every season of my life. Through tiny hurdles and the biggest obstacles.

Huge victories and the smallest wins.

"No, I don't. Maybe I'm not sure how to hold this blessing. Not when it scares me so much."

A soft smile pulled to her lips, and she reached out and tucked a wayward lock of my hair behind my ear. "The things that are the most important are what scare us the most."

"No wonder I'd been terrified of Royce the first time I saw him," I said.

"He sure looked plenty scared of you, too."

My head shook. "No, Mama. I was a means to an end. Insurance."

"Are you sure about that?"

My spirit screamed, thrashing and toiling, my mind etched with his expression from that night. "He admitted it himself."

"Love makes us do drastic things, Emily." She stood, dusted off the back of her shorts, and stretched out a hand to help me to standing. "Makes me wonder about the lengths he would go to for you."

"I haven't heard from him in four weeks, Mama. He hasn't even tried to explain himself. Left the band without a word. We don't even know if the original contract is gonna stand."

I'd found out from Detective Casile the magnitude of the changes that had been made to our contract.

The way it'd given them the right to cut any member loose at any time.

Karl had wanted Richard gone. I shuddered at the thought of the way he'd wanted to have control over me.

Rumors had been running rampant about the dissolution of Mylton Records. That its future was uncertain. We had no idea where we stood, our attorney instructing us to hold tight until he had more information.

Not that the contract was my main concern. But Royce knew how important it was to the band. To my family. That it was what was supposed to have brought us together in the first place.

"The silence speaks volumes, don't you think?" I said.

Mama touched my face. "Maybe you should listen to what it's saying."

It was just after seven that evening when I was coming down the stairs and there was a light tapping at the front door. Twilight poured in through the windows, spilling pinks and grays and muted light into the quieted house.

My pulse spiked, drummed an extra beat. I sucked it down, increased my pace as I took the last couple steps to the front door. I peered out the side window onto the porch, trying to fight the unending disappointment that it wasn't him.

That he'd really left me.

That what I'd thought we'd shared hadn't been real.

Confusion narrowed my eyes when I saw a woman standing at the door, hair tied in a haphazard knot on top of her head as she peered around, anxiously taking in her surroundings.

Well, a young woman.

A very young woman who was shifting on her feet and chewing at her bottom lip.

I reached for the lock and turned it.

A strange sort of energy lit in the air when I opened the door.

Familiar but different.

She lifted her gaze.

Dark, dark eyes tangled with mine.

The color of onyx.

Though hers didn't glint white flames. They held a warm, simmering amber.

My chest clutched and my spirit gave, tendrils reaching for her as if it'd found a fiber it didn't know it'd been missin'.

"Hi," she said, so quiet, her voice so timid and unsure.

I swallowed around the thickness in my throat, as if it might hold back the emotion rising fast.

A flash flood.

"Hi," I barely managed.

"I'm . . . I . . ."

I widened the door. "I know who you are."

Maggie.

I could almost see his eyes glimmer when he'd said it. Compassion and love and loyalty.

"Come in," I told her, realizing how badly my hands were shaking when she angled past me and I shut the door.

A leather messenger bag strapped across her body, she was

wearing simple clothes, jeans and a white tee and white Vans, the girl so sweet and pretty that it was making it hard to remember that hard cruelness of her brother. The only thing I could feel right then was the stunning protectiveness he'd felt for her.

"Would you like something to drink?" I offered.

Awkwardly.

Because what I really wanted to ask was what she was doing here. If Royce was okay. Scream that none of this was fair.

Then I wanted to wrap her up and hug her close and tell her I understood.

But I just stared, watching her carefully, her watching me, as if neither of us knew if the other was going to crack.

"No, thank you. I won't be here long."

Was that disappointment that flashed?

"He doesn't know I'm here. He thinks I'm spending the weekend in Palm Springs with my girlfriends . . . my first trip away by myself," she admitted, a blush pinking her cheeks as guilt clouded her features. "But I couldn't not come. Not after everything he's sacrificed for me."

I nodded slow. "He cares for you . . . so deeply."

She laughed out a disbelieving sound, her gaze cast to the floor before she turned it back on me. "I think I could say the same about you."

Grief clutched every cell in my body, refusing what she claimed and simultaneously wishing that it were true. "He did what he had to do for you, Maggie. I understand it. Have accepted it. I forgive him for it."

I was willing to be one of those pawns on his fingers if it meant him getting justice for his little sister. That she might be able to step out of her home without a sense of fear. That she might have a chance to fly free.

Lines curled across her brow. "You think he used you?"

She said it as if she were actually disgusted by the thought.

"I'm okay that he did."

It was only partially a lie.

The laughter that rolled out of her was quiet. Incredulous affection. "Can I tell you something, Emily? If I can call you that?"

She peered at me, terror and hope brimming in her eyes.

"Of course."

Of course, it was my own terror at what she was gettin' ready to say that sped through my veins.

"I understand that you feel that way. My brother . . ." She almost rolled her eyes as she looked at me as if I would get it—as if we were thick as thieves—the oldest of friends.

"He's . . . intense," she seemed to settle on.

Without my permission, a small laugh pulled from my throat.

"Yeah, just a little bit."

She crossed her arms and started to pace in her own anxiety. "He takes things to the extreme. He was my hero, you know, growing up?"

She glanced over at me.

I remained silent, not sure what to make of her showing up here. Across the entire country.

"I mean, could you imagine your big brother being the lead singer in a band? So cool, and you wanted to be just like him?" She eyed me with a small smirk. "Well, I guess you can."

Warmth spread, a blanket of it, one I wanted to return to her and hold her with.

I liked her. Liked her way too much, which only made every second of this harder.

"I'm sure he was somethin'."

I could only imagine Royce as a teenager. So alive and wild and unruly.

Impassioned by his songs.

Relentless in his commitment.

A devastating force every time he stepped into a room.

"He was gonna be a big deal. Like a huge deal. Everyone knew it, saw his talent. I mean, my father despised him—"

I cringed when she mentioned it, hating that was the kind of home Royce had been raised in.

"So for him to sign Royce's band, they had to be good. But my father . . . he always judged everything by its dollar value. How much money it was going to make him. So, A Riot of Roses? You could bet they were going to be worth a lot."

Her smile faltered a little. "Even when he was giving it his all for the band, working nonstop, doing everything it took to make it big? He was still there for me. Took time for me. It wasn't like either of my parents really gave a crap."

She sucked her top lip between her teeth, like it was a nervous habit. "Even when he got married, he made sure I knew I was still *his girl.*"

I tried not to flinch at the picture that invaded my mind.

Still, I was hugging my arms over my chest.

Trying to hold it together. To be okay with this part of Royce's life when part of me felt like it should have been mine.

"And when he had his daughter—"

I choked, unable to stop the shock, this feeling as if I were being strangled.

The final stake confirming I didn't know Royce at all.

That he'd never let me in.

My hand darted out to the back of the couch to keep me standing.

"He has a child?"

Maggie's face twisted in remorse. "I'm sorry. I-I didn't know he hadn't told you." In discomfort, she fiddled with her fingers. "But of course he wouldn't. He doesn't talk about it. Ever."

I forced myself to look at her.

"He was devastated when he lost her, Emily. Absolutely destroyed."

"How did he lose her?"

Why was I asking this? Torturing myself?

She blew out a shaky sigh, hesitating. She seemed to have to convince herself to continue. "Royce found out that Cory was involved in some bad things with my father. I know I wasn't supposed to know about it, but I heard the two of them arguing in the office. Royce had said he'd kicked Cory out of the band. My father had demanded that he bring him back. Royce had refused. Said he wouldn't stand for the band to be involved in anything criminal. Tensions between my father and Royce had been running high. Getting worse and worse."

She dropped her gaze, paced in agitation, flapping her hands at her sides as if she were trying to shake off the trauma.

"Royce had picked me up that night and told me I was his date for the show. I was so proud, Emily. So proud that I got to stand by him. Just be in his space. I was always his biggest fan. But he had an interview afterward. He'd left me in one of the private rooms backstage. He made me promise not to leave that room until he came back for me."

A tight sob worked its way free of her throat. My soul wept. Pain leeching out, or maybe it was taking on some of hers.

"There was a knock at the door. I . . . I thought Royce had forgotten something. But it was Cory. I tried to shut the door, Emily. I did. But he was too strong. He forced his way in. He'd locked the door behind him, told me Royce was trying to steal what was most important from him, and it was time my brother learned a lesson."

Oh God.

I couldn't handle it.

Her story that felt far too familiar.

The debased, despicable man whose soul was set on desolation.

"Maggie," I whimpered, holding my stomach.

Without looking up, she held one of her hands out toward me, as if she were asking me not to say anything until she could get it out.

Her grief so strong.

Unrelenting in the space.

"He forced me, Emily." Her words turned haggard, grating whimpers. "Forced me. The whole time, he kept saying it was Royce's fault. Like he had a right. And then . . . he . . . "

Her fingertips went up to rake at a spot on her collarbone. "He cut me. Marked me. Told me that I belonged to him."

A shiver of revulsion rocked through her.

She tugged down her shirt to show me the angry X that was almost a perfect match to the one I bore on my hip.

My hand went to my mouth and a tear slipped from the corner of my eye.

But Maggie . . . they were pouring down her face.

"Cory just . . . left me there on the floor," she continued, barely able to speak. "Bleeding and crying and sure that I was going to die."

Her teeth raked over her quivering bottom lip. "Royce found me. I can barely remember anything at that point . . . I was going in and out of coherency. Completely in shock. I just remember him coming through the door and finding me crumpled on the floor. The roar that came out of him before he rushed in to gather me up in his arms."

Her throat bobbed as she swallowed. "I woke up in the hospital the next day. My father was there . . . sitting in the chair beside me."

A tremor rolled through her body. "I just remember . . . remember the coldness that had taken to the room, this feeling that nothing in my life was ever going to be the same. He was so casual, Emily. So callously casual and matter-of-fact while I lay there in that hospital bed. He'd said that Royce had been arrested for attempted murder after an assault on Cory Douglas. An unprovoked assault."

I was trapped by her unwavering gaze, by the truth of what she was trying to convey.

"I'd tried to tell him what happened. I'd begged him. Told him he was wrong. Pleaded with him to believe me. He just pushed to his feet and leaned over me, his voice hard and frigid."

Hers went distant, her eyes pinching at the corners with her own heartbreak.

Her own betrayal.

"My father told me that I'd been carrying a glass down the stairs the night before. That I tripped and it broke and I cut myself. He said that was it. There was nothing more to it. Then he walked out. My own father, Emily. And my brother served a three-year sentence because he was the only one who was willing to stand up and defend me."

Agony clawed. So sharp, sinking in, ripping me to shreds. I was trying not to weep.

For Maggie.

For Royce.

Only she wasn't finished, and I didn't know how much more I could take.

"A month after he was convicted, my brother's wife filed for divorce and petitioned the court for his parental rights to be revoked. Royce was deemed a danger to his family. I'm sure my father paid off the judge to make sure it went through. It wasn't too long after that she and Cory started showing up in pictures together."

Oh God.

I couldn't breathe.

"Cory took everything from him, Emily. His wife. His child. His band. His *freedom*."

"Royce." I couldn't stop the whimper from fleeing through my lips.

Maggie wrung her fingers, cleared some of the roughness from her voice. "When he was released, he was offered a job at Mylton Records as head of A & R, but he was written in as second-in-line. It was the one good thing my mother ever did for either of us, but I'm pretty sure she only did it to absolve her of a little of the guilt she felt for going along with what my father demanded. I always knew Royce had a plan. He'd promised me he would finish what he started, but that it would take time to take down an empire that strong."

A shiver rocked my soul.

This was where I'd become a tool. A puppet in his intricate play.

She must have caught my reaction because she angled her head, a frown pinching her brow.

"After all that, Emily . . . after everything the two of us had been through . . . could you imagine when my brother went to Atlanta to sign an up-and-coming band, a band called Carolina George, and he discovered Cory Douglas attacking their singer? Using her the same way he'd used his sister? He'd lose his mind, wouldn't he?"

Everything lurched.

The ground trembling beneath my feet.

"What are you saying?"

Memories flashed. Me in that hotel room. Someone from room service interrupting the attack.

She edged a little closer. "He came to sign your band, Emily, but instead he found *you*." I stumbled back a step, unable to process what she was telling me. Maggie kept on, her tone dipping in emphasis. "That girl would haunt him. Make an impression he couldn't erase, and he would do everything in his power to make sure he could protect her, too. Just like he protected his sister."

My hands went to my mouth. "No . . . he couldn't have—"

But I knew it. The familiarity I'd felt. The intense warmth. The comfort I'd felt when I'd first seen him at that bar.

As if he'd been sent to find me.

Royce.

"He did, Emily. And I know you don't know me. That you don't trust me or him, but you needed to know. You didn't become a part of the plan. You became a part of the reason. His reason."

Hope and doubt warred, my heart taking off at breakneck speed. "But what about his wife?"

I was gripped by the echo of the night he'd made love to me. When he'd confessed the name, uttered it aloud as I'd traced my fingers over the words forever marked on his chest.

"Anna." I spoke her name like a plea. "He loves her. He told me."

It nearly buckled me in two admitting it.

To give her voice.

Confusion craned Maggie's head, and her eyes narrowed before a tender smile took to her face. "Anna?"

She said it like a question.

I nodded frantically.

She slowly shook her head. "Emily, his wife's name was Nadia. Anna is his daughter."

I was shaking, trembling so hard I could feel it rattling the walls.

Rattling my soul.

"His daughter."

Her smile was somber. "He's had to fight for everything in his life, Emily. For everyone he loves. He lost her, and I hope to God he gets her back. But you need to know, he needs you just as much."

Maggie reached into the flap of her bag and pulled out a massive envelope. "I intercepted this from the attorney yesterday. I thought I should deliver it myself—just in case you had any further doubts."

She handed it to me. Weakly, I accepted it, my knees wobbling and spirit trembling. "What is it?"

She angled her attention toward it. "Something you need to see."

She moved for the door, turned the knob, and paused in the threshold. "It was so nice to meet you. I really, really hope I see you again."

Then she stepped outside and left me there holding the papers that felt as if they weighed a million pounds.

Overcome, I rushed for the high table set up at the wall beneath the stairs, my nerves clanging in desperation as I quickly dumped it out, my heart in my throat and my stomach on the floor.

Frantic, I scanned the paperwork.

The first was a copy of the acquisition of Mylton Records by Stone Industries.

Sebastian Stone's production company.

Royce had let the company go.

What did this mean?

Scrambling, I flipped to another stack sitting underneath.

I jolted in surprise. It was a new contract for Carolina George.

The offer double what it had originally been.

Or we were given the choice to walk away.

Tears blurred my eyes, and my pulse came in rampant, erratic beats. I started to shout for Richard, to give him encouragement that the band was secure.

That Royce had been looking out for us after all.

The way he'd promised.

But I froze when a tiny slip of ripped paper floated free, dancing and dipping until it hit the ground.

Energy surged.

As if he were right there, watching me with those fierce, unrelenting eyes.

I picked it up, hardly able to read the words scrawled on the scrap.

I never knew what it meant
I thought my heart was breaking
Turns out it was only making room for you
So catch me
Catch me when I fall
I'm right here
Waiting for you to catch me when I fall

And I knew . . . I knew it was time to finish our song.

thirty-two

Royce

From the front seat of my car, I stared across the busy street at the fenced-off lot on the opposite side of the road, heart screaming like an engine roaring down the interstate.

My palms slick with sweat.

What was I doing?

Sitting there like some kind of creeper.

But today ... today I found that I couldn't force myself to drive away.

Children ran through the playground, their shrieks and laughter suspended in the heatwaves that clung to the stagnant Los Angeles air. Ricocheting and reverberating.

Shouting of the kind of joy I'd lost four years before. The day my heart had been ripped from my chest and my world had been cast into nothingness.

Thrown into darkness.

Nothing left but a hunger for revenge.

A quest for retribution.

It's funny how people came into your life so unexpectedly and changed everything.

Made you question.

A glimmer of light in the darkness.

She was a star that had shone in the midst of a total eclipse.

Soulshine.

Misery tightened my chest, pressing deeper and deeper into my spirit and clotting my mind. I squeezed my eyes closed against the assault of it. Trying to choke it back. To remind myself why I could never have her. The way I'd used her.

A little girl ran along the fence of the play yard, her head tipped back with laughter and her short black hair cropped around her cherub face.

Pink cheeks and the darkest eyes.

My soul shook.

I stared out the windshield at the child I no longer knew but recognized with every part of me.

Terrified.

Terrified of who I'd become.

Terrified of what I'd lost.

Terrified of my past.

Thing was, I refused to live it for the rest of my life.

It was time to make a change because I couldn't keep going on like this.

I picked up my phone and tapped out the message to my attorney. The one I'd been talking to for the last two weeks.

Getting up the nerve.

Me: I'm ready.

It took all of five seconds for it to buzz back.

Kimpleton: You're sure? This one can't be about revenge.

I stared at the tiny child running in the field, chasing a soccer ball.

My daughter.

My daughter.

Me: With her, it never was.

I tossed my phone back into the console, put my car in drive, and pulled from the curb into traffic.

I was struck with a brand-new feeling. Something so foreign that I wondered if it was real.

Hope.

Dim but gaining in force.

Because someone taught me recently that life isn't about the past. Yeah. It was what shaped you. Formed and fashioned. But it was how you handled it that mattered most.

For the first time in my life, I was going to handle it right.

And I had one more stop to make.

Half an hour later, I pulled up outside the warehouse in an industrial part of the city. A bit seedy and so L.A. that you knew you couldn't be lost. Graffiti covered almost all of the metal siding, most of it done by local artists that had been invited in to do their thing, other pieces appearing overnight, mind-blowing portraits and scenes that shouldn't be possible coming from a can.

But when an artist had the need to create, that creation was unstoppable.

Medium didn't matter.

It was the heart, the passion that did.

Guessed maybe that was what I was riding on when I stepped out of my S7, knees knocking like a fourteen-year-old kid getting ready to get his dick wet for the first time.

Maybe that's what it felt like.

Starting over.

A new experience.

A second chance.

Something that might count in the middle of the destruction raging a path through my insides.

Maggie kept telling me to do something about that vacancy.

To go after what I wanted. To listen to the voice inside of me that was calling out to be filled.

To just pick up the fucking phone and call.

The expression on Emily's face when she'd looked up at me that night promised that I knew better. There was no going back. Too much damage done.

Just prayed she'd find her peace in the middle of it. Understand the reason.

That some part of her would know that I would love her forever.

I took the five concrete steps up to the glass double doors that led into the building and swung open one side to the blaring heavy metal music that screamed from the overhead speakers. It pumped into the waiting room that was nothing but a bunch of dingy couches and overflowing ash trays and the stench of stale beer.

Energy flashed.

A shockwave.

Fingers twitching and spirit rising to take note.

This sense like I was coming home.

The girl behind the reception desk with teal-blue hair and a septum ring and two diamonds in her cheeks pulled her attention up from her phone, her expression morphing from idle disinterest to shock in a second flat.

She shot forward.

I shoved my hands into my jeans' pockets. "Don't have an appointment."

A snort blew from her nose. "You think you need one?"

I cocked my head. "Do you?"

"Pretty sure you can go on back."

It was almost a grin that pulled at the corner of my mouth. I roughed a hand through my hair, walking toward the next set of double doors, shooting her a parting glance and wondering why the fuck I felt nervous. "Thanks."

"No problem."

I pulled open a door to the half-hearted practice going down inside.

Members of A Riot of Roses were spread out, tipping back warm beers and fumbling through a set that I doubted made a whole lot of sense any longer.

Van saw me first, head pulling up from the electric guitar he held on his lap where he sat on a couch. He froze, blue eyes going wide in surprise.

Slowly, he stood and set his guitar aside.

Arsen and Hunter noticed right after, sensing the shift in the air. This feeling that was rushing wide and fast.

My oldest friends.

Arsen's attention jerked up from where he was tuning his bass. "Royce."

Hunter stood from behind the practice kit set up at the far end of the room, carefully, like he had no clue what to make of me being there.

A built-in studio was in the room behind them, production room on the right and the booths to the left.

This place had once been an abandoned warehouse that we'd sneaked into to practice at all hours of the night, punks out living life for ourselves, large and without apology, feeling like thieves causing trouble as we'd chased down a dream.

Had seemed fitting to buy it when the time came right.

Another thing that had been swiped out from under my feet.

Another missing piece.

I stopped inside the door, all eyes on me.

Speculation and fear and hope.

"Royce," Van chanced, tipping his chin toward me in question.

"Hey, man, long time."

"Yeah," he agreed. He eyed me up and down. "You here to play?"

"Heard you might need somebody."

He scratched at his chin before he cracked a grin. "About fuckin' time."

thirty-three

Royce

*I*t was late by the time I pulled up to my house in the Hills. Place lit up where it was perched on a small cliff, a thousand times smaller than that monstrosity a mile up the hill where my stepfather had reigned.

Still, it was perfectly fitting for my role as Mylton Records' head of A & R.

Contemporary luxury with a multimillion-dollar view.

Headlights cutting through the night, I eased into the garage.

I'd stayed at the studio all day and evening, hours passing as we'd just . . . jammed. Going through old songs that had filled me with a gutting sort of nostalgia and new ones that I'd not been partner to, refusing the bitterness and instead embracing the chance.

Choosing life.

Maggie had texted me that she was staying at a friend's tonight. She'd spent the weekend away and had just gotten home yesterday, but she was already out and about again.

Made me fucking glow that she was feeling so confident.

Stepping out of her comfort zone.

Taking the reins of her life and letting it lead her into the future rather than remaining chained to the past.

Of course, made me itch to think about her out on her own, too. Antsy with the onslaught of protectiveness that lined my veins when I thought of her vulnerable.

Worrying like she was a little kid and not the woman she was becoming.

But she didn't need someone trying to shelter her, to keep her under their wing.

Not when she was ready to soar.

Coming to a stop in the garage, I blew out a strained sigh when I cut the engine. The night crept over me, silence echoing back, wrapping me in its loneliness.

I scrubbed a palm over my face, trying to break it up, hoping it would keep down the barbs of pain that spiked. It was only a reminder that I'd taken what I shouldn't have. That I'd gotten greedy and stolen something for myself when that wasn't what this had been about.

Before I lost myself to the desolation, I opened the door and stepped out of my car. The city teemed around me, the trill of bugs in the palm trees that swished in the gusts of wind that blew through the hills and rushed across the valley, the drone of cars a dull hum in the distance.

I pressed the button to close the garage and took the two steps up to the interior door.

Pushing it open, I stepped into the vacancy.

It echoed back across the shining travertine floors.

Though tonight, it was different.

A disorder in the quieted hush.

Angling my head, I peered into the house.

Everything was still, nothing but the bare glow from the lights in the kitchen spilling into the posh living space.

Still, I felt it.

Energy.

Life that stirred the void inside of me.

God.

I was losing it.

I attempted to shove the feeling down. Couldn't get lost in my mind. In the remnants of my bleeding heart.

I pushed into the house, footsteps reverberating across the floor. I started to turn right so I could take the stairs up to my bedroom when I froze.

Awareness pricked my senses.

A skitter of need rustling through the air.

My attention snagged on something on the floor in the foyer.

Edging back, I slowly moved that way, pulse thrumming like a live wire.

Slowly, I knelt and picked up the piece of ripped journal paper, eyes tracing her words.

Come to me
I've been waiting for a break
Looking for something to save me from myself

Emily.

My breaths turned ragged.

Shallow.

Emily.

Fingers twitching with greed, I edged deeper toward the main area of my house, drawn down the hall that led to the great room and kitchen. Emotion crashed when I found another scrap of paper left in the middle of the floor, and I swore, I could feel the ground shake when I knelt down and picked it up, this one inscribed with my handwriting.

Have you been looking for someone
To fill up what you're missing
Who is it who's gonna stop you
From the circle that keeps going 'round

Tremors rumbled, and my eyes were racing, latching onto the next slip that had been left ten feet ahead.

My soul hinged on eternity.

My life a spiral
You sent me spinning
I've lost control
Now I'm questioning everything I think I know

I kept moving forward.
Compelled.
Hooked
Chained.

I already hit rock bottom
Waiting to catch you now
It's you, little mind-wrecker
Trippin' me up long before you could know

I guessed I really was tripping when I edged forward and picked up the next slip that waited close to the open sliding door that led out to the patio.

I'm in a free fall
Don't let me drown
Years spent wasted
Waiting on you to catch up to me
Catching up to you

Tension rippled, energy stretched taut.

Pulling between us. Heart in my throat, I stepped outside onto the patio that overlooked the city.

A negative-edge pool lined the back, the bright teal-blue of the water looking as if it poured off the side, a canvas of city lights that seemed to stretch on forever.

That million-dollar view that made this place worth more than a small fortune.

But it was her . . . Emily, that was the sight.

The view.

The only thing that mattered.

Staggering, gut-wrenching beauty.

Mind-wrecker.

She sat on a stool facing out over the city, wearing a white backless dress that showed off all that silky flesh, blonde curls mounded on her head, a few tendrils dripping down to caress her skin.

My guts fisted in a shock of lust while my spirit screamed for its match.

My chest filling to overflowing.

Love rushing out.

Soulshine.

She had a guitar balanced on her lap, and she was singing softly. Singing slow.

The last words I'd written and left on my nightstand five nights ago. Written when I couldn't sleep.

My soul crushed with how fucking bad I was missing her.

I never knew what it meant
I thought my heart was breaking
Turns out it was only making room for you
So catch me
Catch me when I fall
I'm right here
Waiting for you to catch me when I fall

Her lithe body rocked as she strummed the mesmerizing melody.

She clutched my soul and made me stumble forward a step as she continued to sing our song that had finally been synched.

Years spent wasted
Waiting on you to catch up to me
Catching up to you

Years spent wasted
You were waiting for me
I never knew what it meant
I thought my heart was breaking
Turns out it was only making room for you
So catch me
Catch me when I fall

She looked back at me as she sang the last, the chorus slowing, her eyes filled with a trust I thought I'd never deserve.

So catch me
Catch me when I fall

Jade eyes shimmered in the moonlight. "Will you, Royce? Will you be there for me? To catch me when I'm fallin'? Will you be my life's song?"

It slammed me like a landslide.

The intense love I had for this girl.

Her presence all around me.

Cherries and the sky and the breaking day.

The sun climbing over the darkened horizon.

Blinding and bold.

I moved for her.

Purposed.

Each step desperate in its possession.

Desperate in its surrender.

Because that's what this was.

Possession.

Surrender.

Chills flashed across the skin of her bare back. Goosebumps raced in time with the shiver that rolled through her gorgeous body.

Anticipating my touch.

I edged forward until I was standing right behind her, my chest heaving with the pants that jumped from my lungs. My heart careened as I leaned forward and dragged my nose up along the column of her neck.

Inhaling as I went.

Sweet, sweet, sweet.

Every cell in my body clutched. My words were rough at the shell of her ear. "I want to see you fly."

"I think I've been flyin' since the moment you walked into my life," she whispered into the night, into the shadows that lapped from the pool and tumbled across the stone deck.

My hand spread out over the front of her neck, drawing her back. Her pulse ran wild beneath my touch. "It's me you set free."

Her head shook. "No, Royce. It was you who gave everything to set us free. I know what you did. Why you came for me. You saved me. It was you in that hotel room. And I know what you did for your sister. You fought for us. I know what you did for the band, too."

Energy trembled. "I'd do it all over again, a million times," I told her, mouth moving up and down the column of her throat, unable to stop myself.

Not wanting to.

Surrender.

"I need to know one thing, Royce. I need to know if it is real. If what you feel for me is real or if it's some sort of twisted pity? If you got caught up in the act of protecting me from Cory?"

Teeth grating with restraint, I shifted her around on the stool. Struck by the magnitude of this girl. Her face and those green eyes and her blinding soul.

Slowly, I took the guitar from her and set it aside. I moved back for her and took that precious face in my hands.

"I tried not to love you, Emily. Tried to stay away. Tried to remember my purpose. When it came to you, it was a two-part game. Second I heard you sing, I knew you were probably the most talented person I was ever going to get the honor to work with. I might not have given a shit about Mylton Records, but you? Your band? I wanted to be a part of you being discovered. Then Cory . . ."

My jaw clenched when fury flamed.

Wasn't sure that was ever going to go away.

"I'd come to Atlanta to watch the show. Fitzgerald wanted Carolina George signed that night. I'd gone to the hotel to talk with Richard, see if we could all meet, seal the deal. I was on my way to his room . . ."

My hold tightened on her cheeks, my spirit pitching, reaching to meet hers. "I felt something, Emily. Something that was all wrong. Knew I was going to be on edge because Cory would be there, my old band, wounds too ripe. But it was different. It was *you*."

I swallowed around the jagged rocks gathered at the base of my throat. "I searched through that disorder, not even knowing what I was looking for, moving up and down the hall until I heard you. Your heart and your spirit and then it was a scream."

Old agony and faith flickered through her expression. "When he cut me."

I flinched, hating that he had hurt her but knowing it was how I'd found her. "Yeah."

"Wanted to end him that night . . . part of me wishes that I would have . . . but somehow I managed to stop. To find my focus. To try to see the full plan through because me going back to jail wasn't going to be a benefit for my sister."

My sister.

A grin played at the corner of my mouth when Emily's eyes lit up at the mention of her. And I knew this had everything to do with the little meddler.

Couldn't complain.

"I did my best to pretend like you hadn't affected me that night. That I hadn't felt you in a way I'd never felt anyone before. I was going to see the signing through. Take down my stepfather and Cory and make sure you were safe in the process until the job was done."

My thumb brushed across the tear that slipped from the corner of her eye. "But it was a lie I was telling myself, Emily. Moment I saw you in that bar that night? Something took me over. Something I didn't want to admit. Pretty sure I fell in love with you right then and there."

She blinked through the emotion, her sweet mouth trembling.

"I've never felt someone the way I felt you then. This . . . feeling like I was stepping into something different. Turns out, I was falling into you."

I held her face like the treasure that it was. "And I promise, I will always be there to catch you. Don't want to live my life without you . . . these last four weeks . . ."

I trailed off, unable to describe the brutality of living without her.

Heartbreak slashed through her expression. "I missed you. So much."

Guilt clotted my voice. "I should have told you from the beginning. I was just terrified of failing my sister."

"You should have trusted me to love you," she murmured.

My chest stretched tight, my lips brushing across hers in the softest caress. "What I didn't trust was me loving you."

Attraction flashed at the bare contact.

Love and lust.

I gripped her by the upper thigh, shifting her to make space for myself between those legs that drove me out of my mind.

"But I was a fool. There was nothing that could have stopped me from loving you."

Tears streaked down her face, and I kissed them away, the salty wetness coating my lips. I murmured across her cheeks, "I love you. I love you."

"You are the meaning of every song that I have written," she breathed back.

My chest clutched. Soared and shifted.

I reached out and pulled her face back, needing her to understand before she decided to stay. "My daughter . . ."

"Anna." She whispered it like praise.

Adoration.

It was that very second the girl owned every piece of me.

"Anna." I could barely get her name to break out of the lock of emotion on my tongue. "My daughter is five, Emily, and I haven't seen her since she was nine months old. But I've never stopped loving her. Missing her. Not for a second. The main goal was getting her away from Cory. But now that he's gone? I'm going to fight for her. Know you didn't sign up for a family, but I won't go on living without her in my life."

Emily brushed her fingertips through a lock of hair draping across my forehead, those eyes flickering across my face. "That's exactly what I signed up for, Royce. I signed up to spend my life with you. And that little girl is a part of you."

A smile swam across her teary face. "I want it all, and I want it with you. I want to sing. I want to play. I want a family. Do you want that with me?" she asked, her tone dipping into a plea.

My forehead dropped to hers. "More than anything."

She reached out and took my hands and pressed them both to her flat stomach. "Do you feel that?" she whispered, her gaze peeking up to meet with mine. "*Us* living inside of me? We're goin' to have a baby, Royce."

I squeezed my eyes closed as her words penetrated.

Emotion gripping.

Overpowering.

My throat shook as I swallowed hard.

Her pulse pounded, and she pressed down tighter on my hands that burned against her belly.

"Tell me what you're thinkin'," she quietly begged.

I lifted a hand and spread my fingers out over the back of her head, pressing my nose to hers, lips murmuring my truth, letting myself fall into those trusting green eyes. "I'm thinking I've never been so happy in my entire life."

And I kissed her.

Kissed her with everything I had.

As recklessly as it'd all started. She whimpered, struggling to get as close to me as she could.

My body pressing against hers.

Wanting to consume.

To give.

Love and live.

I angled her head, kissing her deeper, rumbling at her mouth, "Are you happy? Is this what you want?"

She pulled back and forced me to look at her, her fingertips scratching through the stubble on my jaw. "Loving you is the very meaning of joy. Having a family with you is ecstasy."

I pulled her off the stool and into my arms.

Instantly, my hands were everywhere, gripping for fistfuls of this girl.

Kisses frantic.

Hands desperate.

Our tongues danced.

Gave and took.

Two of us were unable to get close enough to the other, pawing and panting our way for the door.

"Ecstasy, huh? That's a good thing because I'm about to make myself at home in paradise."

Could feel her smile beneath my mouth, her breaths growing shorter, need a glow that burned in the middle of us.

"Oh yeah? And where is that?"

"Let me show you."

She was giggling when I swept her off her feet and carried her through my house up the stairs.

Emily looped her arms around my neck, green eyes glinting with adoration and all that hope.

We passed by Maggie's empty room.

Sneaky girl.

I'd have to thank her later, my baby sister looking out for me the way I would forever try to look out for her.

The second I carried Emily through the threshold of my room, the air shifted.

Blood pounding.

Our mouths right back to desperately making their claim.

I peeled her out of her dress while she shoved me out of my clothes, and I couldn't even make it across the room before I was picking her up again and sinking into a chair, the girl quick to straddle me, taking me into that sweet body.

A groan ripped out as she sank down, and I drove a hand into her hair, the other arm wrapped around her waist.

Our noses touched. Our breaths mingled. Our hearts beat in sync.

Every part of us shared.

"Right fucking here."
And I was going to stay right there.
Forever.
Catching her . . .
Catching me.

epilogue

Six Months Later

Little arms held tight around his neck. He held her close, her tiny heart drumming an erratic beat.

"Will you catch me, Daddy? If I fall?"

He wrapped his arms tightly around her, pressed his mouth to Anna's temple. "Of course, I will catch you. That is what I was meant to do."

the end

Thank you for reading *Catch Me When I Fall*

I hope you fell in love with Royce and Emily's story the way I did!

Want more from the Caroline George crew?

Start with their drummer, Leif, in *Kiss the Stars*

http://geni.us/KTSAmzn

Did you love the men and women of Sunder? Start where it all began with Shea and Sebastian in *A Stone in the Sea*

https://geni.us/ASITSAmzn

New to me and want more? I recommend starting with my favorite small town alphas!

Start with *Show Me the Way*

https://geni.us/SMTWAmzn

Text "aljackson" to 33222 to get your LIVE release mobile alert (US Only)
or
Sign up for my newsletter
https://geni.us/NewsFromALJackson

More from A.L. Jackson

Redemption Hills
Give Me a Reason
Say It's Forever
Never Look Back
Promise Me Always

The Falling Stars Series
Kiss the Stars
Catch Me When I Fall
Falling into You
Beneath the Stars

Confessions of the Heart
More of You
All of Me
Pieces of Us

Fight for Me
Show Me the Way
Follow Me Back
Lead Me Home
Hold on to Hope

Bleeding Stars
A Stone in the Sea
Drowning to Breathe
Where Lightning Strikes
Wait
Stay
Stand

The Regret Series
Lost to You
Take This Regret
If Forever Comes

The Closer to You Series
Come to Me Quietly
Come to Me Softly
Come to Me Recklessly

Stand-Alone Novels
Pulled
When We Collide

Hollywood Chronicles, a collaboration with USA Today
Bestselling Author, Rebecca Shea
One Wild Night
One Wild Ride

ABOUT THE AUTHOR

A.L. Jackson is the New York Times & USA Today Bestselling author of contemporary romance. She writes emotional, sexy, heart-filled stories about boys who usually like to be a little bit bad.

Her bestselling series include THE REGRET SERIES, CLOSER TO YOU, BLEEDING STARS, FIGHT FOR ME, and CONFESSIONS OF THE HEART.

If she's not writing, you can find her hanging out by the pool with her family, sipping cocktails with her friends, or of course with her nose buried in a book.

Be sure not to miss new releases and sales from A.L. Jackson - Sign up to receive her newsletter http://smarturl.it/NewsFromALJackson or text "aljackson" to 33222 to receive short but sweet updates on all the important news.

Connect with A.L. Jackson online:

FB Page **https://geni.us/ALJacksonFB**
Newsletter **https://geni.us/NewsFromALJackson**
Angels **https://geni.us/AmysAngels**
Amazon **https://geni.us/ALJacksonAmzn**
Book Bub **https://geni.us/ALJacksonBookbub**
Text "aljackson" to 33222 to receive short but sweet updates on all the important news.

Made in the USA
Columbia, SC
16 September 2023

22963419R00226